A Weekend with Mr. Darcy

VICTORIA CONNELLY

sourcebooks
landmark

Published by Sourcebooks Landmark, an imprint of Sourcebooks, Inc.
P.O. Box 4410, Naperville, Illinois 60567-4410
(630) 961-3900
FAX: (630) 961-2168
www.sourcebooks.com

Library of Congress Cataloging-in-Publication Data

Connelly, Victoria.
 A weekend with Mr. Darcy / by Victoria Connelly.
   p. cm.
 1. Women college teachers—England—Oxford—Fiction. 2. Literature teachers—England—Oxford—Fiction. 3. Novelists—Fiction. 4. Austen, Jane, 1775-1817—Congresses—Fiction. I. Title.
 PR6103.O547W44 2011
 823'.92—dc22

2011015767

Printed and bound in the United States of America
VP 10 9 8 7 6 5 4 3 2 1

To my dear friend, Bridget,
who discovered Pride and Prejudice
with me all those years ago.

'She was the sun of my life, the gilder of every pleasure, the soother of every sorrow.'

—Cassandra Austen of her sister, Jane

Chapter 1

Dr Katherine Roberts couldn't help thinking that a university lecturer in possession of a pile of paperwork must be in want of a holiday.

She leant back in her chair and surveyed her desk. It wasn't a pretty sight. Outside, the October sunshine was golden and glorious and she was shut up in her book-lined tomb of an office.

Removing her glasses and pinching the bridge of her nose, she looked at the leaflet that was lying beside a half-eaten salad sandwich, which had wilted hours before. The heading was in a beautiful bold script that looked like old-fashioned handwriting. *Purley Hall, Church Stinton, Hampshire*, it read.

> *Set in thirty-five acres of glorious parkland, this early eighteenth-century house is the perfect place in which to enjoy your Jane Austen weekend. Join a host of special guest speakers and find out more about England's favourite novelist.*

Katherine looked at the photograph of the handsome red-bricked Georgian mansion taken from the famous herbaceous borders. With its long sweep of lawn and large sash windows, it was the quintessential English country house, and it was very easy to imagine a whole host of Jane Austen characters walking through its rooms and gardens.

'And I will be too,' Katherine said to herself. It was the third year she'd been invited to speak at the Jane Austen weekend, and rumour had it that novelist Lorna Warwick was going to make an appearance too. Katherine bit her lip. Lorna Warwick was her favourite author—after Jane Austen, of course. Miss Warwick was a huge bestseller, famous for her risqué Regency romances of which she published one perfect book a year. Katherine had read them all from the very first—*Marriage and Magic*—to *A Bride for Lord Burford*, published just a month earlier, and which Katherine had devoured in one evening at the expense of a pile of essays she should have been grading.

She thought of the secret bookshelves in her study at home and how they groaned deliciously under the weight of Miss Warwick's work. How her colleagues would frown and fret at such horrors as popular fiction! How quickly would she be marched from her Oxford office and escorted from St Bridget's College if they knew of her wicked passion?

'Dr Roberts,' Professor Compton would say, his hairy eyebrows lowered over his beady eyes, 'you really do surprise me.'

'Why because I choose to read some novels purely for entertainment?' Katherine would say to him, remembering Jane Austen's own defence of the pleasures of novels in *Northanger Abbey*. 'Professor Compton, you really are a dreadful snob!'

But it couldn't be helped. Lorna Warwick's fiction was Katherine's secret vice, and if her stuffy colleagues ever found out, she would be banished from Oxford before you could say *Sense and Sensibility*.

To Katherine's mind, it wasn't right that something that could give as much pleasure as a novel could be so reviled. Lorna Warwick had confessed to being on the receiving end of such condescension too and had been sent some very snobby letters in her time. Perhaps that was why Katherine's own letter had caught the eye of the author.

It had been about a year earlier when Katherine had done something she'd never ever done before—she'd written a fan letter and posted it in care of Miss Warwick's publisher. It was a silly letter really, full of gushing and admiration and Katherine had never expected a reply. Nevertheless, within a fortnight, a beautiful cream envelope had dropped onto her doormat containing a letter from the famous writer.

> *How lovely to receive your letter. You have no idea what it means to me to be told how much you enjoy my novels. I often get some very strange letters from readers telling me that they always read my novels but that they are complete trash!*

Katherine had laughed and their bond had been sealed. After that, she couldn't stop. Every moment that wasn't spent reading a Lorna Warwick novel was spent writing to the woman herself and each letter was answered. They talked about all sorts of things—not just books. They talked about films, past relationships, their work, fashion, Jane Austen, and if men had changed since Austen's times and if one could really expect to find a Mr Darcy outside the pages of a novel.

Katherine then had dared to ask Lorna if she was attending the conference at Purley Hall and it had gone quiet, for more than two weeks. Had Katherine overstepped the boundaries? Had she pushed things too far? Maybe it was one thing exchanging letters with a fan but quite another to meet a fan in the flesh.

Just as Katherine had given up all hope, though, a letter had arrived.

> *Dear Katherine,*
>
> *I'm so sorry not to have replied sooner but I've been away and I still can't answer your question as to whether or not I'll be at Purley. We'll just have to wait and see.*
>
> *Yours truly, Lorna*

It seemed a very odd sort of reply, Katherine thought. If Lorna Warwick was going to be at Purley, surely the organisers would want to know as she'd be the biggest name and the main pull because she was famously reclusive. In comparison to the bestselling novelist, Katherine was just a dusty fusty old lecturer. Well, *young* lecturer, actually; she was in her early thirties, but she knew that people would come and listen to her talks only because they were true Janeites. At these conferences, anyone speaking about Jane Austen was instantly adored and held in great esteem. In fact, any sort of activity with even the lamest connection to Austen was pursued and enjoyed, from Jane Austen Scrabble to Murder in the Dark which, one year, ended in uproar when it was discovered that Anne Elliot had somehow managed to murder Captain Wentworth.

Katherine smiled as she remembered, and then, trying to put thoughts of Purley out of her mind, she made a start on the pile of papers to her left that was threatening to spill onto the floor. It was mostly rubbish that had accumulated as the term had progressed. It was what she called her 'tomorrow pile,' except she'd run out of tomorrows.

With fingers as dextrous as a concert pianist's, she filed, threw away and recycled until she could see the glorious wood of her desk again.

She was just about to pick up her handbag and briefcase when there was a knock on the door.

'Come in,' she said, wondering who was calling so late in the day without an appointment.

The door opened and a tousled head popped round.

'Stewie,' she said, sighing inwardly as one of her students stumbled into the room. Stewie Harper was in his first term studying English literature and he'd spent most of that time banging on her office door.

'Dr Roberts,' he said. 'I hope I'm not disturbing you.'

'No,' she said, resigning herself to helping him out of whatever literary conundrum he now found himself in. 'Come in.'

Stewie looked at the chair opposite Katherine's and she motioned for him to sit down.

'It's the reading list,' he said, producing it from his pocket. 'It says we're to read as many of these titles as possible during the term.'

'Well, as many as you have time for,' Katherine said. 'We don't expect you to spend all your time with your head in a book.'

'Yes but I couldn't help noticing that your book isn't on here.'

Katherine's eyes widened. '*My* book?'

'Yes. *The Art of Jane Austen.*'

Katherine smiled. 'I'm afraid we can't fit all the books on the list.'

'But it's *your* book, Dr Roberts. It should've been on the top of the list.'

Katherine couldn't help being flattered. 'Well, that's very sweet of you, Stewie.'

'Are you writing any more books, Dr Roberts?'

'Not at the moment,' she said.

'But you'll sign my copy, won't you?'

'Your copy?'

'Of your book,' he said, scraping around in an old carrier bag. 'I bought it in town. I had to order a copy.'

'You shouldn't have gone to all that trouble,' Katherine said, knowing that the hardback was expensive, especially on a student's budget.

'It wasn't any trouble,' Stewie said, handing it across the desk to her.

Katherine opened it to the title page and picked up her favourite pen, aware that Stewie's eyes were upon her as she signed.

'There you are,' she said, smiling at him as she handed the book back.

He turned eagerly to the page, his eyes bright. 'Oh,' he said, his smile slipping from his face. 'Best wishes,' he read.

Katherine nodded. 'My very best wishes,' she said.

'You don't want to add a kiss?'

'No, Stewie,' she said, 'because we both know that wouldn't be appropriate, don't we?' Katherine stood up and Stewie took the hint and stood up too.

'Dr Roberts,' he said as they left her office together, 'I was thinking that I might need some extra tutoring. You know—over the weekends—with you.'

Katherine eyed him over her glasses, trying to make herself look as old and unattractive as possible. It wasn't an easy look to pull off because she was strikingly attractive with porcelain-pale skin and long dark hair that waved over her shoulders. Her mouth was a problem too. It was bee-stung beautiful and could be a terrible distraction in class when she was trying to engage her students in her poetry readings. 'Stewie,' she said, 'you don't really need my help.'

'I don't?'

'No, you don't. Your grades are consistently good and you've proven yourself to be an independent, free-thinking student.'

Stewie looked pleased, but then dismay filled his face. 'But surely a student can't do enough studying.'

'You absolutely can,' Katherine assured him. 'Everybody needs a break—that's what weekends are for. Go and have an adventure. Go bungee jumping or parachuting or something.'

'I'd rather be studying with you.'

'Well, I'm going away,' she told him.

'Where?'

'Hampshire.'

'Doesn't sound very exotic,' he said.

'Maybe not but it's a little piece of perfect England. Good-bye, Stewie,' she said, picking up her pace and lengthening her stride.

'Good-bye, Dr Roberts,' Stewie called after her.

She didn't look around but she had the feeling that his eyes were watching the progress of her legs down the entire length of the corridor.

Allowing herself a sigh of relief as she reached the car park, she thought of her small but perfect garden at home where she could kick off her shoes and sink her bare feet into the silky green coolness of her lawn, a glass of white wine in her hand as she toasted the completion of another week of academia.

She'd almost made it to her car and to freedom when a voice cried out, 'Katherine!'

She stopped. It was the last voice—the *very* last voice—she wanted to hear.

'What is it, David?' she asked a moment later as a fair-haired man with an anxious face joined her by her car.

'That's not very friendly. You were the one smiling at me across the car park.'

'I wasn't smiling at you. I was squinting at the sun.'

'Oh,' he said, looking crestfallen.

'I'm in a rush,' she said, opening her car door.

His hand instantly reached out and grabbed it, preventing her from closing it.

'David—'

'Talk to me, Kitty.'

'Don't call me that. Nobody calls me that.'

'Oh, come on, Catkin,' he said, his voice low. 'We haven't talked properly since… well, you know.'

'Since I left you because I found out you'd got married? You're the one who wasn't returning my calls, David. You're the one who disappeared off the face of the planet to marry some ex-student. Nobody knew where you were. I was worried sick.'

'I was going to tell you.'

'When? At the christening of your firstborn?'

'You're not being fair.'

'*I'm* not being fair? I'm not the one who has a wife tucked away in the attic somewhere,' Katherine cried.

'Oh, don't be so melodramatic. This isn't some nineteenth-century novel,' he said. 'That's the problem with you. You can't exist in the real world. You have your head constantly immersed in fiction, and you just can't handle reality anymore.'

Katherine's mouth dropped open. 'That is *not* true!'

'No?' he said. 'So where are you heading now, eh? Purley bloody Hall, I bet.'

'That's my work,' Katherine said in defence of herself.

'Work? It's your whole life. You don't do anything *but* work. Your entire existence revolves around a set of people who've been made up by other people who've been dead for at least a century. It's not healthy.'

Katherine was on the verge of defending herself again but had the good sense to bite her tongue. She didn't want David to launch into his old tirade about how their love affair was doomed long before the arrival of his wife. She knew he'd throw it all in her face—how many early nights had been rejected in favour of the latest Jane Austen adaptation on TV and how often she had burned a much-looked-forward-to candlelit dinner at home because she'd had her head buried in a book. It bothered her when she stopped to think about it long enough because she knew that she was in love with a fictional world. Mr Darcy, Captain Wentworth and Henry Tilney were all creations of a female mind. They didn't exist. Perhaps her obsession with such heroes was because there were so few real heroes, and she was standing looking at a real-life nonhero right then.

'Go home to your wife, David,' she said, getting into her car.

'You know I'd rather go home with you.'

Katherine sighed. 'You should have thought about that before you lied to me,' she said, closing her door and driving off.

Honestly, any man who wasn't safely tucked between the covers of a book was a liability. You couldn't trust any of them. Was it any wonder that Katherine turned to fiction time and time again? Ever since her father had left home when she was seven, she'd hidden from the world around her, nose-diving into the safety of a friendly paperback. Books had always rescued her and remained the one constant in her life.

Before she dated David, she'd had a long-term relationship with an architect called Callum. She'd thought he was perfect and that they'd be together forever, like Elizabeth and Darcy, but he'd been offered a job in San Francisco, and he couldn't turn it down. He asked Katherine to go with him but her mother had fallen ill and she couldn't leave her.

'Follow me out later,' he said, but it hadn't worked out. The weeks passed, telephone calls became fewer, postcards became shorter, and then they stopped altogether. He hadn't even called when she wrote to tell him that her mother had died.

'And that's *real* men for you,' Katherine said to herself as she took the road out of Oxford that led to her village. She thought again about David's words to her. He was unfair. It wasn't as if her whole life revolved around Jane Austen. It was just—well, most of it. But she had other interests. There was her yoga class which kept her in good shape and her weekend jogging with her best friend, Chrissie. And she had lots of other friends who weren't fictional and she was forever attending dinner parties and little get-togethers. It was just that she preferred to spend her free time with her head in a book. She wouldn't be the respected academic she was if she hadn't worked as hard as she had and, as far as she could see, there was no harm in that, was there? She'd made a very good career out of books, for one thing and as far as she knew, she wasn't doing anyone any harm.

Unlike David.

Yes, Katherine might very well be guilty of living a life that was more fiction than reality but at least she didn't lie to anyone. If there was one thing in the world Katherine hated more than anything else, it was a lie.

Chapter 2

Lorna Warwick was just putting the finishing touches on a rather amusing chapter involving a very naughty duke when the phone rang.

'Hello, darling!' a voice chimed. 'Not a bad moment, is it?'

'No, not at all,' Lorna said, saving the chapter and switching the computer off for the day.

'Good, good. Look, I've had a word with the organiser at Purley Hall and he said not to worry, it's your call.'

'Thanks, Nadia. I appreciate that.'

'So, what are you going to do?'

Lorna sighed. 'I'm not sure yet but I'd like to give the writer a break for a while and just be me.'

'You sure that's wise? You'll be letting down a lot of fans, you know.'

'Yes but I'd be letting down a lot of fans if they knew who I really was, wouldn't I?'

'You must be kidding! They'd go mad if they knew the truth,' Nadia said.

Lorna smiled. 'Well, I don't think I'm quite ready to face that.'

'All right, babes. It's your decision.'

'You coming then?'

'Maybe for the Saturday evening dance.'

'Any excuse to buy a new pair of shoes,' Lorna said.

'How well do you know your agent?'

'As well as she knows me.'

Nadia laughed. 'I'll see you at Purley, babes.'

'Okay.'

Lorna stood up and walked across the study to the window that looked out over the garden. It had needed attention for some time. Dandelions yellowed the lawn, grasses had sprouted up in the borders, and brambles tumbled over the wall from the fields beyond. The house needed attention too because Lorna had fired the cleaner two weeks ago, after she'd been caught pocketing pages of the latest manuscript. Now the desk was covered in a fine layer of dust and a potted plant was wilting quietly in the corner.

It was always the same when a book was going well. Boring jobs such as housework and food preparation got neglected. The only thing that mattered was the flow of the story and—at the moment—the story was flowing well. Nadia was going to love this latest one, and no doubt Lorna's editor would too. Tansy Newman of Parnaby and Fox was Lorna's biggest fan and couldn't wait to get her hands on the latest manuscripts. Edits were usually minimal and Lorna was in the lucky position to be consulted about everything from jacket design to publication date—hardbacks were released just before Christmas, and paperbacks in time for the summer holidays. Lorna was lucky; her advances were legendary and her royalties substantial. Not all writers were in such a good position.

For a moment Lorna looked at the bookshelves that lined the study walls. They were filled to capacity with hardback editions, paperbacks, large print, audio books, and foreign editions that included German, Spanish, Japanese, and Russian. It was an impressive collection considering that the first novel hadn't been received at all well in the press.

'Lorna Warwick is attempting to cash in on the fact that Jane Austen's Regency is a perennial favourite,' one critic wrote, 'but what we have here is a cheap imitation. It's soft porn dressed in a little fine muslin.'

The words had stung bitterly until the book had become a bestseller in the United States and was now seen as the forerunner in a very popular genre of Austenesque literature which included sequels, updates on the six classic novels, and the sort of sexy books that Lorna wrote. It was a huge and much-loved industry.

Lorna's fingers brushed the spines of the UK editions. Each featured a sumptuously clad heroine. 'All breasts and bonnets,' another critic had declared, after which sales rocketed. The public couldn't get enough of the feisty young heroines and devilishly handsome heroes and, of course, the happy endings.

Lorna loved writing. Nothing could beat the day-to-day weaving of a new story or getting to know characters that might captivate the readers' imaginations as strongly as they did their creator. But there was more to being a writer than writing, and Lorna was under increased pressure to handle publicity, hence the agent's phone call about the conference. Year to year, those publishers had tried to persuade their favourite writer that it would be a great idea to attend.

'Incognito, if you must,' they'd said, but Lorna hadn't been at all sure about it. The public face of publication had never been appealing. Writing was a private thing, wasn't it? One didn't need to be endlessly signing copies and giving talks. What was there to say, anyway? Surely the books spoke for themselves, but Lorna's publisher had often spoken of how writers were now seen as celebrities.

'The public has to be able to *see* you.'

'Oh, no,' Lorna had said. 'I don't want anybody to see me.'

What was to be done about Purley Hall? A part of Lorna was desperate to go. Being a writer was a lonely job and it would be good to get out and actually talk to real live people for once. That part would be fun, wouldn't it—to get away from the study and meet people?

'Katherine,' Lorna suddenly said. Katherine was going to be there. Her letter had made it very clear that she'd love to meet her favourite author, and a part of Lorna wanted that very much too. Over the months, they'd become very close, sharing secrets and talking about their hopes for the future. Maybe it was the fact that they were writing letters—beautifully old-fashioned, handwritten letters that one savoured and kept. It wasn't like receiving an email one reads and deletes. These were proper letters on high-quality paper that the writers took time to fill. They had crossings out and notes in the margins and funny PS's too. They were to be reread and treasured just like in the time of Jane Austen when letters were a vital means of staying in touch with loved ones.

If there was one good reason for Lorna to attend the conference, it was Katherine.

Suddenly her feet thundered upstairs to the bedroom where a wardrobe door was quickly opened and clothes were pulled out and flung onto the bed. What to take? What should Lorna Warwick take to the Jane Austen Conference? That was a question that was easy to answer because although Lorna gave very few interviews and never gave out author photographs, it was obvious how the public perceived their beloved author. Nothing but velvets and satins would do in rich jewel colours with sequins and embroidery. Old-fashioned but with a quirky twist. A fascinator wouldn't be completely out of place or a sparkling brooch in the shape of a peacock. Shawls, scarves, a pair of evening gloves, perhaps even a shapely hat. Shoes that were elegant but discreet. That kind of thing people would expect.

Lorna wasn't going to wear any of those things, though. Velvets and satins were instantly rejected and shawls were totally inappropriate and the reason was simple. Lorna Warwick was a man.

Chapter 3

IT WOULD HAVE BEEN VERY UNFORTUNATE IF ROBYN LOVE HAD turned out to be anything other than a romantic. As it was, she fit her name perfectly, choosing to read nothing but romances, wearing only feminine dresses, and renouncing any film that didn't have a happy ending.

Life for her was never as good as it was in fiction. A good story beautifully told was always preferable to reality. For Robyn, nothing came close to the highs she got when reading. Her reception job at a small college in North Yorkshire tickled only the surface for her and she could never wait to get home and stick her head in a favourite book and for her, the very pinnacle of literary perfection was Jane Austen.

Some took their pleasures in the spin-offs and Regency romances told by modern authors but Robyn was a true Janeite who preferred her Austen undiluted.

'If only she'd written more,' Robyn would often say with a sigh. The big six just weren't enough. There were the shorter stories too, of course, but they weren't the same as the big novels, and the letters and endless biographies just didn't give the same satisfaction; they were takeaways rather than a three-course meal.

They might fill a gap but they left you feeling unsatisfied and wanting more.

There was never enough. No matter how many versions of *Pride and Prejudice* or *Persuasion* there were—whether for the cinema, TV, or theatre, she would devour them. Each one was different, shedding some new light onto Austen's world and her characters. Whether it was *Pride or Prejudice* or *Bride and Prejudice*, *Emma* or *Clueless*, Robyn would unplug the house phone, turn off her mobile and tune in for her allotted slot of pure happiness.

There were favourites, of course. Who could forget Colin Firth's brooding Mr Darcy from the 1995 BBC version? But equally, Matthew Macfadyen striding across the meadow at dawn could be the recipe for many a happy sleepless night. There was Jennifer Ehle's witty and intelligent Elizabeth and Keira Knightley's youthful exuberance. How could one possibly choose? It entirely depended on what mood you were in. One thing was for sure, though: there could never be enough. Robyn had often wondered what it was about Austen that inspired such devotion. In these modern times of CDs, DVDs, computer games, iPods, and the Internet, there were still people who preferred to sit down in a quiet corner and read a Jane Austen novel.

Perhaps it was the irresistible blend of wit, warmth, and romance that did it. Robyn had never stopped to analyse what it was that gave her such a buzz. She knew only that when her mind was immersed in the Regency period, her twenty-first century problems evaporated. Well, most of them.

It was late afternoon before the Jane Austen Conference in Hampshire, and Robyn was standing in her back garden behind the row of friendly Yorkshire terraces that overlooked fields and allotments. She had shed her work clothes which had consisted of a white shirt and navy skirt and was wearing a knee-length dress in a floaty floral fabric. Her long hair was unpinned and blowing around her face in a tangle of curls, and her bare feet had been thrust into a pair of sparkly sandals.

Her garden was quite unlike all the others in the terrace. They were mostly given over to neat lawns lined with bedding plants or patios housing tubs of begonias but Robyn's was home to her chickens, and her obsession with Jane Austen extended to her feathered friends. There was Mr Darcy—the obvious name to be chosen by an Austen addict for her first rooster, except it wasn't a terribly fitting one as he soon turned into something more approaching a villain, and Robyn had to rethink his name, eventually coming up with Wickham, the villain of *Pride and Prejudice*. The trouble was that Robyn liked sandals and bare feet, and Wickham had a fascination with her toes, pecking at their painted extremes with great vigour.

He was now 'Wickham the chicken,' and his ladies were also named after characters from *Pride and Prejudice*. There was Lizzy, the bright young thing who was quite aware of her surroundings and always the first to raise an alarm. There was the tiny chestnut called Lydia because she was always running away. The supercilious lavender grey was called Lady Catherine. The speckled hen was Mrs Bennet, for she was always fussing around the others like a typical mother hen, and the pale gold was Miss Bingley because she had an air about her, and Robyn was convinced that she looked down her beak at everyone else.

Robyn looked at them all now, pecking around the garden in the sunshine. She loved watching them and could spend many a happy hour reading in her deck chair, listening to the funny little noises they made.

'You ready, then?' a friendly voice called over the low fence.

'Hi, Judith,' Robyn said, smiling at her elderly neighbour who kept an eye on the chickens when Robyn was at work and whenever she went away.

'You sure this isn't going to be too much bother?' Robyn asked.

Judith put her hands on her hips. 'I've brought up four sons single-handedly. I think I can manage a few bantams.'

Robyn laughed. 'I can't thank you enough. It's a real weight off my mind. You're like an auntie to these chickens.'

Aunty Judith shook her head, obviously not approving. 'You just enjoy your weekend. You work too hard, you do. You need to get out more.'

'That's what Jace is always saying.'

Judith's mouth straightened into a line. 'You're still with him, then?'

Robyn blushed. She knew how her neighbour felt about her errant boyfriend. He'd never managed to endear himself to the old woman—not since the time when he woke her up with his drunken singing at three in the morning and then vomited all over her prize roses.

'I thought you were going to break up with him.'

'I will,' Robyn said.

'You've been saying that since that young Lydia was an egg.'

Robyn sighed. It was true. She'd been meaning to sort things out with Jace for some time. Indeed, she'd been on the verge of saying something only last week but he obviously picked up on things and decided to safeguard his position by suddenly being nice to her and buying her the biggest box of chocolates she'd ever seen. He'd eaten most of them himself but it was the thought that counted, wasn't it?

She'd been going out with Jace since school, and it was more of a routine now rather than romance. Jason Collins or 'Jace' as he preferred to be known, for years insisted that his pals called him 'Ace,' but it had never taken which didn't surprise Robyn in the least. For one thing, he still lived with his mother in a house on the edge of Skipton. It was a lovely property with three large bedrooms and a garden that Robyn's chickens would adore, but a young man of twenty-five shouldn't still be living with his mother, having all his laundry done and meals cooked by her. It just wasn't natural. Not that Robyn had ever felt the urge to live with him—oh, no! But if she was ever going to live with somebody, then it would be someone who was a little bit more independent than Jace.

And I could never marry him, anyway, Robyn suddenly thought. *For one thing, I'd be Mrs Collins!* She grinned naughtily as she thought of the ridiculous character of Mr Collins in *Pride and Prejudice*. Robyn Collins. It would never work; it was just another one of the tragedies about their relationship, but the biggest tragedy of all was the fact that she didn't love him anymore.

She tried desperately to think about their early, heady days together when they were at high school. Holding hands under the table during lessons, the secret kisses in the corridor on the way to class, and the little love notes that were constantly being confiscated by infuriated teachers. Where had all that love gone? Had it not been strong enough to leap the gulf between adolescence and adulthood? Had it been left behind with homework, teenage mood swings, and compulsory PE?

'I'd better get moving,' Robyn told Judith, shaking the images of the past from her mind. 'Jace'll be here in an hour, and I want to get packed before then.'

'Well, don't you go worrying about this lot,' Judith said, nodding towards the chickens. 'They'll be fine.'

'Thanks,' Robyn said with a smile before heading indoors.

The terraced cottage was cool and dark after the brightness of the garden, and Robyn headed upstairs to her bedroom at the front of the house. Packing was simple—as many dresses and books as she could fit in her suitcase. She never liked to go anywhere without a copy of one of Jane Austen's big six. *Persuasion* was usually a favourite because it was slim and easily slipped into a handbag but *Pride and Prejudice* was her preferred choice if room permitted because it never failed to raise a smile, whether she happened to be waiting for a train that was more than an hour late or sitting in the dentist's office knowing that the drill was awaiting.

She sighed with pleasure as she placed a copy of each of the novels in her case. Well, she couldn't go to a Jane Austen Conference without one of each, could she? She'd chosen her oldest versions that didn't mind being beaten up a bit in transit. There was the copy of *Sense and Sensibility* with the coffee stain over the scene where Willoughby scoops Marianne up in his arms, and the edition of *Emma* that had taken a tumble into the bath and was now the shape of an accordion.

Her newer copies of the books were downstairs, their covers shiny and pristine and the spines only faintly cracked. Nothing was more perfect to Robyn than a brand-new copy of an Austen novel.

'Rob!' a voice called from downstairs.

'Jace?' Robyn said in surprise.

'Well, of *course* it's Jace!'

Robyn's mouth screwed up in frustration. He was early.

Leaving her packing, she ventured downstairs and was surprised to see that Jace had been doing some packing of his own.

'What's that?' she asked.

'A suitcase, dopey,' he said, dropping it to the floor and ruffling her hair before grazing her cheek with a stubbly kiss. 'I'm coming with you.'

'What?' she asked, following him through to the living room as he settled himself on the sofa, kicking off his shoes and putting his feet up on the coffee table.

'I'm coming with you,' he said, giving a loud sniff. 'Going to drive you down to Hereford.'

'Hampshire,' Robyn said.

'Can't have you getting the train on your own, can I?'

'But I've got my ticket.'

'Doesn't matter,' he said.

'But Jace—it's such a long way, and it sounds as if you don't even know where Hampshire is.'

'I'm making a weekend of it. Booked a B and B just down the road from your Parley Hall place.'

'Purley Hall.'

'That's it!'

Robyn frowned. This was the last thing she expected and the very last thing she wanted. The Jane Austen weekend was her own special sanctuary, and Jace was the last person she wanted to share it with.

'It's really not your sort of thing at all,' she told him. 'And I doubt there's room for you at the conference. All the places are booked.'

'I'm not coming to the conference, silly! No *way!*'

'Then what are you going to do?'

He shrugged as he picked up the remote control and switched on the TV. 'Just hang out,' he said.

'Hang out where?'

'Wherever you want me to,' he said, giving a lascivious wink. 'We don't spend enough time together. I thought it would be nice to have a weekend away.'

'But we won't be together, Jace. I'll be at the conference—*all* weekend.'

'There'll still be time to see each other, won't there?'

Robyn stared at him. What was this? Jace had never been the sort to suggest a weekend away together before. Maybe he'd guessed she wanted to break up with him. Maybe this was his way of trying to smooth things over.

'Got a beer?' he asked.

Robyn walked through to the kitchen and retrieved a can of beer from the fridge. What on earth was she going to do? The thought of Jace 'hanging out' anywhere near Jane Austen country was just frightful.

'Any crisps?' he asked as she entered the room with the beer.

She shook her head.

'Nuts?'

She returned to the kitchen and came back with a bag of fruit and nuts. Jace grimaced. 'No salty ones?'

'No,' she said, wincing as he placed his beer can on her newest copy of *Pride and Prejudice*. He saw where she was looking.

'Oh sorry, babes,' he said, picking it up. Robyn saw the dark circle embossed on Elizabeth Bennet's face and couldn't help noticing that Jace's feet which were now sockless, were dangerously close to the BBC DVD of *Persuasion*, a personal favourite of hers.

With such atrocities as these before her, she thought it best if she left the room.

Chapter 4

WARWICK LAWTON PICKED UP THE LAST LETTER HE'D RECEIVED from Katherine Roberts and read it again. The smile didn't leave his face until the very end when he gave a weary sigh and scratched his chin. She didn't know, did she? She had absolutely no idea that Lorna Warwick was a man. Why should she? The biography in the front of his novels was as fictional as the novels themselves, and nobody but his agent and publisher knew the truth because as far as his professional life went, he was a recluse, shunning the media and turning his back on book signings. Even his close friends didn't know the truth. They were aware only that Warwick wrote 'some drivel or other' and never pushed him for any more information and that was just the way that Warwick liked it. Not that he was ashamed of what he wrote—certainly not. He loved his books. After all, if he weren't passionate about his characters and their fates, how could he expect his readers to love them?

His late mother, Lara Lawton, had taught him the pleasure of reading and writing. She'd been an actress although she'd never risen to the great heights that her name and beauty had always suggested to the young Warwick. *Lara Lawton*. It should have been a name emblazoned across a thousand theatres, a name that dominated the cinema screen and was splashed across magazine covers. Instead she'd swum in the shallows of the world of film and television, taking bit roles here and background roles there.

'And always a book in her hands,' Warwick remembered. There was so much time for her hanging around sets and his mother had been a passionate reader, telling him the plots of all the novels she read and encouraging him when he sat down one day, determined to rewrite the story of *Wuthering Heights* and give it a happy ending that had more to do with Hollywood than Brontë. His mother had been delighted with the result and persuaded him to write some of his own stories. At first he did it to please her but he soon found that it also pleased him and that had been the beginning of his writing career.

The fact that he'd chosen to write historical romances still amazed him and he often wondered if he should turn his attention to thrillers or crime or something a bit more masculine but his mother's early influence had been too powerful and all those evenings together spent watching Jane Austen and Daphne du Maurier adaptations and films like *Dragonwyck* and *Gone with the Wind* had left their mark.

Now he was sailing high in the bestseller lists and leading a double life as a woman. For a moment, he wondered what his mother would make of it all. What would she say if she knew her little boy was known by the majority of the population as Lorna? She'd probably laugh—that lovely, silvery laugh of hers that had always made him laugh too.

His friends would laugh as well. He dreaded to think how much they'd laugh if they ever found out. Warwick Lawton writing as a *woman*! The same six-foot-two Warwick Lawton who went rock climbing and abseiling with his mates on weekends, swapping his keyboard for the feel of a bit of Peak District gritstone under his fingers? Surely not! But if he were honest, he rather liked the duality of his nature. It was like playing a game. One minute he was Warwick, speeding up the motorway in his latest fast car with a tangle of ropes and harnesses in his boot; the next he was Lorna researching women's undergarments in the early nineteenth century.

Of course the charade would be even funnier if he could share it with somebody, and he often wondered if the day would come when he could tell Katherine about it.

'And therein lies the problem,' he said to himself. What was he going to do about his little secret?

His bags were packed for Purley Hall and his agent had sorted out a last-minute room for him and he was leaving in less than an hour but he still hadn't made up his mind what to do about Katherine.

For a moment, he sat absolutely still, listening to the gentle tick of the grandfather clock in the hall. It was the heartbeat of the house and always made him feel calm and in control of things which wasn't how he was feeling at that time.

'Oh, God!' he suddenly exclaimed. Could it be that he was a little bit in love?

He let the thought somersault around in his brain before dismissing it. How could he possibly be in love? He'd never even met the woman although he had to confess to having Googled her, discovering a photograph of her outside St Bridget's College, Oxford, with a bunch of very stuffy-looking men in tweeds. And she was beautiful. He closed his eyes for a moment as he remembered the long chocolate-coloured wavy hair, the dark eyes in a pale face, and a rosebud mouth that was smiling at the camera. Very heroine-like, he thought, instantly casting her as his next vibrant leading lady and saving the photograph to his hard drive.

He'd sat down to read through all her letters again the night before, and one thing had struck him: she was a remarkable woman and he wanted to get to know her better. The way she wrote about books, the way she spoke about—well, *everything*—stirred him. She was passionate about things and wasn't afraid to express those feelings, unlike so many of the women in his past who never really had much to say at all. Take Fiona, the shopaholic: all she ever talked about was her nails and her shoes. Or Lindsay, the interior designer. Warwick had learned more about cushions and pelmets in the four months they'd been together than he'd had any desire to know.

No, Katherine wasn't like any other woman he'd met. She was sweet and smart and had a rapier wit that tickled him pink, and they'd shared such secrets. She trusted him.

She trusted Lorna, Warwick thought. *You aren't the person she thinks you are. Would she tell you all these secrets if she knew you were a man? Would she divulge such feelings if she realised that you were a male with a string of hopeless relationships behind him?*

That was the problem he had with the weekend that lay ahead. What was he going to do about Katherine?

He sat down in his office chair and surveyed the letters before him.

'I love getting your letters. It's so wonderful to know that there's somebody out there who understands,' he read from one of them.

'I really feel that I can trust you,' he read from another. *'You're a really good friend, Lorna, and that's just what I need at the moment.'*

'I can tell you everything and that's a real comfort. That means so much to me,' she'd written in another.

Things had soon become intimate between the two of them and Warwick had spent mornings pacing up and down for the post to arrive when he should have been working.

'*My first big love was my next door neighbour—how clichéd is that?*' Katherine had written just over a month before. '*I let him kiss me on our first date and it was horrible. It nearly put me off for life! But I didn't give in until I was at university. I fell madly in love with a year-three student who seduced me in the library when he was meant to be locking up! I'll never forget looking up at all those books and hoping that the spirits of Thomas Hardy and Emily Brontë weren't glowering down at me. Gosh! I've never told anyone about that before!*'

Warwick smiled as he remembered the confession—it had been the first of many.

He had to admit that the letters had a strange effect on him. They'd gone from the letters of a fan to the letters of a friend in a very short space of time, but they were more than that now. Even though he'd never met her, he felt incredibly close to Katherine and he didn't want to do anything to jeopardise that.

Warwick swallowed hard. This wasn't going to be easy. However he played it, the fact remained that he'd been replying to Katherine's letters under false pretences and had led her to believe that he was a woman. His string of terrible girlfriends had become boyfriends. Fiona's obsession with fashion had morphed into Tony's obsession with motorbikes, and Lindsay's cushions had become Lennie's cushions (Lorna had been horrified to discover that Lennie was gay). Katherine had been sympathetic and supportive of Lorna's hapless love life, offering advice when appropriate. '*Lennie's cushions sound like the perfect Christmas present for that awkward aunt of yours,*' Katherine had written. She'd put her trust in him completely, hadn't she?

Warwick let out a long, weary breath as he thought about the strange situation he'd managed to get himself into. It was like something from one of his books, he thought. Actually, the idea of a woman writing to a man but thinking she's a woman was a pretty good idea for a book, he thought with a grin, but then he felt guilty for even thinking about using his dear friend for the basis of his art. Still, he jotted it down in a notepad before he forgot it. A writer should never turn a good idea away just because it might offend somebody.

Chapter 5

To be stuck in a car with a loved one for more than two hundred miles would be a challenge at the best of times, but being stuck with the most impatient driver in the world when what you most wanted to do was break up with him was an impossible situation.

'I told you I should've come by train,' Robyn said as Jace honked at the driver in front of him for not moving away fast enough at a set of lights.

'What are you complaining about? We're making good time.'

Robyn sighed and did her best to relax. They'd left North Yorkshire just after ten in the morning and registration for the conference was at five o'clock, followed by tea and an official welcome by Dame Pamela Harcourt which Robyn didn't want to miss under any circumstances.

She was also hoping that they would have time for a slight detour to Steventon so she could see the church where Jane Austen had been baptised and spent her earlier years, but she wasn't sure how Jace would respond to such a proposal. Poking around churches with literary connections wasn't his sort of thing at all. He'd much sooner check into his bed and breakfast and head for the nearest pub to sink a few pints, then have an evening belching in front of the TV.

Robyn opened her handbag and pulled out the information sheets about the conference. After the tea and welcome, there was a chance to mingle before dinner and then there was a choice of watching either Emma Thompson's *Sense and Sensibility* or Simon Burke's version of *Persuasion*.

'Ooooo!' Robyn sighed.

'What's up?' Jace asked. 'Not another lady's stop.'

'No,' she said. 'Just choices to be made for tonight.' She didn't bother to go into details. He wouldn't understand. How could a woman choose between Hugh Grant's bumbling Edward Ferrars and Rupert Penry-Jones's smouldering Captain Wentworth? That was the trouble with Austen—there were too many wonderful heroes. It was hard enough deciding which book to read next and which hero to fall in love with again, but it also made real life hard too, for no man could live up to Austen's heroes, could they? Where was a girl going to find a man as patient as Colonel Brandon or as witty as Henry Tilney? And could one ever truly hope to find that elusive of all men—Mr Darcy?

Robyn smiled to herself. If the truth were known, she rather preferred Mr Bingley to Mr Darcy. He was—in Jane Austen's own words—*amiable*; there was nothing complicated about him and Robyn liked that. You didn't have to do any emotional wrestling with Bingley. He liked dancing. He smiled a lot. He didn't go around insulting anyone and making a hash at proposing to a woman. In short, he was just the sort of man Robyn was looking for.

But you have a man, a little voice inside her suddenly said.

But I don't want him, she replied.

Then you should tell him.

I've tried!

Then you haven't made a very good job of it, have you?

Robyn took a sideways glance at Jace. His eyes were narrowed into angry slits as he focused on the road ahead and then gesticulated at a car that was overtaking them. Mr Bingley would never gesticulate, Robyn couldn't help thinking. He was far more likely to articulate.

'Upon my honour!' he might declare. 'I have never met with so many unpleasant drivers in my life.' He would shake his head and think nothing more of it, probably declaring that a ball was in order and that he'd make the arrangements forthwith.

Yes, Robyn thought, Bingley was—as Jane Bennet had told Elizabeth—'just what a young man ought to be.'

Slowly coming out of a daydream in which she was wearing a white empire-line dress and dancing with Bingley, Robyn saw the sign announcing that they had crossed into Hampshire. At long last, she'd arrived in Jane Austen country.

Turning around to retrieve the road atlas from the backseat, she flipped to the right page and made a study of the area. Almost at once she found Chawton, perhaps because she'd circled it in bright red ink. There was already a planned trip to Chawton from Purley Hall on Saturday and Robyn was so excited about it that she felt sure she'd burst with joy but she longed to see the church at Steventon too.

'Jace?' she said, her voice gentle.

'What?' he snapped back.

'I've got an idea.'

'What sort of an idea?' he asked. 'A naughty idea?'

'No,' Robyn said. 'A detour idea.'

Jace frowned. 'I don't like detours. I like going from A to B, and A to B today has been one hell of a drive.'

'I know it has,' Robyn said sweetly, 'and you've been brilliant, but this is such a tiny detour, you'd never even notice it.'

Jace's frown didn't budge, but he tutted and sighed. 'All right, then. Where do you want me to go?'

Robyn was tempted to answer something rude to that particular question but said, 'Take the next right,' instead, and soon they were driving through the narrow lanes of Hampshire with tall hedge-rows and sunny fields on either side of them. The landscape was far less dramatic than Robyn was used to in the Yorkshire Dales but she loved its gentleness. With its pretty village pubs, cute cottages and stone churches, it was perfect and just what tourists thought of when they imagined Jane Austen's England.

As they passed an old wooden stile to the side of the road, Robyn could easily imagine Elizabeth Bennet hopping over it on her way to visit her sister, Jane, at Netherfield. For a moment she wondered whether she dare ask Jace to stop the car so she could walk across a couple of fields until her eyes shone like her favourite heroine's but one look at Jace changed her mind. He wouldn't understand and she'd better not push her luck after getting him to agree to the detour to Steventon.

It took only ten minutes to reach the little church and Robyn gasped as Jace stopped the car.

'Oh, look!' she said, her eyes wide with instant adoration.

'It's a church,' Jace said.

Robyn did her best to ignore his sarcastic tone. Nothing was going to spoil this moment, she determined.

'Aren't you coming in?' she asked as she opened her door.

'Nah. I'll wait here. Churches creep me out.'

Robyn sighed, but she was secretly glad that he wasn't coming with her. He'd only complain.

Getting out of the car, Robyn stretched her arms and took in a great lungful of warm October air. Theirs was the only car in the dead-end lane and everything was perfectly still and quiet.

She entered the churchyard and looked at the modest little building before her. St Nicholas's didn't shout about its presence in the landscape but it was very pretty, with a tiny crenellated tower in a warm beige stone and a small silver spire. Three arched windows sat above a fine wooden door, and on both sides were two carved faces gazing out over the pathway.

A great yew cast a cobwebby shadow across the front of the church, and Robyn thought of how Jane Austen must have walked by it many times and that made her smile.

After opening the church door and walking inside, she marvelled at the coolness of the building after the warm sunshine and gazed at the beautiful white arches under which delicate flowers had been painted.

A bright brass plaque on the wall to the left announced that Jane Austen had worshipped there. Robyn looked around at the neat wooden pews and walked up the aisle and sat down. Where would Jane have sat, she wondered, sitting in both the front-row pews and sliding along them just to cover all the options. Would she have been paying attention to her father's sermon or dreaming of handsome men on horseback? Was it in this very church that she'd created Elizabeth and Darcy, Elinor and Marianne, and Catherine and Tilney? Were their adventures of the heart conceived in this hushed and humbling place?

Robyn let a few peaceful moments pass.

'Only two hundred years or so separate us,' she said with a

smile. It felt strange to finally be sitting in a place her idol had once inhabited. Other than reading the novels, this was as close as she was ever going to get, wasn't it, to walk in the same steps and sit in the same seats?

At last Robyn got up and looked around the rest of the church, noting the memorial to Jane's brother, James, who succeeded his father as rector. There was also a moving memorial to three young girls, Mary Agnes, Cecilia and Augusta, who all died of scarlet fever in 1848.

'Great-nieces of Jane's,' Robyn whispered, 'whom she never lived to see.'

That was one of the great tragedies about the writer—that she led so short a life, dying at the age of forty-one. How many other wonderful novels might have been written if she'd lived longer? That was the question everyone asked. It was, truly, one of the greatest losses to literature and, although Robyn wasn't particularly religious, she couldn't help sending a little prayer up for Jane.

As Robyn walked back down the aisle, she noticed four beautiful kneelers in sky-blue featuring silhouettes of Regency ladies. Everyone, it seemed, was proud of the Austen connection.

After opening the great wooden door and stepping back outside, Robyn spotted a baby rabbit hopping amongst the graves. She walked around the back of the church which opened onto fields, and then thought she'd better make her way back to Jace.

As she left the churchyard and entered the lane, she suddenly heard the sound of horse hooves on the road. She turned around and saw a great chestnut stallion trotting down the lane, its mane and tail streaming out behind him. But the horse wasn't what captivated Robyn, for sitting astride the horse was the most beautiful man she'd ever seen.

A handsome man on horseback, Robyn thought. Hadn't she been thinking of just that image inside the church? It was as if she conjured him from wishful thinking—as if the magical world of Jane Austen had come to life before her very eyes.

She gazed up at the man as he rode by. His hair was a dark coppery gold underneath his riding hat and his arms were bare and tanned. Robyn could tell he was tall, and he sat proudly and confidently on the chestnut stallion. It really was a sight to behold and as he passed her by, he turned, nodded, and smiled, and Robyn could feel the most wonderful blush colouring her face.

'The man's a lunatic!' Jace yelled as the horse and rider picked up speed and shot across an adjacent field. 'Did you see how close he was to my car?'

'He wasn't anywhere near your car.'

'That horse could have kicked out and done all sorts of damage. He's totally out of control.'

'He's totally beautiful,' Robyn said, and then wondered if they were still talking about the horse.

Chapter 6

KATHERINE HAD JUST DELIVERED HER TWO BELOVED CATS TO a friend in the village and now had the unenviable task of saying good-bye.

'My darling boys,' she said, bending down to fondle them both.

Her friend shook her head. 'Freddie and Fitz,' she said. 'They're unusual names for cats.'

'They're my two favourite heroes,' Katherine said. 'Darcy and Wentworth.'

'Oh, I should've guessed. If they were named after my favourite heroes, they'd be Johnny and Brad.'

Katherine smiled. 'Make sure you feed them that new food I've left. They don't like that old food anymore.'

'You spoil them rotten,' her friend said.

'Of course,' Katherine said. 'That's exactly what they're for.'

'And no doubt I'll spoil them rotten too so don't you go worrying about them,' her friend told her.

It was always hard to leave her boys behind but Katherine had to do just that if she was to get down to Hampshire on time; so, saying her good-byes, she took one last look at her beloved cats and left.

Katherine was getting the train down to Hampshire and being

picked up from the station by someone from Purley Hall. She'd already packed and was looking forward to relaxing on the train. She had always loved travelling by train. It was rather like being suspended in time—you were neither in one place nor another and it was the perfect time to dip your nose in a good book. Which books was she going to choose this particular journey? *Northanger Abbey* and *Persuasion* were the obvious handbag choices because of their slimness, but *Emma* was her favourite and it was always fun to dip in and out of it, rereading much-loved scenes. A naughty twinkle was in Katherine's eyes as she organised her train reading. She knew she should be getting herself in the right frame of mind for her lecture at the conference by swotting up on some last-minute Austen, but the temptation to take a Lorna Warwick novel instead was just too much, so packing the Jane Austen six into her suitcase, she placed a much-beloved Lorna Warwick in her handbag, *The Notorious Lady Fenton*.

It was always hard to choose her favourite book, but there was something rather special about *The Notorious Lady Fenton*. It was kind of like a reversed *Pride and Prejudice,* where Lady Fenton clashes with a spirited but poor gentleman before realising that she's madly in love with him, defying family and friends to marry him. Isabella Fenton had to be one of Lorna Warwick's best creations. She was selfish yet sparkling, proud yet passionate, and she got the happy ending that all great heroines deserve.

Once Katherine had found her seat on the train, she took the beloved book out of her bag and turned to chapter one, hoping that she wouldn't be spotted by any of her colleagues or students as she indulged herself in the most decadent of fiction.

Living in West Sussex and having neither chickens nor cats to worry about, Warwick didn't have to leave his home until the afternoon, driving his black Jaguar through the country lanes at a sedate speed. The car had been his little treat to himself once the US sales for his novels had really begun to take off.

He wondered what time Katherine would arrive and how quickly he would recognize her. How could he introduce himself? Would she even like him as a man? And was he going to use his real name, Warwick Lawton? Was the Warwick not a bit of a giveaway? And what profession should he now have?

All sorts of questions flew around in his mind. He hadn't felt this nervous since dating at university. He felt out of practice at this sort of thing and wasn't sure if he could pull it off. His string of broken relationships over the past few years was surely the evidence that he was meant to be alone. Maybe that was one of the reasons he was a writer: he was far more successful in his own company. But there was something about Katherine that made him want to forget his past failures and try again. She could be worth risking embarrassment, humiliation and rejection for.

If only he had the confidence that he gave to his heroes in his novels, he thought, then he would stride into a room, quickly survey all before him, and draw all eyes towards him, before singling out the woman of his choice, who would, of course, be palpitating with desire by then. He would make his approach, bow, silently admire her décolletage as she curtsied before him, say something immeasurably witty, and then take her hand and lead the first dance.

How easy it was back then, he thought. Men and women had clear-cut roles and were happy to play them. Today everything was muddled. Women didn't want to be bowed to or to be told that they were charming creatures and have their eyes admired.

Or did they?

For a moment Warwick wondered.

The women who were attending the Jane Austen Conference might be different. They might actually want a gentleman who admired the clothes they wore, asked about the books they read and pestered them to play the pianoforte. They'd want a Jane Austen or Lorna Warwick hero, wouldn't they? Wasn't that why they read the books? Wasn't that precisely why there were so many adaptations of Austen's novels—because the female population couldn't get enough?

Warwick grinned at this most amazing discovery. He knew exactly how he was going to play things with Katherine.

Chapter 7

ROBYN WOULD NEVER FORGET HER FIRST GLIMPSE OF PURLEY Hall. They'd rounded corner after corner of twisting country lane, the vast hedges full of rosy pink blackberry flowers when suddenly there it was, red-gold and glorious across the rolling blond fields. It sat in symmetrical perfection, its aspect cushioned by the countryside around it, with honey-coloured fields stretching out in front of it and deep green woods behind it.

'Look!' she exclaimed, pointing out the window like an excited toddler.

Jace looked. 'What?'

'Purley!'

'Where?'

'Where?' Robyn echoed. '*There!*'

'That? I thought it would be bigger.'

'It's perfect,' Robyn said, counting its three visible storeys and its seven sash windows across. 'Twenty-one,' she said.

'Twenty-one what?'

'Twenty-one windows. Or rather twenty. I expect one's a door.'

Jace grimaced. Windows and doors didn't interest him. He took another bend in the road and entered the tiny village of Purley.

There was a row of picture-perfect cottages with dark thatched roofs, a pub called The Dog and Boot, and a pale gold church with a modest steeple.

'Oh, I love it!' Robyn said. 'Isn't it lovely?'

''S all right if you like that sort of thing,' Jace mumbled.

Robyn bristled. Well, she *did* like that sort of thing and it was getting hard to enjoy it all with Jace as her companion. When, she wondered, was she going to get rid of him?

'Where are we going, anyway?' he asked impatiently.

It was then that Robyn saw a discreet wooden sign pointing right. 'Purley Hall,' it read, and there was a handwritten sheet of A4 paper tacked underneath. 'Janeites this way!'

They turned into a driveway that could easily have stretched the length of Robyn's whole village back in Yorkshire. The driveway was lined with mature trees, and there were fields either side of it.

Robyn was almost on the edge of her seat as the driveway widened and the grand front of Purley Hall greeted them.

'Oh!'

'What's wrong?' Jace asked.

'Nothing! Nothing at all,' Robyn said.

Jace tutted and brought the car to a screeching halt, its tyres firing up a shower of gravel. He parked almost—but not quite—parallel with a black Jaguar.

'Someone's got some money,' he said.

'Yes, apparently some people have,' Robyn said, wondering what it must be like.

Robyn got out of the car and looked up at the house. The front was in shade, and a great cedar tree to the left shaded the tennis courts and cast its shadow across an immaculate lawn, its branches sprawling out like dinosaur limbs. A set of croquet hoops had been left out on the lawn and beyond that, Robyn spied a bright blue swimming pool.

She looked up at the house once more, awestruck by the size of its windows, which were as large as the great door, and the triangular pediment at the top which soared into the blue sky above.

'Right,' Jace said, interrupting her thoughts, 'I'm off to the pub.'

Robyn did her best to hide her relief. 'What are you going to do with yourself this weekend?'

He shrugged. 'Come and see you.'

'Oh, but you can't,' Robyn said. 'There are activities all day, and you'd be bored stupid by them.'

'All right, all right, I get the message. I'll call you, okay? You've got your mobile, haven't you?'

Robyn nodded.

Jace leant in to kiss her and gave her bottom and affectionate squeeze. Robyn blushed. It wasn't seemly to have one's bottom pinched at a Jane Austen Conference.

Jace hauled her suitcase out of the boot of the car and handed it to her. 'I won't come in,' he said.

'Best not,' Robyn said.

'I'll give you a call.'

'Okay,' Robyn said, watching as he got in the car, did a boy-racer manoeuvre on the immaculate driveway, and disappeared. As soon as he was out of view, she took her mobile out of her handbag and switched it off.

Warwick had arrived a little earlier than predicted but had been welcomed by one of the event organisers and shown to a very nice room upstairs that looked out over the gardens to the river and fields beyond. Nadia had worked wonders at getting him a room in the house at the last minute, and he marvelled at the beauty of it. It sported an enormous bed in a rich dark wood with a pretty yellow bedspread. Four fabulously plump pillows caught his eye and promised a sweet slumber that night.

He looked around the room, and a pretty mahogany dressing stand inset with a porcelain bowl in blue and white caught his eye. He knew that such a piece of furniture would have been common in a Regency gentleman's bedroom, and he took delight in the fact that he was to be its owner for the next few days although he was also glad that he had a modern en suite with power shower. Jugs and bowls just didn't cut it in the hygiene stakes anymore.

A crystal vase of yellow and white roses stood on the deep windowsill and scented the room with their delicate fragrance, and the walls were painted in a shade Warwick recognised as verdigris—a willowy green that was in keeping with the period of the house and gave the room a wonderfully fresh feel. It was a beautiful room.

Warwick wasn't at Purley Hall to stand admiring his bedroom, though. He had to register and see if Katherine had arrived yet, so quickly changing his shirt, he checked his reflection in the mirror—more out of fear that something might be out of place than for vanity—and headed down the grand staircase to where a table had been set for registration.

'The dreaded name badges,' Warwick said to himself. He didn't have time to create yet another pseudonym for himself, he thought. He was to be Warwick Lawton this weekend. His fate was sealed.

About a dozen people milled around the registration table and more were arriving by the minute. Warwick stood at a respectable distance and watched the goings on. As a writer, he was used to observing, and his height gave him the advantage of being able to see everything. The young girl at the reception table was quizzing an elderly woman about her name badge.

'Norris?' the girl said.

'Yes,' the lady with cloudy white hair said. 'Like in *Mansfield Park.*'

'*Doris* Norris?'

'Yes,' the lady said with a cheery smile. 'I know what you're thinking. It's not very likely, is it? But I wasn't always a Norris, you see. I was Doris Webster. Perfectly normal. But then I met Henry Norris and had the misfortune to fall in love with him so here I am—Doris Norris.'

The young girl grinned, and Warwick could see that she was doing her very best not to laugh. He watched for a moment as Doris Norris pinned her name badge onto her pink cardigan, but then a young woman by the door caught his attention. She had long blond hair that corkscrewed down to her waist. Her face was pale with perfect features set into a slightly anxious expression as if she were asking herself, what do I do now? She was wearing a pretty white dress dotted with daisies, and her feet were encased in a pair of silver sandals. Warwick watched her as she looked around the hall, tiny white teeth biting her lower lip, and a part of him wanted to go help her—to take her bag and say, 'Come this way,' but the writer in him stayed perfectly still and watched.

That was one of the things about being a writer—one always stood slightly apart, listening and watching. It was hard to tell sometimes, if one were really alive, for life seemed to be happening to everybody else, and yet the writer's lot seemed to be one of permanent stillness. Had Jane Austen felt like that? he wondered. With neither husband nor children of her own, had she felt that her role had been to watch others? And had that made her happy?

Her books made other people happy, that fact was unquestionable, but had they made *her* happy?

Warwick shook his head. He might well be at a Jane Austen Conference, but he wasn't ready to get all philosophical just yet. He wanted to have some fun. He wanted to see Katherine. He could feel his pulse accelerate at the thought of seeing her for the first time. She wouldn't know who he was so he couldn't call out to her across the room. He would have the chance to watch her. Wasn't that role his favourite? He could get to know a little bit about her before he said hello.

He smiled. He certainly had the advantage in this relationship, he thought.

'My wheels seem to be jammed,' a voice suddenly boomed across the hallway.

Warwick's eyes fixed on the sort of woman who can only be described as a battle-axe. She had an enormous bosom that was thrust out before her indignantly and a face that seemed to be carved out of angry granite. Warwick watched as she struggled with her suitcase and decided he'd better do the gentlemanly thing and offer some assistance. He was in training for a hero, after all, wasn't he?

Chapter 8

ONCE KATHERINE CLIMBED THE STEPS AND ENTERED PURLEY, the naughty novels of Lorna Warwick would have to be forgotten as the weekend promised wall-to-wall Jane Austen. There was no room there for the imitators, the pastiches or the sequels, however good they might be. This was Purley Hall, and nothing but the original Jane Austen was accepted.

Katherine couldn't help feeling a little sad that Lorna wasn't going to be there. She felt quite sure she'd enjoy the experience. They'd talked so much about Austen's novels in their letters to each other and Katherine knew that Lorna's presence would have made the weekend an absolute treat. How much they would have to talk about! They would probably be like a couple of naughty students, chatting and giggling at the back of the lecture rooms, swapping comments and anecdotes.

I wonder what she looks like, Katherine thought as she entered the grand hall of Purley, marvelling at the double staircase and smelling the intoxicating lilies that sat in their vases like marble sculptures above the fireplace. It didn't really matter what she looked like—Katherine knew that, and yet she'd still Googled the name, only to come up with innumerable images of Lorna Warwick novels from around the world. There were no photographs of the writer—not even on her website. Anyway, she wasn't going to be there so what did it matter?

When Katherine looked around the room, one thing was certain. She might not have any idea of what Lorna looked like, but if she were attending the conference, Katherine was sure to recognise her immediately. It would be like old friends meeting up after years of separation.

As she made her way towards the crowded reception desk, she heard a voice, and a chill iced her spine. Oh, no, she thought as she turned around and saw the woman she'd dreaded seeing: Mrs Soames. They'd crossed paths before, and Katherine remembered all too well the woman who could cloud over the loveliest day just by entering a room. She was the kind of woman who found something to complain about in even the simplest of tasks. Nothing was beyond reproach. Whether it was a day's excursion or a cup of tea, Mrs Soames was bound to find something in it that was worth complaining about.

Katherine did her best to sneak by her as she was shouting some orders at a man who seemed to be crawling underneath her suitcase. She could barely make out a pair of long legs ending in smart brown leather shoes poking out from one side of the enormous suitcase and the top of a tousled head of hair at the other end.

'What do you think you're doing?' Mrs Soames said. '*That's* not going to do any good!'

'I think I can loosen it here,' the man's voice said. 'Yes, that ought to do the trick.'

Katherine watched as the dark-haired man stood back up to full height, pushing the suitcase in her direction as he did so.

'Ouch!' Katherine screamed. 'My foot!'

'Oh, my God! I'm so sorry,' the man said, turning around to look at her. 'Are you okay?'

'No, I'm not okay. You've run over my foot with a two tonne suitcase!'

'I beg your pardon?' Mrs Soames said. 'Oh, it's you, Dr Roberts.' There was no trace of concern in her voice for Katherine's poor foot.

Katherine bent down to rub her bruised toes.

'May I help you?' the man asked, his bright eyes filled with concern.

'You're meant to be helping *me*!' Mrs Soames said, her mouth set in a firm line.

'Of course,' the man said. 'Look, I'm so sorry. If there's anything I can do—'

'Just give me some space,' Katherine said, wincing as she hobbled away with her own suitcase.

Robyn took a deep breath and approached the young girl at the desk.

'Hello. I'm here for the conference.'

'What's your name?' the girl asked.

'Robyn. Robyn Love.'

'Oh! What a gorgeous name!'

Robyn gave a shy smile. 'I'm usually told how strange it is.'

'I've met stranger,' the girl said with a giggle, and Robyn wondered what she meant. 'You've got a welcome pack?'

'Yes, thank you.'

The girl looked down at her register. 'You're in the cedar room. Up the stairs and turn right. It's at the end of the corridor.'

The cedar room, Robyn said to herself. She liked the sound of it.

'Mark will help you with your bags.'

Robyn turned and came face to face with a young man who immediately took her suitcase from her.

'Oh, just a minute, Mark,' the young girl said. 'Here's Dr Roberts. She's just opposite, in the river room.'

Robyn turned to see a beautiful woman with dark hair swept up in a severe bun. She was wearing a crisp white shirt and a knee-length black skirt that was pencil-thin over her shapely legs.

'Hello,' Dr Roberts said to the girl who handed her a badge. She then turned to smile at Robyn. 'Please, call me Katherine,' she said, but then she winced.

'Are you okay?' Robyn asked.

Katherine nodded. 'Some idiot just wheeled a suitcase right over my foot. I fear I'll be hobbling the rest of today.'

'Oh, dear!' Robyn said. 'We'll have to find a handsome Willoughby to carry you up the stairs.'

Katherine laughed. 'I think I can make it up myself.'

Mark picked up Katherine's suitcase and led the two women up the stairs.

'Have you travelled far?' Katherine asked Robyn.

'North Yorkshire.'

'A bit farther than me, then. I've only come from Oxford.'

'You're the lecturer, aren't you?' Robyn said excitedly. 'I've read your book!'

'For pleasure?'

'Oh, yes!' Robyn enthused.

Katherine laughed. 'I'm forgetting that everyone here enjoys Austen. I lecture at St Bridget's in Oxford, and I'm afraid the students there aren't all as enthusiastic about our Jane.'

'It must be a hard job,' Robyn said, full of admiration for her new friend.

'Some of the time,' she said, 'but I'm teaching the subject I love and, of course, I get to come to events like this.'

Robyn nodded. 'I wish I'd had the chance to go to study. I would have loved it. It's one of the reasons I like coming to things like this. I learn so much.'

Katherine smiled. 'Learning is a lifelong pleasure.'

The two women climbed the left-hand staircase which joined the right one in the middle and led them up to the first floor where the bedrooms were.

'This is such an amazing house,' Robyn said, gazing back down the stairs to the hall below, her feet making no sound on the plush red carpet.

'This is called the Imperial Staircase,' Katherine told her. 'One of the finest in the country.'

Robyn suddenly stopped.

'What is it?' Katherine asked.

'That man,' Robyn said, nodding to a dark-haired gentleman at the bottom of the stairs. 'He's been watching us. Do you know him?'

Katherine's gaze followed Robyn's. 'Oh! It's that dreadful man who attacked me with a suitcase.'

Robyn watched as the man turned away. 'He's rather good-looking,' she said.

'Well, if you like that obvious tall, dark, and handsome look,' Katherine said.

'Tolerable but not handsome enough to tempt you?' Robyn asked with a grin.

Katherine's gaze met hers. 'Something like that.'

They walked on, reaching the top of the stairs and turning right down a corridor lined with portraits.

'We're at the end,' Mark said, stopping outside two bedroom doors. 'Dr Roberts here,' he said, opening the door on the right. 'Miss Love here,' he said, opening the door to the left. 'Enjoy your stay at Purley.'

Robyn smiled, confident that she was going to do just that.

Warwick was mortified. Of all the people to run over with a suit-case, he had to go and pick Katherine. What a way to finally meet her. He recognised her instantly, of course, but the memory of the look she gave him was enough to make him give up and go home right then.

He helped Mrs Soames to her room with her suitcase and quickly returned to the hall, hoping to apologise to Katherine again and make some sort of amends, but she was on her way up the stairs by then with the young woman in the silver sandals.

He stood and watched, getting his first proper look at Katherine, and what he saw surprised him. What had happened to the long, luxurious hair he'd seen in the photograph of her online? Instead of cascading over her shoulders, it had been tugged into a tight bun, flattened and lifeless at the back of her head. He took in the business-smart outfit in black and white, and the author in him wanted to rewrite her, dressing her in a vibrant colour and unpin-ning her dark hair.

He watched as she talked to the girl with the corkscrew curls and followed their progress up the stairs. He hadn't meant to stare. That stance wasn't the heroic one he'd planned at all and he felt such a fool when he was spotted.

First impressions were important, he thought, thinking of the disastrous one that had befallen Elizabeth Bennet and

Mr Darcy, and Austen herself had realised the role they played when she'd given *Pride and Prejudice* the original title of *First Impressions*. Warwick groaned. He'd completely missed his opportunity to make a good first impression—*twice*. Still, he was an author and was quite used to rewriting plots that didn't work. He'd just have to wait for another opportunity and make sure he got it right next time.

Chapter 9

THE CEDAR ROOM WAS ABSOLUTELY PERFECT AND ROBYN WAS immediately in love with it, rushing over to the great sash window in excitement and sighing like a lovelorn heroine at the view that greeted her. The perfect emerald lawn stretched before her, and the cedar tree stood sentinel-like to her right.

She looked at the double bed and felt guilty that it was for her and her alone and that Jace would be sleeping on his own, but that certainly wasn't her fault. She hadn't asked him to chauffeur her to and from the conference, had she? It was his fault if he was going to be stuck in a bed and breakfast bored out of his mind for the next few days. Robyn was quite determined that he wasn't going to ruin her weekend. She'd looked forward to it for too long.

Flinging open her suitcase and finding her hairbrush, she entered the bathroom and did a quick repair job on her travel-worn tresses. She'd worn her hair long all her life and couldn't imagine it being any other way. It was much admired and Jace loved it but it did take some upkeep, and Robyn often wondered what life would be like with a nice neat bob.

She emptied her handbag of everything she didn't need, which included two paperbacks and a bumper packet of mints, then left her room.

She was halfway down the grand staircase when she caught the eye of Katherine in the hall.

'Robyn!' she called. 'Come and sit with me.'

Robyn joined her in the hall and Katherine linked her arm through hers.

'Now, we're just like a pair of Austen heroines, aren't we?' she said.

Robyn smiled and the two of them walked to the back of the house and entered the room known as the Yellow Drawing Room. It was filled with mellow afternoon light and the windows looked out over the gardens down to the river.

'I have this view from my window,' Katherine boasted.

'It's beautiful here,' Robyn said. 'I don't think I'll ever want to leave.'

'I know,' Katherine said. 'I always feel like that too. It's part of the magic of the conference. They know you'll be back year after year. It gets ahold of you and never lets you go.'

There were three enormous sofas in the room and lots of armchairs in brilliant colours and filling in the gaps some wooden chairs had been placed to accommodate all the guests.

'How many people are here?' Robyn asked.

'There are usually twenty to thirty, but not everyone stays in the hall. There are only enough rooms here for about eighteen. Everyone else stays in nearby B and Bs.'

Robyn swallowed as she thought of Jace again. She wished she could stop doing that.

'Let's get a cup of tea,' Katherine said, bringing Robyn back into the Austensian world of Purley that was filled with china tea cups rather than the Jace world which was filled with beer cans.

Taking a cup of tea and a piece of sugary shortbread, they sat on a big squashy sofa the colour of lemons.

'Hey, there's that suitcase man again,' Robyn said, nodding towards the door as the dark-haired gentleman walked in.

'Oh,' Katherine said.

'He *is* very handsome, don't you think?'

'He's very clumsy,' Katherine replied, turning away.

Robyn smiled. She could feel a romance coming on; she was quite sure of it. 'He's so fit-looking,' she persisted. 'But not in that awful I-spend-all-my time-in-a-gym way. He looks more like an athlete or something. Nice shirt too, don't you think?'

'I'm doing my best *not* to think about him,' Katherine said.

Just as Robyn was contemplating an Austen-style declaration of love from the dark-haired gentleman to her new friend, a gentleman in a scarlet waistcoat entered the room, stood in front of the window and cleared his throat, instantly hushing the room.

'Ladies and gentlemen, it gives me great pleasure to welcome you to Purley Hall and to the Jane Austen Conference. Please put your hands together to welcome your hostess, Dame Pamela Harcourt.'

A wondrous expectant hush befell the room, quickly followed by a riotous round of applause as all eyes turned to the door and the actress made her entrance.

Robyn felt a strange fluttery feeling in her chest. She was actually nervous. She'd been a fan of Dame Pamela's for years. In her youth, she had played an enchanting Elizabeth Bennet and a dazzlingly wild Marianne in TV adaptations, and now she struck terror into the heart of viewers with her portrayals of Fanny Ferrars Dashwood and Lady Catherine de Bourgh.

Robyn's head swivelled towards the door and her mouth dropped open as Dame Pamela made her entrance in a sweep of lilac. Her silvery hair had been swept up in a full meringue style that was pure theatre, and her smile radiated warmth and pleasure at being the centre of attention.

'My dears!' she announced, her hands raised and sparkly with diamond rings. 'My *wonderful* guests! Welcome to my home which, for this all-too-brief space of time, is your home too. I can't tell you how much I look forward to this weekend every year, and each year is invariably better than the last so welcome to the best-ever Jane Austen Conference yet!'

There was another round of applause and Dame Pamela smiled and began to mingle.

～◦

Warwick didn't stay for the mingling.

Idiot! Imbecile! Stupid, stupid man!

He didn't spare the curses as he left the Yellow Drawing Room. What had happened to him? Hadn't he been going to recreate the role of hero and stride across the room to introduce himself to Katherine? If so, what had happened? Well, once he'd caught sight of her again, he'd frozen. For ages he'd gazed at the beautiful curve of her neck which, as her hair was still swept up into a bun, had been left exposed for the express purpose of tormenting men. Then she'd turned round and caught him staring.

Like a ridiculous school boy, he said to himself, leaving the scene of his crime and flying up the stairs as fast as he could. *What must she think of me? She must think I'm a jerk to be avoided at all costs, and I've not even spoken to her yet.*

When he reached his room, he slammed the door behind him. What was he going to do? What would a hero do, he thought. What would Darcy do? Write a letter, probably, but he couldn't do that. For one thing, Katherine would recognise his handwriting. Anyway, there wasn't time.

He could try explaining himself, but what was there to explain? That he was some sort of neck pervert? She'd have him arrested. No, there was only one way to deal with this, which was to pretend that the whole staring thing hadn't happened at all, rather like Mrs Bennet's sudden memory lapse at the bad behaviour of Lydia once she found out that her daughter was married.

Yes, he thought, the new improved Warwick would banish any bad memories of the old one.

Chapter 10

DINNER AT PURLEY HALL WAS ALWAYS SOMETHING TO LOOK forward to and Robyn's first experience was sending her spinning with excitement as she rushed from suitcase to wardrobe in search of the dress she was going to wear. It was a plain sky-blue dress with only a hint of bugle beads along the neckline and it was rather short for Robyn, just skimming the knees instead of covering her ankles.

She felt on show as she made her way down the stairs, very aware of the bareness of her legs, but then she saw the familiar face of Katherine, and her nod of approval put Robyn's mind at rest. Katherine was wearing a pretty dress in burgundy. Her hair had been unpinned and fell over her shoulders in dark waves.

'You look lovely,' Robyn said.

'So do you!'

'I don't often get the chance to dress up at home,' Robyn said. 'This is rather special.'

'It's one of the things I enjoy here.'

Robyn noticed that the dining room door was open, but people were chatting in groups in the hall before entering.

'We're waiting for the dame,' Katherine told her.

Sure enough, a moment later, a hush descended and all eyes

turned upwards towards the cantilevered staircase. It really was the staircase of an actress, Robyn thought, and an actress who knew how to make an entrance, for as the grandfather clock in the hall struck the half hour, a vision in violet greeted them.

Dame Pamela was a sight to behold at the best of times, but that night she was part superstar, part royalty, in a dress of deepest purple which wafted dreamily behind her, and a diamond necklace that encrusted the whole of her neck so that it seemed to be made more of diamonds than skin.

As was becoming the practice whenever Dame Pamela made an appearance, everybody burst into applause which had the effect of lighting up her face like the most enchanting of queens. She took the arm of a gentleman wearing a suit of midnight blue, and the two of them led the way into the dining room.

Robyn entered and her eyes lit up both physically and meta-phorically because the room was a delight of chandeliers and candles. To be as authentic as possible to Jane Austen, electricity had been shunned and the result was greeted by appreciative gasps from the guests as they entered. It was a room that seemed to stretch forever and Robyn thought she needed at least three pairs of eyes in her head to take it all in. The walls were cream with ornate gold plasterwork on the ceiling that glimmered in the light from the candles. There was an impressive fireplace that hadn't been lit, owing to the continued warmth of the season, but which Robyn could imagine it being the very heart of the house when it was alive and roaring, filling the room with the unmistakable smell of home.

Several grand portraits lined the walls, the pale faces gazing down at the guests with the passivity typical of the painted form. Robyn wondered who the people were and how long they had been staring down from those walls. Were they ancestors of Dame Pamela or had she bought the portraits as part of the house when she moved to Purley?

With a dozen questions swimming around in her head, Robyn took her seat, and her gaze fell upon the beautiful table settings, the flower displays and the silverware. It certainly beat beans on toast on the sofa in front of the television in her little terrace, she thought as she gazed at the vases of pink and white roses that lined the table.

White plates and bowls sat in front of the guests and two crystal glasses waited to be filled. It was all so sumptuous that Robyn was almost afraid to touch anything. She was accustomed to her old scratched dinner plates and a sturdy pottery mug.

'I wonder if we'll see our friend,' Robyn said, eyeing the other guests up and down the length of the great table.

'Who's that?'

'The gentleman who likes staring at you so much.'

'I don't think you can call such a man a gentleman,' Katherine said. 'If you looked up the word *gentleman* in the dictionary, there'd be a picture of him—with a great red cross through it.'

Robyn laughed.

'And if you really want to know where he is, he's over there.'

Robyn looked at the end of the table and saw the dark-haired man. 'I wonder why he hasn't introduced himself yet.'

'I'm hoping he's too embarrassed,' Katherine said. 'I can quite do without such complications, anyway.'

Robyn's eyes widened at this declaration, and she waited, hoping that Katherine might say more, but she didn't and the moment passed as the starters were served.

They were halfway through dinner when things began to get interesting. Robyn was just finishing her last mouthful of pavlova when a gentleman entered the room and quietly made his way to the head of the table. He was tall and his coppery blond hair flopped over his face in a manner that suggested he wasn't a part of the conference. He was wearing a loose shirt, dirt-encrusted trousers, and a pair of boots, and Robyn recognised him at once. It was the handsome man on horseback she'd seen in the lane at Steventon and she watched as he approached Dame Pamela and whispered something in her ear. She made to get up out of her seat, but the man placed a tanned hand on her shoulder and shook his head.

What was that about? Robyn wondered. Did the man work at Purley for Dame Pamela or was he her latest boy toy? It was a well-known fact that the dame liked her men a lot younger than herself, and he was certainly handsome. Nobody could blame her if this was the latest handsome young man she'd chosen to help her learn her lines.

Robyn watched as the man turned to leave the room, his coppery hair catching the light of the candles and giving it the look of a halo.

She tutted at herself. Honestly, what was she thinking of, and why was she looking at his bottom? What would Jane Austen have made of such brazen actions? She'd probably have laughed her head off and then written them all down so as not to forget them, Robyn thought, quite sure that the author would have eyed enough men's bottoms in her time as any other red-blooded woman. Especially in the fashions of her time. It was absolutely wicked but great fun to imagine the young author dreaming of Fitzwilliam Darcy and Captain Wentworth and what they might look like in their breeches. Wasn't that a big part of why the film and television adaptations were so successful—because of the fine display of men's bottoms?

Robyn felt herself blushing and cursed her girlishness. She knew her whole face had a tendency to flame scarlet rather than colour her cheeks a subtle shade of pink and it was most embarrassing. She looked down at her lap for a moment, feeling the colour ebbing away before she dared to look up at the handsome young man again. She loved the way he walked the length of the room with easy strides. He had a wonderful grace that comes from riding a horse well.

Robyn was soon distracted from her quiet admiration because when he opened the door to leave, it almost crashed into his face as a second man stumbled into the room.

'Oh, my god!' Robyn said, her mouth dropping open in horror. It was Jace.

A sudden hush fell over the dining room as thirty pairs of eyes swivelled in the direction of the door as the dishevelled man crashed into a chair, sending its occupant sprawling across the table.

Robyn's blush returned with a vengeance while she watched the scene unfolding.

'Where's my gal?' Jace announced, looking up and tripping over his own feet when he tried to move forward.

'Excuse me!' a voice suddenly boomed. It was the man in the scarlet waistcoat whom Robyn thought of as the master of ceremonies.

'What?' Jace said, standing back up to full height and swaying like a reed in the wind.

'Who are you and what are you doing here?'

'Jace, mate. Who the hell are you?'

A collective gasp of horror rose from around the table at the rude interruption and Robyn wanted to slide quietly under it until it was all over, but it was too late to do anything because Jace had spotted her.

'There's my darlin'! There's my Robbie!'

'Robyn?' Katherine asked. 'Is he yours?'

'No,' Robyn said. 'I mean yes. Kind of.'

Katherine looked confused and Robyn swallowed hard because the whole room was looking at her.

'Really!' the master of ceremonies said. 'I must ask you to leave. This is a private function.'

'Get your hands off me. I'm here to see my gal.' Jace stumbled and swayed across the room, catching hold of the table in front of him when he reached Robyn. 'Babes!' he said. 'I was worried about you. Your phone must be broken.'

'It's not broken, Jace,' Robyn said in a whisper, hoping he'd lower his voice to match her own.

'I had to come and see you—make sure you were all right.'

Robyn stood up. 'You shouldn't be here!'

'I was bored!' he whined. 'I'm stuck in that bloody B and B by myself.'

There were more gasps and mutterings from the guests at the intruder's ripe language.

'I told you not to come.'

'Aw, babes!' he said, making an attempt to hug her, but she swerved out of the way. 'Don't be like that.'

'You should have stayed at home,' Robyn said, anger raising her voice. 'This isn't the place for you.'

'Come with me,' he said, grabbing her wrist.

'You're hurting me.'

'What do you want to be with all these stiffs for when you can be having fun with me?'

'Jace!'

'Hey! Leave her alone.' Somebody stepped in between them and calmly but firmly pushed Jace away from Robyn. It was the handsome man on horseback. 'I think you'd better leave. That's your taxi outside, right?'

Jace's face had turned purple with rage. 'You're that toff whose horse kicked my car?'

Robyn shook her head. 'It didn't kick your car, Jace.'

'You are, aren't you? Is that why you're here?' Jace asked, peering around the man to look at Robyn and almost toppling in the process.

'What are you talking about?' Robyn said.

'I know you women. You don't care who the man is as long as he's on a bloody horse. Put bloody Jabba the Hutt on a horse and you'd all be swooning over him.'

'Jace, you need to lie down.'

'Let's get you into that taxi,' the handsome man on horseback said.

'But I want to stay,' Jace cried, shaking the man's hand off him.

'No, you don't. We'll be watching a film later,' Robyn said. 'You'll be bored out of your mind if you stay.'

'What, a film with one of those infernal dance scenes?'

'Exactly,' Robyn said.

Jace seemed to be considering this information for a moment and, finally, he saw sense. 'When will I see you?'

'I'll give you a call in the morning, okay?'

Jace nodded. He looked as if he was about to fall asleep or maybe just fall.

'Let's get you into that taxi,' the handsome man on horseback said.

'Waitwaitwait,' Jace said, bending forward and grabbing hold of Robyn, placing a slobbery kiss on her mouth before leaving the room.

Robyn sank back down in her chair.

'You okay?' Katherine asked as everyone around the table started whispering to one another, desperately trying to find out what was going on.

'That was terrible,' Robyn said. 'Everyone's looking at me.'

'No they're not.'

'I think I'd like to leave.'

Katherine nodded. 'I'll come with you.'

The two of them left the dining room and Robyn breathed a sigh of relief. 'Thanks for not asking too many questions,' she said.

Katherine smiled. 'If you want to talk about it, I'm here. If not, no problem.'

'I appreciate that.'

They walked up the stairs together.

'You'll come back downstairs for the film night, won't you?' Katherine said when they reached their bedroom doors.

Robyn looked lost in thought for a moment as if she couldn't quite place where she was or who was speaking to her. Finally she nodded.

'Good,' Katherine said, checking her watch. 'Shall I knock for you?'

Again Robyn nodded.

'I must say, I was tempted to watch *Sense and Sensibility* for the hundredth time, but I've decided to wallow in *Persuasion*,' Katherine said. 'What about you?'

Robyn hadn't given it much thought. Although she preferred *Persuasion* as a story, she really couldn't cope with it that night. The scene when Anne Elliot realises that she and her one-time lover, Frederick, are like strangers—worse than strangers because they can never become acquainted—always brought tears to Robyn's eyes and would be just enough to tip her over the edge in front of everybody.

'It was perpetual estrangement.' That line always got Robyn. That was the lump-in-the-throat moment and, if she was ever watching the film in company, a sly finger would dab at the tear ducts and a long soft sniff would try to hide the sadness in her heart.

Perpetual estrangement, Robyn thought. Wasn't that exactly what she wanted from Jace?

Chapter 11

KATHERINE DIDN'T SEE ROBYN BEFORE THE FILM BEGAN and wasn't even sure that she hadn't shut herself away in her room for the rest of the evening. Who could blame her? After the awful scene in the dining room, it would be a wonder if Robyn showed her face again at all that weekend. Poor Robyn. It wasn't her fault. As Katherine chose a seat in the library, she wondered about Robyn's story. The man she'd called Jace didn't seem at all suited to her and it puzzled Katherine why she was with somebody like that. But then, who knew what went on in the heart of another person and what might attract one to another?

Just as the lights were being switched off, Katherine became aware of a presence by her side and looked up into the face of the suitcase-wielding gentleman, except luckily for her, he was without his weapon of choice.

'Is this seat taken?' he asked, his voice low, almost shy.

Katherine shook her head, not wanting to add any words of encouragement or to maintain eye contact.

'I couldn't make up my mind which film to see,' the man said.

Katherine's attention remained fixed on the television as the sad yet serene face of Sally Hawkins looked out at the audience with clear, all-seeing eyes.

'I love *Persuasion,* but *Sense and Sensibility* has so much to recommend it too, doesn't it?' the man went on.

Katherine shifted in her chair.

'A wonderful script,' he said. 'One of the best adaptations of a book ever.'

'Shush!' a woman said from a chair behind them.

'And the young Kate Winslet of course,' he added.

'Young man!' the woman from behind them protested. 'Will you stop talking?'

'Sorry,' the man said.

Katherine allowed herself a very small smile. A young Kate Winslet indeed!

It was strange but, no matter how many times Katherine read the novel or saw the adaptations, Anne and Wentworth's story never failed to move her. It was, perhaps, Austen's slowest story in terms of action, but there was a beauty about its simple structure and its sublimely gentle narration. Anne was one of the most sympathetic heroines in literature because she had made a mistake when young that had almost cost her her life's happiness.

Perhaps that's why Austen's books were so popular, Katherine mused, because her heroines made the most terrible mistakes: they either fell for the bad boys or turned the good ones away. They were real, flawed but forgivable, girls who had a lot of growing up to do and readers loved them because they *were* them.

Which one of us hasn't made a hash of our lives at one time or other, Katherine thought, daring to think about her own doomed relationship with David. The only difference was that Katherine wasn't a fictional character in a novel, and Jane Austen wasn't around to ensure her a happy ending.

'Ah, a happy ending,' the man next to her said.

Katherine jolted out of her private daydream, irrationally thinking that the dark-haired man had somehow read her thoughts.

'There's nothing quite like a happy ending, don't you think?' he said.

'Exactly,' Katherine said, getting up from her chair. 'It leaves one feeling so—' she paused.

'Satisfied?' the man suggested.

'Inadequate,' Katherine said.

The man looked bemused a moment but then, getting up from his chair as the lights were switched on, he held out his hand to shake hers. 'I'm Warwick,' he said. 'And I can personally guarantee a happy ending if you befriend me.'

It was Katherine's turn to look bemused and she did it beautifully, raising a dark eyebrow while fixing him with a stern look.

'Really?'

'Absolutely,' he said with a smile that was quite attractive.

Katherine looked at him for a moment, his hand still extended towards her. He was, she had to admit, rather handsome. He had thick dark hair, clear hazel eyes, and a smile that was part charm and part dare. What the heck, Katherine thought. What harm can there be befriending him? After all, it was only for the space of the weekend. If he was completely mad—and she hadn't ruled it out yet—she need never see him or hear from him again. She extended her hand, placed it in his and shook.

'Warwick?' she said.

'You're called Warwick too?' he said with a grin.

She smiled. 'I'm Katherine. Katherine Roberts.'

'And you're speaking on Sunday?'

'I am.'

'I'm looking forward to it,' he said.

They walked slowly towards the library door together and then, reaching it, stopped.

'Well, it was very nice to meet you, Warwick,' Katherine said, giving him a brief smile prior to heading towards the stairs before he had the chance to say another word.

∾

Warwick was stunned. She'd just walked away—casually and coolly walked away from him—as if he were of no further use to her.

Look on the bright side, he told himself. He'd made contact. He now officially knew her name and she knew his. They'd even exchanged a few words.

'But that was it,' he said to himself. What had gone wrong this time? Was she just totally unimpressed by him and didn't want to engage in further conversation? Had she found him dull and unamusing?

Warwick sighed. How odd it had been to sit in the dark with her for the entire length of the film. It had been a strange sort of agony because he knew the woman and yet he couldn't talk to her. And he *so* wanted to talk to her! They got on. If only she knew it and gave him a chance, but she hadn't. She dismissed him as an uninteresting nobody.

What was he going to do now? He couldn't let her slip away from him so easily, could he? He had to give this opportunity another go.

For a moment he stood in the hallway wondering what his

next move was going to be, and then he remembered something—something he could use to his advantage.

'The letters.'

Katherine's letters were the key to unlocking her. She'd written things in them that revealed the very centre of her personality, and he could use that knowledge to get to know her better.

It was a low-down, sneaky, dishonourable thing to do, but it would probably work a treat.

Chapter 12

KATHERINE DREW BACK THE HEAVY BEDROOM CURTAINS AND looked out over the view that she'd quickly come to think of as her own. The sun was shining and the lake was looking particularly blue, with diamond droplets of light dancing on its surface.

A moorhen tore across the lawn at a tremendous speed, its neck lengthened to cartoonish proportions as it made for the thick clumps of reed by the lake. If she hadn't been asked there as a paid guest, she knew the price of the long weekend was worth it for this view alone.

Turning back to the room with the realization that she couldn't spend the entire break gazing out of the window, she realised how lucky she was and how very precious moments like these were. To be absolutely still and take time to look at the world was something Katherine didn't do very often. She needed this at the moment.

The previous night she'd given in to the emotions she'd bottled up for many weeks and had a jolly good cry. David's announcement that he was married had come at a particularly busy time of term and Katherine had chosen to bury herself in her work and ignore the fact that her heart was broken. The only acknowledgement she'd made had been a slight overdose on her DVD collection of costume dramas—in particular her Austen titles.

The restorative powers of Jane Austen never failed. It was the one thing in life that a girl could rely on, like a good bottle of wine or an expensive box of chocolates. David had dropped his bombshell on a Friday and Katherine had spent the entire weekend on the sofa watching the BBC version of *Pride and Prejudice*—all six hour-long episodes back to back, laughing and crying her way through the trials of the Bennet sisters. Judging by the previous night, however, she obviously hadn't, that weekend, cried herself out over her broken relationship.

'But I have now,' she said, examining her pale face in the bathroom mirror. It was always the same when she was upset—all the colour drained out of her, leaving her looking like a little ghost. She'd have to do a good repair job with the make-up this morning, unless she wanted to terrify everyone at breakfast. She wondered what the dark-haired gentlemen would think if he saw her now. Would he be as keen to talk to her if he saw Katherine Roberts—the damaged version?

For a moment she thought about the man that seemed so intent on getting to know her.

'Warwick,' she said to her reflection. It was an unusual name. She'd never heard of it as a first name before, only as a surname.

'Like Lorna Warwick,' she suddenly said and then laughed. Not that he would have heard of Lorna Warwick. He was probably one of those Jane Austen snobs who ridiculed any other novel that wasn't written by the grande dame herself. So that was the end of their friendship, then. They would have absolutely nothing to talk about if he was a literary snob and couldn't bear to indulge in a bit of Regency fun every now and then. Not that she had been planning to talk to him because she hadn't. The last thing she was looking for was another relationship. She needed a break from men. Well, real ones anyway. Fictional men were fine: they knew their place. You could just pick up a book, flick through to the right page, take your fill of your favourite hero and then return him to the shelf. Job done.

Real men, though, were something to be avoided for the foreseeable future. Look, but don't touch, she thought. No, even looking could be fraught with danger. All romantic interludes began with a pair of gullible eyes and there was no telling where things might lead. Just look at Marianne Dashwood and Willoughby and Elizabeth Bennet and Wickham. Hadn't Willoughby and Wickham been the most dashing, romantic of heroes? Hadn't they been charming and totally above suspicion? Yet they proved to be the most dangerous of men.

'Like David,' Katherine said. Except he hadn't been quite as dashing. He was a middle-aged university lecturer whose hair was receding a little and who could have benefitted from a couple of sessions a week at the gym. Katherine hadn't minded any of that, though. It was his wit and charm that had bowled her over—his unashamed flattery and the old-fashioned way he had courted her. He posted love letters under her office door, handed her books of poetry with his favourites marked by a rose. He took her out to the very best restaurants and bought her little gifts beautifully wrapped.

'But he didn't tell you about his wife,' she said aloud. That was it with men, wasn't it? There was always some hidden horror, some terrible secret that just happened to slip their minds as they kissed you to within an inch of your senses.

'Well, never again,' Katherine said. She would never make the mistake of being taken in by a man.

She smiled with satisfaction at this promise. Once she was home, she'd certainly have lots to tell her dear friend Lorna. Katherine's fingers were almost itching to start the letter right then. Lorna would laugh heartily when Katherine told her about Warwick and how cool she'd been in her response.

'And quite right you were too!' Lorna would surely tell her. 'These men must be put in their place.'

Katherine sighed. If only Lorna were there, she thought. What fun they would have together!

Across the hall from Katherine's room, Robyn was waking up, stretching full length under the warm duvet, and staring up at the beautiful plasterwork above the light on the ceiling. It was a far cry from her own bedroom many miles away in Yorkshire with the strange damp patch that glowered down at her each morning. How lovely it must be to live in such elegance, she thought. Getting out of bed on the wrong side would be impossible when one had sash windows on one side and exquisite pieces of furniture on the other. Come to think of it, it would be hard to get out of bed at all when you owned one as beautiful as the one Robyn was occupying. Did she really want to leave its warm comfort when she could spend the day in bed with Mr Darcy? Or even a whole weekend with Mr Darcy? Now there was a thought and if a girl couldn't get away with that at a Jane Austen weekend, then where could she?

Robyn sat up and pushed her hair out of her face. It was always a bit tangled and springy first thing in the morning, and she needed to tame it before breakfast.

Getting out of bed and taking a shower, she tried not to think about the night before. After Jace's appearance, she'd hidden herself away in her room for more than an hour and then got angry that she was letting him ruin her weekend. She then ventured downstairs and quietly joined the film group just in time to see Colonel Brandon carrying a broken Marianne in his arms. It was one of her favourite scenes, and she always adored the moment when, after her fever breaks, Marianne notices Colonel Brandon in the doorway of her bedroom, seeing him as if for the first time, and thanks him.

As ever, in times of trouble Jane Austen was, in the words her sister Cassandra used to describe her, 'the soother of every sorrow,' and Robyn was able to put all nonheroes out of her mind.

Having washed and dressed, Robyn swapped the beauty of her bedroom for the splendour of the dining room, shyly entering and noticing that she was one of the last down.

'Oh, my dear!' a voice suddenly accosted her. 'We were all so worried about you.'

Robyn nearly died of embarrassment right there on the spot.

'I'm Doris,' the white-haired lady said, taking Robyn's arm as if she were some kind of invalid and leading her to the table. 'Doris Norris. I kept a seat for you.'

'Thank you,' Robyn said, catching Katherine's eye on the other side of the table. She winked, but there was nothing more she could do to rescue her friend.

'We all felt absolutely dreadful for you last night after that young man of yours ruined the evening for you,' Doris said.

'Well, he didn't really—'

'He should be ashamed of himself,' Doris continued unhindered. 'He doesn't deserve a nice girl like you, does he? How long have you two been together?'

'Since school,' Robyn said, not really wanting to launch into the history of Jace and her at the breakfast table.

'He was your first love, was he?' Doris asked. 'I know how that one goes. My Henry was my first love. Well, after Mr Darcy, that is. We met when we were eighteen and were married for fifty-four years.' She paused, probably waiting for the intake of breath that usually greeted this piece of information.

'That's amazing,' Robyn said.

Doris nodded. 'We were in it for the long haul in my day. Not like marriages these days with divorces as easy as pie.'

'But you wouldn't want to be trapped in a dreadful relationship,' Robyn said as she poured herself an orange juice from a glass jug.

'Of course not,' Doris said. 'So you have to choose wisely in the first place, don't you?'

Robyn sighed. As kind as she meant to be, Doris wasn't helping.

Doris took a sip of coffee and gave a little chuckle. 'Your young man,' she said, 'it's not exactly the sort of behaviour we expect at a Jane Austen Conference.'

'No,' a stern-looking woman said from the other side of the table. She had a great cliff bosom and reminded Robyn of a terrifying headmistress she once had. '*Not* the sort of thing we expect at Purley.' She gave Robyn a look to suggest that she'd been responsible for the whole thing. Robyn thought it best to avoid eye contact and eat her breakfast as quickly as possible.

'Don't let Mrs Soames get you down,' Katherine told her when they left the dining room together ten minutes later. 'She likes nothing more than a good moan.'

'She scared me stiff!' Robyn admitted, thinking of the glare that had accosted her over the cornflakes.

Katherine shook her head. 'Don't let her get the better of you. I'm sure she comes to these weekends to find fault, not pleasure.'

'You've met her before?'

'Unfortunately, yes. She usually sits in the front row of my talks, wobbling that great bosom of hers in disdain. She's called Frances Soames and a nastier piece of work I have yet to meet.'

'I'll do my best to avoid her,' Robyn said.

'Come on,' Katherine said, 'we've got a hot date with Mr Darcy.'

Chapter 13

THE MORNING SESSION TITLED UNDRESSING MR DARCY was, perhaps, one of the most popular events at the Purley Hall conference. Given by the History Wardrobe, it was a presentation in which a handsome actor performed a sort of Regency striptease revealing almost everything that a fine pair of pantaloons could hide. It was always something to get excited about, and there was a bit of a scramble for front row seats when the doors to the Gainsborough Room were opened, with Robyn, Katherine, and Doris getting prime positions.

'I've seen this three times now,' Doris said with a naughty smile.

Robyn giggled. 'Well, it's new to me, although I've tried to imagine it a fair few times—usually after watching the Colin Firth production.'

'Is he your perfect Darcy?' Katherine asked.

Robyn nodded. 'I think it's the way his hair curls just a little bit, and I love those intense looks he gives Elizabeth.'

'I can't remember the last time I experienced an intense look,' Doris said. 'But I have a dreadful suspicion that it was from my optician when he was examining me for my new bifocals.'

They all laughed.

'Are you seeing anyone, Katherine?' Robyn dared to ask. 'Any Mr Darcy in your life?'

Katherine cleared her throat. 'No,' she said. 'Not at the moment.'

'What?' Doris said. 'A beautiful young woman like you? You should have at least four of five beaux after you at any time.'

'She has at least one here,' Robyn said, instantly receiving a glare from Katherine.

Doris turned around in her chair. 'Who is he? Is he here now?'

'I can't see him yet,' Robyn said. 'But he's very good-looking.'

'Is he that nice young man with the dark hair?' Doris asked.

Robyn nodded. 'He ran over Katherine's foot with a suitcase.'

'You say that like it's romantic,' Katherine complained.

'Wasn't it just a little bit like Marianne twisting her ankle and being scooped up by Willoughby?' Robyn said.

'No, it wasn't,' Katherine said. 'It was very painful and not in the least romantic, and I'm trying to steer clear of him now.'

A gentleman sat down heavily in the front row next to Doris, but it wasn't the dark-haired man with the lethal suitcase they'd been talking about. It was an elderly man with a shock of white hair that made him look like a guinea pig. He was one of the few men attending the conference and it was a great pity that he wasn't in the mould of a hero.

'What's this talk called?' he asked, turning round to squint at Doris.

'Undressing Mr Darcy,' Doris said.

'What?'

'Undressing Mr Darcy!'

'Undressing? Who's undressing?' he asked, looking quite shocked.

'It's an actor in costume,' Doris explained.

'An actress?' he said, his eyes lighting up.

Doris waved her hand and gave up. He'd find out sooner or later.

Sure enough, as everyone took their seats, a lady in Regency costume entered the room and a hush descended. Robyn smiled as she looked over the long white gown the woman was wearing and a pair of the daintiest of shoes Robyn had ever seen. The woman had delicate fabric flowers in her hair and the whole ensemble made Robyn want to give up her twenty-first century jeans and trainers forever.

The costume historian began the talk by asking audience members what they thought Mr Darcy really looked like because there was very little description of him and his clothes in *Pride and Prejudice*.

'What's she saying?' asked the old man next to Doris. 'Is she the one who's undressing?'

Doris didn't have time to explain because Mr Darcy strode into the room.

'Oh, my, gracious me!' Doris said. 'He's magnificent!'

Robyn giggled. It was as if Doris were seeing him for the first time. Her whole face had filled with wonder, and Robyn couldn't blame her. Standing seven feet tall from the soles of his elegant black boots to the top of his Directoire hat, he was the perfect Fitzwilliam Darcy and with his haughty good looks and his confident pose, Robyn felt as if she'd been transported back in time to the Meryton Ball and that she was seeing the same Mr Darcy that Elizabeth would have seen.

The fun then began when the costume historian started disrobing him.

'That must be the best job in the world,' Doris whispered to Robyn and Katherine.

'I don't know why I didn't think of it,' Katherine said. 'It sure beats marking essays.'

The Regency woman began by removing the hat and coat,

showing off a crisp white shirt and a beautiful gold-striped waist-coat. There were gasps from the audience and Robyn's mouth dropped open. Why didn't men dress like that anymore, she wondered. T-shirts and fleece jumpers just didn't get the same reaction, did they?

The hat had been placed on a little dressing table behind them that was set with an oval mirror and gave the feeling that one was really inside Mr Darcy's private rooms, watching him being disrobed.

The undressing continued with layer after layer being carefully removed.

'That woman's undressing him!' the old man next to Doris said.

'She certainly is,' a woman said with a laugh from the row behind him. 'It's what most of us have come on the weekend for!'

A few giggles came from the audience, especially when Mr Darcy began to unbutton his fall-front trousers. The old man next to Doris was looking a bit flustered at this stage. His face had turned quite red and he looked as if he was about to explode.

Alas, Mr Darcy was going to leave something to the imagi-nation of the audience and the costume historian allowed him to keep his Regency drawers on, asking him to put on his banyan—a very elegant man's dressing gown, resplendent in green and gold. A huge round of applause erupted and as Mr Darcy posed for the audience one last time, the presentation came to an end.

Robyn ventured out of the hall. After the noise and laughter of the Undressing Mr Darcy presentation, she needed to be quiet for a few moments, and she'd been longing to explore the grounds. It was one of the drawbacks of the weekend—there were many wonderful talks and activities, but it left very little time to oneself, and Robyn was eager to see more of Purley.

Once she walked through the great front door, three shallow steps led Robyn down to the gravel driveway where she turned right to follow the gardens under the great cedar tree after which her bedroom had been named. She looked up into its dark green depths and wondered at the people who must have walked by it through the centuries. She always thought of trees as the silent witnesses to history which would sound like a hippie thing, were she to tell anyone so she tended not to.

Rounding the side of the house, she entered a sheltered garden where tiny pink roses tumbled over a wall that had mellowed to a beautiful orange-red and was crumbling happily around the edge of the garden. A great herbaceous border overflowed with autumn flowers in deep oranges and hot pinks, and Robyn followed a gravel path that led to three white seats in a secluded corner, inviting guests to sit and absorb the loveliness around them.

Beyond the formal garden, the grounds spread down to the lake and the open fields. It was the sort of view very few people could hope to own, and Robyn felt privileged at being there and owning a little bit of it for the space of a long weekend.

She followed a formal hedge around the back of the house, and that's when she spotted the stable block. Walking towards it, she saw that it was a perfect square of redbrick buildings with a large arched gateway above which sat a squat clock tower. The time on the clock was wrong, but everything else was right, Robyn thought as she entered the yard and looked at the friendly faces of the half dozen horses peering at her from their shady stables. There was a dappled grey with pale eyes and a beautiful chestnut with a white blaze, and then there was a horse that looked exactly like Black Beauty, with a dazzling white star above his eyes.

Robyn had always loved horses; then again, she'd always loved any animal. She stood for a moment, wondering whom she should say hello to first, finally choosing the grey with the pale eyes.

'Hello, my lovely,' she said, stroking the grey muzzle that was as soft and warm as living velvet. 'Aren't you a beauty?' He nodded his head which made her smile. 'You understand me, don't you?' She reached up to scratch behind his right ear.

'He'll have your arm off if you're not careful,' a voice suddenly said.

Robyn leapt backwards from the stable door and turned around to see a tall man in blue jeans and a torn white T-shirt. It was the handsome man on horseback who'd escorted the drunken Jace from the dining room the night before.

'He won't really bite me, will he?' Robyn asked.

The man laughed. 'Only joking,' he said. 'Wouldn't hurt a fly, would you, Pops?'

Robyn watched as the man leant forward and dropped a kiss on the pale muzzle.

'Poppin's as gentle as they come,' he said. 'I'm Dan, by the way,' he added, turning to Robyn. 'I didn't get a chance to introduce myself last night.' He held out a large hand, and Robyn shook it, her tiny hand quite lost in his.

'I'm Robyn,' she said. 'Robyn Love.'

Dan's eyebrows rose a fraction. 'Really?'

'Yes.'

'Love by name, love by nature?' he asked.

Robyn felt the beginnings of a blush creep over her cheeks and turned to face the horse again. 'You didn't tell me *your* last name,' she said, changing the subject as quickly as she could.

'Harcourt,' he said.

Robyn turned to face him. 'Like Dame Pamela,' she said, remembering that he might be the actress's boy toy, but he was clearly more than that. She'd gone and married him! So this was Dame Pamela's secret husband, was it? Robyn's brain raced. No, that couldn't be right, could it? She'd been Pamela Harcourt for longer than this man had been alive.

'What's the matter?' he asked, clearly seeing her confusion. 'You don't think I'm Pamela's husband, do you?'

'No!' Robyn cried. 'I mean, I didn't think anything.' Suddenly, she felt like Catherine Morland in *Northanger Abbey* when Henry Tilney realises that she suspected his father of murdering his mother. How did that heartbreaking line go? *'If I understand you rightly, you had formed a surmise of such horror as I have hardly words to—Dear Miss Morland, consider the dreadful nature of the suspicions you have entertained.'*

How awful! Was Dan as appalled at her as Henry had been at Catherine?

'Let me put you right,' Dan said, interrupting her thoughts. 'I'm Pammy's little brother.'

'Oh,' Robyn said, a modicum of relief in her voice.

'We share the same father—as do half the population of England. I fear our father will not stop until his last breath has left him.'

Robyn gave a little smile. 'I'm sorry… I didn't mean to…'

'Don't worry about it,' Dan said. 'It's a mistake that's been made before, and dear Pammy's gone out with guys far younger than me.' He shrugged his shoulders, and then his sunny expression vanished. 'Hang about. I seem to have lost my two friends,' he said. 'Moby? Biscuit? Here, boys!'

Robyn watched as two dogs came running into the yard. There was a tiny Jack Russell terrier who was a blur of chestnut and white and a much older golden Labrador whose gait was decidedly slower than his companion's.

'*There* you are,' Dan said, bending to pat the old dog while the younger terrier jumped wildly around his legs.

'Which is which?' Robyn asked.

'Well, this mad ball of fur is Biscuit,' Dan said, grabbing the terrier and placing him on his shoulder, where the dog perched with ease, making Robyn laugh. 'And this is Moby.'

'Moby?'

'Moby dog.'

Robyn grinned. 'I like it,' she said, crouching down to pat the old dog. 'And you all live here?'

'Kind of,' he said, running a hand through his coppery blond hair. 'I've got a little place right here.'

'In the village?'

'In the stables,' he said, nodding to the clock tower. 'Just a couple of small rooms, but it's nice to get away from London.'

'And that's where you live normally?'

'Hard to tell,' Dan said, lifting Biscuit off his shoulder and placing him on the ground, where the little dog scooted off to chase a pigeon that had dared to land nearby. 'I've got this so-called luxury flat—all glass and chrome. It's got a deluxe kitchen, all the mod cons you could dream of, and it overlooks the Thames, but this is the place I want to be.' He looked thoughtful for a moment. 'Smell that,' he suddenly said.

Robyn inhaled. 'What is it?'

'Do you like it?'

Robyn took another good big sniff. 'Yes,' she said. 'I do.'

'It's horses. That's the best smell in the world, isn't it? Horses, hay, and leather.'

'And London doesn't smell like that, does it?'

'Nope,' he said, reaching forward to stroke Poppin's head. 'Pammy's been great—she's always wanted these stables full of horses, and I get to look after them.'

'And the place in London?'

'I guess I should rent it out. I don't really use it much. I jacked in my city job months ago.'

Robyn smiled.

'What?'

'I guess that's something I'd like to do too,' she said.

'You work in the city?'

'No. A town in Yorkshire, but the job bores me silly.'

'And what would you like to do?' he asked.

Robyn started. She'd never been asked that question before. 'What would I like to do? Well,' she paused. What could she possibly say? That she'd like to sit in her garden all day with her Jane Austen novels, watching over her chickens? You couldn't make a living from that, could you? 'I guess something wonderful. Something inspiring. Something that means you're not always looking at the clock, wondering how long it is before you can go home.'

Dan nodded. 'I know exactly what you mean. When I came down to Purley, time suddenly took on a new dimension. It's amazing. I get up in the mornings and don't feel that knot of dread in my stomach. It might sound corny but each day really is a gift when you can spend it here with the horses. I love it. I could never go back to London.'

Robyn nodded. 'You're so lucky,' she said. 'It's a magical place.'

'It is,' he said, and they looked at each other for a moment.

'Well, I'd better be—' Robyn started.

'How's your—' he said at the same time.

'Sorry?' Robyn said.

'I was just going to ask if your friend's all right. After last night, I mean.'

Robyn bit her lip. Jace. He always had to go and spoil things, even when he wasn't actually there. Here she was, surrounded by animals in the most perfect of settings, talking to a handsome man who could easily have stepped out of the pages of a novel, and Jace had to go and rear his ugly head. 'I'm sure he's fine,' she said.

'You haven't spoken to him?'

Robyn shook her head. 'I'm guessing he's having a lie-in.'

'And he's your…?'

Robyn's eyes widened a fraction. Don't make me say, she thought. 'It's complicated,' she said at last. 'He shouldn't be here at all. Things are…'

Dan raised a hand in the air. 'I didn't mean to pry. You don't have to explain to me.'

'It's okay,' she said. 'It's just hard to explain.' She looked down at the ground, knocking her left sandal against her right. 'Jace has always been around,' she said. 'I can't remember a time when I didn't know him.'

Dan nodded. 'What does he do?'

'As little as possible.'

He laughed.

'I really should be getting back,' she said, not really wanting to leave at all. For the first time that weekend, she wasn't thinking about Jane Austen but rather about the handsome hero before her.

'Maybe I'll see you later,' he said. 'I'm usually hanging around here somewhere, unless I'm taking one of the horses out.'

Robyn smiled. She wanted to say that she'd be back as soon as possible, but that wouldn't have been very heroine-like, would it? But it wasn't every day that a man like Dan walked into your life.

And not only is he handsome, but he loves animals too, she thought, recalling how he'd kissed Poppin's pale nose, and his delight when the dogs appeared. He wouldn't make jokes about eating her darling chickens for tea, would he?

'Okay,' she told him as casually as possible. 'I'll see you later.'

Shading her eyes from the sun, she made to leave the stable block. And she almost maintained her nonchalance until the very last moment when she turned around to look at him once more.

He was staring right back at her.

Chapter 14

WARWICK WAS BIDING HIS TIME. HE'D DONE NOTHING MORE than nod and smile at Katherine from across the breakfast table. He sat a couple of rows behind her in the Undressing Mr Darcy session, and he didn't even try to corner her during the first coffee break of the morning. Oh, no. That wouldn't be cool. He didn't want to come across as some sort of a stalker. He'd wait for the right moment before he made his move. It was sure to come soon enough.

After the first session that Friday morning, nobody believed that things could get any better and they were quite right. Whoever's idea it had been to invite the Reverend Ernest Hepplewhite to speak about the portrayal of the clergy in Jane Austen's novels, that person would surely be hiding in embarrassment. Undressing Mr Darcy was a tough session to follow for even the most charismatic of the speakers, so the dull and monotonous reverend was doubly boring and many a yawn had to be stifled.

Warwick completely switched off after just three minutes. Instead, he found himself mentally sifting through Katherine's letters.

She likes literature that doesn't take itself too seriously, he thought; hence her addiction to Austen. She likes my novels, he thought with a grin, especially the ones with the strong heroines who speak their minds and never compromise. She likes fine food but doesn't eat out very often because she doesn't like eating alone. Her favourite novel is *Persuasion* because it shows that everybody is entitled to a second chance and that love, goodness and patience are rewarded. But Anne Elliot isn't her favourite heroine. She can never make up her mind as to whether it is Elizabeth Bennet or Emma Woodhouse. Like most Austen fans, she adores Elizabeth's spirit and wit, but Emma's self-confidence and charm always win her over. And her favourite hero? Mr Darcy, of course, and not because of his good looks or his fortune but because he works so hard to protect Elizabeth's loved ones.

As the Reverend Ernest Hepplewhite droned on, Warwick continued his tour through Katherine's letters, revealing the inner-most thoughts and feelings she had shared with him. Remembering them, he felt very privileged at having her as his friend. Now he had to endeavour to deserve her friendship all over again.

As the reverend came to the end of his talk, the sound of polite applause rippled through the room before everyone made a hasty exit. Warwick was one of the first out and stood at a vantage point where he could see everyone. Katherine was one of the last people to come out. She was talking to a woman wearing a cerise jumper that made her look like an inflated beetroot, and Warwick soon identified her as the dreadful woman with the temperamental suit-case, and he could see that Katherine looked desperate to get away from her. This was the moment, Warwick thought.

'Ah, there you are, Katherine!' he said, bustling in and taking her arm, placing it on his. 'Do excuse us,' he said with a cheery smile to the cerise woman.

Warwick pushed his way through the crowded hallway until they were at the foot of the left-hand staircase.

'Excuse me!' Katherine said indignantly.

'I'm sorry,' Warwick said, 'but you looked as if you needed rescuing back there.'

'And what if I did?' she said, her hands placed on her hips.

Warwick noticed how shapely her hips were in the little black dress she was wearing. It was a figure-hugging number with a scooped neckline, and she was wearing a single gold bangle and a pair of small gold hoops in her ears. Her hair was loose and shiny and her lips painted a dark red. She looked amazing.

'I—erm—can't help but rescue beautiful women in danger.'

'Oh, really. Have we stepped back a couple of centuries or something?' she said.

'Naturally. We're at a Jane Austen Conference,' he said, giving her his best smile. 'If a heroine can't be rescued here, then it's a very poor do.'

She smiled back.

He looked into the big brown eyes and felt quite lost for a moment. Don't screw up now, he told himself. You've almost got her.

'So what did you think of our reverend, then?' he asked.

Katherine looked thoughtful for a moment. 'Interesting,' she said at length.

'No, really?' Warwick said. 'I was almost comatose.'

'You really didn't find anything of interest in his talk?' she said, her forehead creasing into a frown.

'Did you?' Warwick said. 'Come on! The man was boredom personified. He was Mr Collins but without the entertainment value.'

Katherine laughed.

'You know I'm right!' Warwick persisted.

'Okay, okay. It was the worst talk I've ever had the misfortune to sit through.'

Warwick laughed. 'Well, I'm glad you agree with me. Personally, I think our reverend would be just the sort of character Jane Austen would have placed in one of her novels and had such fun with.'

'You're a fan of her novels, then?'

'Of course. Why else would I be here?'

'Oh, I don't know,' Katherine said. 'You might be a journalist out to find some easy targets or a speaker with a new angle.'

Warwick shook his head. 'I'm simply a fan,' he said.

'That's rather rare,' Katherine said.

'What?'

'A man openly admitting he's an Austen fan.'

Warwick's eyes narrowed. 'Isn't that a bit of a sexist remark?'

'Not at all,' she said. 'It's an honest one. It's usually women who are the ardent fans—who openly declare their love of the books. Men usually have some sort of an agenda.'

'Really?'

'Yes. In my experience.'

'Then perhaps I'll change your mind,' Warwick said, 'because I'm an ardent fan who isn't ashamed to shout it from the rooftops. Jane Austen is my favourite writer.'

'And mine,' Katherine said.

Warwick nodded. He was thinking about the letters again and had the naughtiest of urges to steer the conversation towards his own books.

'In fact,' Warwick said, 'I was going to buy a replacement copy of *Sense and Sensibility* from the bookstall. Mine's falling apart.'

'They have a bookstall?' Katherine's eyes lit up. 'They've never had one before.'

'It's by special demand, I hear.'

'Then I think I may have to take a look,' she said.

Warwick led the way. The table had been set up in the corner of a small ground-floor room that was obviously a library.

'Oh!' Katherine declared as soon as she entered. 'Wonderful.'

Floor to ceiling shelves were all stuffed with books—a mesmeric sight to any reader—and Warwick and Katherine were instantly captivated.

'What I'd give for a space like this for my books,' Katherine said.

'I think my library's about this big,' Warwick said.

'Really?' Katherine said.

Warwick frowned. He'd said too much.

'What do you do? You didn't tell me.'

'No,' he said. 'I—er—collect. Old books.'

'You're an antiquarian?'

He nodded.

'Do you have any early Jane Austen editions?'

'Oh, no,' he said. 'They're few and far between.' He swallowed hard. Did he sound convincing?

'Wouldn't it be amazing to have a first edition? Just imagine owning a first edition of *Pride and Prejudice*. What are the chances of getting one? Have you ever seen one? Are they horribly expensive?'

Warwick turned away. He was way out of his depth here. What on earth had made him say he collected books? 'There we are!' he suddenly said, doing his best to divert Katherine's attention to the bookstall.

It worked.

'I thought this room couldn't get any better,' Katherine said, making her way hastily towards the table on which was spread a vast number of books. As well as several different editions of the original six Austen titles, there were biographies, spin-offs, sequels, cookbooks, books about fashion, books about Hampshire, Lyme, Regis, and Bath and—Warwick was mightily relieved to see—row upon row of Lorna Warwick books.

Warwick watched Katherine's face to see if she'd noticed them. It would be impossible not to, of course, with their gorgeous jewel-coloured covers, but would she admit to being a fan at the Jane Austen Conference?

It was then that he noticed that the girl behind the table was flipping through one of the Lorna Warwick titles, *Mistress of Carston Abbey*. It was one of his raciest titles. Looking up, he caught her eye and she blushed, returning the book to the display.

'Don't tell Aunt Pamela, but I can't stand Jane Austen,' she said. 'But I love these!'

Warwick smiled. Because of his secret identity, he didn't get to meet fans of his books and it was a wonderfully strange feeling to hear from a real-life reader right in front of him.

'And they're selling well?' he dared to ask.

'Oh, yes! This one's doing well,' the girl said, pointing to the pile of *Wicked Lords and Ladies*. 'But this one's outselling them all—even *Pride and Prejudice*.'

Warwick grinned. It was *The Wedding Scandal*. It was his best-selling title to date in the US and he was hoping that UK sales would follow. It was especially gratifying to hear that it was even outselling Austen's most popular title.

He looked around the room at the small crowd of people who were hovering there, wondering who had bought it. There must be a dozen or so people walking around with it in their handbags, he thought. Fans. He had fans there and they had no idea that their favourite author was walking amongst them. The thought made him smile.

'Disgusting!'

Warwick was suddenly brought out of his smug little musings by this one word which had been spat out somewhere behind his left shoulder. He turned around to see the woman in the cerise jumper with the enormous bosom. She glared up at him, obviously not having forgotten or forgiven him for having apprehended Katherine before.

'Whose idea was it to sell this tat at Purley? It's a disgrace!' the woman complained, her bosom heaving in consternation.

'Just ignore her,' Katherine whispered to him conspiratorially. 'She moans at anything and everything.'

'But some people really think these titles have no business being here,' he said. 'What do you think?'

'Well, I...'

Katherine sounded hesitant. Would she admit to reading them? he wondered. She was there in her capacity as a lecturer from Oxford, after all. Would he gain a confession from her?

'I have been known to read a few,' she whispered, adding a little giggle.

Warwick nodded. 'I thought as much.'

'Do you read them?' she asked.

'Well...' Warwick paused. He hadn't expected her to ask him. 'I suppose you could say that.' There, he thought. That wasn't lying, was it?

'You do, don't you? You're a secret fan! I *knew* it!'

'How?'

'Just the way you were eyeing the covers. You should've seen your face. I bet you've got shelves of them at home.'

Warwick laughed.

'You have, haven't you? I bet you love them just as much as I do.'

'Then you're a fan?'

Katherine suddenly blushed. She obviously hadn't meant to say so much. 'I'm really not meant to like this sort of book, you understand. I'd be horse-whipped from my college if anyone found out.'

'I just can't understand book snobbery. It's something Jane Austen couldn't understand either, isn't it? She spoke out against it in *Northanger Abbey*.'

'Yes!' Katherine said with feeling.

'I mean, a novel displays "the liveliest effusions of wit and humour,"' he quoted.

Katherine nodded with great enthusiasm. '"Conveyed to the world in the best chosen language,"' she finished.

Warwick smiled. 'And I agree.'

'And so do I,' Katherine said.

They looked at each other and smiled. Warwick had done it. They were friends.

Chapter 15

KATHERINE BARELY HEARD A SINGLE WORD OF THE NEXT TALK. A little old lady with a shrill voice was talking about dating and courtship in Jane Austen's time and making it seem the dullest subject on the face of the earth, but maybe Katherine was being unfair and not giving her a chance. Maybe even if this had been the Undressing Mr Darcy session she wouldn't have been able to pay attention because her mind was elsewhere.

She was sitting next to Warwick and, as if that wasn't enough of a distraction, she kept thinking about their conversation. How easy it had been to talk to him, she thought. It was a terrible cliché, but she couldn't help feeling that she'd known him for far longer than the couple of days they'd spent at Purley together, and yet their first few encounters hadn't been auspicious.

Like Elizabeth and Darcy, she thought. How quick we are to make a judgement about somebody, and how very wrong we can be, she thought, casting a quick sideways glance at Warwick. He caught her eye and smiled and she smiled back. He had a very nice face and his smile was the kind that could easily get a girl into trouble. His voice was nice too. It was deep and velvety and she could just imagine him reading to her and how easy it would be to lie back and let the words wash over her. His hair was so cute too—it was very dark and slightly wavy which gave it a tousled look that made her want to run her fingers through it.

As the little old lady shrilled on about the importance of dancing for meeting a prospective partner, Katherine mused on the unexpected situation she found herself in. Honestly, she hadn't meant to be flirting with the opposite sex this weekend, especially not with somebody called Warwick. All the Jane Austen warnings were there: he was tall, dark, handsome, and charming. He'd casually mentioned his Jaguar was parked outside which meant that he was also rich and—the very clearest warning of them all—his name begin with *W* and, as any Austen fan will tell you, that *always* means trouble.

Wickham, Willoughby, and Warwick, Katherine thought. *Wicked Warwick,* she added, but then smiled. The only wicked thing about him seemed to be his grin. And where was the harm in flirting, anyway? Jane Austen had been a huge fan of flirting, and it wasn't as if she was planning on anything coming of it anyway. A bit of flirting might be just what she needed. Flirting was fun, and she hadn't had any fun for what seemed like an age.

But I shall not fall in love again, she told herself. *Not this weekend. Not so easily. No matter how sexy his voice or how strong his arms look, I shall not fall in love!*

Katherine was adamant. Although this weekend was partly work for her, it was also pleasure and as long as she took care not to take things beyond a little flirting, what possible harm could there be?

Towards the back of the room, Robyn was also finding it hard to concentrate. The shrill-voiced woman was having a go at *Sense and*

Sensibility's Marianne Dashwood for her immodest behaviour, to which Robyn took exception. She'd always felt that Marianne took so much flak for behaviour that today would be seen as positively shy and retiring. She had only been a young romantic girl who had fallen in love. Was there anything wrong with that?

For some strange reason, the handsome man on horseback flashed into her mind at that moment.

Dan Harcourt.

That was a good name, wasn't it, she thought.

With his floppy coppery hair and his smiling eyes, he'd quite taken her breath away. Plus there'd been the horses and the dogs. Any man who loved animals got a big tick by his name as far as Robyn was concerned. Perhaps that was one of the reasons Jace had lost favour over the years. He never went near her chickens and was forever making fun of them. What was it he called her birds—her scrawny-necked Sunday lunches? It wasn't the way to win her over at all.

Looking through the rows of heads in front of her, Robyn saw Katherine sitting next to the dark-haired gentlemen. Boy, he was persistent, wasn't he? Had he forced his presence upon Katherine yet again or had something changed and were they now friends? She watched them for a moment and saw them turn to each other and smile. Okay, things had definitely changed.

Perhaps Purley was weaving its magic upon them. Or was it the Jane Austen effect? The world always seemed much rosier when Jane's presence was felt.

'Well,' Warwick said, getting up and clapping his hands together, 'that was another riveting talk. Perhaps she's a relative of our friend the reverend.'

'Shush! She'll hear you,' Katherine said, a little of the lecturer coming through in her rebuke.

The two of them left the room together.

'She had a voice like a tin whistle,' Warwick said.

Katherine tutted him but couldn't help giggling too. 'Where do they get these speakers from?'

'At least it bodes well for you. I mean, unless you're as bad as that.'

Katherine's mouth dropped in mock consternation, her hands resting on her hips.

'Only joking!' he said, and she hit him playfully on his arm.

Lunch in the dining room was an elegant but understated affair with a buffet table heaving with bowls of pasta and salad and large plates of ham, jacket potatoes, quiche, and a fine selection of bread and cheese. There were jugs of iced water and cordial on the tables and blackberry tarts for dessert. Dame Pamela—who was forever buying beautiful dinner services—had chosen one in a warm terra-cotta colour, and everything had the glow of autumn about it.

Katherine and Warwick stood in line together, cutting slices of quiche and fat rings of baguette for each other, swapping smiles and little giggles as they walked the length of the buffet.

Sitting down at the table, they tucked into their food and for a few minutes their minds wandered in differing directions. Katherine glanced up and down the table. It was nothing short of amazing that an author who had been dead for almost two hundred years was the sole reason for all these people gathered there. Wasn't it incredible that these people and many millions more around the world were still reading Austen stories and were inspired enough by them to sign up for a weekend such as this? That one simple provincial woman had reached out and touched so many was nothing short of miraculous.

But it was about more than the books now. They'd taken on quite another dimension, hadn't they? They were far more than just words on a page; they were whole worlds that ardent fans populated in their day-to-day lives. The characters were their friends. Readers could imagine exchanging witty barbs with Elizabeth Bennet, sharing book recommendations with Catherine Morland, and flirting with any one of the handsome heroes. That was the thing about Jane Austen's books—they felt intimate, like a cozy chat with a best friend. Readers always felt exceptionally close to the characters as if they were extensions of the readers themselves or at the very least family members.

Glancing at some of the people sitting at the table, Katherine wondered what lives they led and what role Jane Austen played in them. Perhaps she'd get a chance to find out in one of the sessions that afternoon, an informal discussion in which people could talk about their favourite book.

Katherine thought about the first time she discovered Austen. She was lucky. She hadn't been force-fed it at school by some work-worn teacher who made pupils read passages in class, listening to them as they stumbled over the prose, making no sense and taking no joy from it. No, Katherine had watched the old black-and-white film version with Laurence Olivier and Greer Garson. She completely fell in love with it, even though the costumes had been more *Gone with the Wind* than *Pride and Prejudice*. The next time she was in her local library, she sought it out, devouring it eagerly before buying the first of many copies that would accompany her through the daily grind of life.

The other novels had quickly followed but nothing could

ever compare to that first book. It was the sweetest of reads, and no matter how many books were still out there to be discovered, Katherine felt that nothing would ever come as close to stirring her imagination again. Other than the Lorna Warwick books, of course.

'I've been thinking,' Warwick said, interrupting Katherine's thoughts. 'Your name is rather Austensian, isn't it? Was your mother a fan too?'

Katherine nodded. 'She was indeed. She always adored Catherine Morland from *Northanger Abbey*, but I'm afraid she got the spelling wrong so mine's with a *K* rather than a *C*. Can you believe that? Out of all the wonderful Austen characters, my mother named me after the daydreamer because she thought the names Jane, Emma, and Anne were too plain. And Fanny was a nonstarter, and I'm not sure she could spell Elizabeth.'

'It's a lovely name,' he told her.

She smiled. 'Just so long as you don't call me Kitty Cat.'

'Ooooo!' Warwick said, sucking in his teeth. 'I'm not going to ask who called you that in the past.'

'Good,' she said.

'Names can be tricky, can't they?'

'They certainly can,' she said, taking a sip of water. 'Yours is very unusual. How did you come to be called Warwick?' Katherine watched as he too took a slow sip of cordial as if delaying his answer.

'I have no idea,' he said at last. 'I guess my mother just liked the sound of it.'

'It's a good sound,' Katherine said. 'It sounds like a hero's name.'

'Like an Austen hero?'

'Perhaps,' Katherine said. 'Elizabeth and Warwick,' she said. 'It has potential, certainly.'

He grinned. 'I'm glad you think so.'

Katherine finished the last of her quiche. 'Have you heard of the Republic of Pemberley?' she said.

'That's a website, isn't it?'

She nodded. 'It's the home on the Web for rather a lot of Janeites. It's an amazing place, and you can find out all sorts of information there. We could easily put your name up for discussion. Which novel would Warwick—er...'

'Lawton.'

'Which novel would Warwick Lawton most easily fit into? And would he be a colonel, a captain, or a sir? That could make for hours of happy discussion.'

'And this is somewhere you frequent?'

'Well sometimes,' Katherine said. 'Usually when I'm in my office at college and I'm meant to be marking essays, I have been known to be chattering away on the discussion boards.'

'But nothing beats the real thing, does it? Nothing beats conversation.'

'No,' Katherine said. 'That's why these weekends are so amazing. I can try talking to my students about Jane Austen but half of them will be busy scribbling down everything I'm saying and won't have anything interesting to say themselves and the other half will be asleep.'

'A good listener is hard to find.'

'Yes,' Katherine said, and her eyes met Warwick's.

'And I'm a good listener,' he said. 'You can tell me anything.'

Katherine watched as a very cute smile lit up his whole face. She was beginning to believe that she could, indeed, tell him anything, and it was a very nice feeling. How often in this world could you find someone you could trust?

Chapter 16

ROBYN HAD TOSSED AND TURNED IN HER BED THE NIGHT before and had spent the whole morning umming and ahhing about the next session at the conference.

Join us for an informal discussion about the works of your favourite author. Don't forget to bring a book!

That invitation sounded far too much like school to Robyn. Reading, for her, was a very private experience and although she was enjoying talking to people at the conference about her favourite books, the thought of addressing a big group seemed terrifying. Everybody would be looking at her, and she was sure to blush and get all tongue-tied. No, she would definitely have to give it a miss which was a shame as she'd have liked to have heard other people talk about their favourite scenes and characters but perhaps she could catch up with the gossip later with Katherine, if she wasn't in a corner being monopolised by the dark-haired gentleman.

Perhaps she could take her book out into the gardens and find a quiet seat somewhere and enjoy some choice scenes from *Pride and Prejudice* on her own. They'd been told that the gardens of Purley were at their disposal, and it would be a shame not to make the most of them, Robyn thought. She smiled to herself. There could be few things so lovely as reading Jane Austen in a beautiful English country garden.

Her silver sandals crunched across the gravel driveway as she walked around the side of the house, under the great cedar tree. How blissful it was to have the gardens to explore. As much as she adored her own patch of chicken-filled garden at the back of her Yorkshire cottage, it couldn't compare to this. For a moment she thought of Jane Austen's letter written from her brother Edward's country house. She'd written about the pleasure in having so much space 'all to myself.' That's how Robyn felt now, except it seemed that she didn't quite have it all to herself.

As she saw a brilliant blue of a swimming pool, she was aware that there was somebody in it, splashing happily in the sunshine. It was in a secluded corner of the garden, and Robyn couldn't resist taking a quick peek, walking along a path that cut through a thick green hedge.

Her heart almost stopped. She hadn't quite known what to expect. A couple of children, perhaps—nieces of Dame Pamela's on their holiday—or one of the conference attendees who liked the idea of a swim more than the discussion group. But it wasn't children and it wasn't anyone from the conference either. It was Dan Harcourt, the handsome man on horseback, except he wasn't on horseback, and he was no longer wearing a shirt or jeans.

For a moment Robyn didn't move but watched, spellbound, as Dan swam the short length of the pool, moving with the grace of a dolphin and turning perfectly as he reached the end of each length. Up and down he went, oblivious to the world around him and Robyn standing watching him.

Finally he surfaced, his tousled head breaking the water and his bright eyes sparkling from the exercise.

'Robyn?'

'Hello,' she said, smiling shyly.

'Chuck me that towel,' he said.

'What?' Robyn asked.

He smiled. 'My towel. It's behind you.'

'Oh!' Robyn said, seeing the large cream towel on the white bench behind her. She put her copy of *Pride and Prejudice* down. It was obvious that she wasn't going to get any reading done, and she didn't want it to get wet. Grabbing the towel, she turned back to the pool where Dan was emerging, heaving himself out with astonishing speed.

Robyn swallowed hard. She didn't know where to look or rather she did, except she didn't think it was what she should be doing. This was more graphic than Darcy after his dip in the lake at Pemberley or Edward Ferrars chopping wood in the rain, for Dan Harcourt was completely shirtless, and he wasn't wearing breeches either.

His body was tanned and toned and glistened with water droplets. It was the most beautiful body Robyn had ever seen and nothing like the pale white one of Jace's which was slightly flabby around the edges. This body was that of someone who kept himself in shape although not by spending hours at a gym, contorting his muscles into unnatural bulges. This body reminded Robyn of the glorious chestnut stallion he'd been riding the day she saw him at Steventon Church. It had a natural elegance and strength that didn't looked forced but was totally compelling.

I'm staring, she thought. *I mustn't stare! But where else can I look?*

'This is my luxury,' Dan said as he rubbed the massive towel over himself. 'Pammy hardly uses the pool which is such a waste. I virtually have it to myself, and it's brilliant on warm days like this.'

'Yes, I bet it's nice after all your hot work in the stables. You must get very—erm—hot,' she said, biting her tongue and trying not to think of Dan doing hot, sweaty work in the stables.

'Have you come for a swim yourself?' he asked.

'Oh, no. I came out to read,' she said, turning and nodding to the white seat on which lay her beloved copy of *Pride and Prejudice*.

Dan clocked it. 'It's a truth universally acknowledged, eh?'

'You've read it?'

'No more than that opening sentence, I'm afraid, but I've seen my sister's adaptation.'

'She's the very best Lady Catherine I've ever seen,' Robyn said. 'Is she?'

Robyn nodded and watched as Dan slung the towel over his left shoulder. Blushing, she looked away. 'I should—I should really be—'

'Oh,' Dan said, seeming to sense her embarrassment. 'Don't let me disturb you. I was just going.'

'You're not disturbing me. It was me who disturbed you, I think. I can find somewhere else.' She walked to the seat and picked up her book. The grounds of Purley were quite extensive enough that she wouldn't need to be tripping over Dan all the time.

'Robyn?'

She turned around and almost crashed into him. 'Oh!' she said. She'd thought he was still standing by the pool.

'Stay and talk to me. I don't often get to talk to anyone. Moby and Biscuit aren't great conversationalists, and the horses never have much to say.'

Robyn smiled. 'I... erm—'

'Would it make you feel more comfortable if I got changed?' he said. 'I've got my things over there.' He nodded towards a small tile-roofed building behind the pool that had two white columns covered in roses. 'There's a shower in there. I won't be long.'

She watched as he walked away and then she sat down on the pretty white seat.

What are you doing? You should be inside discussing the finer points of fiction, not skiving in the garden eyeing up the stablehand.

Robyn opened her book and flipped through the pages to her favourite scene: the bungled first proposal of Darcy. Concentrate, she told herself, and stop thinking about Dan. She loved this scene. She loved how Darcy managed to say absolutely everything he shouldn't and yet feel such conviction that he must be honest with Elizabeth. How very much they hurt each other! Their words were used like weapons, and as amusing as it was to the reader, it was heart-wrenching too but there was more to it than that. It could truly be enjoyed only on a second read because you knew that these two individuals would battle the odds and see their mistakes and get their happy ever after together. A first read always had the wince factor and made the reader think, *Don't say that!* Darcy voicing his feelings about Elizabeth's inferiority and how it would degrade him to marry her, and Elizabeth's declaration that he was 'the last man in the world' that she could marry.

The moment that always caught Robyn with its emotion was Darcy's *'You have said quite enough, madam. I perfectly comprehend your feelings, and have now only to be ashamed of what my own have been. Forgive me for having taken up so much of your time, and accept my best wishes for your health and happiness.'*

Perhaps that's what made *Pride and Prejudice* so popular; because its hero and heroine go through so much. They suffer and they learn about themselves and about each other. They're not perfect but they're identifiably human, and they can find perfection through being with each other.

Robyn mused on these thoughts, her eyes no longer on the page but staring out across the lawn that stretched down to the lake.

'Okay?' a voice said.

Robyn jumped. It was Dan, now dressed in a pair of faded jeans and a dark grey T-shirt, his towel scrunched up in a ball by his side. 'Hi,' she said.

'May I?' he asked, nodding to the bench. She nodded, and he sat down, taking the book from her. 'Mind if I have a look?'

'No. Be my guest.'

Dan flipped through to the opening chapter and read the three short pages. Robyn watched him, wondering what he was making of them. It was generally true that Jane Austen was a girls' thing but there were a number of men at the conference so she obviously had her male fans.

Just not Jace, she thought. He'd never be a fan. Robyn remembered the number of times she tried to get him to read a book by Austen. There was that time when he said, 'Okay, okay, just leave it on the coffee table.' The trouble was, he'd left it on the coffee table too. It was the same with the films. She'd casually leave one running when Jace was due to call. He'd come in, glare at the TV in distaste, mumble something about 'those infernal dance scenes,' and switch to the nearest sports channel.

What would Dan make of the phenomenon that was Jane Austen? Robyn twiddled with a length of curly hair as she awaited his verdict.

Finally, he looked up from the book and laughed. 'I like this Mr Bennet character,' he said. 'I think he has a hard time of things. I like this bit. "I have a high respect for your nerves. They are my old friends. I have heard you mention them with consideration these twenty years at least."'

'Yes,' Robyn said. 'Dear Mr Bennet. He has so much to put up with.'

'I like it,' Dan said. 'I'd like to read more.'

'Really?'

'You sound surprised.'

'I am surprised,' Robyn said.

'Why because I'm a man?'

'Yes, absolutely!'

Dan laughed. 'You think we all hate books?'

'No—not that—just Jane Austen.'

'But this is really funny. I like funny things. Life can be too serious sometimes, can't it?'

Robyn nodded. 'Jane Austen is the cure for most things in life, I find.'

'Can I borrow it?'

Robyn's eyes widened. Her book? Her special copy of *Pride and Prejudice*. Well, one of them.

'Sorry,' he said, handing the book back to her. 'I'll get my own copy.'

'Oh, no!' Robyn said, suddenly realising how mean she must have seemed to him. 'Please—borrow it.'

'You sure?' he asked.

She smiled and pushed the book firmly towards him. She'd suddenly realised that if he borrowed the book, she'd have a very good excuse to talk to him again.

'Thanks,' he said. 'This will be a real treat. I don't read much fiction but I promised myself I would when I left my old job. In

London, it was always the boring old trade magazines and newspapers that took up my time and I never got a chance to read a novel but I'm a quick reader so I'll get it back to you as soon as I can.'

'Oh, there's no rush,' she said.

'But you leave on Monday,' he pointed out.

Robyn sighed. 'Oh, yes,' she said.

'Purley weaving its spell over you?'

'I think it is,' she said, and her gaze locked with his. His eyes were a wonderful golden brown and danced with light and life.

'I felt the same way when I used to visit. It got harder and harder to leave, and so I just didn't bother.'

'You're lucky,' Robyn said. 'I wish I could stay.'

He smiled at her. 'Me too,' he said. 'I mean about you—staying.' He laughed.

Robyn liked his laugh. It was a big happy sound that was totally natural.

'Is this what all women want, then?' he asked.

'What?'

Dan held up the book.

'Romances?' Robyn asked.

'No,' he said, turning to page two again. '"A single man of large fortune."'

'Ah, you've found us out.' She giggled. 'It's what Mrs Bennet wanted for her daughters. You'll have to read more to find out why.'

'And today? What do women want today?'

Robyn looked at him. 'I don't think you'll find the answer to that question in a book.'

'But what do you want, Robyn?'

Robyn swallowed and wondered why he was so interested in her. Not that she minded. She liked it. Jace never asked her any questions like that. The only sort of questions he asked were, 'What's for tea?' or 'Have you got any ketchup?'

'What do I want?' she said. 'Well, I'd like a job that I love in a place that I love.'

'And you don't have that at the moment?'

Robyn shook her head. 'My job's just something I get through.'

'And what about your—er—friend?'

'Jace?' Robyn took a deep breath. 'I don't know what he wants but I don't think we want the same things. Not anymore.'

'He doesn't understand Austen?' Dan said, a little twinkle in his eyes.

'No,' Robyn said. 'But worse—he doesn't understand me.'

They fell silent for a moment. Robyn looked out towards the lake and watched as a pair of white swans descended from the sky, their great wings booming. They made a wonderful skidding splash together and then folded their wings up to form the most perfect of shapes.

Suddenly Robyn was aware that Dan was staring at her.

'What?' she asked in a whisper-soft voice.

'How can he not understand you?'

Robyn looked at him for a moment and then turned away, not knowing what to say to him.

'I'd better get back,' she said at length, standing up.

Dan stood up beside her. 'Thanks for the book,' he said. 'I'll take good care of it.'

'You'd better,' she said and gave a little smile before walking away.

As she skirted the side of the hall, she realised that her heart was beating at an alarmingly fast rate.

'Oh, my goodness!' she said to herself, trying desperately not to let her mind float back to the image of Dan climbing out of the pool. She wasn't going to think about that long, toned body, and she certainly wasn't going to think about the way the water had glistened on his arms and his chest. That wouldn't be right at all, would it?

Just as her mind was illicitly travelling south, her phone beeped. She'd dared to turn it on for half an hour and sure enough, there were half a dozen voice mails and text messages from Jace. She read the latest one.

Want to see you tonight. Will call in at 8 p.m.

Robyn groaned. It was as if he knew what she'd been up to.

Chapter 17

KATHERINE NOTICED ROBYN'S ABSENCE IN THE INFORMAL discussion group as everyone took their places in a big circle around a table in the library. For a moment she wondered where her friend might be, but then Warwick came in and sat down next to her and Robyn was forgotten.

She'd really been looking forward to discussing Austen with mature people. Often she was left frustrated by the apathy of her students at college when presented with the very finest of literature, and there were very few people she could discuss her passion with, other than the virtual friends online at the Republic of Pemberley. That's why weekends like this were special. The only problem was that one had to share them with the likes of Mrs Soames, Katherine thought, seeing her archenemy walk into the room and sit in a chair opposite her. Katherine sighed. She'd been hoping that Mrs Soames might be having a prolonged siesta.

Mrs Soames was one of those people who rub you the wrong way as soon as they look at you. She had a large stony face with screwed-up eyes that fixed themselves on you and did not let go. It was most unnerving to have her in one of your lectures, and she'd always be sitting in the front row too, dying for you to make a mistake which she'd invariably spot and put right. And she moaned about everything. 'Can't we change the chairs around? I can't face the window.' 'It's too cold in here.' 'It's too warm in here.' 'We haven't been told where the toilets are.' On and on it went, a never-ending tirade against the world and everyone in it.

Katherine did her best to avoid eye contact with the old harridan as Dame Pamela entered the room to lead the discussion. As usual there was a polite round of applause as the actress took a seat. She was wearing a beautiful, floaty dress and shawl the colour of raspberry sorbet, and her shimmering silver hair was swept up and topped off with a deep red rose. She was every inch the glamorous star, and Katherine—who'd previously been rather pleased with her appearance in her figure-hugging emerald dress—felt positively dowdy in comparison.

'Thank you!' Dame Pamela began. 'This is always one of my favourite parts of the weekend. It's our chance to swap thoughts and ideas about our favourite, *favourite* books. Jane Austen left us with six perfect novels and even though it is a regrettably small collection, it still provides us with ample material to get excited about. Who would like to start our session? Perhaps someone would like to tell us about their favourite novel—their "own darling child," to quote Jane.'

At first everyone was quiet. It was a phenomenon known to every lecturer and teacher—nobody ever wants to be the first to speak.

Finally dear old Doris Norris took the plunge, holding up a brand-new copy of *Northanger Abbey*. 'This,' she said, 'is my favourite. I admit it wasn't when I first read it but I've warmed to it over the years for its humour and its wonderful heroine, Catherine.'

'And its hero,' a woman next to her said.

'Ah, yes! The wonderful Mr Tilney,' Doris said with a sigh. 'Who can resist a man who knows so much about muslin?'

A ripple of laughter ran around the room.

'But that's a brand-new copy of the book,' someone else said, nodding to Doris's copy of *Northanger Abbey*. 'I'm guessing you've worn out your last copy.'

Doris nodded. 'It fell into a canal from a holiday barge. I can't think how many copies I get through but I always make sure that there's a little bit left over from my pension to buy new books. I'm sure you'll all agree that they're one of life's necessities.'

Everybody nodded.

'I once dropped a copy of *Persuasion* off the Cobb in Lyme Regis,' a woman named Rose said. She was in her fifties and Katherine had spoken to her briefly the night before and had learnt that she was at the conference with her sister, Roberta. 'What a terrible waste,' she continued. 'I kept looking for it, as if it might wash up on the beach but it was the last I saw of it.'

'Well, wait until you see the state of mine,' somebody else said, holding up her own much-loved copy of *Persuasion* which had a cover that was creased and curling and a spine so cracked that the title had been completely lost. 'This goes everywhere with me. It lives in my handbag, and I daren't leave the house without it. I'd rather be without my mobile or my lipstick. It's my greatest fear to be made to wait somewhere—a doctor's waiting room or a terrible traffic jam—and not have my favourite Austen with me.'

'I'm just the same,' Roberta—Rose's sister—said. 'Only it's *Sense and Sensibility* that comes everywhere with me. I've worn out three copies now but I keep them all. They're like old friends.'

'I know just what you mean,' Dame Pamela said. 'Whenever I'm on location and there's all that dreadful hanging around the set, I just dip into a bit of *Pride and Prejudice,* and the time whizzes by. In fact, I'm almost sorry when I'm told I'm wanted on set.'

Everyone laughed.

'*Pride and Prejudice* is my favourite too,' a woman with a husky voice said, bending down to retrieve a pile of books from an I Love Mr Darcy shopping bag. 'And I've got quite a few copies,' she said, presenting the group with her different copies. There was a pretty pastel-coloured copy, the BBC TV tie-in edition featuring Colin Firth and Jennifer Ehle, the Joe Wright film tie-in featuring Keira Knightley and Matthew Macfadyen, and innumerable other versions, including some gorgeous foreign editions.

'Do you read all the foreign ones, Carla?' Rose asked.

'Oh, no,' Carla said, 'but I have to have them for the collection. And there's more, too.' Everyone watched in anticipation as she delved into the depths of her bag and brought out book after book after book. Katherine guessed that Carla was in her late forties, and she was very chic with vanilla-blond hair cut in a classic bob. She was wearing an expensive-looking tailored jacket and skirt, and the diamond on her ring finger was the size of a small egg. But that wasn't what was mesmerising the gathering—her books were holding everyone's attention. They comprised the collection of a true Austen aficionado. The titles were varied and wondrous. There were spin-offs and sequels and just about everything else you could imagine with a vague connection to the beloved original, *Pride and Prejudice.*

Katherine read the titles as they emerged: *Mr Darcy's Diary*; *Mr Darcy, Vampyre*; *The Other Mr Darcy*; *Pemberley*; *Darcy and Elizabeth: Nights and Days at Pemberley*; *Mr Darcy and Me*; *Mr Darcy Takes a Wife*; *Mr Darcy Presents His Bride*; *The Darcys and the Bingleys*; *Darcy's Temptation*; a copy of York Notes on *Pride and Prejudice*; as well as a copy of *CliffsNotes, SparkNotes,* and an 'A' level study guide. Carla even had a copy of *Pride and Prejudice and Zombies* which had been the cause of many a heated discussion already amongst die-hard fans.

'I have lots more,' she said, 'but I couldn't carry them all.'

Katherine, like everyone else, gazed in amazement at the collection.

'My house is absolutely chock full,' Carla said. 'Shelves are double stacked. I bought a bookcase last year and piled it high, and the whole thing collapsed.'

'I've got books in every room—even the bathroom,' Roberta confessed.

'You mustn't keep books in a bathroom. It's not good for them,' Doris said.

'But it's good for me! I love reading in the bath,' Roberta said. 'It's the only time I can get naked with Mr Darcy.'

Everyone laughed except her sister, Rose, who looked quite shocked by this admission.

'So do we have any favourite scenes from *Pride and Prejudice*?' Dame Pamela asked.

'The first proposal,' someone said.

'That's mine too.'

'Oh, yes!' Roberta said. 'I love how shocked Elizabeth is that Darcy has been in love with her for so long and yet she hadn't realised.'

Everyone nodded and sighed with bliss as they remembered the scene.

'I like it when Elizabeth upsets Lady Catherine and she says, "Obstinate, headstrong girl! I am ashamed of you!"' Rose said.

'I liked that scene too,' Dame Pamela said with a mischievous sparkle in her eyes.

'And we loved you in it!' Doris said.

Katherine nodded, remembering the very fine performance of Dame Pamela in the role. Hadn't she won a BAFTA for it?

'I like the bit where Darcy strides across the field at dawn and proposes to Elizabeth again,' an elderly lady at the far end of the room said.

Mrs Soames sighed in exasperation. 'That's the film! That scene isn't in the book.'

'Are you *sure?*'

'Quite sure.'

'But I remember it so vividly.'

'No, it's Matthew Macfadyen you're remembering so vividly,' Mrs Soames said.

'And so do we all,' Katherine said with a little laugh. She was enjoying herself immensely. Although she'd thought that the conversation would be far more serious in tone, she couldn't help being amused by the turn it had taken.

Roberta got up from her chair and picked up one of the Austen spin-offs Carla had presented the group with. 'I can never make up my mind about these, but they do look very tempting,' she said, flipping through a copy of *Mr Darcy, Vampyre.*

'But they're not Austen,' Mrs Soames said.

'I know they're not Austen,' Roberta said.

'But it's the next best thing,' Carla said.

'*Nothing's* the next best thing, I fear,' Dame Pamela said. 'We just have to accept that six perfect novels are all we're ever going to get.'

'What about Georgette Heyer?' Rose said. 'I like Georgette Heyer's books.'

'A very poor substitute,' Mrs Soames said.

'Or Barbara Cartland?' someone else suggested.

'Did someone say Barbara Cartland?' Mrs Soames boomed, her bosom rising like a tsunami.

'I *like* Barbara Cartland!'

'How can we be talking about Jane Austen one minute and Barbara Cartland the next? We'll be talking about that dreadful Lorna Warwick next. Have you seen they're selling her books here at Purley?' She nodded towards the book stall at the other side of the room. 'It's a complete travesty!' Mrs Soames said.

'But how can something so enjoyable be bad?' Rose said. 'Didn't Jane Austen say as much?'

'Yes she did,' Doris said. 'In my own favourite book, *Northanger Abbey.*'

Katherine nodded. 'She said that a novel displayed "the greatest powers of the mind" and "the liveliest effusions of wit and humour conveyed to the world in the best chosen language."'

The group looked suitably impressed by Katherine's ability to quote.

'What do you think?' Dame Pamela said, looking straight at Warwick.

Warwick looked up, and Katherine realised that he'd been particularly quiet throughout the discussion and had gone quite red in the last few minutes. Maybe he was just shy, although he hadn't struck her as being the shy type.

'You okay?' she said, leaning towards him.

He looked at her and nodded.

'It's not often that we get a male perspective on Austen,' Dame Pamela said. 'What do you think of all these spin-offs and sequels? All these Georgette Heyers and Lorna Warwicks?'

The whole group turned to Warwick, awaiting his answer. Katherine, too, was keen to hear it.

'Well, I... er... I think that there's room on the shelves for all sorts of books,' he said. 'As Katherine said, Austen thought the novel a great invention, and who are we to argue with her?'

A few people nodded but Mrs Soames didn't look convinced.

'What do you think, then?' Dame Pamela asked, seeing Mrs Soames shaking her head vehemently.

Katherine sighed. Some people should never be asked for their opinion, for they were sure to give it at very great length.

'I don't think Austen had all novels in mind when she said that,' Mrs Soames said, her face stiff with irritation. 'There are novels and there are novels.'

'What do you mean?' Carla asked.

'I mean that some aren't worth the paper they're printed on. They're cheap, trashy tat,' she said, her words stabbing the air like knives.

Warwick cleared his throat.

'You don't agree?' Dame Pamela said, obviously seeing how uncomfortable he was.

'No, I don't,' he said.

Everyone waited, expecting him to say something else but he didn't.

'So you don't read anything other than Jane Austen?' Carla said to Mrs Soames.

Mrs Soames shot her an evil look. 'And what's wrong with that?'

There were a few titters from the group.

'But that's so boring!' Carla said, flicking her vanilla-blond hair.

'It's not boring,' Mrs Soames said. 'I'm just a specialised reader. I don't like anything else.'

'Okay!' Dame Pamela said, clapping her hands together with an astonishingly loud sound. 'Any other favourite books or scenes?'

A few other people divulged their favourite moments which

included Emma's shenanigans with her boot while trying to match-make Mr Elton and Harriet, Catherine discovering the laundry list in *Northanger Abbey,* and Wentworth's letter in *Persuasion.*

'But he's not the most romantic of heroes, is he?' Roberta said. 'I mean, he's wonderful but he isn't a patch on Darcy.'

'Colin Firth, don't you mean?' Carla said. She seemed to have a knack of turning every conversation back to *Pride and Prejudice.* 'I think he has to be the definitive Darcy, doesn't he?'

'Especially when he dives into the lake,' Roberta said with a grin that split her face in two.

Mrs Soames shifted uneasily in her chair. 'How is it that every conversation about Jane Austen inevitably turns to Colin Firth in a wet shirt?'

The room was suddenly filled with laughter and whisperings about the famous scene. Mrs Soames, it seemed, was the only one to complain.

Chapter 18

ROBYN WAS IN HER ROOM GETTING DRESSED FOR DINNER AND dreading the approaching arrival of Jace. It just wasn't convenient. There was dinner and then there was the much-looked-forward-to quiz night. How was Jace meant to fit into such a line up?

She thought about calling him to ask him not to come but she knew she'd be wasting her time. No, she thought, she was better off getting on with the evening as best she could and getting rid of Jace as soon as she could—whatever time he made his appearance.

She chose one of her favourite dresses in a sunburnt orange. It reminded her of a sunset, and she liked the way it skimmed over her body without clinging too much. It was threaded through with silver and caught the light. Throwing a long scarf around her shoulders in case the evening got cool, she checked her reflection. Her face had a little more colour in it than usual. Had she caught the sun or was she still flushed from her earlier swimming pool encounter?

'Stop thinking about him,' she told her reflection.

Why? a little voice inside her said. *You like thinking about him. It makes you happy.*

'It makes me confused!'

What's confusing about it? He's a handsome man and you're single, aren't you? Or you soon will be. That's what you're planning, isn't it? You're going to break up with Jace so why feel guilty about eyeing the next man?

'I'm not eyeing him!'

Oh, rubbish! I saw the way you looked at him—all doey-eyed and lovelorn.

'I was not!'

Were too!

Robyn shook her head. 'This is ridiculous! Can't I have a polite conversation with a man without suspicions being raised? It doesn't mean I fancy him.'

But you do, don't you?

Robyn stared hard at her reflection, her eyes wide and questioning. 'I don't know how I feel,' she whispered but as those very words left her mouth, images of Dan strayed through her mind. His smile. His eyes. His body! She couldn't shut them out.

You do know how you feel. You do! the little voice said, and Robyn sighed. Maybe that's what was bothering her—the realisation that she was a little bit in love.

'I am not going to leap from one relationship to another,' she told her reflection.

Why not? He's perfect!

'How do you know that?'

You've only to look at him to know that!

'That is so shallow!' Robyn said.

But you've talked to him and you've got to agree that he's pretty amazing, right? He adores animals—you've seen him with those horses and dogs. He even showed an interest in Pride and Prejudice! *What more could you ask for?*

124

Robyn sighed. This was awful. She always shied away from getting herself into awful situations, and here she was, right bang in the middle of one, and it was all her own silly fault.

Katherine had been anxious for Warwick since the group discussion. He hastened out of the room before she had a chance to talk to him which seemed odd behaviour because they'd been getting on so well, and she imagined them lingering a while longer in the library together after the group dispersed.

Well, there was nothing as strange as men, she thought as she brushed her hair and changed into a dress the colour of blushing roses. She'd bought it for her first date with David. He picked her up, gave her a single red rose, and drove her to a beautiful out-of-the-way restaurant in the Cotswolds with views of the rolling countryside. Katherine thought she was being spoiled but looking back, she realised that she was probably just being hidden. He wouldn't have wanted to risk being seen in a restaurant in Oxford, would he?

'Bastard,' she said as she smoothed down the dress. She hadn't worn it since but she hadn't been able to discard it. She might well hate David but she couldn't hate the dress. It was too lovely to be rejected because of its misfortune in having been worn in the company of an idiot.

She left her room and headed downstairs for dinner and spied Warwick at the foot of the stairs. Was he waiting for her? she wondered. He looked up as she walked towards him.

'Hello,' he said.

'You disappeared,' she said with a frown.

'I'm sorry. I had to make a phone call.'

'Oh,' Katherine said. She had the feeling that he wasn't telling the truth. 'I'm afraid us ladies can be a bit scary when we start talking about heroes,' she said. 'Was it awful?'

'No,' Warwick said. 'A little scary,' he said, 'but mostly enjoyable.'

'You left so suddenly at the end,' she said. 'I didn't know what happened to you.'

He smiled at her. 'Shall we go into dinner?'

She nodded but she didn't want to let the subject drop. 'It must be odd being one of the few men here,' she said. 'Does it make you uncomfortable?'

'Why should it?'

'Well, you didn't exactly join in much with the discussion.'

'Neither did you.'

'I said more than you did,' Katherine said, realising that they were beginning to sound like an old married couple.

'But you didn't stick up for Lorna Warwick, I noticed.'

'Ah,' Katherine said. 'I know I didn't, and I feel like a traitor but I have to put my great reputation as a doctor of literature first. Only you know the true feelings I harbour for Lorna Warwick's work.' She gave him a wink.

He grinned back at her, and everything seemed to be okay once again.

As they were entering the dining room, Katherine saw Robyn.

'Hey, Robyn!' Katherine called.

Robyn stopped and turned around.

'You okay?' Katherine asked as she approached. 'You look a bit red.'

'Oh, I'm fine,' Robyn said, self-consciously touching her face with the back of her hand. 'It's just… erm… warm.'

'We missed you at the discussion group.'

'I decided to take a walk.'

Katherine nodded and suddenly remembered her manners. 'This is Warwick,' she said. 'Warwick, my friend, Robyn.'

The two of them shook hands.

'Did the group go well?' Robyn asked.

'It was brilliant!' Katherine said, telling Robyn about the great row that had ensued. 'Poor Warwick here was quite embarrassed by it all. I'm afraid it's the same thing every time a bunch of women get together and Mr Darcy is mentioned.'

Robyn smiled.

'Are you sure you're okay?' Katherine asked again, noticing that her friend was looking distinctly uneasy.

'Yes,' she said, but then she sighed. 'Well, no.'

'What's wrong? Is it your friend?'

Robyn nodded. 'I'm afraid he's threatened to drop by again.'

'Oh, dear,' Katherine said. 'Can you ignore your phone and hope for the best?'

'You saw what happened the last time I tried to do that.'

'Ah, yes. Well, maybe he'll entertain us all again tonight,' she said, making an attempt at humour.

'That's exactly what I'm afraid of,' Robyn said.

Warwick realised that he had not responded well in the group discussion. In fact, his behaviour could have given him away completely, but he'd little suspected that a discussion about the books of Jane Austen would turn into a personal attack on him. He'd never experienced that before. As a writer with a hidden identity, he never put himself out into the world as Lorna Warwick and so had never faced that sort of criticism before. He'd had bad reviews, of course—every writer had to learn to take the bad along with the good—but Mrs

Soames had been a whole new level of critic. Her words had been vicious and vitriolic. It had been a scary experience, and Warwick hadn't dared to defend himself for fear of being found out so he'd run away. It was the only option he thought safe.

But Katherine had definitely suspected something. He was quite sure that she didn't suspect anything close to the truth, but she still seemed a little out of sorts with him. He'd have to charm her again.

'You know, there were some interesting points made in that group today,' he began.

'Oh?'

'Yes,' he said. 'Everyone has their own idea about what makes the perfect novel and the perfect hero.'

Katherine nodded.

'I wonder what it is about a certain novel that ticks the boxes for a reader. I mean, for me, a story can have the most fascinating plot in the world, but if the narrator's voice is dull, then the plot counts for nothing. For me, authorial charm is everything.'

'Oh, my goodness!' Katherine said. 'That's exactly what I've always thought.'

'Really?' Warwick said, remembering the phrase Katherine had used in one of her letters. He was taking a risk by quoting it back to her but she was unlikely to remember it exactly and it seemed to be working for she was nodding and smiling as if he'd just said the most profound and intelligent thing in the whole world.

'If the language chosen to tell the stories doesn't engage me, then I really don't care what happens in terms of plot or the characters,' she said.

'They're just stories, aren't they?' Warwick said. 'Stories anyone could tell with no skill or charm about them, and who would want to bother with such stories?'

'That's exactly how I feel,' Katherine said, clattering her cutlery down on her plate and giving Warwick her full attention which he liked very much. 'Language—especially English—is such a powerful tool and all too many writers abuse it by using bland words and appalling clichés.'

'And that's part of the great charm of Austen, isn't it? Her warmth and her wit could carry you through any story,' Warwick said, really getting into his stride now. He was enjoying himself immensely, pushing all of Katherine's buttons and watching her soar with joy.

'Well, it's certainly no accident that she's still being read two hundred years after her first book was published,' Katherine said, her face beaming as she talked about her favourite subject. 'Few authors can hope for such success.'

'Indeed,' Warwick said, clearing his throat. 'I suppose it must be every author's dream.'

'I often wonder what Jane did dream of when she wrote her books,' Katherine said. 'Did she know that they would touch so many people and be read for hundreds of years after she'd put her pen down for the last time?'

'This is what I think,' Warwick said, digging deep and trying to remember the letter he was thinking of. What was it Katherine had said? 'I think she wrote the stories that meant the most to her. I think that's what every good writer does and that passion they feel communicates itself to every reader, irrespective of age or race or the century they're born in. It's timeless.'

Warwick watched in wonder as Katherine's beautiful mouth dropped open. Her dark eyes were sparkling with animation. She was glorious!

'That's amazing,' she said. 'That's *exactly* what I've always thought.'

Warwick nodded and tried his best to look nonchalant about the whole thing. She was hanging on his every word and he was enjoying it immensely.

'You know,' he said, 'it's wonderful talking to you about books. I feel like—I don't know—we have a connection.'

Katherine smiled sweetly but didn't say anything. It was time to push things even further, Warwick thought.

'I feel I can really talk to you and, I must say, that's a new experience for me.' He shook his head, looking thoughtful. 'I've had a bit of a disastrous past with women, I'm afraid. I've been let down a lot.' He paused, wondering if she'd jump in.

'Me too,' she said quietly.

'Really?' he said.

She nodded. 'I'm afraid so.'

He sighed. 'Then I apologise on behalf of my sex. I only hope that you haven't given up on all of us.'

She looked up at him. 'It's funny you should say that. I was just telling my friend, Lor—telling a friend—that I was going to give men up. I think it's safer to stick to fictional men sometimes. But I was advised against it.'

'Then you have a very sensible friend,' Warwick said with a smile. It was just what he'd wanted to hear.

∽

It was shortly after Robyn had finished her main course that her phone vibrated in her handbag.

'Oh!' Doris Norris, who was sitting to the right-hand side of Robyn, exclaimed loudly as the tiny handbag waltzed over her foot.

'Sorry,' Robyn said.

'Is that your vibrator?' Doris asked, and the whole table went silent for a moment, with everyone staring at Robyn. 'Your vibrator phone?' she added with an innocent little smile.

'Vibra*ting*,' Robyn said, her cheeks flushed yet again. It was probably best to leave the room, she thought, pushing her chair away from the table and making a hasty retreat. Dessert would have to be sacrificed.

She left the dining room and walked out into the hall. She didn't need to check her phone because she could see Jace's car from the window, parked at a peculiar angle right in the middle of the driveway, with no thought of aesthetics or etiquette. She watched him from the safety of the hall for a moment. He was tapping the steering wheel with an anxious hand. He didn't look happy.

Robyn took a deep breath and opened the door, walking down the steps and crunching across the gravel before knocking on his window.

'Jesus!' he shouted, unwinding the window. 'You scared me half to death.'

'Did you want to see me or not?' Robyn said.

'Of course I bloody want to see you! What sort of a question is that?'

'Because you don't look very happy.'

'I'm not very happy,' he said. 'Get in the car, Robyn.'

'I'm not leaving Purley.'

'Just get in the car. I want to talk to you without the whole world watching,' he said, nodding to his rear view mirror. Robyn turned to see what he'd spotted, and she groaned when she saw the half dozen faces staring back at her from the dining room.

Reluctantly because she didn't feel like sharing a small space with Jace, she got into the car. 'What is it?'

Jace turned around in his seat and looked at her. His face looked pale as if he'd had an argument with the sun and refused to see it ever again. His hair was messy too and looked like it hadn't seen a comb for a number of weeks.

'I've been bored out of my mind,' he said. 'There's nothing to do down here. Hertfordshire's boring.'

'Hampshire,' Robyn said. 'We're in Hampshire.'

'Well, Hampshire's boring.'

Robyn frowned. 'What have you been doing?'

'Dunno,' he said with one of his shrugs. 'Hanging around, mostly. Talking to the barman.'

'Oh, Jace!'

'What?'

'There's so much to see around here.'

'Like what?'

'Why don't you go to Chawton? We're going there tomorrow.'

'What's at Chawton?'

'Jane Austen's cottage.'

'What do I want to see some old cottage for?'

'Because it's beautiful and interesting and was the home of one of the most famous writers in the world,' Robyn said, but she could tell that she wasn't making an impression. 'Well, what about Winchester? You could go shopping.'

'On my own?'

'Why not?'

'Because it's boring,' he said sounding very much like a whining child. 'Why don't you come with me?'

'What?'

'Come with me to Winchester tomorrow. Come now and stay at the B and B with me.'

'Jace, I can't.'

'Why not?'

'Why not? Because I'm enjoying myself here. I've been saving up and looking forward to this weekend all year. You know I have. I'm not about to walk out and stay in some crumby B and B when I've got a great room here at Purley.'

'Well, let me stay here with you.'

Robyn sighed. 'You know I can't.'

'Aren't you bored?' he asked, scratching his messy hair.

'No.'

Jace tutted. 'I just want to be with my gal.' He reached across and picked up her hand.

'But we never talk when we're together,' Robyn said and then swallowed hard. She hadn't meant to say something that confrontational. Not that night. Not in the middle of her Jane Austen weekend.

'What do you mean?'

'Nothing,' she said quickly.

'No, Robyn. You meant something by that. I'm not thick. What did you mean?'

'Jace, I've got to get back.'

He wouldn't let go of her hand. 'I know what you're thinking,' he said. 'I'm not good enough for you, am I? I'm not smart like all those people in there who read all those posh books and know which knives and forks to eat their soup with.'

Robyn tried not to giggle; he was being deadly serious.

'You've always thought that, haven't you? And you're right. I know I'm not good enough for you. But I was once, wasn't I? When you needed me. I was good enough for you then when there was nobody else, wasn't I?'

'Jace, don't.' She pulled her hand away from him. 'Don't talk about that. Not now.'

'You never want to talk about it.'

Robyn sat perfectly still for a moment. This was horrible. He was putting all sorts of bad memories into her head and she didn't want them there. This was her special weekend away from all that. It was a time to escape into the safe and beautiful worlds of Elizabeth and Darcy and Elinor and Edward. She didn't want it to be about Robyn and Jace.

'Look,' she said at last. 'I've got to be back for the quiz. It's one of the highlights of the weekend.'

He stared at her for a moment and she couldn't tell if he was going to let her go without a quarrel or if he was going to start up again.

'All right, all right,' he said after a protracted silence. 'I know when I'm not wanted.'

But did he? Robyn wondered. Did he *really*?

She got out of the car and Jace did too. It was terrible timing because across the front lawn, walking out of the lengthening shadows, was Dan leading a grey mare with Moby and Biscuit following behind. Robyn watched and it seemed that everything was happening in slow motion as Dan raised a hand and waved across to her, a smile lighting up his tanned face.

'Who the hell is he?' Jace demanded.

'Dan.'

'Dan?'

'He works here.'

'He's that bloody horseman, isn't he? The one that nearly half killed my car.'

Robyn rolled her eyes. 'Night, Jace,' she said and walked as quickly as she could back to the hall before he could even think about kissing her good-bye.

Chapter 19

THE JANE AUSTEN QUIZ NIGHT WAS ALWAYS ENTERTAINING AND as soon as dinner was over and desserts had been consumed and coffees drunk, everybody made their way to the library, where chairs had been placed around little tables.

'Groups of three!' Dame Pamela shouted above the excitement. 'Groups of three.'

Katherine and Warwick looked at each other in despair.

'Where on earth can Robyn be?' Katherine asked, her hands on her hips as if she were searching for a naughty student rather than her new friend.

'I think she's been abducted by that mad boyfriend of hers,' Warwick said.

'Don't say that,' Katherine said. 'I'm sure he's capable of such a thing.'

The figure of Mrs Soames appeared in the library doorway and they watched in undisguised horror as she made her bosomy way across the room towards them.

'Oh, no!' Katherine said to Warwick.

'Lord preserve us!' Warwick said.

'We've *got* to find another partner. Quickly!'

It was too late.

'Ah, there you are, Dr Roberts,' Mrs Soames said. 'I thought you'd have approached me by now to make up a team.'

Katherine physically blanched at the cheek of the woman.

'*My* team always does well in the quiz,' she continued, manoeuvring her bosom with all the menace of an army vehicle.

Katherine looked up at Warwick as if he might be able to find a way out of their predicament, but with a miraculous sense of timing, she saw her saviour.

'Robyn!' she yelled across the room, waving madly to catch her attention before she was grabbed by somebody else. 'I'm terribly sorry, Mrs Soames, but we already have a team.'

Mrs Soames turned around to see the approaching figure of Robyn. 'That slip of a thing?' she said in disgust. 'She can't possibly know as much as I do.'

'But *she's* our friend,' Katherine said pointedly.

Mrs Soames's mouth wrinkled up like a pug's bottom. She turned around as fast as her enormous bosom would allow her and walked away in search of somebody else to harass.

'Boy, are we glad to see you,' Katherine said, squeezing Robyn's arm. 'Where were you?'

'Trying to get rid of Jace,' she said.

'Everything okay?'

Robyn sighed. 'For the moment.'

'Well, you've just saved us from the dreaded Mrs Soames,' Warwick said.

Katherine nodded. 'There's a quote from *Mansfield Park* that I always remember in the presence of Mrs Soames. "We must prepare ourselves for gross ignorance, some meanness of opinions, and very distressing vulgarity of manner."'

They all burst into laughter.

'Girls,' Warwick said, 'we'd better find a table before the quiz starts.'

Robyn looked a little uncomfortable. 'Are you two sure you want me in your team? You'll probably know so much more than me!'

'Rubbish!' Katherine said.

'You're as much of a fan as we are,' Warwick said, leading them to a table by the window at the far end of the library. 'And it's my experience that fans know far more than professionals.'

'What's your profession?' Robyn asked him.

'He's an antiquarian,' Katherine said.

'Then you'll know *far* more than me,' Robyn said.

'Take your seats!' Dame Pamela called across the sea of heads. 'There should be pens and paper on each table.'

'Gosh, I'm quite nervous,' Katherine said.

'*You're* nervous?' Robyn said.

'Let me tell you a secret,' Katherine said, and three heads leant in close together. 'I may be a lecturer, but I always get nervous before every single lecture—every single seminar. It never gets any easier.'

Robyn's mouth dropped open. 'Really?'

'Really,' Katherine said.

Dame Pamela, who was standing underneath an enormous portrait of herself on one of the few walls in the library that wasn't covered in books, held her hands up for silence which came instantaneously.

'Ah, the power of a dame,' Warwick whispered.

Dame Pamela beamed a smile around the room as she let the question sheet flutter in her hand. 'This is probably my favourite part of the conference weekend,' she said, 'but I'm sure to say that about the trip to Chawton tomorrow and the dance the day after that. There's something very special about our quizzes, though, and just to whet our appetite, the prize tonight is a special collector's edition of Jane Austen's novels for each team member.' She held up one of the beautiful box sets of white and gold books. There were sighs of appreciation and people picked up their pens in anticipation. 'And a signed and framed photograph of me in the role of Lady Catherine de Bourgh.'

Warwick grinned at Katherine.

'She gives those out every year,' Katherine whispered. 'I think she had too many printed.'

'We'll start off with some easy questions to warm you all up,' Dame Pamela said.

'You be the scribe, Robyn,' Katherine said, pushing the piece of paper towards her, together with the pen.

'Where was Jane Austen born?' Dame Pamela asked.

Robyn beamed. 'I know that one!'

'Go on, then,' Katherine said, 'write it down.'

'Steventon—here in Hampshire,' she whispered, and Katherine and Warwick nodded in agreement.

'Question number two,' Dame Pamela said. 'Still nice and easy. How many brothers and sisters did she have?'

'One sister,' Robyn whispered.

'I knew you'd be good at this,' Katherine said with a grin

'But I'm not sure how many brothers. There were lots, weren't there?'

Katherine nodded. 'Six,' she whispered, and Robyn wrote down the answer.

'Imagine sharing a house with six boys,' Katherine said, shaking her head.

The questions continued, getting progressively harder. It seemed that the collector's editions of the Jane Austen novels and the signed photographs of Dame Pamela weren't going to be easily won.

'Now for the next section,' Dame Pamela announced. 'It's our quote quiz, where you have to name the speaker and the novel the quote is from. We'll start with a nice, easy one. "He is a most disagreeable, horrid man, not at all worth pleasing. So high and so conceited that there was no enduring him."'

'Mrs Bennet!' the whole room chanted, and there was a ripple of laughter as pens scribbled down the answer.

'I did say it was easy,' Dame Pamela said. 'Just to warm you up for the tough ones. So here's the second quote,' Dame Pamela said. '"One half of the world cannot understand the pleasures of the other."'

'Emma!' Katherine said without a moment's hesitation.

'From which novel?' Warwick asked with a grin.

She pulled a face at him.

'Next quote,' Dame Pamela said. '"It is a great comfort to find that she is not a poor helpless creature, but can shift very well for herself."'

'That's about Catherine in *Northanger Abbey*, isn't it?' Warwick queried.

'But who said it?' Robyn asked.

'It's her mother,' Katherine said. 'Mrs Morland.'

Robyn wrote down the answer.

'And the last quote,' Dame Pamela announced. '"This is always my luck! If there is anything disagreeable going on, men are always sure to get out of it."'

'Oh,' Robyn said. 'Is that Mrs Bennet?'

Katherine shook her head. 'Too astute for Mrs B. I think it's Anne's sister in *Persuasion*, the one who's always complaining.'

'Mary? Mary Musgrove,' Warwick said.

'The very one,' Katherine said, and a smile passed between them that had quite the effect of banishing Robyn's very presence.

'You've all survived the quote round, but the questions are getting a little tougher now. We have a real mixed bag in this section so be warned. In the previous section, you should have written the number of brothers and sisters Jane Austen had. Now you must name them all.'

'Oh, lordy!' Robyn said.

'No, no,' Katherine said. 'We can do it. There was Cassandra—obviously.'

Robyn nodded. 'And Edward—the one who was adopted by the Knight family. Who else was there? We need five more names.'

'Charles,' Warwick said.

'Yes and Frank—or Francis—and George,' Katherine said.

'And Henry and James,' Robyn said. 'I remember that because it's like that American writer's name.'

'We've got them!' Katherine said. 'Well done, team.'

'Okay, everyone?' Dame Pamela asked after a couple of minutes. 'Was that enough time? Right, next question. What was the original title of *Northanger Abbey*?'

'Ah,' Katherine said, 'it was *Susan*.'

Robyn scribbled down the answer, hoping it was right. She wanted to win those books.

'Now,' Dame Pamela continued, 'this will test even the most dedicated Janeite. In *Pride and Prejudice*...' she began.

'I thought she said it would be hard,' Mrs Soames was heard to say from her table. 'There's nothing hard about *Pride and Prejudice*. A true Janeite like me knows it inside out.'

'So you might think,' Dame Pamela said. 'In *Pride and Prejudice*,

Mr Collins reads to the Bennet girls after dinner. What is the name of the book he reads from? And there's an extra two points if you can name the author of the book.'

Silence fell upon the library. Even Mrs Soames looked stumped.

'I told you it was for true Janeites,' Dame Pamela said with a silvery laugh.

Katherine frowned at Warwick and he frowned right back at her.

'I have absolutely no idea,' Katherine said, 'and I thought I knew that book inside out.'

'That's what everybody thinks,' Warwick said. 'Robyn? Any ideas?'

Robyn bit her lip and then smiled before writing something down on their answer sheet and passing it to the two of them.

Katherine read the words she'd written. '*Sermons to Young Women* by Dr Fordyce.'

'Really?' Katherine said, impressed. 'I had no idea, and I've read that novel so many times.'

'How did you remember that?' Warwick asked.

Robyn gave a little smile. 'I read it in *Jane Austen for Dummies* just last week.'

Katherine and Warwick grinned.

'Fordyce's book was terrible,' Robyn continued in a whisper, lest any other teams hear her answer. 'It encouraged women to be submissive and everything.'

'Like that's never a good thing, you mean?' Warwick said and received evil glares from both Katherine and Robyn.

A few more questions came and went and Robyn's writing hand was beginning to get sore, but she battled on for her team and for the chance to win those books.

'And final question,' Dame Pamela announced at last. 'We all know the opening sentence of *Pride and Prejudice,* but what's the last sentence? It's a long one, I know, so we don't expect it to be word perfect, but the person who gets nearest to it will get five points.'

There was much intaking of breath from around the room.

'Over to you, Katherine,' Warwick said.

'Don't leave it to me! I'll need all the help I can get,' she said. 'Okay, it's about the Gardiners and Derbyshire. I remember that much.'

'And how much Darcy and Elizabeth love them,' Robyn chipped in. 'I'll write that down.'

'And there's a lovely phrase about them coming together,' Warwick said.

'How does it go?' Robyn asked, her pen hovering hotly over the paper.

Warwick's mouth became a firm line of concentration. 'Something about the Gardiners bringing Elizabeth to Derbyshire and so "uniting them."'

They each took it in turns to examine the strange sentence they had cobbled together.

'Does this look right?' Warwick asked.

Katherine looked at it again. 'It looks like it could pass muster.'

'And that's the end of the quiz,' Dame Pamela said a few minutes later. 'Make sure you have your group's name on the top of your paper before handing it to Higgins,' she said, motioning to her right-hand man who, that evening, was wearing a mustard-coloured waistcoat with the brightest gold buttons ever created.

'We haven't got a name!' Robyn said.

'It has to be Austensian,' Katherine said.

'Of course,' Warwick said. 'How about The *Pride and Prejudice* Posse?'

'Eeew, that's really awful,' Robyn said with a giggle. 'What about Darcy's Girls?'

Warwick cleared his throat.

'Ah, yes sorry.'

'We want something that's fun but that encapsulates the whole feel of Austen,' Katherine said.

They sat pensively for a moment.

'I know. How about Bennets and Bonnets?' Katherine said with a grin.

Warwick grinned and Robyn nodded as she wrote the name proudly in block capitals across the top of their answer sheet and then handed it to Higgins the butler when he came around.

'Well, that's that,' Robyn said. 'Our fate is sealed.' She might as well have been talking to herself because Katherine and Warwick were staring at each other as if nobody else in the room existed, least of all Robyn.

Glasses of mulled wine were served together with the prettiest of chocolates as Dame Pamela's team of quiz markers got to work and Robyn sat sipping and nibbling, her eyes trying to avoid the lovebirds before her.

How amazing the library was, she thought, staring up at the great height of the bookcases all around the room, her eyes taking in all the coloured spines. They looked like real books too—books that Dame Pamela had bought individually and actually read— not books she'd bought by the metre to impress guests, as some country house owners did. How Robyn would love to have such a room! At present, her little terrace could accommodate only a couple of modest-sized bookcases, but they were her pride and joy, filled with books that she thought of as her friends. And how she would love to add the collector's editions to her little family.

At last Dame Pamela took up her position again to read out the results. 'In third place, with twenty-two points, is Darcy's Girls.'

Robyn gasped. 'They stole that name from us!' she said, turning round and seeing that it was Mrs Soames's little gang.

'I wouldn't be a bit surprised,' Katherine said, quite sure that Mrs Soames had probably been listening in on some of their answers to the questions too.

There was a round of applause as Dame Pamela motioned for Mrs Soames and her team to collect signed photographs of herself.

'In second place, with twenty-seven points, is Purley Queens,' she said, and the group members—Rose, Roberta, and dear Doris Norris—made their way to collect their own signed photographs.

'Great group name, ladies,' Dame Pamela said, greeting each of them with an air kiss before handing them their signed photographs.

'And that just leaves the winners,' Dame Pamela said.

Robyn looked at Katherine and took a deep breath.

'With an astonishing *thirty-five* points, it's Bennets and Bonnets!'

Robyn squealed with delight and practically leapt out of her chair. Katherine and Warwick stood up and they all hugged each other before going to receive a powdery kiss from Dame Pamela and collect their signed photographs and collector's editions of the six Jane Austen books.

'They're gorgeous!' Robyn said with a sigh of delight as she was handed her prize. 'Thank you.'

'You're entirely welcome, my dear,' Dame Pamela said. 'You are a true Janeite.'

Chapter 20

ROBYN WAS FLOATING WITH HAPPINESS AT HAVING BEEN ON the winning team of the quiz and she wanted to take her much-prized new books up to her room. As she left the library, she was greeted by many congratulations and much cooing over the beautiful white-and-gold books, and even the snooty remark from Mrs Soames that the books were inferior to a set she'd bought recently couldn't touch Robyn.

Reaching her room, she thought about the two teammates she left downstairs. Everyone had been mingling and chattering away after the quiz—apart from Katherine and Warwick. Robyn wasn't sure what they were talking about, but it looked much too intimate and intense for a third person to join in.

She walked across to her window and saw a glorious full moon behind the cedar tree, casting enormous shadows across the front lawn. It was like a scene from a nineteenth-century poem, Robyn thought, and she knew she had to go outside and be a part of it.

In true Austen style, she grabbed a warm shawl to wrap around her shoulders and headed down the stairs and out the front door. When she rounded the side of the house, her soft shoes crunched lightly on the gravel. She could hear the chatter and laughter from the library and spied the scene through the window as she passed. There was Doris Norris, her face wonderfully red from the consumption of mulled wine, and Higgins the butler walking around the tables with a small silver tray laden with yet more chocolates. And there—in their quiet corner of the room—were Katherine and Warwick. Robyn watched them for a moment. It was like a silent film, with the hero and heroine about to divulge something very important.

'Where's the volume switch when you need it?' Robyn said in frustration, but she didn't really need to hear what they were saying. She could see it in Warwick's eyes and the way he was holding Katherine's hand.

She turned away, feeling that she shouldn't be watching anymore—that she'd strayed somewhere she shouldn't be. Taking a deep breath of balmy night air and hugging her shawl around herself, she took the path under the great cedar tree, passing by the swimming pool that had been covered over since Dan's swim. Wouldn't it be wonderful to have a midnight swim, she thought. But then her mind strayed to places it shouldn't, and she thought it best that she move as far away from the pool as possible.

She entered the garden, her shoes sinking softly into the grass. The house was behind her now, and she turned to look at it. Most of the windows glowed with light, and it seemed to be smiling as if it were happy to be filled with people.

She walked across the lawn, found a bench to sit on and gazed up at the great fat moon, allowing her eyes to adjust until she could see the deep clear sky studded with stars. Living in Yorkshire, she was used to seeing the heavens unadulterated by light pollution. It was one of the joys of rural living, but the sight of it never failed to leave her awestruck.

She was wondering if she was looking at the same stars that Jane Austen would have once looked at, when she heard a voice.

'Hello there,' it said softly from somewhere in the great hedge.

Robyn sat up abruptly, as if she'd been caught napping. 'Dan?'

He stepped out of the shadows and the moonlight lit him up, casting his tall shadow across the lawn as he walked towards her. 'I thought I'd find you in the garden tonight,' he said.

She looked up at him, curiosity in her eyes. 'Did you?'

He nodded. 'I had a feeling you'd like moonlit nights.'

'You mean you thought I'd be a silly old romantic?'

He motioned to the bench and when she nodded, sat down beside her.

'Moonlight was really important in Jane Austen's time,' she said. 'They arranged events like dances for when the moon was at its brightest because it helped them travel at night. I don't think their roads were very good.'

'No motorways lit up by lights,' Dan said.

'Exactly,' Robyn said. 'Imagine what it must have been like.'

'I often go riding by moonlight,' Dan said.

'Do you?'

He nodded.

'But not tonight?'

'No. I thought I'd miss you if I went out.'

She looked at him, surprised by his admission. What did he mean? But he didn't elaborate and seemed to be thinking about something else now.

'Pammy loves these events,' he said. 'She loves a house full of guests. It's what these places were built for, really. Although she loves having it to herself too, but not all the time. She's such a gregarious person and can't bear to be alone for long.'

'It's certainly wonderful being a guest,' Robyn said. 'I feel like I've stepped back in time. Like I might have arrived here by carriage in the moonlight.'

They sat for a few moments, each looking out across the silvery lawn towards the lake.

'How are you getting on with *Pride and Prejudice*?' Robyn dared to ask.

Dan smiled.

'You haven't read it, have you?' she said.

'I have!' he said. 'Just not all of it.'

'And you won't, either, will you?'

He looked affronted. 'What makes you say that? Because I'm a man?'

'Yes,' Robyn said.

'That, Miss Love, is outrageously sexist.'

'But terribly true, I'm afraid.'

Dan laughed and then turned to look at her, his eyes fixing on hers. His face had a stern expression that was somewhat unnerving.

'What?' Robyn said.

Dan's eyes narrowed as he continued to stare at her. 'I'm just wondering if you have a pair of fine eyes.'

Robyn's eyes—fine or not—widened with delight. 'That's the phrase Darcy uses to describe Elizabeth's eyes! You *have* been reading it!'

'Well, I told you I had. Don't sound so surprised.'

They sat in silence for a moment.

'I'm sorry,' she said at last.

'For what?'

'Not believing you,' she said. 'I guess I was judging you by— well, what I know of men.'

'And that's not much?'

She stared at him. 'Are you insulting me?'

'No!' he said quickly. 'Just making an observation—like you did about me.'

She smiled. 'I suppose that's fair, then.'

'What I mean is—' he stopped.

'What do you mean?'

He shifted his legs in front of him. 'Well, it seems to me like you've been with this man of yours for some time now. Am I right?'

Robyn adjusted her shawl around her shoulders. 'How do you know that?'

He shrugged. 'Just your body language around each other. If you don't mind my saying, you look as if you annoy the hell out of each other and have been doing so for some time now.'

Robyn was shocked by his audacity and stared at him openmouthed.

'If you don't mind my saying,' he repeated.

'And what if I do?' she asked.

'Too late now,' he said with a small smile. 'I've said it. Me and my big mouth.'

Robyn sat back on the bench and pouted.

'Why are you with him?' Dan asked.

'Why are you asking?'

'Because I want to know,' he said simply. 'You don't look suited. You don't look happy.'

'It's not really any of your business,' she said.

'Maybe not,' he said. 'But I care about you.'

She looked at him. He was staring into the distance, and she stared at his profile which seemed to be carved out of marble in the moonlight—so perfectly formed. This man—this handsome stranger—cared about her.

'Why?' she said, the word escaping her before she had time to check it.

He looked around, and his face was filled with surprise at her question. 'Why? Because I like you. You're a romantic, like me, and you're as much in love with Purley as I am. You don't mind getting covered in dog hair, and you like the smell of horses as much as I do. And I like talking to you. I really like being with you. It feels...' he paused. 'Right. Is that a good enough reason?'

⁓

Perhaps it was the second glass of mulled wine that did it but Katherine didn't think so. She knew what it was. It was Warwick— pure and simple. His charm, his mischievous eyes, that wicked smile, and the fact that she and he seemed perfectly attuned to each other. It was like Marianne and Willoughby in the heady early days.

Yes, but look what happened to them! a little voice told her.

No, don't! another little voice said—the voice she really wanted to hear. *Just enjoy it.*

The two had been swapping secret little smiles for what seemed like an eternity. First he would look up and catch her attention, and it would seem casual, but then he would hold her gaze for a fraction longer than was necessary. She'd look away, enjoying the flirty flustery feeling that she was sure was colouring her face.

It wouldn't be long before she lifted her gaze again, and there he would be—looking right at her. Katherine felt like a teenager all over again. It was the same heady feeling that comes from knowing that the attraction you are feeling for somebody is returned two-fold. And it was not knowing what was going to happen next, like a great book that keeps you turning pages as you're held in suspense.

When Warwick leant across the table in the library and took her hand in his, Katherine's skin seemed to catch fire. How long it had been since somebody had touched her in that way! It was so simple a gesture, yet the message it sent was irrefutable.

'I want to take you upstairs,' he said in a voice barely audible in the chatter around them, but he needn't have uttered a single word, for she understood him perfectly, and they got up to leave.

'Won't you join us, dear?' Doris Norris asked them as they walked by her table. 'We're making a team to play cards, just like in Jane Austen's time. You wouldn't want to miss that, would you?'

'Katherine needs to lie down,' Warwick told Doris in a firm voice that was going to brook no opposition.

'Oh, dear,' Doris said. 'Not feeling well? Too much of that mulled wine, I expect. Wasn't it delicious?'

Katherine almost gasped at Warwick's lie and couldn't get out of the room fast enough. Once at the stairs, Warwick took her hand in his and they laughed their way to the top, and then things became serious.

'You shouldn't have said that,' Katherine said, feigning outrage.

'Why not? You didn't want to stay and play cards, did you? Because if you did, we can go back downstairs.' He held her gaze, and his eyes were dark and intense.

'You're teasing me,' she said.

'I'd never do that,' he said, the tiniest of smiles playing around his mouth. 'Well, I might,' he added. 'In the right circumstances.'

Still holding her hand, he let his fingers circle the delicate skin of her palm until she felt quite weak with desire, and then he led her to his bedroom, fishing his key out of his pocket and opening his door.

There were no lights on, but none were needed, for the curtains were open and moonlight spilled into the room, casting its magical silvery light onto the bed.

Warwick closed the door behind them and took a step towards her. 'You're so beautiful,' he whispered to her, moving closer and holding her face in his hands.

They felt warm against her skin, and she closed her eyes as he bent down to kiss her.

Katherine shivered with pleasure at the touch of his lips.

'I couldn't keep my eyes off you all evening,' he said, his fingers stroking the oh-so-soft part of her neck before trailing through her dark hair. 'You've bewitched me.'

'Warwick,' she said, his name sounding delicious on her tongue, 'I didn't expect this. It's all happening so quickly.'

'I know,' he said. 'I know.'

'This weekend—I—it's all so—so…' she struggled to find the right words and failed. Here she was, a doctor of literature, and she couldn't express herself. Well, not in words, anyway, so she kissed him again and allowed her hands to circle around to his shoulders. He felt strong and muscular. Was this from the rock climbing he'd been telling her about? If so, she was deeply appreciative of what the Peak District could do for a man's physique. She felt her pulse quicken when she touched him.

'You're okay with this?' he whispered. 'Because we can slow things down if you want. We don't have to hurry things. You're worth waiting for, Katherine.'

Katherine smiled. 'You haven't had to wait that long for me,' she said.

'I've waited my whole life for you,' he said.

She closed her eyes at his words. They weren't the most original in the world, she knew that, but nobody had ever said them to her before, so they sounded like the most exquisite poetry.

His lips hovered over hers, and she felt the warmth of his breath. Did she want to slow things down? Was that what she really wanted? She moved a fraction of an inch towards him and pressed her lips against his.

'I'm okay with this,' she said.

'And this?' Suddenly Warwick was kissing her neck.

'Yes,' she gasped. 'That's okay too.'

She was floating, and it was the best feeling in the world. It was—dare she think it—even better than a good book.

Robyn got up from the bench and walked across the grass. The moonlight seemed to be pulling her towards the lake, and she didn't try to fight it.

'I'm sorry if I pried,' Dan said, following behind her. 'You're not mad at me, are you?'

'No, I'm not mad,' Robyn said. 'It just feels strange.'

'How do you mean?'

'That you've been watching me, making these observations about my life.'

'If you don't mind my saying, I think most of the people at this conference will have been making observations about your friend's performance the other night.'

Robyn sighed and gazed up into the deep, dark sky. 'You're probably right,' she said. 'It's so unfair. I came here to escape all that, but it won't let me be.'

'What won't?'

She turned her attention away from the heavens and looked back at the earthy yet equally celestial Dan.

'Jace,' she said. 'It's all a mess. You're right.'

'I'm sorry,' he said.

'And I've been trying to sort it out. I really have. Except I keep making a mess of things. It's like some terrible farce. The harder I try, the worse it becomes.'

'Have you told him how you feel?' he asked.

'Not in so many words, but I've dropped quite a few hints.'

Dan shook his head.

'What?' she asked.

'Some people can't take hints, and your friend strikes me as one of those types. You'll have to be more direct with him. Tell him straight that you're not happy.'

Robyn looked out across the lake. The moon was reflected perfectly on its surface. 'It's not easy being honest.'

'No,' Dan said, 'but it doesn't look very easy being dishonest either, not from what I've seen.'

They were quiet for a moment and in the distance, far across the fields, an owl hooted.

'Why do things become so complicated?' Robyn asked.

'Because we let them,' Dan said. 'We let things get out of hand. It's very easy to do.'

'Has it happened to you?'

'All the time. It's happening right now.'

Robyn stared at him. 'What do you mean?'

'I can feel things are about to get even more complicated,' he said in a voice barely above a whisper.

Robyn didn't get the opportunity to ask him what he meant

again because he bent down towards her and kissed her, very sweetly and very firmly, on the mouth.

'Gosh,' she said a moment later.

'Have I gone and complicated things even more for you?'

Robyn nodded slowly. 'Yes,' she said. 'I think you have.'

Chapter 21

THERE WERE TWO PILES OF DISCARDED CLOTHES ON THE FLOOR of the Temple Room and the kissing had started in earnest. Katherine felt she had left her old self back in Oxford and a new, uninhibited woman was emerging, and it felt wonderful. When Warwick kissed her, it felt like a perfect piece of heaven had landed on her lips and she didn't want it to stop—ever.

At first their kisses had been light and feathery soft, the sort of kisses that send tingles everywhere at once. But things became more intense, and Katherine and Warwick ripped each other's clothes off faster than if they'd been on fire.

'Katherine!' he'd groaned as he took his first glimpse of her, and her heart raced at her first sight of him.

What would Jane Austen have made of it all? Perhaps it wasn't the right moment to think about darling Jane. It seemed almost sacrilegious to be doing such things at the Jane Austen Conference. Shouldn't the two adults be downstairs playing cards and discussing whether Jane and Bingley would really have been financially abused by every passing tradesman and servant?

Katherine didn't want to think about books now, though, unless it was one of those hot scenes from one of Lorna Warwick's books. That's what this was reminding her of—a wonderfully abandoned scene of lust on a night that could easily pass for summer, where lips kissed hungrily and hearts beat wildly behind thin muslin gowns.

~♥

Down by the lake, Robyn was feeling dazzled and dazed and while it wasn't a totally terrible feeling, it was one she hadn't anticipated.

'What are you thinking?' Dan asked her.

Robyn shook her head slowly. 'I *can't* think.'

'I haven't overstepped the mark? I haven't gone and ruined things, have I?'

Robyn looked up at him. He was tall, and a funny thought occurred to her, even though she'd just protested that she was unable to think. What if they were to spend the rest of their lives kissing each other? Surely he'd get a bad back or a crooked neck from stooping down to kiss her. Well, she couldn't be responsible for that. It would be too awful.

'You're so tall,' she said.

He laughed. 'What a funny thing to say!'

She started to walk because she didn't trust herself standing still anymore. If she continued to stand there in front of him, she'd be sure to kiss him again, and she didn't want that. Well, she did, but she shouldn't, should she? It wouldn't be right. *Oh, what a mess! Keep moving. Don't look at him.*

They walked along the banks of the lake until they came to the wooden bridge that crossed onto the island. It was too tempting and before she could think of the implications and complications, Robyn was walking across it towards the round temple whose white columns were bright in the moonlight. There were roses climbing up the temple, but it was impossible to tell if they were pink or white. They smelled of heaven on the warm night air.

'Aren't they perfect?' she said.

'There was a wedding here last weekend,' Dan said. 'The bride wanted roses everywhere.'

'They've lasted all this time?'

'No,' he said. 'But Pammy saw them around the temple and insisted we had some for this weekend too. I think she'll always want them here now. Flowers are a particular weakness of hers.'

'And every woman's,' Robyn said. 'Even if we say they're not. One of my friends is always complaining that flowers are a waste of money, but you should see her face when she receives them. Her boyfriend sent her a huge bouquet at work last month, for her birthday. She couldn't stop smiling all day.'

Robyn bent to inhale the sweet perfume of one of the huge pale blooms. 'I love how silent flowers are.'

'What's that?' Dan asked.

'You know… how *quiet* they are. I mean, this is so beautiful, and yet it doesn't make a song and dance about it, does it?'

Dan laughed. 'Well, I never thought about that before. You are a strange one,' he said.

Robyn frowned at him.

'But wonderful,' he said.

Robyn gave a nervous little laugh. 'No I'm not. I'm a mess and a muddle, and I don't know what I'm doing half the time.'

Dan grinned. 'You're not going to put me off, you know.'

'Put you off what?' Robyn asked.

'Kissing you again.'

There was no escaping him as he lightly pushed her against one of the temple columns and his mouth sought hers. She closed her eyes and felt she was floating in a great sky filled with roses. Her senses were overwhelmed, and when he moved away from her, she felt as if she were going to float away—far across the fields and woods.

'You okay?' he asked.

'I don't know,' she said. 'I feel all floaty.'

Dan smiled. 'Me too.' He bent forward and stroked her hair, his fingers twirling her long curls. 'Your hair reminds me of honeysuckle.'

She looked up at him in surprise. 'Jace says it reminds him of noodles boiling in a pan.'

Dan frowned. 'That's the most bizarre thing I've ever heard.' He sighed and removed his hand from her noodly honeysuckle hair. 'Tell me about him.'

'Must I?'

'I think you must.'

Katherine lay back on the white pillows of Warwick's bed and stared across at the window through which the moonlight was streaming. She felt caught up in some sort of dream world and didn't dare move for fear of waking up.

Warwick was asleep beside her, and she could hear his breathing—deep, slow, and satisfied. She smiled. She hadn't felt so relaxed in—she was going to say weeks but if she were perfectly honest, she didn't think she'd ever been so relaxed in her whole life.

Well, she thought, she hadn't expected a night of wild passion when she packed for the Jane Austen weekend. She thought it would be a weekend of polite conversation over cups of tea, rather than having one too many glasses of mulled wine and ending up naked in a stranger's bedroom.

But he's not a stranger, she thought, sitting up in the bed and looking at him, his dark hair falling across his face and his skin marble pale in the moonlight. She felt as if she'd known him for aeons. It was a strange but wonderful feeling, and it was hard to imagine a time when she hadn't known him. Had it been only two short days?

It had never been like this with David, she thought, and she knew why now—because he was always in a hurry to leave her. 'Things to do,' he always said, but it was more like the other woman he had to get back to. They never spent an entire night together.

Smiling to herself as she sneaked out of bed, Katherine padded across the room to the tray where there was a kettle and a bottle of still water. She took the top off and poured some into a glass and drank it down in one go. She'd forgotten what a workout making love could be. Had it put a sparkle in her eyes? she wondered. Did she have that wonderful bloom that had been absent for so long?

She walked across to the window, carefully hiding herself behind the folds of the heavy curtains, in case somebody was out there in the shadowy gardens. What a magical place Purley was, she thought, and how caught up in its spell she had become. But wasn't that going to make it all the more difficult to leave when Monday finally reared its ugly head?

Katherine didn't want to think about that right now—or did she? When she returned to Oxfordshire, she would be researching her latest nonfiction book about Jane Austen and would certainly have plenty to keep herself busy. But she couldn't stop wondering if Warwick wanted to be a part of her world.

For a moment she fell into a Warwick reverie of autumn bike rides around the golden Cotswolds and picnics in the hills and of long warm nights like tonight. But maybe she was getting ahead of herself. Just take things slowly, she thought.

She smiled. That was a laugh, wasn't it, after hopping into bed with him after so short a time?

She looked around the room and her eye caught a big black notebook on the dressing table. She turned to look at Warwick. He was sleeping on his front now, his head swallowed up in his pillow. Like most women, Katherine couldn't resist poking her nose into things, especially things like a notebook that had been left out with the intention of being nosed at although she was aware that it was horribly wrong of her.

Tiptoeing across the carpet, she opened the book, but it was too dark to make out anything inside it so she took it back to the window where the moonlight lit up the pages of writing. It was a bit of a mess. His handwriting was terrible and there were crossings out and great blobs of ink as if half a dozen fountain pens had committed suicide on his pages.

'Anna Conville,' Katherine read. 'Laurence. Louis.' The names were written down the left-hand side of the first page and Katherine wondered what they were. Perhaps they were names of friends or maybe they were authors Warwick was searching for as part of his trade as an antiquarian.

'She always wears black,' she read. That was curious, Katherine thought. Why would somebody need to write that fact down?

'Louis is the fourth marquis,' she read on the next page. That was even more curious. Perhaps these were names of important clients who were after rare first editions or something.

Katherine looked at the writing and frowned. There was something vaguely familiar about it, but she couldn't quite think what. Maybe it reminded her of one of her student's badly scrawled essays.

Warwick suddenly stirred and afraid of being caught holding the notebook, Katherine hastily returned it to the dressing table.

She should really return to her own room, she thought. It would be the right thing to do. But she didn't want to do the right thing, so she walked back across the room and slipped into the bed again next to Warwick and closed her eyes for the most perfect night's sleep of her life.

~

Out in the gardens, Robyn and Dan had left the temple on the island and were walking slowly back to the house. A shadow partly clouded the moon at one point and they'd been thrown into darkness, but Dan reached out and took Robyn's hand and he hadn't let go of it since.

'So how did you two meet?' he asked.

'Jace and me?' Robyn asked, knowing that's exactly what he meant but not really wanting to take the conversation in that direction. 'We've always known each other. Since school.'

'High school?'

'Preschool,' Robyn said. 'We went to the same nursery, then the same primary and high school. We weren't really friends—not until high school—but he's always been there somewhere in the background of my life.'

'When did you start going out together?'

'Just before high school finished.'

'And was it all—'

'Look, Dan, do you mind if we don't talk about it?' Robyn said. 'It's been such a perfect night. I don't want to spoil it.'

He stopped walking for a moment and with her hand still firmly in his, looked at her. 'But you're not happy.'

'I am right now.'

'That's not what I meant.'

She sighed. 'I know what you meant.' And then she did something that was completely out of character but that the moment was demanding. She stretched up on tiptoes and kissed him. Was it to shut him up or was it because she simply had to kiss him? She wasn't sure, and Dan wasn't complaining either way.

Chapter 22

WHEN KATHERINE NEXT WOKE UP, SHE WAS STILL IN Warwick's bed, but his side was empty.

'Warwick?' she said, sitting up and brushing her hair out of her face. She could hear the shower in the ensuite and decided that it might be a good time to get dressed and return to her own room. Lord only knew what she looked like. She hadn't taken her make-up off the night before. There was a pretty good chance that Warwick had kissed most of it off, but she had a feeling that her eyes would look like giant bruises, and that was never a good look.

Getting out of bed and trying to locate the right number of clothes in the right order, Katherine caught sight of her reflection in the mirror on the dressing table. She looked wonderfully dishevelled. Her face was flushed and her eyes—although panda-like, as she'd suspected—were sparkling with mischief.

She dressed quickly and then opened the bedroom door, peering outside first to make sure there was nobody around to see her escaping from a room that wasn't hers. That just wasn't the behaviour of a guest speaker from Oxford, was it?

Robyn, too, had woken up with a smile on her face. Her mouth still felt swollen from kissing although she thought that was probably being fanciful. Still, as she put her fingers to her lips, she couldn't help being a little fanciful and imagining Dan's lips had left their impression upon them. She'd never been kissed like that before in her life and she knew she never would be again, unless she did something about it.

Flinging herself under the shower, Robyn thought of the position she found herself in. It wasn't what she'd expected from a weekend in Hampshire; that was for sure. Who would have thought that she'd fall in love at the Jane Austen Conference, although, now she thought about it, it seemed like the most perfect thing in the world.

It wasn't perfect by any means, though, was it? Robyn knew that and Dan knew it too, and he'd tried to find out what was going on last night, hadn't he? Did that mean he really cared about her and thought they had a future together? Robyn couldn't see how it would work. For a start, she lived in Yorkshire. She had a home there with chickens! She couldn't just up and move, could she? No matter how much she'd fallen in love with Dan and Purley.

She smiled as she thought of Purley. It was a beautiful place. Perhaps she wasn't in love with Dan at all but had fallen for his home. Hadn't Elizabeth confessed to have fallen for Darcy at the time that she first saw his home, Pemberley?

As she got dressed, she promised herself that she wouldn't stress about the two men in her life. Yes, there were some decisions to be made—and sooner rather than later—but she could forget about them for the space of a morning. After all, it was the morning she'd most been looking forward to: the trip to the Jane Austen Museum in Chawton. She had seen photographs of the redbrick cottage and watched all the home movies on YouTube, but visiting the real place herself was going to be beyond compare. Her visit to the little church at Steventon had been exciting enough, but to walk through the rooms where Jane had lived many of her years and written all her adult fiction was going to be the most wonderful experience that couldn't come quickly enough, and Robyn was one of the first to board the coach that had been hired for the trip to the Hampshire village.

Oh, what is everyone doing? she thought, looking back at the house and wondering why everyone wasn't champing at the bit to get going like her. Where were they all? What was more important than getting to Chawton?

She checked her handbag for her camera. She'd already checked to see that it was there three times. It had been charged up that very morning after she deleted every single photo that she no longer needed. There must be plenty of room to capture everything, she thought. Would 418 images be enough, though? There was always her mobile phone as a backup, which also took pictures, except she hadn't recharged that. Oh, dear! Would she have time to nip back up to her room and charge it? But then she'd lose her place at the front of the coach, and it might actually leave without her. She couldn't risk it.

'You're becoming paranoid,' she whispered to herself. 'Just relax and enjoy the day.'

She looked at the faces of her fellow day-trippers as they got on the coach. Were they as eager as she was? It was hard to imagine that anyone could possibly be looking forward to it as much as she was. Some had been coming to the conference for years, and Chawton must surely be quite commonplace to them by now.

She smiled as Doris Norris boarded.

'Ah, my dear. How are you?' she said, taking the seat next to Robyn.

'I just wish we'd get a move on,' Robyn said. 'I can't wait to see Chawton.'

'You'll love it,' Doris said. 'You know, I've been five times now, and I never tire of it. It's the most beautiful place in the world to me.'

Robyn's eyes widened, and she felt guilty at supposing that the day would be special only to her. Of course, true Jane Austen fans would get something out of every single visit, no matter how many times they'd been before. Just to spend time in the place that their idol had once inhabited was enough.

'And how did you enjoy last night?' Doris asked. 'Your team did well.'

'Yours did too,' Robyn said.

'Those books were beautiful,' Doris continued.

'They are lovely,' Robyn said. 'I shall always treasure them.'

'But we didn't see you after that. Did you go off for a little walk?' Doris's eyes were twinkling and, for a moment, Robyn wondered if she'd been spied out in the garden with Dan.

'Yes, I... er... I went for a walk.'

'A moonlit walk,' Doris said. 'I remember those.' She looked wistful for a moment. 'My Henry and I used to take walks in the moonlight when we lived on the north Norfolk coast. Have you ever been there? It has the most amazing beaches that stretch for miles. Acres and acres of sand that are quite magical in the moonlight. Of course we were younger then, and it didn't matter if we got a bit of sand here and there.' She gave a little chuckle, and Robyn's eyes widened in delighted surprise.

It was then that Katherine boarded the coach. Robyn caught her eye and smiled. She'd been looking forward to finding out what had happened to her the night before, especially as Warwick climbed the steps of the coach right behind her and the two of them took a seat together towards the back. Robyn grinned. Perhaps Katherine had had as magical an evening as she'd had.

When everyone was finally on the coach, including a dashing Dame Pamela wearing fuchsia from head to toe, they left Purley, going down the tree-lined driveway and turning out into the lane. How long ago it seemed since she'd driven up that driveway with Jace, Robyn thought, and how she dreaded leaving with him once the weekend came to an end. Being at Purley was like living on a little island—one seemed far removed from the rest of the world and its troubles, and it was something that one could get used to very easily.

Once they reached the main road, the atmosphere on the coach reminded Robyn of a school outing, with everyone seeming to harbour the feeling of being let loose from their everyday routines. Chatter levels escalated and as the bus entered the village of Chawton, every pair of eyes strained to be the first to see the cottage.

The village was lined with pretty cottages but Robyn knew what she was looking for, and her first glimpse didn't disappoint. Sitting on a quiet curve of a road, Jane Austen's house seemed to overlook the whole village, and Robyn thought what a perfect position it was for a writer. Jane would have been able to see so much of village life from the many sash windows. A low brick wall surrounded a very pretty garden full of flowers and trees, and Robyn couldn't wait to get inside and walk in the steps of its former owner.

'It's so pretty,' she said, and Doris nodded.

Robyn's heart rate accelerated, and she was the first off the coach once it parked. The group from Purley had been split into two—the first was to tour the house while the rest viewed the garden, outbuildings, and shop. Robyn was in the second group.

Along with most of the others in her group, she made a beeline for the shop and although she was eager to get into the house, the shop was a good substitute and was pure heaven for any Austen fan.

It was a long, low-lying building with beams and white walls and shelves stuffed with books. *Books!* Robyn's hand reached out and grabbed one after another. She owned all the Austen titles, countless times over, but she could never resist picking up the latest editions. Then there were all the wonderful books *about* the books—biographies, titles about life in Jane Austen's time, collections of her letters, travel guides to Bath, recipe books, and more. Robyn's eyes were well and truly boggled as she took a copy of each title from the shelf and flicked through it.

I have to have this one, she thought, spying a title that was new to her. *And this too. I can't leave without this.*

Then she saw the diaries, a collection of fictional accounts from the viewpoint of Austen's heroes, and her hand reached out to *Mr Darcy's Diary* by Amanda Grange without a moment's hesitation. Hadn't Carla been talking about that title to her? Well, she had to have that, didn't she? And she couldn't *not* buy *Colonel Brandon's Diary* alongside it. He was a special hero, after all, and the portrait of him on the cover was particularly dashing. But could she buy those two and leave Captain Wentworth to sulk on the shelf? The answer was no, and Robyn grabbed a third book which joined her two nonfiction titles and made her way to the till, looking around the shop in case she'd missed anything.

The brooding image of Colin Firth as Mr Darcy stared back at her from every direction. Robyn had never seen many items featuring the handsome face. There were "I Love Mr Darcy" bookmarks and Mr Darcy mugs, posters, notepaper, and even thimbles. Colin Firth was everywhere. Robyn wondered what he thought about being seen as the quintessential Darcy, and was Matthew Macfadyen put out by it all?

Just as the assistant was popping her books into a bag, Robyn ran across the shop and grabbed a couple of Darcy bookmarks. Well, if you had books, you had to have bookmarks, didn't you?

There were one or two Austen snobs in the group from Purley who looked down their noses in the most condescending of fashions at some of the shop items, but most of the group loved it, gathering up great armfuls of tea towels and spending inordinate amounts of time deciding which Mr Darcy bookmark to buy.

Robyn watched for a moment as Roberta and Doris stood in front of the shelves housing the DVD film adaptations.

'Oh! Have you seen this one?' Roberta asked.

Doris laughed. 'I've seen *every* one. And if they made a hundred more, I'd see those too.'

Robyn nodded. It was the same for all true fans. There could be a new version of *Pride and Prejudice* every month, and the fans would still want more.

She left with her goodies and walked into the stable that housed the lovely little donkey carriage Jane Austen would have ridden in, wondering what she would have made of it all—the museum, the coach loads of tourists, and the innumerable books that had been written about her. What would she have thought of the shop paraphernalia and the rows of DVDs and the Mr Darcy mugs? It was sad that she would never know about the huge industry that existed because of her imagination.

What would she have made of all the films? Would she have fallen in love with the actors just as so many women did? Would she have had favourites? And what would she have made of the famous wet shirt scene in the BBC version of *Pride and Prejudice*?

It was a game Robyn often liked to play: what would Jane Austen be like if she lived in the twenty-first century? What kind of books would she read now? What kind of music and television would interest her? Would fans queue around the block for her at book signings like they did for JK Rowling? Would she endorse Darcy figurines and theme parks? Jane World or Austen Land, perhaps with *Northanger Abbey* ghost rides and a Mr Darcy waterlog.

Robyn walked into the garden, gazing up at the pretty cottage and admiring the flame-coloured flowers in the borders. What changes would Jane see were she to visit today? Robyn wondered. Certainly the signpost announcing Jane Austen's Cottage wouldn't have been there or the Cassandra's Cup tearoom across the road. If only Jane could visit the present. What changes she would see! And what would she make of computers? Would she have shunned her scratchy quill and steel-nibbed pen in favour of a laptop, sitting by the window tapping lightly on the keyboard, exchanging emails with Cassandra when they were apart and putting her day-to-day observations on Twitter?

Robyn had many questions that would never be answered, but perhaps the most persistent one was, *would Jane have liked me?* As a reader, one always felt close to the authors, as if they were telling their story just for you. They were born to entertain only you, and their characters became your friends. You trusted your narrators and shared the most intimate of moments with them, so you naturally assumed that you knew them. But what was Jane really like? Would she and Robyn have been friends had they ever met?

'I hope so,' Robyn said quietly to herself as she sat on a seat in the garden and gazed at the white sash windows that Jane would once have looked out of.

Chapter 23

KATHERINE AND WARWICK WERE IN THE FIRST GROUP TO TOUR the house and amongst the first to enter its rooms. As soon as they were out of sight of the room steward in the drawing room, Warwick grabbed Katherine's hand and pulled her towards him, kissing her firmly on the mouth.

'Warwick!' she protested, but it was rather feeble as protests went because he kissed her again straightaway and she didn't complain. Well, not at first. Not until they heard footsteps behind them. 'Really,' she said, 'in the home of Jane Austen! There must be a law against such things.'

He grinned at her. 'And what's wrong with that? I'm sure our author would have approved. Wasn't love the key to all her books?'

'I just feel so guilty,' Katherine said, self-consciously straightening her hair in case she'd been ruffled.

'Why?'

Katherine thought for a moment. 'I suppose I think of this place as being a bit special. It's almost like a church.'

Warwick smiled.

'You don't think I'm crazy?'

'No,' he said. 'I know exactly what you mean.' They smiled at one another and then moved on through to the dining parlour, where a small table and chair had been set by the window.

'This was the room she wrote in.'

'It's lovely,' Warwick said. 'Nice and bright although I couldn't write next to a window that looks out over the village.'

'Do you write?' Katherine asked with a smile.

Warwick frowned. 'I mean, if I were a writer, I think I'd be distracted by a window. I'd be too interested in watching what my neighbours were getting up to. I'd have to have my back to the window.'

'I wonder how she wrote,' Katherine said. 'I mean, did she mind people interrupting her? Could she enter the world of her book and shut everything else out? There's that gorgeous scene in the film *Miss Austen Regrets* when Cassandra walks into the room while Jane is writing, and she stops and her pen is hovering over the paper until her sister leaves. I love that. I think I'd be like that if I wrote fiction.'

'Have you ever wanted to?'

'What, write fiction?'

Warwick nodded.

'No. I'm quite happy with my nonfiction. I like researching the facts. Fiction is my escape at the end of a long day. I don't think I'd ever want to write it. What about you?'

Warwick shrugged. 'I love books. I love reading them and buying them and selling them.'

'But not writing them?'

'I don't know,' he said, clearing his throat.

But Katherine wasn't really listening. She was looking at the grand portrait of one of Jane Austen's brothers, Edward Knight, the one who'd been adopted by a rich family.

'How strange it seems to us now to send one of your children away to be raised by somebody else—with their name too.'

'And their fortune,' Warwick pointed out. 'If Edward hadn't left the Austens and become a Knight, his mother and sisters wouldn't have had this cottage.'

'No,' Katherine said. 'I wonder what would have happened to them.'

'Jane and Cassandra would have had to marry.'

'Oh!' Katherine said. 'And if Jane had married, she probably wouldn't have written. She'd have had another role to play.'

'I guess so.'

'Thank goodness for the Knight family then and for Edward.'

'But what if Jane *had* fallen in love?' Warwick asked. 'What if she'd met the right man and married?'

'Then I don't think we would have the books.'

'Would you make that sacrifice—for the happiness of Jane?'

Katherine bit her lip. 'You mean, would I rather she'd married the man of her dreams and never written a word?'

'Yes.'

'I don't think she would have done it,' Katherine said at last. 'I don't think it was in her. I think her writing was everything. No man could have been loved more than her darling books.'

'You really think so?'

Katherine nodded. 'And thank goodness for that,' she said, moving on to the next room.

❧

When Robyn finally entered the cottage, she had to remind herself to keep breathing. She simply couldn't help holding her breath. This was it, she thought—the moment she'd so long anticipated— and it was every bit as magical as she imagined it would be.

The rooms were small but full of light and there was much to look at. It was lovely to see all the bits of furniture and imagine things being used by Jane, especially the little writing desk by the window.

There were many items in the house that 'may have' been owned by Jane and things such as chamber pots that were 'typical' of her day, but a very special item in the museum collection had belonged to Jane and had been very special to her, a beautiful topaz cross. It was in a drawer in a room called the vestibule, which was a kind of hallway, and Robyn gasped as she opened it. She'd heard about the cross before. Three were in the drawer: a large one that had belonged to Edward Knight's wife and two smaller ones bought for Jane and Cassandra by their brother.

Robyn looked at them with quiet wonderment, longing to touch Jane's cross and place it around her own neck, to feel those warm yellow gemstones against her skin. But she could only look at them tucked safely in the display drawer so close it was tantalizing.

Moving upstairs, Robyn entered the room that had once been Jane and Cassandra's bedroom. It was a modest-sized room, about the same size as Robyn's own bedroom, and it felt funny to be standing there with its replica bed, closet and chairs. A framed lace collar hung on one of the walls.

'Worked by Jane Austen,' Robyn read with a wistful smile, imagining the author's hands at work on this very piece that was in front of her.

In another room was a patchwork quilt that Jane, her sister, and their mother had made. Robyn gazed at the floral-festooned diamond shapes made from old dresses belonging to them and their nieces. Which patches would have belonged to Jane? she wondered. She was transfixed. It was so bright and pretty that she longed to stroke the warm fabric, but behind glass, it was safe from the hands of fans. Just as well, really; otherwise things would be ruined in no time. No matter how well-intentioned people were, they still had an urge to reach out and physically touch the past.

⁓

As Robyn made her slow progress around the rest of the house, Katherine and Warwick were in the gift shop.

'Look!' Warwick said, holding up a hardback. 'They have your book.'

Katherine looked at him wide-eyed. 'Shush!' she said. 'Put it back.'

'But I'm going to buy it. I want you to sign it for me. You should sign all these. They've got…' he counted, 'five.'

Katherine shook her head.

'They should know who's standing in their shop.'

'Warwick!'

'Aren't you proud of your book? You're being stocked at Jane Austen's house!'

She smiled. 'Of course I'm proud; I just don't need everyone to know about it.'

'You're funny,' he said.

She shook her head. 'I'm sure you'd be the same. Writers are very modest people, you know. If we weren't, we wouldn't be writers; we'd be performers or something, shouting our talents from every platform.'

'But you're speaking this weekend,' he said.

'And it's a rare exception to my rule,' Katherine told him. 'I love these weekends. I can be who I really am.'

'And what's that?' he asked.

'A Janeite,' she said and then sighed in delight. 'It's just so wonderful being able to say that out loud. You know, if I so much as hinted such a thing at St Bridget's, I'd be flogged. They'd chase me across the quad and I'd never be allowed to darken the name of fine literature again.'

Warwick smiled. 'I hate book snobs.'

'So do I,' she said. 'At least there's a good range of fiction here although I can't see any of Lorna Warwick's.'

'It doesn't surprise me.'

'No? But I'm sure they'd sell well here. Maybe we should suggest it.'

'No!' Warwick said.

'Why not? You were all for me announcing myself a minute ago. Why not do our friend Lorna a favour?'

'I want to see the garden,' he said, scratching his nose and looking uncomfortable.

Katherine hastily bought a Jane Austen recipe book, a book about manners, and when she was quite sure Warwick was out of sight, an I Love Darcy bookmark.

'Got anything nice?' he asked her when she joined him.

She nodded. 'Just some more books for the collection,' she said, hoping he wouldn't look inside her bag.

'I wish I could show you mine,' he said.

'Your books?'

He nodded.

'Do you have a shop? I'd love to see that.'

'No,' he said. 'Everything's done from home.'

'I guess that's easier these days,' she said. 'So many lovely old bookshops are closing, but I guess rents make things difficult. Did you used to have a shop?'

'Er, no,' he said, stopping to read a notice board in the garden about the flowers on display.

'How many books do you have at any one time?'

'Thousands,' he said. 'I can't stop buying. Like you.'

'I expect you've got a lot more than me, though,' she said. 'What's your favourite?'

'I rather like those roses,' he said, pointing to the profusion of delicate blooms that encircled the cottage door.

'No!' Katherine laughed. 'Book! What's your favourite book?'

'Well, I have some first edition Walter Scotts.'

'Wow! I'd love to see them. Maybe I could visit some time.'

'Well,' he said, 'I'm not sure that's a good idea. The place is a mess; it really is.'

'Perhaps you just need a woman's touch,' Katherine said. 'I'd be happy to help. I love a good sort out—especially if it involves books.'

'You don't need to do that,' Warwick said, tugging on his right ear and looking decidedly uncomfortable.

'But it would be fun.'

'It wouldn't,' he said. 'Trust me.' He cleared his throat, his mouth twisting into funny shapes.

Katherine thought it best not to pursue the matter. He was obviously rather embarrassed about his untidy collection of books.

'I think I'll take a walk down to the church,' Warwick said. 'Before the coach is due to leave.'

Katherine nodded. 'I'm going to stay here for a while,' she said. 'I'll see you later?'

She watched him and sighed as he left the garden. She hadn't meant to make him feel uncomfortable, and she regretted having pushed herself forward. Still, she thought it would be fun to see his collection of books, and she'd misguidedly thought that he'd want to show it to her.

'The mystery of men,' she thought as she left the gardens to get a pot of tea at Cassandra's Cup.

~

Warwick's strides were long and fast as he left Chawton Cottage. He didn't really want to see St Nicholas's Church or Chawton House and he'd already paid his respect to Jane Austen's mother and sister—the two Cassandras—in the churchyard. He just needed to get away.

Why did Katherine always bring the conversation around to books? Okay so they were attending a literary conference and book talk was bound to be high on the agenda, but things had been getting a little too close for comfort back there, and he felt that her eyes were burrowing into his very being. Had she been suspicious, he wondered, or was he just being paranoid? She had no way of knowing who he really was.

Passing a row of pretty cottages on his right, he dared to look back. Katherine was nowhere in sight, and he breathed a sigh of relief. He needed a few moments to get himself together.

'What an idiot I've been!' he cursed to himself. What do you think you're playing at? This isn't a game—this is real life, and if she ever finds out what you've done—

But how could she? He wasn't going to tell her. Not yet, anyway.

'So what's the plan?' he asked himself, thinking of their night together and how completely he had lost himself with Katherine. She was everything and more than he had dreamed of, and he could never risk hurting her but if he wanted to have a future with her, then she'd have to know the truth. There was no alternative, was there?

Unless I give up writing and start up a business as an antiquarian, he thought. She was actually worth it too, wasn't she? She would be worth giving up everything for, but could he really do that? No, probably not. Writing was in his blood; he had a feeling sometimes that his very veins were filled with ink. He couldn't give that up no matter how much in love he was.

'What a mess!' He cursed. This really was turning into a frighteningly Lorna Warwick–like plot but with one alarming difference: he wasn't at all sure it was going to have a happy ending.

When Robyn finally surfaced from the house and entered the sunny garden, she felt wonderfully mellow and replete, as if she'd eaten a fine meal and couldn't possibly manage anything else, but then she remembered St Nicholas's Church and knew she couldn't leave until she paid her respects to the two Cassandras.

It was a pleasant walk along the lane, and Robyn smiled at the pretty thatched cottages, their gardens full of autumn blooms. How wonderful to live in Jane Austen's village, she thought, or was it a pain with ardent fans like herself peering over their walls and trying to see in through the windows?

She continued down the lane, passing a school and more houses and then a field full of shire horses. Next came the great sweep of driveway that led to Chawton House, the one-time home of Jane Austen's brother, Edward. Flanked by neat emerald grass, the drive led the eye to a hint of house at the end of it, three storeys high with great mullioned windows and a cavern-like door.

Walking down the driveway, Robyn wished she could visit the house, but it was the church she'd come to see, and she took a small path to the right and entered by the latch gate.

The two graves she was looking for weren't hard to find, because a group of people were standing in front of them with cameras. Standing side by side at the back of the churchyard in a wonderfully sunny spot, the markers were of simple pale stone declaring the departure of Cassandra Austen and Cassandra Elizabeth Austen. Jane's mother had lived to the ripe old age of eighty-seven and her sister had lived until seventy-two. How much longer they'd had than Jane, Robyn thought, and how sad that the three of them had been parted in death. Jane and her sister had been close, and it seemed strange that Jane was in Winchester so many miles away from her beloved Chawton.

After walking around to the front of the church, Robyn entered, instantly recognising a few people from the conference. It was then that she noticed Warwick sitting in one of the pews, his head bent. He hadn't seen her come in and at first she thought he was praying. It wasn't until she stood beside him that she saw he was writing. He was using a spiral-bound notebook, and his black pen was moving across it at a furious pace. Mesmerised, she watched him for a few moments, wondering what he was writing.

When he looked up at last, he almost leapt right out of the pew.

'Robyn!' he said, closing the pad and placing it quickly in the pocket of his jacket before standing up and raking a hand through his dark hair.

'Hello,' she said. 'You writing?' It was a silly question, but she didn't know what else to say. 'I mean, is it a journal?'

'Well sort of,' he said. 'Have you seen the graves? I was just going to look at them.'

'Yes, I've seen them,' she said.

'I'll see you back on the coach then,' he said, making a hasty exit from the church.

Robyn watched him go and then realised that Katherine wasn't

with him, which made her remember Dan. Wonderful handsome
Dan with kisses warmer than the sun and hands that made her skin
tingle all over. She hadn't thought about him for hours, and that
surprised her, but like everything in her life, he had to get in the
queue behind Jane Austen.

After a very good pot of tea, Katherine left Cassandra's Cup and
made her way to the coach. She had a little wobble on the way,
wondering if she had time to nip back to the Jane Austen shop and
double-check that there wasn't something she overlooked, but she
thought better of it and went meekly on her way to the coach.

Warwick was already on board, and Katherine suddenly felt
anxious.

'Hey!' he said to her as she approached.

She hesitated a moment, and he seemed to sense it.

'You okay?' he asked.

She nodded and sat down beside him. 'You went off,' she said
without preamble.

'To the church,' he said. 'I told you.'

'Yes, I know,' she said. 'But it was the manner in which you went.'

'I don't understand.'

'No,' she said, 'neither do I.'

'Katherine? What's wrong?'

She turned to look at him, and his eyes were so large and dark
that she could easily have lost herself in them and forgotten all her
worries, but she didn't. 'What's wrong?' she said. 'That's exactly
what I was going to ask you. Are you regretting what happened,
now you've had time to think about it?'

'What do you mean? Of course I'm not regretting it!'

'Because you've been very strange,' she said with an undisguised pout.

'When?'

'In the garden—before you went to the church.'

'I'm sorry,' he said, and he really did sound like he was sorry. 'I wasn't aware of that.'

'It was like you didn't want to talk to me anymore.'

He shook his head. 'No, it's not that at all! It's just I didn't want to talk about work, you know?'

Katherine's eyes narrowed as she tried to understand him. 'You should have said something. Why didn't you say something? I've been brooding for the past hour, and I'm not the kind of woman who takes to brooding kindly.'

He dared a little smile and picked up her hand, bringing it to his lips to kiss it.

'I won't ever make you brood again,' he said.

'You'd better not,' she said, and sitting back in her seat, she allowed herself to be kissed before the coach started to fill up.

Chapter 24

AFTER A LATE LUNCH BACK AT PURLEY, ROBYN VENTURED OUT into the sunshine. It was blissfully warm, and the sky was the shade of blue one dreams about on dark winter days.

It had been a wonderful morning at Chawton, but it was equally good to be back at Purley. Robyn really felt that she was slipping into a new way of life in Hampshire. *How easy it would be to live here*, she thought, staring out across the immaculate lawn and the neat flower beds.

It was then that a chestnut and white flash of fur darted towards her. It was Biscuit.

'Hello, little fellow,' Robyn chimed, bending down to fuss over him. He jumped up onto her knees, making her laugh and nearly sending her toppling onto the grass. He gave a little jump, licked her face, and then sprang off her lap and ran a few circles, heading back towards the stable block whence he came, turning back to look at her every now and then. It was as if he were trying to get her to follow him. Robyn laughed. Maybe Dan had trained him to do just that. Maybe Biscuit was Dan's furry matchmaker and she didn't need much encouragement to obey.

Walking under the clock tower into the stable block, she

inhaled deeply the scent of horses. Dan was right—it really was the best smell in the world, especially on a warm autumn day when everything smelt horsy and warm and the scent of hay carried on the breeze.

Robyn noticed that Biscuit had disappeared, but she spied Moby, the golden Labrador, and went over to give him a fuss.

'Where is everyone, Moby dog?' she asked as he pushed his considerable weight against her leg while she rubbed his belly.

'Did I hear a friendly voice?'

Robyn looked up. She'd definitely heard Dan, but she couldn't see him anywhere.

'Dan?'

'Over here.'

Robyn turned to one of the stables and saw his bright coppery head of hair appear above a stable door.

He grinned at her. 'Come and say hello,' he said.

Robyn walked across the yard and entered the stable.

'This is Minstrel,' Dan said, patting the bay horse that was happily munching a bale of hay. 'One of our new recruits, aren't you, boy?'

'He's gorgeous,' Robyn said. 'How many horses do you have here?'

'Six that belong to Pammy and three others whose owners live locally.'

Robyn watched as he finished grooming the gleaming coat, his bronzed arms covered in a light layer of dust and his bright hair flapping about as he moved. It was rhythmic and mesmeric, and when he finished, she felt quite dazed.

'I missed you,' he said.

'When?'

'Since we said good night.'

Robyn smiled and watched as he put the body brush down and wiped his hands down the front of his jeans. He was wearing a dark T-shirt that was fraying around the neck in a particularly provocative way, Robyn thought, gazing at his throat as if it were the most beautiful thing she'd ever seen.

'Robyn,' he whispered, and before she could think to say anything, his arms were around her and his mouth had claimed hers in the sweetest kiss. He was firm and gentle at the same time, and Robyn had never felt safer in her life. When she finally opened her eyes, he was gazing down at her as if she were the centre of the entire universe. She smiled up at him, her hands placed on his chest.

'So what's on, this afternoon?' he asked, his hands stroking her hair. 'When do I have to give you up again?'

Robyn looked thoughtful as she tried to remember, but it was distracting when a handsome man was kissing her neck. She tried to concentrate but found that all she could focus on was the hotness on her skin from his touch. Gently she pushed him away. 'Dan!' she chided.

'What?'

'I'm trying to think.'

'And I'm trying to kiss you. It's very important.'

'There's some talk about the Regency bonnet and a lecture called What Can We Learn from Jane Austen?'

'Lots,' Dan said. 'There, now you know the answer, you can come out riding with me.'

'What?'

He stood back up to full height, leaving her neck and her lips alone for a moment. 'Come riding with me. It's a perfect afternoon, and I could show you some of my favourite spots. There's a little place by the river across the fields from here. You'd love it.'

Robyn laughed at the ease of his invitation. 'But I'm at the conference.'

'So skip class!' he said. 'It'll be fun.'

'I've never been riding before,' Robyn said.

'Then it's high time you did.'

'But what if I fall off?'

'You won't. I'll put you on Poppin. He's as slow and gentle as an autumn breeze.'

'But I don't have a hat or boots. I don't even have trousers with me.'

'That's okay,' Dan said. 'We've got loads of riding gear in the tack room. Come on!'

Robyn found that she was wearing a huge smile; it was hard to refuse such an offer.

Sure enough, at the back of the tack room there was an old clothes box stuffed with trousers, jumpers, and hats, and innumerable pairs of riding boots stood at attention beside it. Dan left her to change, and Robyn found the most suitable clothes, choosing a sky-blue jumper, a pair of brown jodhpurs, and smart black boots. Twisting her hair back, she popped on a riding hat and left the makeshift changing room. Dan was tacking up the grey horse he'd promised her, and Robyn approached them, feeling a little shy.

'Hey!' he said, turning around. 'You look great!'

'Liar!'

'No, you really do.'

Robyn shook her head. 'Everything's just a little too big.'

'Is the hat okay?'

'Oh, the hat's fine.'

Dan approached her and fidded with the hat, making sure it sat snugly and that the straps were okay. 'The hat's the main thing,' he said, and a few minutes later, he had put his own hat on and all that was left was to mount the horses.

Robyn's horse, Poppin, was the docile grey that she'd met the first time she entered the stable block.

'He's one of Pammy's favourites for Sunday rides around the fields,' Dan said as he lowered the stirrups for Robyn.

'Pammy—Dame Pamela won't mind, will she?'

''Course not. It's good that they get exercise. Now come over here and say hello.'

Robyn reached out a hand and stroked Poppin's grey muzzle. 'He's lovely. Can I keep him?'

Dan laughed. 'If he were mine, I'd give him to you right now.'

'Who will you be riding?'

'Perseus.'

'That's a very grand name.'

Dan nodded. 'The hero from Greek mythology who slew Medusa. I think Pammy was playing the goddess Athena when she bought this one. Everything had to be Greek.'

'Is he the chestnut?' Robyn asked, remembering the striking image of Dan on horseback the first time she saw him.

'He is. He's a very special horse, but he needs a firm hand. Now,' he said, standing behind Robyn, 'place your hands like this.' He took Robyn's hands and guided them. 'With your foot in the stirrup, I'll give you a leg up, okay? Just swing yourself up into the saddle, making sure you clear Poppin's rump. He's got quite a sizeable one.'

Robyn grinned, but she could feel her heart racing at the prospect of leaving the ground.

'On three,' he said. 'One, two, three!'

Robyn was officially launched and travelling at an alarming speed before hitting the saddle with a bum-numbing thump.

'Okay?' Dan said.

'Not the softest of landings,' Robyn said, grimacing. 'Sorry, Poppin.'

'He'll survive. He's had bigger bottoms than yours landing on his back.'

Robyn blushed. She was well aware that her derriere was very much on display in the jodhpurs, and Dan must have enjoyed a very good view as he swung her up into the saddle.

'Okay,' he said, grabbing her fingers. 'Reins like this. Just have a walk around the yard whilst I get Perseus. Use your knees to squeeze him into motion.'

Robyn's brow furrowed in deep concentration. She felt far from the ground, and she didn't want to land on it from such a great height. It felt strange, and yet there was something wonderfully exciting about it too. This was a new Robyn—Robyn the horsewoman who could gallop across the countryside, clearing every gate in sight. Well, maybe not today.

As she managed to move Poppin into a walk, she slowly began to build up her confidence.

'Don't keep looking down at the ground!' Dan called from Perseus's stable. 'Not unless you want to end up there. Look in the direction you're heading.'

Robyn did what she was told. Yes, that was better. She did a few more circuits of the stable yard, getting used to turning left and right and maintaining her balance although she did have one or two wobbles that nearly unseated her.

'Feel ready for the great outdoors?' Dan asked as he led Perseus out of his stable and swung himself into the saddle with such ease that it took Robyn's breath away.

'Come on, boys,' Dan said, giving a whistle for the dogs to follow.

'Will they be able to keep up?' Robyn asked.

'We won't be doing anything beyond trotting,' he said. 'Not with this being your first time.'

Robyn was relieved to hear it. Although she couldn't think of anything more romantic than galloping across the fields of Hampshire with the wind whipping back her hair, she wasn't at all sure she'd be able to play out such a dream without ending up on her bottom in the middle of a ditch.

Dan led the way out of the stable block and down the driveway. Robyn took a quick look back at Purley Hall, wondering if anyone would notice her sloping off on horseback when she should be attending the next lecture.

Taking a left out of the driveway, they walked down the lane, the wonderful sound of hooves clopping on the road surface, until they came to a bridle way.

'This way,' Dan said, and they turned the horses onto a track lined with trees on one side and open fields on the other. Moby and Biscuit led the way, the little terrier a blur of fur and the old Labrador sticking his head in the undergrowth at regular intervals. Robyn's face was bisected by the biggest of smiles. This was the last thing she expected when she booked a weekend at Purley, but how wonderful it was! Wasn't life extraordinary? One made plans, but then fate came along and said, 'Actually, *this* is going to happen today.'

Robyn looked ahead at the tall straight back of Dan and straightened her own back in response. She wanted to look the part, even if she didn't feel it. He looked at home in the saddle and so—well—handsome. What was it about a man on a horse? she wondered. Perhaps it was the unique bond between man and beast that just didn't happen between a man and a car. Or perhaps it was the clothes. Dan certainly looked damned fine in a pair of jodhpurs. Maybe that was the real reason. Those figure-hugging trousers were wonderfully reminiscent of men in Jane Austen's time. Certainly one couldn't help noticing how snugly they fit over his bottom, especially as Perseus broke into a little trot and Dan's bottom did a little dance in the air.

'Okay?' he called to her.

Robyn, whose eyes were still fixed on Dan's rear, had been so preoccupied by the vision before her that she almost toppled out of her saddle when Poppin moved from walk to trot. Mercifully it didn't last long, and they returned to a sedate pace that allowed her to get her breath back.

'Are you remembering to keep looking in the direction you're heading?' he asked.

'Yes,' Robyn said, and that was the main problem, wasn't it?

'You're doing really well,' he said, turning around in his saddle and throwing an easy smile in her direction. 'You sure this is your first time?'

'Well, other than the obligatory donkey ride on the beach, yes!'

'You'll probably feel it in the morning, but I hope it'll be worth it.'

Robyn was quite sure it would be worth it, for where would she rather be than with the amazing man she'd just met?

As the bridle way opened out into a field, Dan pointed to the far side. 'The river's down there,' he said, turning around to look at her. 'It's the most perfect place in the world. You'll love it.' He gave a smile that made her heart somersault in anticipation, and she knew that he was right—she was going to love it.

Robyn wasn't the only one to have ducked out of a talk that afternoon. Warwick had decided that he knew all he wanted to know about the Regency bonnet and decided that a quiet cup of tea in his room was in order. He needed some time to himself to get his thoughts in order. Things hadn't gone well that morning. First, he'd felt himself compromised by Katherine's questions and responded badly to them, shutting down completely and upsetting her which was the last thing he wanted to do.

'You're lucky she's still speaking to you,' he told his reflection in the dressing table mirror.

Then Robyn had caught him writing in the church. As he'd entered the driveway that led to the Great House at Chawton, he'd thought of an idea for a scene and had to write it down. It was an occupational hazard as a writer. Ideas didn't always wait until you were sat at your desk with everything to hand—they sprung upon you when you were in a supermarket queue or driving your car. Well, Warwick was prepared for that eventuality and always carried a pen and pad with him so he wouldn't lose the moments when inspiration struck.

'But what if she'd read what you were writing?' he asked himself. What if Robyn had been quietly looking over his shoulder? She might have discovered his true identity right there and then and run to Katherine and blown his cover.

He'd been careless and sloppy—he'd even left his notebook out in his bedroom. What if Katherine had seen it? How would he get out of that one? No, he had to be more careful. He couldn't risk her finding out who he really was until he sorted things in his own mind first.

A knock on the door startled him.

'Hey!' he said as he opened it and saw Katherine standing there.

'Can I come in?'

''Course.'

He watched her enter the room, her dark eyes glancing around. 'I like this room,' she said.

'I like having you in it,' he said, walking towards her and kissing her.

'Warwick,' she said, inching away from him, her tone firm, 'I think we need to talk. I mean, there's something I want to say.'

'Okay,' he said. 'Sounds serious.'

'Well, it is, I suppose.' She sat on the stool by the dressing table, and he was glad that he'd moved his notebook. 'I can't help thinking how quickly the time is going.'

He nodded. 'That's because we've been having fun.'

'I know,' she said, 'and it's all been wonderfully unexpected.'

He watched her as she twisted her hands in her lap.

'What is it?' he asked, sitting on the edge of the bed.

She looked across at him. 'I'd like to see you again,' she said. 'After this weekend.'

'And I'd like to see you again too.' He watched as she let out a deep breath. 'Did you really think I wouldn't?'

'I wasn't sure *what* to think,' she said. 'I thought this might just be one of those crazy holiday-type flings, you know?'

'I don't do those,' he said.

She smiled. 'Neither do I.'

'Then that's settled,' he said and, although he was smiling at her, he could feel his panic rising and was only just managing to keep it in check.

Chapter 25

Seeing the countryside from the back of a horse was a totally new experience for Robyn. After the first terrifying ten minutes, she began to settle in the saddle. Dear Poppin was the gentlest of rides and hadn't bolted or tried to throw her into a bramble bush as she feared he might.

And the views! She could see for miles across the fields and hedgerows of Hampshire and felt very close to the trees, as if she were a bird floating somewhere between the earth and the sky.

As they followed the field around, she caught a glimpse of Purley Hall across a great golden field, its rosy walls bright against the trees behind it. How beautiful it was, sitting in perfect harmony in the landscape, and how funny to think of Katherine and Warwick somewhere within its walls while she was outside with Dan. She took in a deep breath of autumn air and slowly exhaled.

It was then that she saw the curve of a river.

'Nearly there,' Dan said. 'You coping okay? Not too sore?'

'I'm fine,' Robyn said. 'Everything's fine.'

She followed as he and Perseus led the way across a grassy bank, stopping under the shade of a line of trees and watching as Dan dismounted. Okay, she thought, that was quick.

'Your turn,' he said. 'You can't stay up there all day.'

'But I'm not sure how to get down.'

'It's a piece of cake. Just take your feet out of the stirrups, keep hold of the reins and grab ahold of the front of the saddle. You want to lean forward and swing your right leg over Poppin's back and try to bounce when you hit the ground, bending your knees.'

'That's a lot to remember,' Robyn said, biting her lip as she tried to put it all into practice.

'There you go,' Dan said a moment later as she returned— wobbly legged—to the ground. His hands were around her waist and she turned to face him, her neck stretching back as he bent down to kiss her. Unfortunately they were still wearing their riding hats and the peaks crashed into each other, causing them both to erupt into laughter.

Dan removed his hat and unclipped Robyn's, freeing her hair and allowing for a far less dangerous embrace.

'Shall we try that again?' he asked, and she nodded, giving in to the most perfect kiss in the world. She felt as if the whole heat of the sun was in that kiss and, when she finally opened her eyes and they parted, she thought she would swoon like a heroine and have to be scooped up from the ground.

'I'll just sort out the horses,' he said.

Robyn nodded and walked across the riverbank, finding a warm patch of grass to lie down in. Moby and Biscuit were far too busy to sit down. Moby had found a shallow bit of bank and was lapping from the water, and Biscuit was up to his tail in a clump of grass that probably hid a multitude of watery rodents.

Dan joined her on the grass, stretching out his long legs and flinging his head back to the heavens. Robyn looked up at the sky through the leaves of an oak tree. She'd never felt so peaceful.

'This is wonderful,' she said with a sigh. 'I can see why you left London.'

Dan made an appreciative sound. 'You couldn't slope off on a horse in the middle of the afternoon in the job I used to do.'

Robyn propped up on one elbow and gazed at him. He was flat back, his right arm shielding his eyes from the sun and a long blond grass sticking out of his mouth. 'You're so at home here,' she said. 'You seem to be made of the earth.'

Dan sat up and laughed. 'You say the funniest things!'

'Do I?'

He nodded.

'It's just—well, you look so tanned and—'

'Dirty?'

'I wasn't going to say that!'

'I know. But I am. Look!' he said, holding out his arms for her to inspect. 'Permanently covered in horse dust and hair.'

Robyn looked. They were the most perfect arms in the world— strong, bronzed, and intensely huggable. She felt as if she could lose herself quite comfortably in them for at least three eternities. Quickly turning away before she lost her senses completely, she gazed at the river, its clear waters flowing in a direction Robyn could only guess. In the rush of day-to-day modern life, it was easy to forget that such places existed, but they were there—it was just a case of making time to see them. Pleasures like this didn't change with the centuries. People still longed to feel the earth beneath their feet and the sun on their backs. Robyn knew that Jane Austen and her sister went walking every day in the countryside, and perhaps that was why Elizabeth Bennet was such a keen walker too.

'"Crossing field after field at a quick pace, jumping over stiles and springing over puddles with impatient activity,"' she recited.

'Pardon?' Dan looked across at Robyn.

'I'm just remembering how Elizabeth Bennet loved to walk in the country.'

'Ah, the amazing Miss Bennet.'

Robyn frowned. 'She wouldn't have been called "Miss Bennet"—that was the title given to the eldest daughter, Jane, in *Pride and Prejudice*. Elizabeth was the second eldest.'

'I stand corrected,' Dan said.

Robyn grinned. 'Sorry. Didn't mean to get all boring and precise.'

'But you can't help it?'

'I can't,' she admitted with a laugh. 'Not where Jane Austen's concerned. I mean, I'm not an expert but I know a thing or two and I hate it when people get things wrong. Is that awful?'

'Not at all,' he said.

Robyn chewed her lip before her next question. She'd been dying to ask it for ages. 'Have you read any more?'

'I have,' he said.

She waited patiently. Was he going to say anymore or did he hate everything about the book and hate her for asking him about it?

'Poor Elizabeth has just been proposed to by Mr Collins and Mr Darcy. Very badly,' he said.

Robyn laughed with as much relief as pleasure that he seemed to be enjoying it. 'Aren't they the worst proposals in the world? Poor Lizzy!'

They were quiet for a moment and Robyn listened to the sounds around her. Biscuit was snuffling along the riverbank, the horses were munching the grass behind them, and the gentle flow of the river played as a constant soundtrack over it all.

'Have you ever been proposed to?'

Robyn started from her reverie. She hadn't expected to be asked such a question. She sat up and turned around. Dan's bright eyes were fixed on her.

'Have *you*?' she asked, keen to deflect the question away from her but equally keen to know his answer.

'Do you mean have I been proposed to or have I done the proposing bit?'

'Either. Both.'

Dan's clear eyes fixed on the river for a moment before he replied. 'I'm afraid I've had a string of doomed relationships,' he said.

'Doomed?'

He nodded. 'I was a bit of a workaholic in London. Always had my eye on the next big client I could get on board. Didn't leave me much time for dating, I'm afraid. I'd forget I was meant to be meeting someone because I'd get so tied up at work.'

'Oh, dear,' Robyn said.

'Yes. It didn't go down well with the women in my life, but there was one special girl and I swear I really made an effort for her. I'd leave work only two hours late and everything.' He gave a wry grin.

'What was her name?'

'Holly.'

Robyn waited for him to continue, but he didn't seem to want to. 'Did she propose to you?' she asked with a half-smile.

Dan shook his head. 'But I nearly proposed to her. I bought the ring, booked a table for two at her favourite restaurant overlooking the Thames, left work on time for once, and then I waited.'

Robyn cocked her head to one side. 'What happened?'

'She never showed up,' he said with a shrug. 'It wasn't until a month later that I found out she left town that very night with a mutual friend.'

'Oh, Dan! That's awful!'

'Well, it was at the time, but it's worked out for the best. I wouldn't be sitting here in the middle of a field with you if she'd shown up and said yes. I'd probably have worked myself into an early grave too, with the hours I was doing.' He sighed. 'It probably wouldn't have worked out anyway. For a start, she's allergic to dogs and I couldn't be without a few furry companions, could I?' He picked up Biscuit, who had given up hunting for rodents and flopped by his master. Robyn watched as he placed the little dog on his lap and tickled his ears.

'So what about you? Anyone ever popped the question to you?'

It was her turn to answer and she couldn't, not now that Dan had revealed all. Robyn shook her head. 'No,' she said.

'So there are no plans to marry Jace?'

Robyn sat quietly for a moment. 'I think not,' she said at last with a strange kind of laugh. She could feel Dan's eyes on her and looked up to meet them.

'If there's anything you want to talk about, I'm a good listener.'

'Thanks,' she said, 'but I don't think there's very much to say, really.'

Moby, who'd been patrolling the riverbank, came and flopped down next to Robyn. She reached out and stroked his golden head.

It was then that her phone beeped. She'd forgotten that she transferred it from her skirt pocket to the shirt she was wearing and cursed the action when she saw the text.

'Leave it,' Dan said, but it was too late.

'Got u a prezzy. C u tonite.'

'Is it from Jace?' Dan asked.

Robyn nodded. 'He's coming over tonight,' she said. 'I wish he wouldn't.'

'Then tell him not to.'

'I would if I thought it would make any difference.'

'You want to get back?'

Robyn shook her head and lay back on the grassy bank, her bare arm resting along the warm length of Moby. She wanted to stay like that for as long as possible. Tonight would come soon enough.

Chapter 26

'I'VE NEVER DONE ANYTHING LIKE THIS BEFORE,' SAID KATHERINE from underneath the soft folds of the duvet on Warwick's bed. One minute they'd been chatting about whether Purley Hall resembled any of the grand country houses in Jane Austen's novels and if that was why Dame Pamela had bought it and then, the next minute, they'd been urgently entangled on the bed together.

It was a good job that they'd both decided that they could well do without the afternoon discussion group about which Austen character you were most like because they never would have made it downstairs in time. Katherine's hair was, once again, a victim of passion and was cascading over her shoulders like beautiful brambles, and Warwick's room was something to behold, too.

'So,' Katherine said, pushing her dark hair out of her face in a vain attempt to restore some sort of personal order, 'we might have missed the talk, but I still want to know.'

'Know what?'

'Which Jane Austen character you're most like.' She could see a little smile lifting the corners of Warwick's mouth.

'I don't think that's for me to say.'

'What do you mean?'

'Well, isn't it all very subjective? I mean, isn't every man going to say he's Darcy and every woman say Elizabeth?'

Katherine sat up in the bed, hugging the duvet to her. 'I don't think so.'

'Okay then, who are you?'

Katherine took a moment to think. 'Well, I'm smart. I'm witty. I'm a good friend. I'm passionate about books and I love to walk.'

'Elizabeth Bennet!' Warwick said. 'I told you—*Every* woman thinks she's Elizabeth Bennett.'

Katherine laughed and lay back on the pillow.

'So, who do you think I'd be?' Warwick asked, curving an arm around her body.

'Now, that's interesting,' she said. 'You're obviously handsome so you could be any of the heroes, really. But I can't make out much about your private life so for all I know, you could be a Willoughby or a Wickham.'

Warwick's mouth dropped open. 'No! Really? You really think that?'

'I'm only joking!' Katherine laughed. 'Perhaps you're more of an Edward Ferrars, and there's something you're not telling me because you can't.'

'What makes you think I'm not telling you everything?'

Katherine's eyes widened. 'Because you aren't.'

'I just don't like talking about my work, that's all.' He moved his arm away from her and sat up, swinging his legs out of the bed.

Kathcrine watched him and was scared that she'd upset him again. 'I'm sorry,' she said, sitting up once more. 'It's just I'm really interested in what you do.'

Pulling on his trousers, he turned and smiled at her. 'You're forgiven,' he said. 'And I will tell you more about it some time. Just not this weekend. I want this weekend to be about us.'

'It *is* about us,' she said.

'I know,' he said. 'I just don't want it spoiled by anything.'

'What could possibly spoil it, silly?'

He looked at her for a moment and then leant across the bed to claim another kiss. 'Nothing,' he said. 'Nothing at all.'

The gala dinner on Saturday evening was always a bit special. Guests at the conference weekend usually dressed up for dinner, but everyone made an extra special effort on Saturday. There was an array of beads, sequins, and glimmering jewels and—for the men—tuxedoes and bow ties. Dame Pamela was sparkling in silver, a diamond choker clasping her neck and a brooch the size of an ostrich egg blinding everyone who looked at it.

After showering the very last vestiges of hay and horse from her personage, Robyn changed into a figure-hugging dress the colour of rosé wine. She twisted her hair up and away from her shoulders and fixed it with a large rose clip that matched her dress and wore a pair of art deco-style earrings that glittered as much as Dame Pamela's diamonds but had cost a fraction of the price.

As she descended the staircase and walked across the expanse of hallway into the dining room, she felt as though she'd stepped into a film set. Everything was beautiful. Candles were ablaze everywhere, and mirrors gleamed, reflecting the rich colours of all assembled.

Everyone was chattering and cameras flashed from all directions. Robyn smiled at the scene but wished that Dan were there to share it with her. When they'd parted at the stables, she felt glum and hadn't wanted to return to the hall at all, especially not when he kissed her again.

'I should go,' she'd said as she stood perfectly still. Immovable.

'I guess you should,' he said.

'Come and see me again?'

'Of *course*!' And then it had hit her. What was she doing? She was falling in love with another man when she hadn't even finished with the other one. And what did she think was going to happen there? Even if she did manage to break up with Jace, how did she think things would work out with Dan? He was based here—in Hampshire—and she was miles away in North Yorkshire. How was that meant to work? Long-distance relationships were never a good idea.

Looking at everyone as they walked into the dining room, Robyn felt a little lonely. She knew she wasn't the only person who was attending the conference on her own, but suddenly everyone seemed to be in pairs. There were the sisters Rose and Roberta, Mrs Soames and that other awful woman who didn't seem to approve of Robyn at all, and Warwick and Katherine, of course. Still, maybe she'd sneak down to the stables after dinner and see Dan again.

The thought of another visit excited her, and she took a seat at the table with a big smile on her face that grew even further when Katherine sat next to her.

'Hello!' she said brightly. 'How are you? Feels an age since I saw you.'

'I'm fine. You okay?' Robyn asked, nodding to Warwick as he took a seat to Katherine's right.

Katherine leant closer. 'I'm afraid I skipped class this afternoon.'

'Really?'

Katherine nodded, and a sweet blush coloured her cheeks. 'With Warwick.'

Robyn gasped.

'Oh, I haven't shocked you, have I?' Katherine said, grabbing Robyn's hand and squeezing it.

She shook her head. 'No!' Robyn said. 'It's just that—well—I kind of skipped class too.'

'I can't say I blame you. I mean this afternoon wasn't the most riveting.'

'With Dan.'

'What?' It was Katherine's turn to gasp.

'The guy who works in the stables,' Robyn said.

'Oh, *yes*! I've seen him. Robyn, he's gorgeous!'

'I know!'

'So you were with him?'

She nodded. 'He took me out riding. It was wonderful. I didn't want to come back.'

The two of them sat grinning at each other for a moment.

'There must be something in the air here,' Katherine said.

'I think it's the Jane Austen effect,' Robyn said.

'Really?' Katherine said, a quizzical expression on her face.

'We're spending the whole weekend reading about romance and handsome heroes and happy endings—it's bound to do something to our brains.'

'You think it makes us susceptible to love?'

Robyn gave a little laugh. 'That's certainly what's happening here, isn't it?'

Katherine took a deep breath. 'This isn't exactly what I expected from a Jane Austen weekend, you know.'

'Me neither.'

'I thought it would be all books and talks.'

'Me too!' Robyn said.

'I never thought I'd fall in love.'

'Me neither.'

Katherine threw a quick glance at Warwick. 'It's rather wonderful, isn't it?'

Robyn smiled and nodded, and it was then that the dinner was served.

~

It was a perfect dinner. The starter was light and sublime, the main course sumptuous and satisfying, and dessert ravishingly chocolaty. Robyn was folding her thick linen napkin and looking forward to her cup of coffee when she heard a strange noise.

'What on earth was that?' somebody asked from across the table.

Conversation died down as everyone's attention was drawn to what was going on beyond the dining room. Something was happening in the hallway—some sort of clattering, crashing, and shouting. Katherine turned to Robyn, and they gave each other perplexed smiles, but then Robyn's face drained of all colour when she heard a voice.

'Goddamn door!' it yelled. 'Go on, boy! Get through there. Giddy up!'

It was Jace, and Robyn could only guess what he was up to; however, she didn't have to wait long to find out, for the dining room door crashed open, and in charged a horse.

'Perseus!' Robyn cried.

Sure enough, Perseus—the chestnut stallion—was in the house and more alarmingly, Jace was on his back.

There was a collective gasp from the table. Cups and cutlery were dropped in alarm, and several guests leapt out of their seats.

'What in heaven's name is that?' the elderly gentleman with the guinea-pig hair shouted, adjusting his glasses in an attempt to find out.

'It's a horse!' Rose exclaimed, grabbing her napkin and wielding it as if it were some kind of shield. 'It's a horse!'

'Jace!' Robyn cried. What on earth was he doing on Perseus, and how did he get him into the house? She saw that Perseus was wearing his saddle and bridle so perhaps Dan had just brought him back from an evening ride.

'Robyn!' Jace called back, almost falling forward onto Perseus's neck.

'What are you doing, Jace?' Robyn leapt out of her chair and ran towards him.

'I came to see you! You like a man on a horse, don't you? I know you do! And I wanted to get it right. It's got to be right, see,' he said, his words slurring together.

'You might've broken your neck. You can't ride a horse!'

'I'm doing all right, aren't I? I've not fallen off!'

Robyn was beside herself. The whole dining room was in disarray, with guests jostling each other in an attempt to reach the safety of the other side of the room. Only a few brave people remained seated, staring in shock at the scene before them. Robyn turned to see if somebody was going to make a helpful suggestion, but even Dame Pamela seemed immobilized.

'Jace—'

He held up a hand before she could say anything else. 'No, listen,' he said. 'I've got something to tell you.'

She watched as Jace fumbled in his jacket pocket.

'Jace—*please* get down.'

'No way! I'm up here now. I'm gonna do this properly.'

Flustered, Robyn didn't dare look around the room at the diners. Goodness only knew what they were thinking.

'Robyn Love,' he said. 'I know I'm not good enough for you.

I know I'm not one of your heroes from a book. I'm just a regular guy who doesn't know his Darcy from his elbow. But I love you, and I want to marry you. Will you be my wife?'

He reached down out of the saddle and handed Robyn a tiny blue box.

Oh, dear Lord, please let me be wrong, Robyn thought, dreading opening it because she knew what was in there. But what else could she do? Absolute silence filled the dining room as everybody looked at Robyn and Jace, mouths and eyes wide open, not wanting to miss a single second.

Robyn did the only thing she could do and opened the box with shaking fingers. Sure enough, sitting on a velvety cushion was a diamond ring, three bright stones that winked at her in the candlelight.

'Well?' Jace said, grabbing hold of Perseus's mane as he swayed forward. 'Will you marry me?'

This can't be happening to me, she thought. *Please* let me wake up.

'Jace—I—' Robyn began, her words catching in her throat.

'*Will you marry me?*'

The words stabbed through her. She turned to look at the guests around the table and huddled in the far corners of the room. Everyone's faces had softened. All were waiting for her to say something—for her to say 'yes.'

'Yes,' she said, her voice a little squeak.

As soon as the word was out, there was a deafening round of applause. Somebody gave a very fruity wolf whistle, and everyone stood, making a mad scramble towards her, patting her on the back, kissing her cheeks, and generally frightening her to death.

'Careful of the horse!' Warwick's voice suddenly cut above the noise. Instantly everyone moved backwards, and Robyn noticed that she wasn't the only one to look anxious—Perseus was looking a little unnerved too.

'He's going to poo!' somebody cried from behind her.

'Get that animal out of here!' somebody else shouted, and everyone watched in horror as Perseus's tail rose an inch.

'Oh, my God,' someone said with a gasp, and everybody watched as Perseus extended his very impressive equipment and a loud gush of urine splashed onto the carpet. Those who had dared to remain seated at the table moved as fast as was humanly possible to the other side of the room as the amber stream continued.

'What's going on down there?' Jace asked from above. 'He's taking a piss, isn't he?'

Robyn winced, quite sure that people shouldn't swear at a Jane Austen Conference.

Everyone was gasping and whispering, horrified and amused at the same time. What would Dame Pamela think? All eyes had turned from the young lovers to the grande dame, who was looking decidedly perplexed, her eyes two wide circles in her face.

But then she burst out laughing, her body bending forward as if it could not support itself. Everybody stared as she continued to laugh, the merry sound filling the room.

'That,' she said, 'is the funniest thing I've seen in a long time!' And off she went again, laughing and laughing until everyone else joined in. Everyone except Robyn. She stood, immobilized, staring at the row of diamonds before her.

'Put it on!' Jace shouted above the laughing.

Robyn looked up at him. He was staring down at her with such a tender expression that she couldn't do anything other than obey him. The laughter died down a bit and the diners began to return to the table, partly in the hope that coffee was about to be served and partly because they were aware that the carpet underneath Perseus was now pungent.

'I suppose we should try to get this horse outside,' Dame Pamela said at last. She approached Perseus, her beautiful jewelled shoes squelching on the carpet, and held a hand out to him, stroking his white blaze. 'Dan!' she suddenly said. Robyn turned to see Dan enter the room. He'd obviously been running, and he wasn't looking very happy.

'Get off that horse!' he yelled, glaring at Jace.

'Oh, man! Here comes the cavalry,' Jace said.

Dan reached up towards Jace.

'Take your hands off me, pal!'

'Then get off this horse before I pull you off!'

Jace, who was wobbling like a Weeble, didn't need to be told twice. If he didn't get off now, he was very likely to fall off at some point soon. Everyone watched as he tumbled onto the floor, almost crashing into Dame Pamela.

'This is outrageous,' Mrs Soames said. 'I've never seen anything like it in my life. I shall be formally complaining about this.'

Dan stepped to one side, holding Perseus's reins in one hand and reaching out to move Robyn out of the way as he turned the horse to face the door.

'Oi! That's my future wife!' Jace shouted before collapsing onto the floor, perilously close to where Perseus had left his mark.

'Someone get him to bed,' Dame Pamela said. 'Higgins—would you kindly do the honours? We'll make up a bed for him in the West Drawing Room. I think it very unlikely that he'll be able to make it upstairs, and he won't be able to do much damage in the drawing room.'

Higgins the butler, who'd been watching the proceedings from the relative safety of the door, was wearing an expression that didn't altogether agree with Dame Pamela's words.

'Dan, get poor Perseus out of here.'

Dan nodded and led the horse away.

Robyn watched as he turned his back to look at her, his hurt visible in his eyes.

Chapter 27

'POOR ROBYN,' KATHERINE SAID.

'What makes you say that?' Warwick asked. They were standing by the window in her bedroom. It was the first time he'd been in her room.

'Didn't you see how miserable she looked?'

'I did notice that she wasn't smiling. Perhaps she was just in shock,' he suggested.

'Shock? She doesn't love him, Warwick!'

'How do you know that?'

'Because she's in love with somebody else.'

Warwick stared at Katherine. 'How do you know that?'

'Because she told me.'

'Who's she in love with?'

'The guy from the stables.'

'That strapping chap who came in for the horse?'

Katherine nodded.

'But she's only just met him.'

'And I've only just met you,' she said.

He smiled at her, walked towards her, wrapped his arms around her, and pulled her close. 'So you have.'

'It can happen very quickly, you know,' she said.

'You don't need to tell me that,' he said.

'It's probably something to do with this place. Maybe there's some sort of spell on it that makes everyone fall in love.'

'I haven't noticed anyone swooning over Mrs Soames yet.'

Katherine giggled. 'Maybe Higgins the butler will take a shine to her.'

Warwick laughed, and then something caught his eye. There, on Katherine's bedside table, was a copy of *The Notorious Lady Fenton*. Without thinking, he walked across the room and picked it up.

'Have you read it?' Katherine asked.

'Yes,' he said. Well, that was a truth of sorts, wasn't it?

He flipped through the pages, noticing a Mr Darcy bookmark placed at the front.

'Oh,' Katherine said. 'You weren't meant to see that.'

'Don't tell me, you bought it for a friend?' He smiled as he saw Katherine's embarrassment. 'If they made an Elizabeth Bennet one, I would have bought it.'

'I love this book,' she said, taking it off him and opening it about halfway through. 'This scene,' she said, 'at the ruined castle. It's wonderful.' She handed the book to Warwick and he skim-read the words he knew so well. He could remember the day he'd written them. He hadn't been too sure of the scene himself. Was it too over-the-top Gothic? Would his editor accuse him of hamming it up? But no. Tansy—the toughest editor in town—had adored it, and Lorna's readers had too. He'd known because the letters arrived by the sackful. And now here was dearest, loveliest Katherine singing the scene's praises too. It was too much. He knew he shouldn't push things, but the writer in him wanted to hear more.

'So what was it in particular you liked about it?'

Katherine took the book off him again. 'Everything, really,' she said. 'The atmosphere Lorna Warwick creates—it's sinister but sexy at the same time. I love the little touches, like Isabella's fingers brushing the stone walls, and the way the moonlight makes the gargoyles seem alive.'

Warwick smiled.

'Did you like it?'

'Oh, yes. I did. It's not a bad piece of writing, I suppose.'

'That's nice to hear. I mean, I know you're a Jane Austen fan, but it's good to hear a man praise a woman's work. It's rare when that happens. There's so much snootiness when it comes to reading, isn't there?'

Warwick nodded. It was no good. He was feeling bad again. Bad and wicked and foolish. But he was an author, and an author loves to be praised, and here, standing before him, was an ardent fan, and he couldn't help wanting to hear more from her. Was it really so wicked?

'Which other scenes did you like?' he asked, trying to sound nonchalant.

Katherine cast her eyes up to the fine plaster ceiling. 'I liked the scene where Isabella confronts Sir John. She just dazzles in that scene. She reminds me of Elizabeth when she turns down Darcy.'

Warwick couldn't help smiling. 'I know exactly what you mean.'

'And the wolfhound scene is hilarious. And the ending, of course. I love all of it. It's my favourite Lorna Warwick book, and there isn't a bad sentence in it.'

Warwick swelled with silent pride at her words. How wonderful it was to hear her thoughts. Of course, she'd told him all about her favourite book when she wrote to him as Lorna, but it was different hearing the words when you were in the same room.

Something occurred to him. Would Katherine confess such a thing? If he pushed her just a little, would she tell him about writing to Lorna Warwick?

'It's a shame Lorna Warwick doesn't know how much you love the books,' he said, watching her closely for her response.

'Oh, I'm sure she gets loads of letters from fans.'

'I don't know,' Warwick said, stroking his chin. 'Writers aren't exactly pop stars, are they? They lead such hidden, secretive lives. I mean, Lorna Warwick doesn't even go to public events, does she?'

'No, I don't believe she does.'

'I bet her mailbag is sorely empty,' Warwick said. 'I bet she'd love to hear from someone like you.' He watched as Katherine gave a little smile. 'What?'

'Nothing,' she said, doing her best to hide her expression.

'Tell me,' he said.

'There's nothing to tell.'

'Are you sure?' he asked, wondering if she would give up her great secret.

'Well, maybe I could tell you, but you have to promise that it doesn't go any further.'

'Of course,' he said. 'I promise.'

'I wrote a fan letter to Lorna Warwick.'

'Really?' he said, quite impressed at how convincingly surprised he sounded.

Katherine nodded. 'I couldn't help it. I just had to get in touch. Is that silly of me?'

'No!' Warwick said with probably a little too much enthusiasm.

'It's just... well... I can't write to Jane Austen, can I? And Lorna's books always make me feel so happy. They take me right out of myself, just as a good book should, and I really wanted to tell her that.'

'So did she write back?'

Katherine smiled. 'She did!'

'Really? What did she say?'

Katherine gave Warwick a quizzical look. 'I rather think that's between me and her, don't you?'

'Oh, come on!'

'I'm not telling you.'

Warwick walked towards her and placed his hands on her hips.

'You can't get around me that way,' she said.

'No?' he said, bending to kiss her.

'Or that way.'

But the truth of the matter was he didn't mind. Either way, he was a winner.

⁓

It was the longest night Robyn had ever known. For most of it she sat on the window seat, staring out of the window onto the lawn. The moon was somewhere behind the cedar tree, and its shadow was thrown across the grass, eerily beautiful.

Robyn hadn't bothered to put a light on when she gave up on the idea of sleeping. The silver-edged darkness suited her mood, but there was something she wanted to do now so she crossed the room to switch on the lamp by her bed. A small yellow circle of light warmed the room, and Robyn picked up the little blue box that sat on the bed stand. She'd taken the ring off her finger and placed it in the box as soon as she was in the privacy of her room. Now she opened it again and looked at the three tiny but perfect diamonds. She was surprised at Jace's choice—it was a genuinely beautiful ring and not a choice she would have expected him to make. Not that she spent any time thinking about the sort of engagement ring Jace would pick out for her. That prospect had never crossed her mind. But what was she to do with it, and more importantly, what would she do with the life that would follow if she accepted the ring?

For a moment she tried to imagine what life would be like as Mrs Jace Collins, but the vision was too disturbing. She thought of the beer cans that would be placed on her beloved Austen books. The Saturday match would replace *Sense and Sensibility* on the television. He wouldn't want her reading in bed, and she knew for a fact that he objected to her posters: the Gwyneth Paltrow *Emma* one in the kitchen, the Greer Garson *Pride and Prejudice* one in the kitchen, and the Matthew Macfadyen one in the bedroom. They'd all have to go. She would be the one to compromise; she knew that. But these little things wouldn't matter so much if she truly loved him. She wouldn't miss a few posters and she could learn to ration her film consumption—she was sure she could.

'If I loved him.'

But you don't love him, the little voice inside her said, and she knew it was true. She didn't love Jace.

You love somebody else, the little voice went on.

Crossing to the window again, she looked out across the darkened driveway towards the stables and remembered the hurt look on Dan's face as he left the dining room earlier that night. How different he had been from the smiling, laughing man of their afternoon ride. She'd been happy, sitting on the grassy bank with him, gazing up into the sky, and letting the conversation flow as easily as the river, yet just a few hours later, she felt as if she was the most miserable girl in the world. And how perverse it seemed to be miserable after having a proposal of marriage and being given a beautiful diamond ring! Wasn't it what every girl dreamed of?

'Oh, God!' Robyn cried, screwing up her eyes and shaking her head. She was in such a muddle, and there was only one thing she wanted to do, and that was to see Dan. She had to talk to him and explain things. It couldn't wait until the morning.

She was wearing her favourite old floral pyjamas with the red wine stain down the front which was probably a secret best kept to herself. Grabbing her jeans, she dressed quickly, pulling on a T-shirt and a cotton jumper and thrusting her feet into a pair of sandals.

She unlocked her door and crept out into the hallway, closing and locking her door as quietly as possible. It felt strange walking around Purley in the middle of the night. The whole house was sleeping, and few lights had been left on. As she stood at the top of the great staircase, Robyn hesitated. Maybe she should return to her room and wait until morning. She wasn't even sure if there were alarms set in the house or if the front door would be locked. She could imagine how embarrassing it would be to wake everyone up with some screaming alarm on top of all the trouble she'd caused already. But something told her she'd be all right, and she simply had to talk to Dan. She couldn't bear for him to think badly of her for a single second longer than he had to.

Glancing around to make sure nobody had stirred, she crept down the stairs, her flat sandals silent on the thick carpet. It was easy to imagine oneself the mistress of the house at this time of night, with nobody else around. How amazing to live in such a place! What must that be like? Robyn wondered. Did Dame Pamela drift around the rooms swathed in chiffon, pretending to be a queen? Not that she needed to. She was already movie star royalty and had a title. She didn't need to pretend.

Stepping into the hallway, which was lit by only a single lamp on a gold console table, Robyn inched her way towards the front door. Well, she thought, she hadn't set any alarms off yet. It was looking promising.

The front door was, indeed, locked, but the key was in place and the two large bolts were easy to draw. Within moments she found herself at the top of the steps overlooking the gravel driveway and the moonlit lawn. She closed the door behind her and walked towards the stable block, her sandals crunching lightly on the gravel.

All of a sudden, it dawned on her that Dan might be asleep. She was assuming that he was as upset and unable to sleep as she, but what if he'd wiped her from his mind and was dreaming of somebody else already? He might not want to be disturbed. She chewed her lip but continued to walk. Even if he didn't want to see her, she had to talk to him and clear things. It was the only way.

After entering the stable block under the clock tower, she looked around her. All was quiet and all was dark. Dan wasn't sitting by a lit window brooding about her at all. He was sound asleep, wasn't he?

The sound of barking broke into the night, causing Robyn's heart to race. It was Biscuit, and soon Moby joined in, creating a horrible canine chorus that threatened to wake the whole of Hampshire.

'Who's there?' Dan's voice came from his room in the clock tower and Robyn saw a light come on. She heard footsteps, together with a charge of dogs, and a door opened and light spilled into the stable yard.

'Dan!'

'Robyn?'

She took a step forward into the light.

'What are you doing here?'

Chapter 28

KATHERINE WASN'T SURE WHAT HAD WOKEN HER UP BUT WHEN she saw the sleeping figure of Warwick beside her, she was glad she had awakened. It was wonderful to wake up in the middle of the night with a handsome man in her bed and it was something that didn't happen very often. With her workload and her luck with men, she'd been woefully short on male company over the last few years which probably explained why she'd catapulted herself into this relationship with undisguised gusto.

For a few blissful moments, she watched him as he slept. He had the most gorgeous dark hair she'd ever seen and the sort of eyelashes women spent a fortune trying to create. And he was there next to her. How had that happened? Was this her prize for having suffered the lies and treachery of David? Was she in line for some pure unadulterated joy at last?

One of the most exciting things about the whole weekend was that Katherine would have the pleasure of living it all again when she wrote to Lorna Warwick. She couldn't wait to tell Lorna all her news. What would the great author say? Would she approve of such things or would she be shocked by Katherine's behaviour? No! You couldn't possibly shock a romantic novelist, could you?

Thinking back to some of the steamy scenes she'd written, it would take a lot to shock her, Katherine thought.

Slipping quietly out of bed, Katherine opened her bag and took out a notepad and pen and went to sit at the dressing table by the window, switching on the lamp as quietly as possible. She was feeling restless and thought she might as well start her letter to Lorna now.

Dear Lorna,

Forgive the notepaper, but I'm writing this from Purley Hall in Hampshire. The Jane Austen Conference has been something of a surprise this year, and I only wish you were here to share it. I think I've fallen in love! I know—I said it was never going to happen again, and I truly believed it wouldn't. I wanted a good long break from men after the whole David debacle, but this has just—well—happened!

His name's Warwick—like your last name! Isn't that funny? I've never met a Warwick before. It's quite a distinguished sort of name, isn't it? A real hero's name, I think. Rather like something out of Jane Austen. I can just imagine it. Captain Warwick Lawton. I wish you could meet him. Well, I wish I could meet you too. It feels as if we've already met somehow, but I was hoping you'd be able to make the conference. It would have been fun to finally meet you and—

'What are you doing?'

Warwick's voice startled her. She turned around and saw him sitting up in the bed.

'Nothing. Go back to sleep!'

'Are you writing?'

'Yes,' she said.

Warwick gave a little chuckle. 'You look very Austensian sitting there in the lamplight with your writing paper and pen.'

'I didn't mean to disturb you. Sorry,' she said. 'Go back to sleep.'

'What are you writing?' he asked.

She sighed and closed the notepad, returning it to her bag with her pen. 'Nothing,' she said, slipping back into bed next to him. She snuggled up against him, he kissed her forehead, and she closed her eyes. She could finish her letter to Lorna another time.

In the stable yard, Robyn was beginning to wish she hadn't left the warmth of her bedroom.

'You'd better come inside before you freeze to death,' Dan said. He could obviously see her shivering.

Robyn entered the tiny hallway where Moby and Biscuit were wagging furiously at their midnight visitor, their tails beating against her legs in the confined space. A wooden staircase led up from the door, and Dan led the way. It was only then that Robyn realised he was wearing shorts and a T-shirt.

'I woke you up,' she said, getting quite an eyeful as she followed him upstairs.

'Not really,' he said.

His voice sounded strange—strained and unnatural. It wasn't the voice she'd grown used to over the past couple of days.

'I didn't mean to disturb you.'

'You're not disturbing me,' he said as they reached the top of the stairs. Robyn looked into the room that greeted her. It was a small loft-like room with white walls and exposed beams everywhere and a beaten-up sofa at its centre onto which Biscuit bounced.

'Off!' Dan told the little dog, who shamefacedly jumped off and returned to his basket in the corner of the room.

There was a tiny kitchen sink by a small window that overlooked the stable yard; a cooker; a fridge; a shelf crammed with mugs, bowls, and plates; and another full of cookery books. He hadn't told her he liked to cook but then again, they'd known each other only a frighteningly short time, and she realised that there was an awful lot she didn't know about the man. Suddenly she felt shy at being in his home so late at night but tried not to show it as she looked around, noticing a door at the far end of the room that she guessed led to the bedroom and bathroom.

'It's small but it's home,' Dan said, as if reading Robyn's thoughts.

'It's nice,' she said. 'You've got it nice.' She took in the painting of a horse on the far wall and looked at the two dogs curled up in their baskets, now that the excitement had died down. What more did anyone need? Robyn wondered how it compared to the plush London apartment he'd once lived in. She'd bet that place hadn't smelled of horses.

Dan motioned for her to take a seat and she sat on the little sofa.

'Do you want a tea or a coffee?'

She shook her head. 'I'm restless enough as it is.'

'I've got some chamomile tea somewhere. Pammy got me a box when I first came down from London. She said I had the city jitters and needed to calm down.'

'Did it work?'

'I don't know,' he said. 'It tasted of wee so I poured it away.'

Dan came and sat next to her on the sofa, his long bare legs stretched out in front of him. It was very distracting. The room was lit by a single low-wattage lamp and the intimate atmosphere was making Robyn feel uneasy but she hadn't gone there to sit around feeling awkward. This wasn't about just her anymore, and she had to think about how Dan was feeling.

She took a deep breath. 'I wanted to say sorry,' she said, her voice barely audible above the snores emanating from Biscuit and Moby's respective baskets.

'You don't have to explain anything to me,' Dan said.

'Yes, I do.' Robyn leant forward and looked at him. 'I didn't plan for any of this to happen. I'm not saying that as an excuse, but this has all taken me by surprise.' She sighed. 'Jace was never meant to come here. I was trying to break up with him, you see, and I think he got wind of that. He started turning on the charm a bit. Well, not much. But he insisted on driving me down here and then he went and booked a room nearby, determined that we should make a proper weekend of it together. He's been hard to ignore, but I've been doing my best; I really have.'

'Why didn't he come on the weekend with you?'

'Are you kidding? He can't stand Jane Austen. He'd be a nightmare. He can't even bear to be in the same room when I'm watching one of the film adaptations.'

'But we sometimes do things to please the ones we love,' Dan said. 'I once put on a suit and sat through four hours of opera to please a girlfriend.'

Robyn gave a little smile. 'Jace isn't like that. If he doesn't like it, then it must be rubbish.'

They were quiet for a moment, the sound of the dogs snoring filling the silence.

'I had no idea he was going to propose to me. I really didn't. It completely took me by surprise. And the horse and everything!' Robyn's eyes widened as she remembered. 'That's the most romantic thing he's ever done in his entire life.'

'It's the most stupid thing he's ever done. He could've got his neck broken. He's lucky Perseus was in a good mood,' Dan said.

'I know,' Robyn said. 'I was worried for him, but he looked happy. I think it's one of the very few times he thought of anyone but himself.'

'So you didn't know he was going to propose?'

'Of course not!' Robyn said. 'I've never given him any encouragement, especially in these last few weeks. If anything, I've been trying to distance myself from him.'

Dan looked at her, his forehead furrowed.

'What?' Robyn said.

'You said yes.'

Robyn swallowed hard. 'I know.'

'But you're not wearing his ring.'

'I know,' Robyn said. She looked at Dan. His eyes were narrowed, and she wasn't sure if he was about to shout at her or kiss her.

'I've got something for you,' he suddenly said, getting up from the sofa and walking across the room. He picked up a jacket that had been thrown over the back of a wooden chair and Robyn watched as he reached inside the pocket and brought out a little red box. It was the second time that evening that she'd seen a man do that, and she felt nervous, which was ridiculous, really. Dan wasn't about to propose to her, was he? No! He couldn't be. The thought was ridiculous. Besides, she told herself, the box he was holding was too big to hold a ring. Unless it was a hideously huge, expensive ring.

Dan cleared his throat. 'I went into Winchester after our ride this afternoon. There were a couple of things I had to pick up, and I dropped by a friend's shop. He has a funny little place selling antiques at the back of the cathedral. Well, not antiques as such. More junk, really. But you never know what you're going to find there. Pammy loves it in there. She's always picking up little bits of costume jewellery. Anyway,' he said, taking a step forward, 'I saw this, and it made me think of you.' He held out the little red box and Robyn took it, looking up into his eyes.

'I don't know what to say,' Robyn said.

'Better take a look at it first,' he said with a little smile, and Robyn opened it up to reveal the prettiest brooch she'd ever seen. It was a perfect silver horse racing along with its tail and mane flying out behind him.

'It's lovely!' she said. 'I've never been bought anything so pretty.' She looked up at Dan and smiled. 'Thank you.'

'It's only silver,' Dan said. 'I know it can't compete with a diamond ring.'

'Up until today, that ring is the only real gift Jace has ever bought me.'

Dan looked perplexed. 'He's never bought you a gift?'

'Well, he usually gets me practical things. Last year, for my birthday, he bought me a milk pan. It's not very romantic, I know, but I did need one.' She gave a little smile. 'But it's nice to be spoiled now and again, except I don't think I've done anything to deserve this, Dan.'

'Why should you have to deserve something? I saw it and I thought of you. That's all. You don't have to earn it. I wanted to get it for you. Buying it was a purely selfish thing, really.' He sat back down on the sofa next to her and Robyn took the brooch out of its box and handed it to him.

'Pin it on for me,' she said.

He unhooked the clasp, and she pointed to the spot on her

jumper, watching as his long fingers brushed the material. 'There,' he said a moment later. 'You now have a horse galloping across your breasts.'

Robyn giggled and then saw Dan's sudden embarrassment as he realised what he'd said.

'I'd better go,' Robyn said, standing up. She walked to the top of the stairs but as soon as she started to descend, Dan's hand grabbed hers.

'Don't go,' he said. 'Stay with me.'

She looked around at him. With her on the second step of the stairs and him above, he looked taller than ever, and she knew that it wouldn't be hard to stay with him but before she could say anything, he pulled her back up the stairs and was kissing her, his mouth covering hers and preventing any protestations. It was so easy. She didn't want to be anywhere else but there with this man, and she didn't want to be doing anything else.

So what was the problem?

'Dan!' She pushed away from him, tears stinging her eyes.

'Don't go,' he said, his voice quiet and controlled but Robyn was fleeing down the stairs and was out of the stable yard before he could stop her.

Dan was quick to follow, stopping only to pull a coat over him, and Moby and Biscuit were in hot pursuit too, sensing a scene of great excitement.

'Robyn!'

She didn't stop but she didn't need to because Dan was by her in seconds and had blocked her way.

'Dan—don't!'

'You're not going like this. You came to see me tonight, and we've hardly said a word to each other.'

Robyn realised that he was right. She'd meant to give him a proper explanation about what had happened with Jace, except she hadn't.

'I'm really sorry, Dan. I didn't mean to drag you into this mess.'

'You didn't,' he said. 'I dragged myself and willingly. I want to be with you, but you've got to let me know what's happening. I can see you're not happy with Jace. *Anybody* can see that. And yet you tell him you'll marry him. What's going on?'

'You don't understand,' Robyn said.

'No, that's right, I don't understand because you're not telling me anything. What's his hold on you, anyway?'

Robyn stood silently for a moment. 'You want to know what his hold on me is?'

Dan nodded.

'He's been kind to me.'

'Kind? Buying you milk pans and not letting you be the person you truly are?'

Robyn shook her head. 'I'm grateful to him,' she said. 'He helped me at a time when I needed it.'

'What time?'

She sighed. She didn't want to go into all that now but looking at Dan and thinking about the time they'd spent together, she realised that he had a right to know.

Chapter 29

WHEN HE WAS QUITE SURE KATHERINE WAS ASLEEP AGAIN, Warwick got out of bed. He took a sip of water and then walked towards the window, looking out across the great expanse of lawn that was silvered by the moonlight. He then looked back at the sleeping form of Katherine and smiled. Her dark hair had spilled out across his pillow, and she looked peaceful.

How long ago it seemed since he'd known the quiet contentment that he was feeling. His relationships of the past had always been more about fun than anything else. They passed the time nicely enough and he never had anything to complain about but then again, he'd never felt the way he felt about Katherine. There'd been one woman who came close. Alison. Warwick had met her on a research trip in Austria. She'd been sitting by the bar in the hotel and he had bought her a drink and they'd spent the whole evening talking. They'd gotten on well—they really had—and yet there hadn't been that spark he felt with Katherine. Their relationship had lasted almost a year. She lived in Glasgow, which was a fair old way from Sussex, but they'd made the effort to meet when she was on business in London, but it had all fizzled out.

He sighed. That was as close as he'd ever come to a long-term relationship. It was rather pathetic really, considering the number of years he'd been on the planet, but perhaps things were about to change.

Watching Katherine as she slept, he thought about the confidences they'd shared in their letters and how close they'd become.

He remembered one letter in particular when she'd been feeling down about the married man she'd been involved with. David, wasn't it? Warwick had wanted to drive up to Oxford that minute and punch him in the nose. How dare somebody upset her so much! He could still recall whole sections of the letter.

He'll never ever know how much I loved him, she'd written. *Or how much I was willing to give him. For the first time in my life, I was thinking about the future—the long-term future. I was thinking about children—can you believe it? I'm so angry with myself. How could I not have seen the man he really was?*

Warwick swallowed hard as he remembered her words, but he reassured himself that he wasn't another David. He just had a little bit of explaining to do at some point; that was all.

How he valued that openness in her! She'd held nothing back from him in her letters—well, she'd held nothing back from Lorna. They really were the very best of friends, and it was killing him that he couldn't tell her that now. If only there was some way he could get back into bed with her and confess everything. If only he could be sure of her response.

Katherine stirred in her sleep, and he saw her eyes opening. 'Warwick?'

'Hello, sleepyhead.'

'What time is it? Are you okay?'

He nodded and walked back to the bed, leaning over to stroke her face. 'I've never been better,' he said, and got back into the warm bed beside the woman he was fast falling in love with.

Outside in the garden, Robyn was wishing that she hadn't left the warmth of her bed. If she'd stayed there, she wouldn't be facing the questioning eyes of Dan, would she?

'Okay,' Robyn said with a sigh. 'I'll tell you about Jace if you really want to know.'

'I really want to know,' Dan said. 'Shall we sit over there?' he asked, motioning to a bench near the cedar tree.

Robyn nodded, and they walked across the lawn to reach it, Moby and Biscuit trotting ahead of them, taking a walk in the moonlight in their stride.

'I don't know where to begin,' Robyn said.

'The beginning's usually a good place.'

Robyn sighed as she sat down. Her eyes had adjusted to the moonlit night, and she felt a sudden calmness, sitting under the great tree with Dan. Somehow she knew she could trust him.

'It happened at high school,' Robyn began. 'You'd never believe it, but I was rather shy then.' She looked at Dan.

'And rather shy now,' he said.

'Well, a little, I guess. But imagine that tenfold. It wasn't an easy time. I was a bit of an easy target with my hair.'

'Your hair is beautiful,' Dan said.

'But it's very easy to pull.'

'I thought that sort of thing only happened at primary school.'

'You don't know the type of high school I went to,' Robyn said, remembering the constant teasing and endless jokes made about her long locks. 'Anyway, this isn't about my hair. Well, it began with my hair, I suppose. Jason—Jace—came to my rescue when beastly Ben Harris was making my life a living hell one lunchtime.'

'What happened?'

'Jace punched him.'

'Oh!'

'He got a week's worth of detentions. He was lucky he wasn't suspended, really or expelled.'

'And that's why you fell for him? Jace the hero flying to your rescue?' Dan asked.

'No, it wasn't that, actually, but it certainly made me notice him. I'd known him before that, of course. We used to take the same bus to school, and everyone knew everyone else, but it was only after that that we really became friends.'

Robyn paused for a moment and looked down, noticing how bright her silver brooch looked in the moonlight.

'You okay?' Dan whispered.

She nodded. 'It was that summer when things started to go wrong. My brother, Scott, had finished sixth form and was hanging around the house driving Mum crazy. She wanted him to get a job, but he just spent most of his time in bed. We all kept teasing him, saying he was a good-for-nothing lay about. Dad called him a bed potato. We laughed about it, really. We all thought he was just being a moody teenager. We didn't realise he was ill.'

Dan frowned. 'What happened?'

Robyn looked up at him, and there were tears in her eyes. 'He died,' she whispered. 'It was all so quick. He started complaining about headaches. They were getting worse. He was having trouble with his vision and he wasn't eating, and it turned out he had a tumour. He died a week before Christmas.'

'God, Robyn! I'm so sorry.'

She nodded. 'It was years ago and yet it still makes me sad to think about it. And, you see, Jace was the only good friend I had at that time. Most of my other friends seemed to just melt away.

It was so horrible. I think some were afraid to talk about it, in case I broke down in front of them. They didn't know what to say or do. And then others were sweet for a day or two—making a fuss over me with cuddles and kisses—but then they forgot about it all. For them, it was time to move on, and I couldn't bear it because I *couldn't* move on—not for ages. Scott was my only brother and I missed him every day, and Jace was the only one who seemed to understand. He got me through it. He let me talk and cry for hours. I'd tell him the same things about how I missed Scott and how guilty I felt about it being him and not me. And I must have driven him mad because I was always asking the same question over and over again—why, *why?*' Robyn paused. 'I've never forgotten Jace's kindness. He was so sweet and attentive.'

Dan squeezed her hand, and they sat in silence for a moment. Finally he spoke. 'If you don't mind my saying, it seems to me as if Jace has never let you forget that either, from what you've told me about him.'

'What do you mean?' Robyn said with a sniff.

'You don't want to be with him, do you, let alone marry him? And yet you said *yes.*'

Robyn looked confused.

'He's playing on that kindness of yours. He knows you're not happy with him yet he had the effrontery to propose to you and to expect you to say yes!'

Robyn stood up. She didn't like the angry tone of Dan's voice.

'I'm sorry about your brother—I truly am. Nobody should have to go through something like that and I'm sure Jace was a good friend to you.'

'Yes, he was,' Robyn said.

'But you've more than paid for that one kindness with years of your own, Robyn. He can't expect any more from you. You can't build a relationship on guilt!'

'But he was there for me when nobody else was.'

'So say thank you and buy him a bottle of wine.'

'It's not as easy as that.'

'Why not?' Dan asked. 'I'll tell you why not—because you're not letting it be easy.'

Robyn started walking back towards the hall. She didn't want to hear any more of this.

'Robyn!' Dan said as he chased after her, the dogs following at his heels.

'You've got to let me sort things out by myself, Dan. I can't think at the moment.'

'Listen to me! Tell me you're not going to go through with this.'

Robyn looked up at him. His face was filled with concern. 'I don't know what I'm going to do.'

'That's not good enough.'

'Why?' Robyn said. 'Why are you so concerned about me and the decision I make?'

Dan gave her a look so intense that she almost stumbled backwards. 'You have to ask me that?' he said. 'Don't you know? I love you!'

'You can't love me. We hardly know each other.'

'What's that got to do with anything? You've known Jace for years, but you obviously don't love him,' he said.

'You can't presume to know how I feel.'

'What are you talking about?' Dan said. 'You've more or less said how you feel about him yourself, and what the hell have you been doing with me if you're in love with Jace? Tell me that!'

Robyn stood perfectly still and silent for a moment. 'I don't know,' she said at last. She could almost feel her heart caving at the feebleness of her statement. It wasn't what Dan deserved to hear, and she knew that it wasn't the truth either.

'Danny?' a voice suddenly called across the lawn. It was Dame Pamela in a dressing gown and slippers. 'You'll wake everybody up! For heaven's sake—come inside, you two.'

Robyn turned to Dan. She was desperate to say something—anything—that would give him some understanding of how she felt about him, but the moment had slipped away.

'Oh, my dear! You're frozen!' Dame Pamela said as she approached them, placing an arm on Robyn's shoulder. As soon as she made the observation, Robyn started to shiver. She watched as the great actress took in the dishevelled state of her brother, standing barefoot in the middle of the lawn with a coat gaping open to reveal his T-shirt and shorts.

'What's got into you two?' Dame Pamela asked. 'My goodness!'

'It's all right,' Dan said. 'It's over.'

Robyn blanched at his words and watched as he took off with the dogs towards the stables.

'Dan!' Robyn called after him, but he didn't stop. He didn't even turn around. What just happened? What had she done? One minute they'd been sharing confidences and she'd felt close to him—telling him things she'd never told anyone else. The next minute, he was walking away from her, declaring it was over.

She felt hot tears stinging her eyes as she watched him go. Was that really it? She swallowed hard, and her throat felt tight and lumpy. Dame Pamela took hold of her arm and led her inside.

'Come this way, my dear,' she said, and Robyn had no choice but to follow. It was obvious that Dan didn't want to talk any more that night, and Robyn was concerned that he didn't want to talk to her ever again. What had gone wrong? She hadn't meant for things to turn out this way, truly she hadn't, and her heart ached when she thought of the parting look on his face.

'What have I done?' she said out loud.

'Oh, you've probably just fallen in love,' Dame Pamela said, 'like we all have in our time.'

'I've made such a mess of things.'

'We'll get them sorted,' she said. 'Come along now.' She led the way up the stairs and along a corridor beyond a door marked Private. Ordinarily, Robyn would have been fascinated by a secret tour of an actress's home, but she was feeling washed out and worn down and couldn't muster any enthusiasm. She barely noticed the plush red carpet that lined the corridor as if leading them to some glittering premiere or the framed photographs of Dame Pamela with the great and the good. There she was with two other great dames, Judi Dench and Maggie Smith, and there with the gorgeous Rupert Penry-Jones on the set of the recent adaptation of *The Importance of Being Earnest*, and there she was with the dazzling Princess Diana. Robyn saw none of these, for her thoughts were turned inward.

When the two women reached a door at the end of the wing, Dame Pamela opened it.

'We won't be disturbed here,' she said.

Robyn walked in and saw that it was a library. She frowned. There was a library downstairs, wasn't there?

'This is my own personal library,' Dame Pamela explained, as if reading her thoughts. 'I keep my special reading copies here.'

Reading copies, Robyn thought. So what were the books downstairs? Then again, she had several copies of each of her Jane Austen novels, didn't she? Some were old favourites read time and time again until the spines cracked and the pages became loose. Perhaps these were Dame Pamela's loose-paged books.

Robyn looked around the room and noticed there was a table at the far end completely covered in scripts, papers, and odd bits of jumble.

'Do excuse the mess,' Dame Pamela said, obviously noticing the direction Robyn was looking in. 'Paperwork has never been my strong suit. Now, I think a little brandy is in order.'

'Oh, no, Dame Pamela, really—'

'Nonsense, child. Take a seat,' she said, motioning to a beautiful dusky pink chaise lounge.

Robyn sat down. It was on odd sort of seat to be offered, and she perched on the end of it rather than sprawling down its length.

'I always like a little brandy in the evenings,' Dame Pamela said, and Robyn watched as the woman walked across to one of the numerous book shelves and removed a thick leather-bound copy of *A Midsummer Night's Dream* and retrieved two crystal glasses and a bottle of brandy. 'Don't tell dear old Higgins about this,' Dame Pamela said. 'He thinks he's in charge of the household spirits, and I'd be sorely reprimanded if he ever discovered my secret stash.'

Robyn watched as Dame Pamela poured two generous measures into the tumblers.

'Here,' she said.

'Thank you.' Robyn took the glass and sipped, feeling the wonderfully warming effect of the drink as soon as she swallowed.

Dame Pamela took a hefty sip of brandy and sat down in a yellow armchair opposite Robyn.

'So, you're in love with my little brother, eh?'

Robyn almost swallowed her second mouthful of brandy the wrong way.

'I wouldn't blame you,' she went on. 'He's a peach, isn't he? And he has a good heart too. Not like dreadful Julius or that appalling Gervais. I have quite a few brothers, you know, but Dan's the only one I'd recommend to anyone.'

Robyn had to smile at that.

'Ah, yes!' Dame Pamela went on. 'Love's a wondrous thing. I've been in love so many times. Oh, *so* many times!' she said. 'And I still remember all my dear lovers,' she said, her eyes misting over and her voice lowering as if she were about to divulge a secret. 'But there's always one who remains special, isn't there? For me, that was—well, I don't need to tell you his name. But he was perfect. We were so right together. Everything was an adventure, whether we were trekking in the Himalayas or shopping for groceries. We made each other laugh—*all* the time. It was blissful. It really was. But that's not to say that we didn't have our trials because we did. We fought like Richard Burton and Elizabeth Taylor. That's just the way life is, isn't it? Of course we broke up,' she said with a sigh. 'He got married and has a rather famous son now, but you don't need to know all that.'

Robyn wished she'd go on. It was lovely listening to her talk.

'So, back to you, my dear,' Dame Pamela said.

'I'm so sorry for all the trouble I've caused,' Robyn said. 'I'm sure Jace is too. It's just he doesn't really think things through. It's a difficult time for us, you see.'

'And all this nonsense with him proposing!' Dame Pamela said. 'What was all that about? I mean, he went about it the right way. I've never seen anything so impressive in my life. But he must know you don't love him.'

Robyn nodded woefully. 'I think that's exactly why he did it.'

'And you said *yes*!'

'I know!' Robyn said, hanging her head in shame. It was like being cross-questioned by Dan all over again. 'And I don't have any answers.'

'What do you mean, you don't have any answers? You must know why you said yes.'

Robyn took a deep breath. 'Everyone expected me to.'

'Oh, rot!'

Robyn flinched at Dame Pamela's response.

'You shouldn't have felt pressured by a bunch of strangers into saying something that went against your better judgement although I can see why you did it. I dread to think what that chap of yours might have done if you'd said no, but you must think about the future here, and if you don't love him, you'll have to tell him.'

'I know I will,' Robyn said.

'Look, my dear, if you don't mind my saying, you're in an awful muddle, and you're the only one who can get yourself out of it. I wish I could help you more, but I can't. We have to sort these sorts of problems out for ourselves, don't we? Now, get the rest of that brandy down you and get a good night's sleep. Perhaps you'll be able to see things clearer in the morning.'

Robyn nodded, hoping Dame Pamela was right.

'Jace?' she said.

'Don't worry about him. He's snoring for England in the West Drawing Room.'

Chapter 30

'WARWICK?' KATHERINE WHISPERED HIS NAME AND GAVE HIS shoulder a gentle squeeze.

'What time is it?' his voice mumbled into the pillow.

'Time to go,' she said.

'Can't be.'

'It is.'

He sighed and rolled over, his hair flopped over his face. How adorable he looked, Katherine thought, hoping she looked half as cute first thing in the morning. But adorable or not, he had to get out of her room and back to his own.

'Come here,' he said, pulling her into a warm embrace that was impossible to resist.

'I have to get up,' Katherine said firmly, but she wasn't really making any progress. 'I've got my talk this morning.'

Warwick looked at her. 'So you have, Dr Roberts.'

'Don't call me that.'

'Why not? It's rather sexy. I'm in bed with a doctor.'

'Warwick!'

'Brains *and* beauty!'

'*Warwick!*' she grabbed ahold of her pillow and bashed him.

'All right, all right, I'm going,' he said, leaping out of bed.

Katherine watched as he hurriedly got dressed. Who was this glorious man who had come into her life, she wondered, and in the past, did Regency heroines watch their Regency heroes getting dressed?

'I'll see you later, doctor,' Warwick said, winking as he fastened his belt.

Katherine flopped back on her pillow for a moment and sighed. How could she possibly think about giving a talk when all she could think about was Warwick? And he was going to be there too, sitting in the room staring at her with those big brown eyes. She was going to have to tune him out if she was going to get through her talk with anything approaching professionalism.

After showering and dressing in a conservative white blouse and pencil-thin black skirt, Katherine took some time applying her make-up and then wondered what to do with her hair. Ordinarily she pinned it back when giving a talk, but Warwick had said how much he liked it when she wore it loose. She experimented. Up? Down? Up? Down?

'Down,' she said at last, letting the dark waves spill over her shoulders. She put on an extra lick of lip gloss and then sat by the window overlooking the lake and pulled out her notes for her talk. This was the real purpose of her stay at Purley Hall, but it had been very easy to forget it after meeting Warwick. Love had definitely taken precedence over literature this weekend.

Despite not falling asleep until the early hours, Robyn had woken just before seven and felt strangely awake. Dame Pamela's glass of brandy had, indeed, helped her sleep, and she was feeling much more able to cope with the world now that it was a new day.

After getting out of bed and pulling on the jumper she'd worn the night before, she saw the horse brooch again and stroked its silver body with her fingers, recalling Dan's face when he left her the night before. She closed her eyes because the image was too painful to bear.

'Dan,' she whispered.

But there was something—somebody—she had to put before Dan that morning, and it was Jace. What was she going to do about Jace?

'What would Elizabeth Bennet do?' she asked the empty room.

She took a cushion from the little armchair by the window, picked up her prize books, sat on the window seat, and took out the beautifully bound edition of *Pride and Prejudice*. Running her hands over the white and gold cover, she thought how there were few more beautiful things than a new edition of a favourite book.

Robyn might have missed the lecture titled What Can We Learn from Jane Austen? but she didn't need some stranger to tell her what she already knew. *Pride and Prejudice* was a novel about proposals: good proposals, bad proposals, and ill-advised proposals. Robyn had read and remembered them all, and she flipped through her pristine copy to find the scene she knew she had to read again. It was Elizabeth Bennet's refusal to marry the odious Mr Collins.

'You could not make me *happy, and I am convinced that I am the last woman in the world who would make* you *so.'*

Robyn loved Elizabeth's strength in that scene. It was one of the acts that endeared her to readers. As well as being clever and witty and the very best of sisters, Elizabeth was independent and brave. In a time when marriage was the only real career option available to women, Lizzy had risked everything by turning down a suitor who would have provided her with a good living.

And then there'd been the shock of Charlotte Lucas's acceptance. It made Robyn shudder, no matter how many times she read it. It was Charlotte's only chance at a life to call her own, wasn't it? What was it she told Lizzy? 'I ask only a comfortable home.'

Robyn stared out of the window down onto the emerald lawn and thanked her lucky stars that she was a modern woman. No matter how much she loved to read about Regency women and fancy herself dressed in sprigged muslin, in truth that life had been much tougher for a woman. No, the twenty-first century might lack the manners and the genteelness of courtship, but at least a woman could make decisions about her future without the fear of being penniless.

The fact was that Robyn didn't need Jace to provide her with a home. She had one on her own and unlike Charlotte Lucas in *Pride and Prejudice*, she had many options open to her. She didn't need to marry Jace so why had she said yes? Was it really only because everyone had been expecting her to say yes? Just imagine if she'd said no. What would have happened then? She tried to picture the scene with Jace sitting up high on Perseus, his smile filling his face. He'd been sure of her response, hadn't he? Maybe that's why men frequently proposed in public places—there was far more chance that a woman wouldn't turn them down, for fear of humiliating them. But a woman couldn't risk tying herself to the wrong man just to save a few minutes of humiliation, could she?

Robyn sighed. It was more than that, wasn't it? She still had the old nagging feeling about being tied to Jace. He was all she'd ever known. He was safe. Okay, so he didn't set her heart on fire and he annoyed the hell out of her most of the time, but they knew each other and that level of knowledge was a strange kind of comfort.

'Like my job,' Robyn acknowledged.

Everything had always been simple. She went to the same school her mother had. She took the first job she was offered and had been there ever since, and she'd known no other man except Jace. She always took the easy option because change was scary, wasn't it? But change could be wonderful too—Jane Austen had shown her that. Elizabeth and Darcy had had to learn so much about themselves and change their whole way of thinking about each other before they could be truly happy together. Anne Elliot had changed from a dependent and naïve woman to one who knew her own mind and wasn't afraid to make her own decisions, and dear Catherine Morland was able to put aside her childlike view of the world and embrace a reality that would include her beloved Henry Tilney.

A great many of Austen's books were about growing up and learning. Her happy endings didn't come about by chance but through change which was something Robyn had never been happy embracing. Until now.

Now she knew what she had to do.

Warwick was singing in the shower. He liked singing, but only when he knew nobody was listening. Today it was Queen's 'Somebody to Love,' and his voice was echoing in a manner that he thought wonderful, a fact any neighbour would have strongly disputed.

It had been another wonderful night at Purley, and Warwick couldn't help smiling when he thought about how he'd spent the whole of it with Katherine. How warm and wonderful it had been in her company! There was something—dare he say it—*settling* about being with her. He felt at ease with her although he really shouldn't because he still had to tell her the truth about himself.

'And I will. I'm sure I will. At some point. Things will work themselves out,' he told his steamy reflection without managing to convince himself. 'Just let me enjoy this weekend.'

But it wasn't to be. As soon as he was dressed, his phone beeped. It was a text from Nadia Sparks, his agent.

'May come to the ball after all! Will call u. N x'

Warwick swallowed hard. Nadia was talking about the Sunday night dance at Purley. It was always a special event, and people from the publishing world did tend to gate-crash. But Nadia mustn't be one of them, he thought, quickly ringing her number. It went to voicemail, and he hung up, cursing loudly. This was the last thing he'd expected. As much as he adored his agent, he really didn't want her there. She represented Lorna Warwick, and he wasn't Lorna Warwick this weekend—far from it—and anything that threatened that fact should be avoided at all costs.

It was eight o'clock when Robyn walked down the stairs. Nobody was around except Higgins the butler, who this morning was sporting an indigo waistcoat with bright silver buttons.

'Good morning, miss,' he said.

'Good morning,' Robyn said. 'I was going to see Jace—my… erm… fiancé.'

'Of course, miss. Follow me.' He led the way towards the library and then opened a door that Robyn hadn't noticed before.

'The West Drawing Room,' he explained. 'I took the liberty of serving breakfast in here for you both.'

'Oh, thank you,' Robyn said, noticing a tray that had been placed on a little table for her and Jace with cereal, fruit, toast, tea, and juice. It was far more than either of them deserved, after all the trouble they caused.

Higgins the butler gave a little bow and left the room, and Robyn turned to see Jace, his tousled head half-hidden in his bedding. She sat on a chair beside the makeshift bed, wondering if she should wake him. It would be much easier if she didn't, she thought. But that wasn't the way forward, and Robyn was determined that things were going to be sorted out once and for all.

'Jace!' she whispered. He didn't stir. '*Jace!*'

'Huh?' He was suddenly bolt upright, his hair sticking up in all directions at once. He winced when he felt the onset of a hangover. 'Oh, it's you,' he said, not sounding at all pleased to see the woman he'd recently proposed to.

'Well, of course it's me. Who did you expect?'

'I thought it might be that strange man in the weird waistcoat. He was clattering about in here before, but I pretended I was asleep. He kept clearing his throat.'

'That's Higgins the butler. He's made us some breakfast.'

Jace got up, pushing his blankets aside and suddenly realising that he was naked. 'What the hell?'

'Your clothes have all been washed and pressed. Look,' Robyn said, motioning to a chair where they were all neatly laid.

'Blimey. I should come here more often,' he said, getting up and dressing quickly.

'You shouldn't have come at all,' Robyn said after a pause.

He turned round. 'What do you mean?'

'What were you thinking about, Jace?'

He zipped his trousers up and stared at her as if she were speaking a foreign language.

'What was I thinking of?' he said, his forehead furrowed. 'You. I was thinking of you.'

'But you never have before.'

'What are you talking about?'

Robyn sighed. 'We've got to face facts. Things aren't working out.'

He didn't say anything for a moment because he spotted breakfast and was tucking in. 'Have some of this toast, Rob. It's fab.'

'Jace!'

'What?'

'It's not working.'

'Well, come and sit over here then,' he said.

'I'm not talking about breakfast. I'm talking about us.'

Jace's mouth dropped open, still half-full of toast.

'Don't look at me like that,' Robyn said. 'You know the way I feel. You must do. It's not been right for ages, and I'm really sorry, but I should have said something before. It's just I didn't know what to say.'

Jace finished eating his mouthful of toast before gaping at her again. 'But you said yes. You said you'd marry me, Robyn.'

She nodded. 'I know, and I'm so sorry.'

'You're not wearing the ring,' he said, glancing at her hand.

'No.'

'I want that ring back,' he said.

Robyn frowned. 'You'll get your ring back.'

Jace's face was a kaleidoscope of emotion. It went from confused to disbelief to anger to fear.

'I don't want the ring, Rob. It's yours. I want you to have it, and I want you to be my wife!' He'd forgotten about the food in front of him and was kneeling beside Robyn, clasping her hand in his. 'You can't do this to me. I love you!'

'No, you don't, Jace. You really don't.'

'How can you say that? You don't know how I feel.' His face was pale and his eyes had a hollow look that was almost haunting.

Robyn sat forward a little. 'We've just got used to each other,' she said. 'We've never known anyone else.'

'And what's wrong with that?'

'Nothing. If we really loved each other, but I don't think we do. We're so different.'

'But that's a good thing, isn't it? Yin and yam and all that.'

'Yang,' Robyn corrected him.

Jace sighed. 'I know I'm not as smart as you and I know I don't read all them books and stuff, but I do love you, Robyn. I really do.'

Robyn looked at Jace. His eyes were swimming with tears and at the sight of them, Robyn's welled up too.

'I'm sorry,' she said. 'I'm really sorry.'

He looked down at his shoeless feet for a moment, not saying anything, but then he looked up. 'I was there for you, Robyn when nobody else was.'

Robyn should have known it was coming, but a part of her was hoping Jace wouldn't stoop so low at a time like this. She closed her eyes, wondering how to handle things, and decided that remaining calm was the only way.

'I know you were. And I can never thank you enough for that. You were my very best friend.'

'Some way to treat your best friend,' he said.

'I can't marry you out of gratitude!' she said, finally getting angry. 'Can't you see that would never work?'

'There's someone else, isn't there?' he said, his face flooding with sudden colour.

'There isn't anybody else,' Robyn said, trying desperately hard not to complicate things even more. 'This is about you and me.'

'Is it that bloody horse guy? 'Cause if it is, I'll sort him out.' Jace was on his feet and heading for the door.

'You're not listening to me, Jace! It's got nothing to do with him or anybody else.'

Jace stopped and turned around.

'I just don't love you,' she said.

There was a dreadful moment of silence and Robyn watched as Jace closed his eyes. He finally seemed to be listening to her.

Chapter 31

Katherine couldn't manage much for breakfast. It was always the same before giving a talk—nerves always got the better of her. She'd be able to eat like a pig afterwards, but nothing more than a cup of tea was manageable beforehand.

'I was half expecting to see a horse in here this morning,' Doris Norris said with a chuckle as she entered the dining room.

Rose and Roberta followed her in.

'Well somebody has done a very good job cleaning up after him,' Rose said.

'Thank goodness,' Roberta said. 'We wouldn't want to smell that whilst having our scrambled eggs.'

'How is the bride-to-be this morning?' Rose asked Katherine as she sat down next to her.

'I haven't seen her yet,' Katherine said, hoping Robyn was all right and wondering what had become of Jace.

'I bet she has that wonderful bloom of young love,' Rose said wistfully.

Katherine didn't respond and Rose instantly picked up on it.

'You don't think so, Dr Roberts?'

Katherine pushed her spoon around her cup of coffee. 'I think she has a lot to sort out,' she said.

'You don't think our dear Robyn's happy?' Rose's sweet face creased with concern. 'But she said yes.'

'So did Princess Diana,' Katherine said, and got up from the table to end the interrogation.

She returned to her room for a quick tidy up, wondering if she should knock on Robyn's door to see if she was okay. But perhaps that wasn't a good idea. If it were Katherine, she'd want some space to work things out in her own time without the interruption of well-meaning strangers. Instead, she focused on what she always did before a talk. Not having a last-minute look at the notes as some speakers might do, oh, no. There was only one thing to read at a time like this—one perfect passage of prose that never failed to work its magic on her and help her remember that the world was a beautiful place and why her specialised subject was the work of Jane Austen, and that was her favourite passage from *Persuasion*: Captain Wentworth's letter to Anne.

'You pierce my soul. I am half agony, half hope.'

Ah, Katherine thought, Mr Darcy might well claim nine out of ten readers' hearts, but one mustn't forget the deep passion of Captain Wentworth.

'I have loved none but you... You alone have brought me to Bath. For you alone I think and plan.'

Katherine loved that! This was Austen at her romantic best and Katherine adored Anne's response.

'Such a letter was not to be soon recovered from.'

This was the sort of stuff to stir even the wintriest of hearts and although Katherine needed to calm herself before a public talk, this heartfelt scene was irresistible and gave her both peace and optimism.

In the West Drawing Room, Robyn was in desperate need of soothing in the form of Jane Austen, but there was one last scene to endure before she could escape to the safety of the books in her room.

'I think it's best if you go,' she said, wishing Jace would move away from the door so she could make a run for it.

He nodded slowly and relief flooded her at how well he was taking everything.

'How are you going to get home?' he asked.

'Oh, I brought my train ticket with me.'

'Just in case you broke up with me?' he said, his tiny smile telling her he wasn't going to put up a fight.

'I didn't plan this, Jace.'

'I know,' he said.

There was an awkward moment when neither of them knew what to say. They'd been together for many years and now it was ending. What *did* one say in such a situation?

'I guess I'll see you around,' he said at last.

'I'm sure you will,' Robyn said and watched as Jace nodded. He didn't look very happy, but at least he was looking more resigned.

'Wait here whilst I get the ring,' Robyn suddenly said.

Jace shook his head. 'Keep it.'

'No, it wouldn't be right.'

'Keep the ring, Robyn. It's yours.'

She picked up his hand and squeezed it gently. 'Thank you,' she said and then leant forward and kissed his cheek.

While she headed for the stairs, she thought how lucky she was that she'd managed to get away without a far bigger scene. Maybe they'd all been played out over the last couple of days and there was no more drama left in Jace.

'And thank goodness for that,' she said to herself as she began to climb the stairs, not daring to look back down.

'Robyn—wait!'

Robyn froze halfway up the stairs.

'I can't,' he said, and she turned around to face him. 'I can't just let you go like this.'

There were a few people walking down the stairs to get ready for the talk and a few more leaving the dining room after breakfast. Robyn had to get rid of Jace. She couldn't risk another scene so she let him approach her.

'You've got to go, Jace. It's over. Please, you've got to see that.'

'Give me one more chance,' he said. 'Just one more.'

Robyn shook her head.

'*Please!*'

She was heading back up the stairs again but this time, Jace followed her and people were starting to look. They recognised him, didn't they? And they were no doubt expecting to be entertained once more.

'Jace, you've got to accept that things are over,' she said.

'But all the years I've been with you—you can't just throw them all away.'

'But you weren't with me,' Robyn said. 'You were still living with your mother.'

His eyes narrowed at her comment. 'Is that what this is about—me living at home? Well, that's going to change, isn't it? As soon as we're married, we'll be together. You'll see! Everything will be different then.'

'You're not listening to me! I'm not going to marry you,' she said. 'And I can't miss any more of the conference talking about it.'

'Robyn—*please*,' he said and his eyes filled with tears. 'Forget

253

about this conference for one second and think about *us*. All you ever think about is bloody Jane Austen. How come I always have to play second fiddle to fiction? I'm fed up of it. It's not right.'

A torrent of emotions was building in Robyn and she knew that she could no longer remain silent.

'You just don't get it, do you? And you never have. That's one of the problems here! You can't see that this conference is part of who I am. And my books too and all the film adaptations you hate so much. How could you ever think we could live together when you don't get that? You've never understood it, have you? And you've done everything you can to make me feel guilty. But I can't change. I am who I am, and Jane Austen is as much a part of me as the blood that pumps through my body. Her words are my life and I can't be with somebody who doesn't understand that. I just can't.'

Jace looked a little thunderstruck at her words as if he knew that he was the one who was going to have to back down on the point. 'But I can change,' he said, running a hand through his hair in desperation.

'No, you can't,' she said, 'and I wouldn't ever ask you to because that's not fair. We're just two very different people who don't belong together anymore. You must see that!'

They were silent for a moment and Robyn noticed that Jace's eyes had filled with tears and her own were vibrating with them too. She reached up and touched his face. 'Please,' she said, and he looked at her, his eyes so big that it almost hurt her to look at them.

'I can't bear it, Robbie.' His voice cracked as he called her by her nickname.

Robyn took his hands in hers and squeezed them. 'We've got to move on,' she said. 'This isn't good for us anymore.'

'But I won't ever see you again, will I?' he said in a voice that was barely audible.

'Of course you will,' Robyn said.

He shook his head. 'You'll meet someone else. I know you will.'

'You will too,' she said, 'but that doesn't mean we can't still be friends. Really good friends.'

'It won't be the same,' he said.

'No, it won't be.'

They were absolutely still for a few moments, their hands still interlaced and their foreheads almost touching. The people who had been watching the scene from the bottom of the stairs turned away as if they knew they were intruding on a very private scene.

Robyn let go of Jace's hands and closed her eyes for a moment. When she opened them, she saw that Jace was walking down the stairs.

'Jace!' she called, running after him.

He stopped and turned to look at her.

'Are you okay?' she asked.

He took a deep breath and sighed it out. 'I want you to be happy. I really do,' he said, 'and if I can't make you happy then we shouldn't be together.' He sounded calmer, as if all his fight had drained out of him.

'But we *can* still be friends, can't we?' Robyn said.

Jace nodded. 'I'd like that,' he said, and he gave the tiniest of smiles before crossing the hall.

As Robyn watched him go, she felt tremendously sad as if a little part of her had left along with Jace. She'd done most of her growing up with him—they'd been at school together, they got their first jobs together, and he was there when she left home; it was strange to think that their time together had come to an end.

When she felt a hand give her shoulder a gentle squeeze, she knew who it would be.

'Are you all right, my dear?'

Robyn turned around to face Dame Pamela. She produced a beautifully embroidered handkerchief for Robyn, who dabbed her eyes with it. She would have liked to have trumpeted into it too, but it was far too fine a handkerchief for that sort of abuse.

'I'm so sorry, Dame Pamela,' she said. 'I'm doing nothing but causing scenes this weekend.'

'Nonsense, my dear. It's not your fault. Now, come along with me.'

She led Robyn back upstairs and took her to her special library. It was a little early in the day for brandy, Robyn thought, but that wasn't the plan.

'Why don't you have a little rest here?' she said, motioning to the chaise lounge on which Robyn had sat the night before. 'I always find this room so calming and—believe me—there've been many times when it's been my refuge. Just take as long as you like. I'm going to go down to Dr Roberts's talk, but I'll be back up later. I'll get Higgins to bring you a cup of tea and some breakfast. I bet you didn't have yours this morning, am I right?'

Robyn gave a sniff and nodded. 'Thank you,' she said and watched as Dame Pamela left, finally allowing her tears to flow freely as soon as the older woman was out of the room.

If only Jace had left and not followed her upstairs. She'd never forget that awful haunted look on his face and she couldn't help remembering Jace's accusation that he'd always played second fiddle to fiction.

Robyn closed her eyes. It was true, wasn't it? There were few people who knew her as well as Jace did. Was it normal to fixate on novels so much? Was it normal to spend so many hours of one's life thinking about fictional characters? The conference she was attending told her that hers wasn't the only head spent thrust in a book for a goodly proportion of one's life, but that fact wasn't necessarily a comfort. Maybe it was a symptom of something more sinister.

'Like I don't have a life of my own,' she said.

But she did. She had her little cottage. Okay so it was rented, but she'd have her own one day soon. She had a job. So what if it wasn't really fulfilling and she spent most of her time watching the hands of the clock crawl around? She could always find another one. And she had her chickens.

'Oh, dear,' Robyn whispered. She was an old maid with a yard full of chickens. Perhaps she shouldn't have been as proud as Lizzy Bennet. Perhaps she should have been sensible like Charlotte Lucas and resigned herself to becoming Mrs Collins.

As she was brooding on her spinsterhood, Higgins the butler came in and placed her second breakfast tray in front of her.

'Thank you so much,' she said. 'I'm sorry to be so much bother.'

'Is there anything else I can get for you, miss?' Higgins asked.

'Oh, no thank you,' she said.

He seemed to hesitate a moment. 'A tissue, perhaps?'

Robyn blinked and suddenly realised that she must, indeed, look a sight. 'Oh, yes. Yes, please.'

He left the room and came back with a bumper box of tissues and as soon as he was out of earshot, Robyn was able to have a good trumpet at last.

Chapter 32

KATHERINE WAS GIVING HER TALK IN THE LIBRARY AND CHAIRS had been set out in neat rows. She walked up and down the beautiful room trying to pace out her nerves. No matter how many times she gave a talk, she always got nervous because each talk and each audience was different and there was no telling how it was going to go.

In one hour, this will all be over, she told herself.

'You all right?' Warwick asked her.

She hadn't seen him enter the room and she beamed him a smile as he approached her. 'I'm fine,' she said.

He gave her arm a quick squeeze before anyone saw.

'Did you hear about Robyn and her fiancé? Ex-fiancé, I should say,' Warwick said.

'No. What happened?'

Warwick told Katherine about the scene on the stairs. 'Mrs Soames told me. Sounds like she had a front-row seat.'

Katherine frowned. 'I wouldn't be a bit surprised. Speaking of front-row seats, I'm betting she'll bag one of these ones.'

'Don't mind if I get one too?' Warwick asked.

'As long as you don't heckle.'

Sure enough, as the room began to fill, in walked Mrs Soames, plonking her considerable bottom on the seat right next to Warwick. He rose an eyebrow and Katherine rolled her eyes heavenwards at his misfortune.

It was almost time to begin and as everyone made themselves comfortable, clearing throats and rustling clothing and bags, Dame Pamela entered the room and the accompanying round of applause filled the air.

'Hello, my dear,' she said to Katherine. 'How are you?'

Katherine exchanged air kisses with the dame and then stood to one side, allowing herself to be introduced.

'Dr Katherine Roberts is a lecturer at St Bridget's College in Oxford and is an expert on the life and works of Jane Austen. She's spoken at our conference in the past and it always gives me great pleasure to welcome her.' Dame Pamela led the applause and Katherine began her talk.

'"It is a truth universally acknowledged that a single man in possession of a fortune must be…"' she stopped, gesturing to the audience to finish the famous opening sentence of *Pride and Prejudice*.

'"In want of a wife,"' the audience chimed, their faces smiling. Well, apart from Mrs Soames, who wasn't looking impressed by Katherine's opening.

'Yes, "In want of a wife,"' Katherine continued undeterred. 'And it's the importance of marriage in Jane Austen's novels that we're going to explore this morning.'

~✺~

Robyn surprised herself by how much she was able to eat and with each mouthful, she began to feel a little more human again. Her tears had dried and she hoped that her face had returned to relative normality again. She hoped she had cried all she was going to cry over

Jace. It wasn't that she was hardhearted—far from it—it was just that she'd known this day was coming for some time and had been carrying the weight of it with her. Now it was over and she felt a strange kind of lightness. She wouldn't have to see him again. She wouldn't have to worry about leaving her films playing on the TV and risking his foot flying through the set. She could leave her precious books lying around without worrying that they'd be spoiled. In short, she could be herself.

She took a last sip of sweet tea before getting up from the chaise lounge. She really should think about getting back to her room to tidy herself up and trying to catch some of Katherine's talk.

It was then that something caught her eye. One of the book-shelves wasn't quite flush. There was a definite gap behind it. Robyn stared at it for a moment and then realised what she was looking at.

'It's a secret door!'

Curiosity got the better of her, and she went to investigate. It was one of those doors that was also a shelf filled with books, and the thrilling thing about it was where it led.

Robyn dared to push it open a fraction and saw a light-filled room at the centre of which stood a large oak desk strewn with papers.

It's an office, Robyn thought, Dame Pamela's private office, and the sight of it made Robyn gasp because it was the most horren-dously messy place she'd ever seen. There were cabinet drawers left half open, spilling their contents onto the floor, and a side table on which sat a mountain of eight-by-ten photographs of Dame Pamela. Robyn peered at them and noticed that they were covered in a fine layer of dust. There was a dark wood settle up against one of the walls, and it was heaped with envelopes. Robyn took a step towards it and examined a couple of them. They were all unopened, and it was then that Robyn remembered Dame Pamela telling her that paperwork had never been her strong suit. She wasn't kidding! The whole place looked more like a museum rather than a working office and no matter how much Robyn loathed her job at the college, her fingers itched to get to work restoring order in Dame Pamela's world and before she knew what she was doing, she sat herself at the desk and began to work.

~

Katherine was examining the difference between the marriages of Mr and Mrs Bennet to that of Mr and Mrs Gardiner in *Pride and Prejudice* when a mobile phone started to buzz from the front row. As a university lecturer, she was quite used to students interrupting her with their ever-present mobiles, and the reprimands were always severe. But it wasn't a student's mobile that was buzzing. It was Warwick's.

Katherine paused a moment as he answered it. 'Sorry!' he mouthed to her, and she watched as he hurried out of the room.

'Well, how rude can you get?' Mrs Soames bellowed from the front row. 'Do continue, Dr Roberts,' she said.

Katherine bristled. She didn't need Mrs Soames's permission to continue.

~

Warwick felt terrible about having to run out of Katherine's talk, but what else could he do? Ever since his agent had left that message threatening to come to Purley, he'd been hoping she'd ring back so he could do his very best to persuade her not to come.

'Warwick, darling! How are you? How's life at Purley?'

'Nadia! I was in a talk!'

'Oh, sorry, hon! Let me call you back later.'

'No—don't go! What's all this about you coming down to Hampshire?' he said, determined to get it sorted out straightaway.

'Yes, isn't it marvellous? My mother-in-law was coming over for lunch today, but she had to cancel. Got a rotten cold, but it's worked out in my favour because I can now come to the dance tonight,' Nadia said.

'It's rather a long drive, isn't it?'

'I've just got my new BMW,' she said. 'I'll be with you in no time at all.'

Warwick scratched his head. How was he going to stop her?

'Are you sure it's a good idea?' he said. 'You know what you're like, Nadia—you always overdo things when there's alcohol around.' There was a pause, and he wondered if he'd overstepped the mark.

'Oh, you are funny!' Nadia said. 'Just because I like a little tipple now and again. I hardly ever get to let my hair down now, do I?'

'I really don't think it's going to be any fun.'

'Whatever makes you say that? Of course it will be fun! You're forgetting that I've been before. What's wrong with you, Warwick? You're acting strangely.'

'Nothing's wrong. I just don't think it's worth your making the trip down here. It's a really dull crowd.'

'No crowd's dull when Dame Pamela's about. Anyway, I promised a client that I'd have a chat with her. I've got a script she might be interested in.'

'Can't you post it?'

'No, I can't. I said I'd give it to the lady herself. Warwick, what *is* the matter?'

'I've told you—nothing!'

'Doesn't sound like nothing!' There was a pause. 'I know what it is—you've met somebody, haven't you? Well, it's about time, I must say. You don't have enough fun!'

'I've not met anyone,' he said, perhaps a little too quickly to sound convincing.

'Well, I'll be leaving later this afternoon,' she said. 'So I'll see you later, darling.'

'Nadia—' But it was too late; his agent had hung up.

~~~

Robyn was about halfway through opening a mound of post and sorting it out into neat piles when she heard her name being called. It was Dame Pamela.

'Oh, *there* you are!'

Robyn dropped the envelope she was holding and looked up in shock. 'Dame Pamela... I... I didn't mean to touch anything.'

'What are you doing?' Dame Pamela asked, her voice curious rather than irate, for which Robyn was heartily thankful.

'I saw the door was open, and I couldn't resist taking a look. I'm *so* sorry. I shouldn't have just come in and made myself at home.'

'You *do* look at home, I must say!'

Robyn shot up out of the seat. 'I'm afraid I have this awful compulsion to tidy things.'

'I wish I did,' Dame Pamela said. 'But, as you can see, this is a sorry state for an office. I can't seem to hold on to my personal assistants, you see. I don't know what it is,' she said, holding her hands up to the ceiling with great theatricality. 'If you know of anyone who wants to be stuck working for a curmudgeonly old actress in the middle of nowhere, you will let me know, won't you?'

Robyn nodded. 'You're looking for a PA?'

Dame Pamela nodded, and then her eyes narrowed. 'You're not looking for a job, are you? You look as if you're doing marvellously well sorting out my mess here.'

'Oh, I have a job,' Robyn said.

'Well, that's a very great shame, I must say,' Dame Pamela said, and the two of them left the room together.

~❦~

Katherine was coming to the end of her talk when she saw Warwick sneak in and take a seat at the back. She wrapped things up, took some questions, and was then greeted to a round of applause and a lovely thank-you from Dame Pamela, who had also sneaked out and sneaked back in. What was going on with everyone this morning? she wondered.

She was just about to make her way towards Warwick when she felt a large hand land on her arm. It was Mrs Soames, and she wasn't looking very happy.

'I read that book of yours,' Mrs Soames said.

'Oh?' Katherine said, dreading what might be coming next.

'Yes,' Mrs Soames said. 'It was very expensive. Luckily I managed to find a copy in a charity shop, and it had a wine stain on page seventeen so I got another one pound fifty knocked off it. You must have been paid handsomely for it.'

Katherine took a deep breath. 'Writers of academic books aren't paid very much at all,' she said. 'And I won't have received anything from your purchase either.'

'What do you mean? I paid three pounds for that book.'

'And it would have all gone to the shop, not to me. Authors don't get a penny from secondhand book sales.'

Mrs Soames's mouth wrinkled unpleasantly. 'Well, that's not my fault, is it? And you can't expect me to pay twenty pounds for a book, not when I can get it for three.'

'Did you have any questions about the book?' Katherine asked. 'Or was it just its price you wanted to query?'

Mrs Soames bristled and her bosom rose in annoyance before she turned around and left the room. Katherine gave a big sigh. These people were sent to try us, she thought. It was the only explanation.

'It was a wonderful talk. *Wonderful!*' Doris Norris said, coming to see Katherine a moment later. 'Lots of amusing moments, and I feel I've learned so much.'

'Thank you,' Katherine said, her smile restored to her once more after the Mrs Soames encounter.

'You young women today are simply marvellous. Careers and everything! It's wonderful. Simply wonderful!'

Katherine smiled and watched as Doris went off to talk to Rose and Roberta at the other side of the room.

And there was Warwick, coming towards her looking apologetic.

'I'm so sorry!' he said.

Katherine's eyebrows rose. 'If a student's phone goes off during one of my seminars, there's the severest penalty to pay,' she said, her hands on her hips in her perfect lecturer pose.

'Please, feel free to reprimand me,' he said with a naughty grin, making Katherine smile.

'Are you okay?' she asked as they left the room together. 'You seem a bit jittery.'

'Probably just need a cup of coffee,' he said.

'Then let's go and get one.'

He nodded but there was something about him that looked different. He looked slightly out of place all of a sudden. Probably something to do with that phone call, she thought. He really was a man of mystery, wasn't he?

As soon as the thought entered Katherine's head, it occurred to her—not for the first time—just how little she really knew about him.

Chapter 33

JUST BEFORE DAME PAMELA HAD LEFT ROBYN AT THE FOOT OF the stairs, she'd leant forward and given her the sort of hug one could normally expect only from a mother. It had almost brought tears to Robyn's eyes again.

'You've been so kind,' she said.

'Oh, nonsense!'

'I can't believe how much trouble I've caused.'

'My darling girl, you've been an absolute poppet, and nobody blames you for anything. I'm just glad things have finally sorted themselves out.' Dame Pamela gave her a smile, but there was a look in her eyes that Robyn didn't quite understand. 'I only wish there was more I could do for you.'

'But you've done so much already.'

Dame Pamela smiled. 'And it's been the very least I could do. Now, why don't you go and see Dan?'

'Dan?'

Dame Pamela nodded. 'He'll want to know, won't he?'

'Yes,' Robyn said, 'but are you sure he'll want to see me? We didn't exactly part on good terms last night.'

'Yes, but that was last night and this is today, isn't it?' Dame

Pamela said.

Robyn wasn't quite sure how that made any difference.

'Of course he'll want to see you. If I know my little brother at all, I'd say he adores you so go and see him right away. Then you can ask him to the ball tonight, can't you?' There was a naughty twinkle in Dame Pamela's eyes, and it was soon reflected in Robyn's own.

Robyn saw him as soon as she walked under the clock tower into the stable block. He was bending down with his back to her, cleaning out one of Poppin's back hoofs. She watched him for a moment, and he was completely absorbed in his work, his coppery hair flopping over his face and his muscles straining as he worked. Would he want to see her? His sister seemed to think he would, but Robyn wasn't so sure. The look on his face the night before was burned deeply into her brain, and it was hard to imagine that he'd want to see her ever again.

'Okay, Pops, all done,' he said, letting go of the hoof and straightening up.

Robyn caught his eye and gave a hesitant smile. 'Hello,' she said.

'Robyn!'

She slowly walked towards him and as she did so, Biscuit and Moby appeared out of nowhere and crashed into her with enthusiasm. She bent to fuss them. At least they were still talking to her—in their own particular doggy way, she thought.

Dan ran a dusty hand through his hair and looked at her, obviously waiting for her to say something, but Robyn didn't know how to begin. At the beginning, of course, she thought to herself. Isn't that what Dan had told her?

'I've broken up with Jace,' she said.

Dan's eyes widened at her words. 'Really?'

She nodded, and then something occurred to her. 'It's a bit like Jane Austen,' she said. 'She was engaged once. Not for long, though. They think it probably lasted about twelve hours.'

'Like your engagement, then?' Dan said.

'I know. Isn't it weird?' Robyn said, realising the similarities for the first time.

'So what happened to Jane Austen?' Dan asked, and he looked genuinely interested.

'Well, she'd accepted a proposal from a rich man called Harris Bigg-Wither. He was even richer than Mr Darcy, and she and her mother and sister would have been looked after for life. But she changed her mind in the morning and withdrew her acceptance.'

'Why?'

There was a sadness in Robyn's eyes as she answered him. 'I think she said yes with her head but no with her heart.'

'Like you?'

'I said yes because I was scared of what Jace would do if I said no.'

'But you're not scared now?'

'No,' she said.

There was a moment's pause.

'I can't see that ever having worked out,' Dan said. 'Between Jane Austen and that guy, I mean. Can you imagine? *Pride and Prejudice* by Jane Bigg-Wither!'

'I know. It's a terrible name for a writer, but everyone thinks that she wouldn't have written at all if she'd married.' Robyn inwardly sighed in relief at the ease with which they were talking again.

'So it all worked out for the best?' Dan said.

'From a reader's point of view, I guess it did.'

'Things usually do, you know.'

'What?' she said.

'Work out for the best.'

Robyn nodded. 'Anyway, Jace has gone.'

'Back to Yorkshire?' Dan asked.

'I hope so. I don't think I could handle another of his surprise visits,' she said.

There was another pause where they stood staring at each other, inching around the subject with caution.

'Are you okay?' Dan asked at last.

'Everyone keeps asking me that,' Robyn said.

'That's because everybody cares.'

'I'm not going to break, you know.'

'I know that,' he said and he gave her a little smile. 'Look, I wanted to say sorry about last night.'

'Me too,' Robyn said.

'I was just worried about you. I knew you weren't happy, and I wanted to protect you.'

'You sound like Colonel Brandon,' Robyn said.

Dan frowned.

'*Sense and Sensibility*,' Robyn explained. 'He's forever rescuing one of the heroines, Marianne Dashwood.'

'Ah,' he said.

'But I don't need rescuing,' she said. 'I can look after myself.'

He nodded. 'I know.'

Robyn reached out and gave Poppin a pat. He was standing patiently as the two of them wrestled awkwardly with their emotions.

'I've got your book,' Dan said suddenly. '*Pride and Prejudice*. I finished it last night.'

'Really?'

'Couldn't sleep. I got up and made a cup of that dreadful chamomile tea and sped through to the end.'

'What did you think?'

'It still tastes of wee.'

'No!' Robyn said. 'Not the tea! What did you think of the book?'

'Brilliant! Really brilliant. Had me hooked. Couldn't wait to see if Darcy and Elizabeth were going to get together after his bungled proposal.'

'I know!' Robyn said. 'Every time I read it, I always feel sure they're never going to get together after all the awful things they've said to each other.'

'But they do,' he said.

'Yes.' Robyn's eyes met his. 'They do.' For a moment, she thought that Dan was going to rush forward and kiss her. His eyes looked at her with intensity, and she longed to feel that warmth and excitement that she felt when they embraced, but he stood perfectly still and she looked down at the ground, trying to calm herself before she spoke again.

'I've actually come to ask you something,' she said.

'Oh?'

'Would you like to go to the ball with me?'

'Pammy's ball?'

'It's tonight.'

'I know. I usually try to make sure I'm out of the way.'

Robyn looked disappointed.

'It's just that Pammy always tries to rope me in to dance with all the old dearies. You know how it is at these things—the women always outnumber the men.'

'I know,' Robyn said, 'which is why I'm here to bag myself a partner.' She grinned, and he grinned back at her.

'I'm a terrible dancer,' he said.

'So am I,' she said. 'We're being taught some of the dances later this afternoon, but I'll be sure to forget them by this evening.'

'Then we'll be treading on each other's toes?'

'Most definitely,' she said.

'Sounds great,' he said. 'I'll see you later then.'

Robyn gave Poppin one last pat and then left the stable block with a veritable spring in her step.

⁓

After a session of Jane Austen Scrabble in which Doris Norris managed to place the word *wax* on a triple word score, everybody met in the library for dance lessons led by Grace Kaplan, a sprightly sixty-year-old who could turn even the most reluctant dancer into a Regency John Travolta in the space of ninety minutes. Dame Pamela had rushed out to the stables and insisted that Dan take part too, so Robyn and Katherine were amongst the lucky few who had male partners.

Katherine tied her hair back and was looking forward to following in the dainty footsteps of some of her favourite heroines, but she noticed that Warwick was still not quite himself.

'It'll be fun,' she said to him, squeezing his hand in hers as they lined up for the first dance.

'Oh, I know,' he said, flashing her a quick smile that seemed all surface and no substance. She followed his line of vision to the driveway outside.

'Are you expecting someone?' she asked.

'What?'

'You keep looking outside. I was wondering if you're expecting someone.'

'Me? No.'

'Oh,' she said. 'You just seem a little distracted.'

'No I'm not,' he said, turning his attention to her again.

'You're not hiding something from me, are you? A Lucy Steele isn't going to suddenly come crawling out of the woodwork, is she?'

'Lucy Steele?'

'Edward Ferrars's secret fiancée,' Katherine said with a little stab at humour.

'Oh, yes. Of course,' he said, and then he seemed to realise what she was getting at. 'Good grief, no!' he said. 'What do you take me for?'

'Not a married man, I hope!' she said with a laugh, but she was secretly remembering her horror at having found out the truth about David.

'Me—married? You must be joking!' Warwick said.

'Well, that's all right then,' Katherine said and they turned their attention to Grace, who proceeded to give them a set of instructions more complicated than the Dashwood family tree.

By the end of the session, everyone was gasping for a cup of tea. Toes had been stepped on and fingers had been crushed in pursuit of Austensian perfection, and now most of the participants were able to execute rather accurate versions of several country dances. Even Dan managed to surprise himself, contorting his tall frame into any number of elegant movements, much to the envy of all the women who did not have the fortune of being his partner.

'Is he your new beau, then?' Doris Norris asked Robyn once Dan had left the library to return to the stables.

'We're just good friends,' Robyn said.

Doris Norris smiled. 'Just good friends. Like Emma and Mr Knightley, eh?' she said with a chuckle.

Robyn blushed, and it was then that she realised that there were decisions to be made. Her relationship with Jace was well and truly over, but was she really ready to leap into another one?

Chapter 34

THE SUMPTUOUS SPLENDOUR OF THE SUNDAY NIGHT DINNER was partially eclipsed by the promise of the Purley Ball later that evening. It was the only thing people were talking about and Robyn couldn't help being excited at the prospect of dancing with Dan all evening. She was thankful that he was still talking to her after all that she'd put him through. What a weekend it had been, but she wasn't going to think about any of that tonight, and she wasn't going to worry about what would happen tomorrow when she had to leave Purley and catch the train back up to Yorkshire.

She couldn't wait to go upstairs and put on the dress she'd chosen. An hour before dinner, Dame Pamela turned the library into a wonderful sort of dressing room where rail upon rail of wondrous Regency-inspired dresses and outfits had been wheeled out of storage. Katherine hadn't been sure if they were historically accurate or not, but they were certainly beautiful.

Robyn chose a dress in a lovely shade of rose pink with pretty puff sleeves and a silky ribbon tied under the bust, and Katherine chose a traditional white, its square neckline daringly low cut and trimmed with silver braiding. Warwick resisted Katherine's urges to don a pair of breeches and a cravat but gave in to wearing a fine waistcoat in a thick duchess satin over his own choice of shirt and trousers.

Of course it wasn't compulsory to choose a costume—guests could wear what they wanted—but the chance to wear something that made you feel as if you'd stepped right out of the pages of an Austen novel was too good an opportunity to miss, and there'd been a mad scramble for the prettiest gowns.

It was going to be a hugely romantic Regency affair and after dinner was over and everybody changed, walking down the staircase in their peacock splendour, they all made their way towards the Great Hall. It was a room that new guests to Purley had not yet seen. The huge white double doors that had remained closed over the weekend were flung open to receive everyone, and the room was greeted with gasps of delight as they entered. The walls were peach coloured, the white plasterwork was stunning, and the ceiling was embossed with thick whorls with cupids firing their arrows at the guests below. At its centre hung an enormous chandelier. Robyn gazed up into its depths. It looked like a frozen waterfall and sparkled and danced with light.

Everywhere, candles and mirrors reflected the guests and gave the impression that the room stretched to infinity. It was the most beautiful, most over-the-top scene Robyn had ever cast eyes on. She was breathless and speechless. Was this how Catherine Morland felt the night she attended her first ball in Bath? She looked around at the other guests. There was Rose and Roberta, both sporting feathery fascinators that bobbed about whenever they turned their heads. Carla was resplendent in bottle green and gold. Even Mrs Soames managed to look glorious in a lilac satin gown, her fan held over her bosom which was threatening to burst from its Regency confines.

Robyn loved the way that her taffeta dress flowed coolly over her legs and she delighted in the way it rustled as she moved.

A string quartet struck up and filled the space with music, and she saw Grace Kaplan in a stunning sky-blue dress, there to make sure her work that afternoon wasn't wasted and that everyone was up and dancing.

'It's just like the Netherfield ball!' Robyn heard Rose exclaim as she clasped her fan to her chest in delight, and Robyn had to agree with her. It was like a scene from a very expensive movie, and everyone looked like a star that night, not just Dame Pamela Harcourt. Gasps of delight issued forth as she made her entrance. She looked enchanting. Her hair was piled up on top of her head Marie Antoinette-style, and she was wearing a silver dress that sparkled with beads. Diamonds dripped from her ears, throat, and wrists.

'I'm not sure how Austensian she looks,' Roberta said.

'Yes,' her sister Rose agreed. 'More ostentatious than Austen, I think.'

Robyn saw Katherine across the room and went to join her, and the two embraced, great smiles plastered on their faces.

'But there aren't enough men!' Katherine said with a sigh.

'Where's Warwick?' Robyn asked her.

'On his way. I knocked on his door but he wouldn't let me in. I'm not sure what he's up to.'

'Oh, I think I know,' Robyn said, nodding to the other side of the room as Warwick made his entrance.

Katherine gasped when she saw him and Robyn smiled in delight.

'I don't believe it!' Katherine said. 'He said he was only going to wear the waistcoat.'

Warwick wasn't wearing just the waistcoat but was sporting the full period works which included a very snug pair of breeches and a cravat that made him look very Darcy-like.

'Don't say a word,' he told Katherine as he approached her, waving a finger of warning lest she was about to laugh at him.

'But you look wonderful,' she told him.

Robyn watched as the two of them embraced and took to the floor.

'Where's your lovely young man, then?' Doris Norris asked, appearing at Robyn's elbow. She was wearing a pretty gown in primrose yellow and a lovely cameo necklace.

'We split up,' Robyn said.

'I know that,' Doris said. 'I meant that hunky young man from the stables.'

Robyn's eyes swept the floor in embarrassment. 'I don't know,' she said.

'What do you mean? There he is!' Doris announced, and Robyn looked up and saw him.

'Dan!' she said softly. He, too, was in authentic costume, except his was more Captain Wentworth than Mr Darcy. He was wearing a deep navy and gold jacket with bright buttons and thick gold braiding along the collar and sleeves. His hair looked even brighter than usual, and his appearance caused an instant stir in the women.

'You can't beat a man in uniform,' Doris said, her cheeks turning quite pink as she took in the wondrous sight before her. 'If only I were a little younger—say forty years younger. My, would he be in trouble!'

Robyn stood completely still. She'd stopped breathing, and it had nothing to do with the tightness of her dress.

'Good evening, Robyn,' Dan said as he approached her with a little bow.

Robyn bobbed him a curtsey. 'I've always wanted to do that!' she said with a smile.

He smiled back at her and then took her hand and led her to the dance floor.

◦◦◦

Warwick looked around the Great Hall not noticing the beauty of the room, noticing only the absence of a certain person. Where was she? This was awful. She could turn up at any moment, and he had to be ready to intercept her.

'Warwick?'

'Yes?' he said, turning to face Katherine.

'You okay?'

'I'm fine,' he said. 'Fine.' He nodded. 'I'm sorry. I'm not being very good company, am I?'

'Well, you do seem a little preoccupied.'

He took a deep breath. 'You look beautiful,' he said, noticing the way her white dress clung to and flowed over all the right places. 'Really beautiful.' He leant forward and kissed her cheek.

'Warwick! Everyone will see!'

'Good! It's our last night here, and I don't want to have to pretend that you're not the most enchanting woman in the whole room and I'm totally besotted with you.' He watched as Katherine blushed. She really did that beautifully, like a heroine in one of his novels. 'Come on,' he said. 'Let's dance.' He held his hand out, and that's when he saw her. She was a wire-thin woman with short spiky red hair, and she was wearing a little black dress that didn't even bother nodding to the Regency period.

'Nadia,' he said quietly.

'What?' Katherine said. 'You know that woman?'

'No,' he said. 'I mean, yes. Sort of.' He shook his head in confusion. 'I've got to speak to her. Wait here. I'll be right back.'

'Warwick!' Katherine shouted after him, but he was already pushing his way through the crowded dance floor, a frown deeply carved on his forehead.

'Ah, Warwick!' Nadia shouted as she saw him approach. 'How are you?' They air kissed, and he gasped as he smelt the alcohol on her breath. 'Get me a drink, won't you, darling?'

He grabbed her arm and took her to one side. 'What are you doing here?' he asked.

'Whatever do you mean? I told you I was coming down.'

'Yes, I know—to see Dame Pamela.'

'And to come to the ball. I'm not going to miss all this, am I?'

He shook his head. 'I don't think we should be here together.'

'Why not? What's wrong with an agent spending some quality time with her author?'

'Because I'm not an author here,' Warwick said through gritted teeth. 'And we've got to decide who you are. You can't be my agent—I'm an antiquarian.'

'Warwick, what on earth are you talking about?' she said. 'Be a darling and get me drink. One of those nice bright cocktails over there,' she said, nodding towards a waitress holding a large tray of jewel-like drinks.

'Don't you think you've had enough already?'

Nadia hiccupped. 'Well, I may be a little merry, but I've only just started.'

Warwick shook his head.

'Don't worry. I won't drive home tonight if you're worried about me. It's just been a long week, and I want to let my hair down a bit.'

'But nobody knows who I am here. You do understand that, don't you?'

Nadia nodded, but she really didn't seem to be listening to him, and it was then that she saw Dame Pamela.

'Ah! Do excuse me, Warwick, darling. There's dear Dame Pamela, and I've got this bloody script to off-load onto her.'

'Nadia!' Warwick called after her, but it was no use; she'd gone.

This was a nightmare, Warwick thought. An absolute nightmare.

Chapter 35

ROBYN WAS QUITE BREATHLESS AFTER JUST HALF AN HOUR OF dancing. She'd worried about feeling the cold in her flimsy gown, but the dancing and the heat from the candles was enough to keep any heroine warm, and when she glimpsed her reflection in one of the mirrors, she saw that her face was glowing.

She'd never realised how complicated dancing could be and now had a new respect for the women in her favourite novels. There were so many things to remember: where to put your hands, how to hold your arms, which way to turn and of course—the real reason for dancing—to converse with your partner. At first, the only words Robyn and Dan exchanged were 'whoops' and 'sorry,' but it was all enormous fun, and the music was almost completely drowned out by the sound of everybody laughing.

Robyn knew that if she hadn't been concentrating so hard on the movements, she would have spent the whole time gazing at Dan. She already thought him the most handsome man she'd ever met but in his Regency naval uniform, he looked so much like a hero from a novel that she was spellbound.

I'm Anne Elliot and he's my Captain Wentworth, she kept thinking as they glided across the floor together, the light from a thousand candles dazzling her eyes. She was having a great deal of fun with him. They chuckled their way through the cotillion, giggled throughout the quadrille, and sighed in delight during the waltz.

'I don't ever want this evening to end,' she said as they drew breath between dances.

Dan clasped her hand in his and brought it to his lips. 'It doesn't have to,' he said.

On the other side of the room, Warwick was wishing the evening would hurry up and end. He'd drunk two cocktails in quick succession and was wondering where he could get a whiskey, when Katherine approached him.

'Hey,' she said, her smile bright but concerned. 'I was wondering where my partner had got to. I've just had to endure a dance with the vicar, and I don't think my toes will ever recover.'

'I'm sorry,' he said, but he didn't want to move because he had a very good view of Nadia and could keep an eye on her. The only problem was, with all the drink he'd been consuming, he was in desperate need of the toilet.

'Are you sure you're okay?' Katherine asked.

He nodded. 'Look, I just have to nip out for one minute, but I'll be right back and after that, we can dance. Okay?'

Katherine smiled. 'Okay,' she said.

He left the Great Hall and hurried along the corridor to the downstairs cloakroom. He had to be as quick as humanly possible. He didn't want to leave Katherine and Nadia in the same room together for longer than was absolutely necessary, although it was highly unlikely that they'd find each other.

'Why should they?' he said, trying desperately to reassure himself. Still, he didn't want to take any chances and hurried back to the Great Hall faster than Lydia's elopement.

～

Katherine had enjoyed all but one dance so far, her partners varying from elderly women to the local vicar, who'd obviously been invited to make up the numbers of men, and not because of his prowess as a dancer. It was terribly thirsty work, and she spotted the very tempting cocktails across the room and headed towards them.

There was a woman in a black dress standing by the table. She had strikingly spiky hair and beamed Katherine a smile.

'Aren't these *heaven*?' she said to her.

'This is my first,' Katherine explained, 'but they do look rather wonderful.'

'I've been looking forward to this evening,' the woman said. 'It's been a long, hard week.'

Katherine looked at her and noticed that her eyes were red. Was it from staring at a computer screen all day or was it from the effect of one too many cocktails? she wondered.

'I'm Nadia,' she said, extending the hand that wasn't clasping her glass.

'Katherine.'

'And you've been here at the conference?'

Katherine nodded. 'I gave a talk this morning.'

'Oh, what about?'

'Marriage in Jane Austen's novels.'

'Ah!' Nadia said. 'The wise and the foolish?'

'Yes,' Katherine said.

'And are you married?'

Katherine blinked. It was rather a forward question. 'No, I'm not,' she said.

'Me neither. No time for all that nonsense. Men are fine as work colleagues but I wouldn't want to take one home with me. Apart from the husband, you understand.'

Katherine smiled.

'Having said that,' Nadia continued, 'they do have their uses, such as dance partners and there's a terrible dearth of them here.'

'Every year, I'm afraid,' Katherine said. 'Dame Pamela does her best to bring them in from the surrounding villages. I've been dancing with the vicar.'

Nadia gave a throaty laugh. 'I'm actually looking for a man myself,' she said. 'A very particular man I seem to have lost.'

'Oh? What's his name?' Katherine asked.

'Warwick.'

'Warwick?'

Nadia nodded. 'You know him?'

'Yes,' Katherine said. 'I do.' She then remembered that it was this woman Warwick had wanted to talk to earlier.

'I seem to have lost him in the scrum.'

Katherine looked around the room, but Warwick hadn't yet returned. 'Well, he told me he was coming right back.'

'Good, good!'

Katherine took a sip of her drink. 'So are you two friends?' she prodded, curious as to how Warwick knew this spiky-haired, cocktail-swigging woman.

Nadia shook her head. 'Well sort of. I guess you could call us friends although he really didn't want me here today. I must say, he can be a little peculiar at times. He values his private time, you see, and I keep forgetting that and come barging right into it.' She paused for a sip of her drink. 'I guess it's more of a working relationship with us too.'

'Oh, you're an antiquarian too?' Katherine said.

Nadia frowned. 'An antiquarian? Good gracious, no! I'm his literary agent.'

Katherine frowned. 'Literary agent?'

Nadia nodded. 'I've represented him for years.'

'I didn't know he wrote,' Katherine said, looking perplexed. She glanced over at the door and saw that Warwick was back in the room but he'd managed to get waylaid by Mrs Soames and couldn't get away.

'No, you wouldn't,' Nadia said. 'It's a big secret, you see.' She giggled and Katherine was sure she could see the bubbles from the cocktail rising in her eyes. 'But I've said too much. *Much* too much,' she said, waving her finger in front of her face as if it might shush her.

'He's a writer?' Katherine said. 'Warwick's a writer?' She was posing the question to herself as much as to Nadia, slowly recognising the signs she'd been seeing all week. She recalled the notebook she'd seen in his bedroom. It was nothing to do with his business as an antiquarian at all, was it? It was a writer's notebook. But why hadn't he told her he was a writer? She loved books—he knew that. She would have loved to have known that he was a writer. Why had he kept it hidden from her?

'Nadia,' she said, 'I've got to know more. What sort of things does Warwick write?'

Nadia shook her head in an exaggerated manner. 'No, no! I can't say. I simply *can't* say! No, no, *no!*'

'Is it fiction?'

Nadia's lips disappeared but her head was nodding.

'He writes fiction?'

'I didn't say anything,' Nadia said, hiccupping dramatically. 'I did not say *anything*.'

'But I would've seen his name, surely,' Katherine said. 'I mean, I read a lot of fiction. I virtually live in bookshops and I spend hours browsing online. I would have noticed a name like Warwick.' Her eyes suddenly widened. 'He doesn't write under his own name, does he?'

Nadia looked startled, her eyes pink with too much alcohol. 'I didn't say that. You can't assume anything. He's sworn me to secrecy and it's quite the best secret in the publishing world.'

'Why's it a secret? Lots of writers use pseudonyms.' Katherine's brow furrowed in contemplation. Why would Warwick use a pseudonym? Did he value his privacy? Or was he writing something he didn't want to admit to? Perhaps he wrote Jane Austen sequels and that was why he was at the conference. He was a huge Austen fan like herself but maybe he was a bit embarrassed about what he did.

For a moment she thought about their time together at the shop at Chawton. He'd seemed particularly uncomfortable there in front of the books and again during the discussion group when Lorna Warwick's books had been mentioned.

'Lorna Warwick!' Katherine suddenly blurted out the name.

'What?' Nadia looked startled.

'Oh my god!'

Nadia clutched at Katherine's bare arm, her fingers grasping her like a falcon's talons. 'I didn't tell you that,' she said, her lips quivering. 'You can't say that I told you that!'

Katherine's eyes doubled in size. 'I'm right, aren't I?'

'You've got to swear you won't breathe a word.'

Katherine stood perfectly still as if she'd suddenly been pinned to the floor. This couldn't be happening. It must be some misunderstanding. She'd had too many cocktails. The music was too loud. There was too much commotion in the room.

'Warwick Lawton,' Katherine said quietly.

'Lorna Warwick,' Nadia said, nodding energetically.

Chapter 36

Mrs Soames was in full spiel about how shocking it was that there were so few men at the ball.

'You'd think that Dame Pamela would have the situation sorted by now, wouldn't you?'

'Well, it's hardly her fault,' Warwick said, his eyes roving the room in search of Katherine. And Nadia. 'I mean, she can't force men to come along to these things, can she?'

'Dame Pamela can be very persuasive when she wants to,' Mrs Soames said. 'Why couldn't she have invited some of those actor fellows she works with?'

'I expect they're all rather busy,' Warwick said, wondering how he was ever going to break free from the woman.

'You'll dance with me, though?' she said, not waiting for Warwick's answer. He blanched as she took his hands in her great meaty ones and pushed him towards the dance floor.

It wasn't until he was stuck in the middle of a dozen spinning couples that he saw Katherine. He was about to smile at her, but it seemed that she'd already spotted him and she wasn't smiling. He did a full 360-degree spin and Katherine still wasn't smiling. It was then that he saw the reason why. Nadia Sparks was standing next to her.

Katherine's mind was reeling faster than Warwick was spinning on the dance floor.

'You're not going to say anything, are you?' Nadia said, swaying a little.

Katherine didn't respond. She wasn't sure she'd be capable of speech ever again.

'I bet you've even read one or two of his books, eh?' Nadia said, her mood suddenly lifting.

'Yes,' Katherine said. 'One or two.'

'I thought so! And they're marvellous. All marvellous! I don't know why he doesn't make it known. I think it would actually improve sales. Not that he's not selling enough as it is. I just think it would really amuse the public.'

'Yes,' Katherine said. 'It would be highly amusing. Like a kind of experiment.'

'What's that?' Nadia asked.

Katherine wasn't listening. Her heart was hammering too loudly because she caught Warwick's gaze from across the room. Instantly she was struck by nausea, and her vision blurred with hot tears. She put down her drink with a shaking hand and left the room as quickly as she could, pushing through the dancing couples, intent on escape before she could make even more of a fool of herself.

From the middle of the room Warwick saw Katherine leaving. Right before she left, she shot him a look that almost punctured his heart. Her eyes had turned into two deadly weapons.

'Excuse me!' he said, dropping Mrs Soames's fat hands and

fighting his way across the room to where Nadia was standing. Actually she was more slumped against the cocktail table, her eyes half-closed.

'Nadia!' Warwick hissed as he approached her.

'Warrwrrick!' she slurred. 'Where've you breen?'

'What have you been saying?' he demanded.

'What do you mean?'

'To that lady—just now—what did you tell her?'

'Nothing!' she said. 'I've been shaying nothing.'

'You told her, didn't you?'

'I didn't tell her anythring!'

'Don't lie to me, Nadia! I saw the look on her face. You must have told her.'

Nadia didn't say anything. She only swayed a little and hiccupped.

Warwick took it as a full admission. 'You idiot! Have you *any* idea what you've done?'

'What *I've* done? It's not me who's breen hiding his identity and pretending to be a woman. Don't you brame this on me, *Lorna*!' Nadia suddenly swayed alarmingly and grabbed hold of Higgins the butler as he walked by.

'Would madam like a chair?' Higgins asked.

'*Madam* is leaving,' Warwick announced.

'But I've not finished my drink,' Nadia said.

'I'm calling you a taxi to the nearest hotel. You're not staying here a moment longer,' he said, taking the drink from her and placing it on Higgins's tray.

'But Warwick!' she said.

'Please, sir,' Higgins said, 'allow me to do the honours.'

'Would you?' Warwick said, thinking that he'd better go in chase of Katherine rather than hanging around for a taxi.

'Of course, sir. I shall see madam is looked after.'

'You're a marvel, Higgins,' Warwick said, slapping the butler on the back before hightailing it out of the Great Hall.

Chapter 37

Katherine wasn't sure what she was going to do. Her mind was whirring wildly and everything around her seemed to have taken on a dream-like quality, as if this couldn't really be happening to her. Only one thing was certain—she had to get as far away from Warwick as she could. The thought of facing him was too much for her. She couldn't bear it—not after the time they'd shared together.

She shook her head, trying to dispel the images of the nights they spent together. How could she have been so stupid? She never gave herself to a man so easily, and yet she walked right into his trap. She'd never felt as betrayed in her life. Even her relationship with David hadn't ended as badly as this. At least he'd only been hiding a wife and not another complete identity!

Katherine entered the main hallway, the music of the Great Hall fading behind her, and slowed her pace a little. How had everything changed so quickly? The whole evening felt as if it were crashing down around her, and the joy that she'd felt earlier at the ball had vanished, as if it had never existed. Now she felt as if the pretty white and silver dress she was wearing was mocking her, and she determined to get out of it as soon as she could.

She made it as far as the foot of the stairs when Warwick caught up with her.

'Katherine—wait!'

She heard his voice and froze and then slowly—very slowly—she turned around to face him. 'Don't come any closer to me,' she said, holding up a hand to stop him. Her voice didn't sound as if it belonged to her. It was icily cold and strangely distant.

'Look,' Warwick said, raking a hand through his hair which was looking somewhat dishevelled, 'I don't know what Nadia's been saying to you, but—'

'Really? You have *no* idea what we've been talking about?' Katherine said, her voice threaded through with sarcasm.

'I didn't mean that. I mean I think I know what she's told you.'

Katherine nodded. 'Oh, you do? So you don't think I was smart enough to work it out for myself? You think you could have just kept up this charade for as long as you liked and I would never have guessed? Is that what you think?' Her eyes narrowed as she looked down at him from her position on the stairs. She saw him swallow hard. 'You lied to me,' she said, and she could feel her heart racing madly. 'Why did you lie to me?'

He opened his mouth to speak, but no words came out.

'All those things you said to me.'

'I *meant* them! It was all true.'

She shook her head. 'Why don't I believe you? How do I know what the truth is from you? Was this some game of yours? Were you using me to research some plot line of a new book?'

'No!'

'Because that's what it feels like! Right now I'm thinking you've just been using me for some warped writer's experiment. Did you enjoy sounding me out about my opinions when you already knew what my answers would be? Did you get some perverse pleasure from that?'

'No! Katherine, I—'

'I can't believe you abused me like that. How could you? How could you break that trust? All those letters we shared!' Her eyes flashed with tears as she remembered them. 'All those things I told you. I *trusted* you! I told you things I've never told anyone else in my life because I thought you were my friend.'

'But I am your friend—*listen* to me!'

Katherine wouldn't be interrupted. 'I thought you were Lorna.'

'But I *am* Lorna,' Warwick said.

Katherine shook her head. 'I bet you were laughing at me behind my back. "There goes Katherine the Gullible." *God!* What a fool I've been! I can't believe I didn't see what was going on. It was so blindingly obvious! I mean, you kept talking about your own books, didn't you? Trying to get me to praise them, for heaven's sake! There were so many things I should've picked up on. I even found your notebook.'

'What?'

'Yes—you were stupid enough to leave it out in your room, and I flipped through it. I shouldn't have, I know that, and I don't know what made me do it, but I thought it was something to do with your antiquarian business.' She gave a laugh that was as far away from being amused as it was possible to get and then she fixed him with dark eyes that were brimful of hurt. 'Do you know what the worst thing about all this is, the thing that hurts the most? You quoted me from my letters, didn't you? I remember it now. You quoted something I wrote to you. And here I was thinking that we were so alike, that we had the same thoughts.' A rebellious tear spilled down her cheek before she had time to stop it. 'And I fell in love with you!'

'Katherine!' he said, his voice filled with anguish. He took a step towards her up the stairs, but she held up her hand again as if she were trying to ward off something inherently evil.

'Why didn't you tell me you were Lorna Warwick? You should have told me. I had a right to know, didn't I?'

He looked at her and for a moment she thought she could see tears in his eyes too.

'I didn't know how,' he said. 'I really wanted to, but nobody knows about it. When you started writing to me, it was fun. I had no idea the letters would continue and that we'd become such good friends. It was a wonderful surprise to me—it really was. But it also made things difficult because I began to fall in love with you, Katherine, and I didn't know what to do.'

'Don't lie to me! I don't want any more lies!'

'I'm not lying. You've *got* to believe me.'

'Why?'

'Because it's the truth. I fell in love with you months ago, and I didn't know what to do about this weekend. Remember you asked me if I was coming? But you were asking Lorna. You weren't expecting *me*. And when I arrived, I tried to talk to you, but you kept brushing me off. I had to get to know you as *me*.'

'And that's why you started using my letters? Bowling me over with how much we had in common?'

'But it's all true. We do have all those things in common; you know we do.'

'I don't know anything anymore!' Katherine said. 'I don't even know what to call you.'

'Warwick. I'm Warwick.'

They stared at each other for a moment in silence, the sound of laughter and music faint in the background from the Great Hall. Everyone else was enjoying themselves.

'You're Warwick,' Katherine said. 'But where's Lorna? Where's the woman I was writing to?'

'She's right here,' Warwick said, his hand on his heart. 'I'm here.'

Katherine shook her head. 'I told her all my secrets.'

'And they're safe with me.'

'I trusted you. I trusted the person I was writing to.'

'I know,' Warwick said. 'And I'm so sorry if I betrayed that trust.'

'If? *If?*'

Warwick hung his head in shame. 'I didn't know what to do so I just kept writing to you. I had no idea this would happen. You've got to believe me.'

She stared at him and then slowly shook her head before turning around. 'I don't want to hear any more.'

'Katherine! Listen to me. This is crazy. *Katherine!* Don't walk away from me. We're best friends, for God's sake! You can't throw that away.'

'I didn't throw it all away!' she said, stopping for a moment to face him. '*You* did!'

'There was nothing else I could've done. Tell me what I should've done.'

'You should have told the truth!'

'When? At what point would you have listened? When we first met here? You would have thought I was a mad man! When I was in bed with you? Would you have stayed? Tell me that! Because I don't think you would have.'

'And when were you planning on telling me? How long could this have gone on for?'

'I don't know,' Warwick said. 'All I know is that we're good together. I've never met anyone like you. You've changed every-thing for me, Katherine. Before I met you, I was just a writer with a string of hopeless relationships that never went anywhere. But then you wrote to me and I swear, my life changed gears. It sounds corny, and I'm not putting this very well—I'm a better writer than I am a speaker—but you gave me something to look forward to. Your letters became my whole life. I couldn't write in the mornings before the postman had called, and then I'd have to answer your letters straightaway. I've never had that experience before in my life, and I know you feel the same way too. I *know* you do.'

Katherine, who had been racing up the stairs, suddenly stopped. She turned to face him and almost crashed into him. 'Don't! I can't listen to any more of this.'

'Please—' he reached out to touch her arm, but she pulled away from him.

'No,' she said, and there were tears in her eyes again. 'Leave me. Just leave me.'

Chapter 38

ROBYN HAD DANCED HERSELF DIZZY, AND HER COMPLEXION was the colour of deep red roses. Still the music continued, and Dan spun her around until she felt featherlight and in danger of floating away.

'You okay?' he asked her.

'I think I need one of those fans,' Robyn gasped. 'I've overheated.'

'How about a turn around the gardens?' Dan suggested.

'You sound just like a Jane Austen character,' Robyn said with a giggle, and the two of them left the room together.

It felt good to be out in the garden. The cool October night air felt wonderfully refreshing on Robyn's bare arms, and she breathed deeply, something she'd forgotten to do when she was spinning around the dance floor.

'I've never danced so much in my life,' Robyn said.

'Me either,' Dan said.

'Did you dance much in London?'

'Are you kidding?'

'You didn't go clubbing?' Robyn asked.

'Do I look like the sort who goes clubbing?'

'Well, not here when you're mucking out the horses,' she said.

'And not there either. I was the workaholic, remember? I'd stay in the office until the cleaners threw me out and then grab some awful takeaway on the way home. It wasn't much of a life, really.'

'And you're not bored here in the middle of Hampshire after London?'

Dan laughed. 'No way! There isn't a moment to be bored with all the horses and dogs to take care of and even if there were, I'd fill it with walking and riding. There's so much to see around here. It's so beautiful.' He smiled. 'People don't talk about Hampshire much. It's not in the same league as the Lake District or the Cornish coast, is it? You don't hear people saying they're going to Hampshire for their holidays but it's a beautiful county. I love the gentleness of the hills and the long, wide rivers. I don't think I could live anywhere else now.'

Robyn smiled. She liked listening to him talk about Hampshire. It was the birthplace and resting place of her dear Jane Austen, after all. But her smile soon faded as she remembered that she'd have to leave it all behind the next day.

They walked around the house until they were in the gardens at the back of Purley. Robyn could smell the scent of late roses on the night air.

'Tomorrow's your last day,' Dan said, making Robyn flinch. It was as if he had read her mind.

'Don't!' she said. 'I don't want to think about that.'

They walked for a few moments, neither talking. An owl hooted in the distance, a long mellow sound, and a little breeze played with Robyn's curls.

'Robyn,' Dan said at last. 'I need to know.'

'What?'

'Are you really going?'

She stopped walking and turned to look at him. 'I've got to. My home—'

'Don't go.'

'Dan!'

'Stay. Stay with me.'

'What? In the stable block? With your dogs and my chickens?'

'Why not?' he said, taking her hands in his and squeezing the very life out of them.

'You're crazy!' she said.

'Crazy about you,' he replied.

Robyn didn't know what to say. It was all too much for her. She'd looked forward to this weekend, and it had exceeded all her expectations; it really had, but then there'd been the stress of having Jace there and the terrible proposal and breakup and the unexpected confusion of falling in love with Dan, she thought.

'We'll find a way,' Dan continued. 'Pammy's got more land than she can shake a script at. There's room for you and a thousand chickens.'

She looked up at him. His face was gentle and earnest. 'But my home's in Yorkshire, not here.'

'Like mine was in London, but it's here now, and I want you here with me.'

'But you hardly know me!'

Dan frowned. 'But I *do* know you. Okay, I might not have known you long, but does that really matter? I only know that it feels right with you.'

Robyn sighed. 'It's just—this is all so unexpected. I mean, I came here with Jace.'

'And you were going to break up with him, which you did,' Dan pointed out.

'I know.' They started walking again, across the grass towards the lake. 'I've not had time to come to terms with all this yet,' she said as she gazed up at the moon. There were a few shreds of thin cloud scudding across the sky and its light wasn't as bright as the prior night.

'What do you need to come to terms with?' Dan asked.

'Everything!' she said. 'You. Me. Jace. I've never been single, you see. I've been with Jace since school, and it's going to be strange being on my own when I get home. I know I've been unhappy with him and we didn't really spend that much time together, but he was always there.'

'And now *I* always want to be there,' Dan said, catching up her hands and spinning her around. 'Always. Always. *Always!*'

Robyn felt like Marianne being spun by Willoughby in the film version of *Sense and Sensibility* as she completed circles before crashing into Dan. They were both laughing.

Finally, once some semblance of normality had settled, Robyn sighed. 'I have to go home,' she said. 'I have to be me for a while. I have to think.'

Dan swallowed and then nodded. 'I don't want you to go, but I know you have to.' He reached out a hand and stroked her hair. 'I'll drop you at the station.'

Robyn shook her head. 'It's okay. I'll get a taxi with the others.'

'You don't want a lift? I can take you on Perseus if you'd prefer.'

Robyn smiled. 'Can we say good-bye tonight? I think it would be easier.'

Dan took a moment before answering her. 'Easier for you, perhaps.'

She took his hands in hers. They were warm, and she knew she never wanted to let go of them.

But I must, she told herself.

'I'm sorry,' she said, 'but I've got to have some time to myself.'

'I know,' he said. 'Can I at least kiss you good-bye?'

She nodded and closed her eyes as his lips met hers.

It was the sweetest kiss she'd ever had, and it took all her courage and resolve to leave him, to walk back to the house without looking around to where she'd left him standing in the shadowy moonlit garden.

~

Alone in her room, Katherine held her head in her hands. Her breaths were shallow and frequent, but she was managing to keep the tears at bay. Had everything really happened or had she had one cocktail too many and imagined it? Warwick Lawton was Lorna Warwick. Lorna Warwick was Warwick Lawton. How had she not seen it? She'd even made a comment about his unusual name and how it was like Lorna Warwick's. For goodness sake, how had she not guessed? She even started writing a letter to Lorna when she'd—or rather *he'd*—been sleeping in her bed!

She flopped down on the edge of her bed and kicked off her shoes and then stood up to take her dress off. How happy she'd been just a couple of hours before when she was getting ready for the ball! How happy and how naïve, she thought.

How could Warwick have done that to her? Had he no heart? How could he have flirted with her so mercilessly and made her fall in love with him?

Katherine closed her eyes. She couldn't believe it. She'd let it happen again—she'd given her heart to a man only to be deceived.

Her mind spiralled back over the previous few days and she remembered opening Warwick's notebook and half recognising the handwriting. Of course! It was the same writing as Lorna

Warwick's letters, except a little more rushed and scrawled. Why hadn't she seen it? All the clues had been screaming at her. Had she deliberately chosen to ignore them?

What hurt her more than anything was the fact that she believed him so absolutely. They'd only been together for such a short time but she sincerely believed that there'd been a connection between them. She felt safe with him and she felt loved. Had that all been an act? Was she just part of some warped writer's experiment? And when exactly had it all started, with her first letter or at some point after that? Had Warwick come to Purley with the express purpose of deceiving her? The thought was too awful to bear.

Suddenly there was a knocking on her door.

'Katherine?' Warwick's voice called from the landing. 'Katherine? Let me in! We need to talk.' He knocked again and when there was no reply, tried the handle, only to find it locked. '*Please!* You've got to give me a chance to explain.'

Explain? What did he want to explain? That he used her? She *knew* that!

'Go away, Warwick,' she said quietly, too quietly for him to hear, and then she sat perfectly still, closing her eyes and her mind to his knocking and his words until—finally—he left her.

Still she remained sitting on the bed, not quite knowing what to do, but then she got up and found her mobile and placed a quick call to the local taxi firm. She felt rude to be leaving without saying good-bye to everyone, especially Dame Pamela and Robyn, but it was the only thing she could do.

Chapter 39

WARWICK WOKE UP WITH A HEADACHE THAT HAD NOTHING to do with alcohol. He groaned and rolled over, wishing he could fall asleep again but knowing it would be impossible. He had to try to speak to Katherine again.

Leaping out of bed, he took a shower and shaved and dressed, and then he left his room with the speed of a man on a mission. It was still early and he was grateful that there was nobody around to stop his progress. He really couldn't handle an encounter with the ebullient Doris Norris or the insufferable Mrs Soames.

It took him only seconds to reach Katherine's room, but he instantly knew that something was wrong because her door had been left open with the key hanging in the lock.

'Katherine?' he called, inching his way inside. The curtains were open and the bed was made, and he knew in an instant that it hadn't been slept in. Katherine had left.

He walked across to the window and looked out over the gardens and down to the lake. There was no getting away from it— he'd screwed up big time. How on earth was he going to sort this one out? And was it something that could be sorted out? He wasn't at all sure it was. It was more complicated than any of his plots.

At least if they got too complicated, he could go back and delete things. You couldn't do that with life. There was no Delete button to help you erase an awkward scene. You couldn't hit Backspace to get rid of all the rubbishy bits. You had to live with the decisions you made.

Warwick leant his head against the window, feeling the cool glass against his skin. Katherine would never forgive him, would she? Well, he couldn't blame her. Being a writer, he was good at seeing things from other people's perspectives, and he could perfectly understand why she'd never want to see him or hear from him again—*ever!* He also knew that he couldn't live with that thought. He loved her. He'd never loved anyone more than her, and he was profoundly sorry that she'd become entangled in such a god-awful mess.

He had to sort it out. How he'd do it was a mystery to him and certainly one that couldn't be solved before a cup of coffee so he left the room and went downstairs in search of one.

Higgins the butler was the first person he saw when he reached the entrance hall.

'Good morning,' Warwick said. 'Did Miss Sparks get to her hotel all right last night?'

Higgins cleared his throat. 'I'm afraid madam was in no state to go anywhere, sir.'

'What do you mean? She's still here?' Warwick said aghast.

'She is indeed, sir. We thought it best to let her sleep it off so we made up a bed for her in the West Drawing Room.'

'Can I see her?'

'Of course, sir.' Higgins motioned in the direction. 'I'll bring you both some coffee, sir.'

'Thank you,' Warwick said. 'That would be most appreciated.'

Like Jace the night before, Nadia was asleep on the sofa, a thick duvet hiding half her head. Warwick didn't want to disturb her but, at the same time, he wanted to shake her until her head fell off.

'Nadia?' he called.

There was no response.

'Nadia!'

A slight groan rose from the duvet and a pair of bleary red eyes greeted him. He wished the sight of it shocked him, but it didn't because he'd seen it many times before. Her spiky hair stood up around her head in a scary halo, making her look thistle-like, and her lipstick had turned into a scarlet streak across her face. It was not a pretty sight.

'Oh, my head! My poor head,' she complained.

'Your head! You're moaning about your head? What about my heart, Nadia?'

She looked confused. 'What's wrong with your heart? Are you ill?'

'No, I'm not ill,' he said. 'I was being poetic.'

'Well don't be. It's too early in the morning to be poetic. I need coffee.'

'So do I,' Warwick said. 'Higgins is bringing us some.'

'Is he the cute butler?'

'Cute? He's seventy years old!'

'Oh, dear,' Nadia said. 'Perhaps he looked cuter after a few cocktails.'

'Nadia!'

'I think I may have made a pass at him.'

Warwick's head dived into his hands in despair. 'I still can't believe what you said.'

Nadia pushed the duvet away from her body and swung her feet onto the floor. 'I'm so sorry,' she said. 'I don't know what possessed me.'

'Alcohol!' Warwick shouted. 'That's what possessed you! Don't you know what you're like when you drink? For God's sake, Nadia, you're a nightmare. You always do or say something you regret.'

'Do I? Do I really?' She looked genuinely mortified at the thought.
'Yes!'

She reached out and squeezed Warwick's arm. 'Well, maybe it's for the best. I mean, it was bound to come out sooner or later, wasn't it?'

'I'd rather it was later,' Warwick said.

'She seemed like a really nice girl.'

'She was a really nice girl,' Warwick said, 'and you've gone and ruined it!'

'Surely not,' Nadia said. 'You just need to explain things to her.'

'She won't listen to me.'

'Maybe she will this morning, now she's had a night to sleep on it.'

'She left last night.'

'Oh,' Nadia said.

They sat in silence for a moment, Nadia's eyes casting around for her shoes.

'I really love her,' Warwick whispered.

'Oh, Warwick!'

'And I don't know what to do.'

Higgins entered the drawing room with a tray holding two cups of strong black coffee.

Nadia looked up, her face instantly flushed red, and she quickly looked away.

Higgins laid the tray down on a table. 'Your coffee,' he announced unnecessarily, and Warwick noticed that the old butler was blushing too.

Robyn was deliberately taking forever to get showered and dressed. It was the last time she'd wake up in the Cedar Room and the last time she'd enjoy the view out across the lawn.

After putting on a poppy-coloured dress and pinning her silver horse brooch to it, she sat on the window seat, looking out towards the stable block. She could just see the clock tower, and the temptation to leave the house and go see Dan once more was overwhelming.

'But I've said my good-byes,' she told herself and getting up from the window seat, she wheeled her suitcase onto the landing in preparation for departure, taking one last look at the room before heading downstairs for breakfast.

As soon as she entered the entrance hall, she heard raised voices and the figure of Warwick appeared from one of the rooms that led off the hall.

'Katherine's gone, Nadia, and she won't be coming back.'

'Well, she would've been leaving today anyway. What's the big problem?'

Robyn watched as a dishevelled-looking woman followed Warwick.

'Robyn!' he said, looking surprised.

'Katherine's gone?' Robyn said. 'Why did she go?'

'Why?' Warwick's eyes widened alarmingly. 'Why don't you ask this woman?'

'Oh, for pity's sake, *don't* start all that again! My head's throbbing!'

'If you hadn't turned up, Nadia, if you hadn't gone and got drunk like you always do and opened your big mouth—'

'She'd have found out sooner or later,' Nadia said.

Robyn looked from one to the other in deep puzzlement. 'Found out what? Why's Katherine gone?'

The hall was beginning to fill with people on their way to breakfast.

'Katherine's gone?' Roberta said as she and her sister Rose joined Robyn. 'Did she have any breakfast?'

'She left last night,' Warwick said.

'But why?' Rose asked.

'Because she found out the truth,' Nadia said.

'Shut it right now, Nadia.'

'Oh, Warwick, it's out now, isn't it? What's the point in hiding it anymore?'

'Hiding what?' Roberta asked.

Nadia took a deep breath. 'Warwick here is Lorna Warwick.'

'Oh my god!' Warwick yelled, as if he'd been shot.

'Lorna Warwick?' Robyn said. 'I don't understand. How can you be Lorna Warwick?' she asked, turning to face him.

'It's his pen name, silly!' Nadia said. 'He writes as a woman.'

Warwick's mouth dropped open. 'Why not tell the whole world while you're at it? Take out a page in *The Times*!'

'Lorna Warwick?' Doris Norris, who'd just entered the hall along with Mrs Soames and half a dozen others, jostled to the front. '*He's* Lorna Warwick?'

'He certainly is!' Nadia said, suddenly looking very pleased with herself. 'It was my idea, too.'

'*Your* idea?' Warwick cried. 'It wasn't your idea! I submitted my first novel to you as Lorna. You had no idea I was a man until I turned up at the restaurant that day.'

'Of course I knew,' Nadia said, blushing furiously.

'Lorna Warwick?' Doris said above their voices. '*He's* Lorna Warwick?'

'That's what they're saying,' Roberta said.

'Well, I never!' Doris said, her hands flying to her face. 'I simply must get my books signed by her. I mean *him*!'

Suddenly the hall filled with excitement and the sound of footsteps up and down the stairs.

'It's Lorna Warwick!'

'Who?'

'Him! That Warwick fellow!'

Warwick's secret was well and truly out and before he could escape, there was a mad scramble to get books signed by him.

'I bought five!' Doris announced, thrusting the bright paperbacks under his nose. 'Put "To Doris," and let me have my picture with him. Here, Rose, take my camera, will you?'

Warwick was surrounded. There was no escape. The public he'd hidden from for so long were making up for lost time.

Nadia left quickly and quietly, sneaking out as Warwick was crushed by fans. Dame Pamela, who'd been informed of the situation by a perplexed Higgins, finally came to his rescue, leading him up for a quiet breakfast in the privacy of her personal library.

'Goodness! I've never known a weekend like this one before,' she said. 'This room's certainly been made the most of.'

Warwick sat down on the chaise lounge, shaking his head in shame.

'You are a man of mystery, aren't you?' Dame Pamela continued with a big smile. 'I must say, I am surprised.'

He moved to the edge of the chaise as a much-needed cup of coffee was placed in his hands.

'I am so sorry, Dame Pamela.'

Dame Pamela tutted and wagged a finger at him. 'Everyone keeps apologising to me this weekend, and I've no idea why. I'm having an absolute ball. This is the best Jane Austen Conference ever!'

'I feel like I've let everybody down,' Warwick said.

'What do you mean? Everybody *loved* your revelation. They were going mad down there. They feel like they've been let in on the best kept secret in the world.'

'I never meant for this to happen,' Warwick said. 'I'm such a private person. I really don't crave attention for my work.'

'Yes, I don't blame you for shunning the public's attention,' Dame Pamela said. 'It can be wearisome having people clamouring after you all the time for your autograph.'

Warwick sighed. 'That's just the sort of thing I wanted to avoid.'

Dame Pamela nodded sympathetically. 'Now, before you leave, you simply *must* sign my Lorna Warwick books for me. I have them all, you know.'

Chapter 40

ROBYN SAT AT HER DESK AT THE COLLEGE WHERE SHE'D BEEN working for more years than she cared to remember. A window overlooked a courtyard that held industrial-sized bins used by the catering students. Behind that was a canal that was looking a murky grey-green. It wasn't much of a view, but Robyn wasn't really looking at it because she was thinking of a place so beautiful that it wouldn't matter if her little window overlooked a sugar-white beach in the Seychelles.

She was thinking of Purley.

October had slipped into November and it was three weeks since she'd left Hampshire, but it seemed like a whole lifetime ago. She often recalled the last lovely glimpse of Purley from the back of the taxi and downloaded a photograph of it from the Internet and set it as her computer background.

She hadn't seen Dan on the morning of her departure. There was one moment as the taxi driver had been loading her suitcase into the boot when she looked across to the stable block and saw Biscuit racing back and forth after a couple of pigeons but there'd been no sign of Dan. But isn't that what she'd wanted?

Time. She'd asked for time, and now she had it in abundance.

There was no Jace to pick up after at home anymore, and her evenings were hers to do with what she liked. She could sit and read or watch exactly what she wanted, without the fear of an irate boyfriend coming in and putting a foot through the TV.

The funny thing was, Robyn would pick up a book or put a much-beloved film adaptation on and then not really pay any attention to it. The pages would turn but the words wouldn't be fully digested, and Mr Darcy would be just a blur on the TV screen.

It was the same with everything she tried to do. Since coming home to Yorkshire, Robyn walked about in a daze, as if she were drifting, merely going through the motions of her day-to-day life, while with every breath in her body, she wished she were back at Purley. Life was happening all around her, but she wasn't noticing much at all. Take that week for example. She didn't notice buying three bruised bananas from the stall on the market. She didn't notice filing all the *M*'s under *N*. Well, not until Bill Cartwright bellowed at her. And she didn't even notice the blouse that she wore inside out. She had only one thing on her mind, and his name was Dan Harcourt.

She'd spent days—*weeks*—thinking about their time together and agonising over how quickly it had all happened. That couldn't be right, could it? Nothing good could happen that fast, she thought. It must have been one of those holiday romances one hears about—brief, beautiful but unsustainable.

The more she thought about it, the more she believed that her time at Purley had been as fictional as her favourite books. It seemed like a dream world to her, and the feelings she experienced there didn't have a place in the real world.

Now, sitting at her desk in the office, she absentmindedly stroked her silver horse brooch. She pinned it to every outfit she wore—whether it was inside out or not. As she felt its smooth coolness beneath her fingertips, she remembered the panic she had the week before when she misplaced it, and there'd been a frantic search to find it. Everyone in the office had been involved until the work placement student, Samantha, found it at the side of a filing cabinet.

Perhaps that's why Robyn's fingers flew up to it with increasing regularity. She needed to be sure it was there.

That evening, after being released from the restraints of yet another day at the office, she fed the chickens in her back garden, marvelling at how bright their colours looked in the last rays of the sun. Wickham was looking a bit out of sorts as Robyn's toes had been put away until next spring, and Lydia and Miss Bingley were squabbling over some poor beetle in the grass that only just managed to escape their brutal beaks.

Inside, Robyn moped about for a while, picking up her prize copies of the Jane Austen novels she won in the quiz night at Purley.

For a moment she thought about Jace and how he would have teased her at having yet more copies of the famous books. She'd seen him the previous week on the high street. She ducked behind a stall selling dog rugs and he hadn't seen her. He'd been with his mum, and Robyn had a feeling that he always would be.

After she pulled out the white-and-gold copy of *Pride and Prejudice*, her fingers rubbed over the embossed cover and spine. It was perfect, but it wasn't as perfect as her old trusted travelling copy she'd leant to Dan and which was all the more precious to her now because he'd held it in his hands for hours, devouring the words as eagerly as she did. She picked it up, turned to the famous first page, and read the very words Dan would have read. *It is a truth universally acknowledged...*

'That a single girl in possession of a great love must be in want of a complete change of lifestyle,' Robyn said with a little smile.

It was no use. She could ignore it no longer. She'd had enough time being herself in her old house in the old town she was brought up in, doing the old job she'd grown to hate. She didn't belong there anymore, and it was finally time to move on.

Before she could think of a reason not to, Robyn grabbed her conference pack and picked up the telephone, dialling the number on the front cover.

'Purley Hall,' a voice said. It was Higgins, and Robyn had to stop herself from shouting his name in her excitement at hearing him again.

'Higgins, it's Robyn Love. I came to the Jane Austen Conference.'

'Good evening, Miss Love. How may I help you?'

'I was wondering if I could speak to Dame Pamela.'

'I'll see if she's available,' Higgins said and put Robyn on hold.

'Robyn, darling! How are you?' Dame Pamela's voice sang down the line a moment later. 'To what do I owe this pleasure? Everything okay, I hope?'

'Oh, yes, Dame Pamela, but I have a question for you.'

'Fire away, my dear. Fire away.'

'Are you still looking for a PA?'

As Robyn waited to hear the answer, she only hoped that she wasn't too late.

In a quiet corner of West Sussex, Warwick was writing himself silly, with novels and letters. In the three weeks since the Jane Austen Conference, he'd written eighteen letters to Katherine, and all of them had been returned to him unopened. He sent them to her home address as well as care of St Bridget's. After the first six came back, he started getting sly, printing out typed address labels and using different envelopes. It worked, and Katherine obviously opened them, but she still returned them, without a single word of her own added to them.

'Goddamnit!' Warwick cursed, highlighting and deleting a whole page of nonsense he'd just typed. It was his new novel, and it hadn't been going well. Nothing had been going well since he left Purley.

Once word was out about his true identity, his publishers had gone to town, making the most of an excellent PR opportunity, and Warwick was expected to do all sorts of interviews for newspapers, magazines, radio, and television. It had been awful. The only thing he got out of it had been to use these forms of communication to try to apologise to Katherine, hoping against hope that she'd be reading, listening or watching.

'I never meant to hurt anybody,' he told Andre Levinson on his chat show. 'It's just that things got out of hand and I couldn't see a way out.'

'I have some very special readers who mean the world to me,' he told the reporter from the newspaper *Vive!* 'And I hope they stay in touch. I really do.'

He'd received five sacks of fan mail after that story went out, but not a single letter from Katherine.

He finally made the decision to visit her, driving from West Sussex up to Oxfordshire, one day. If she didn't respond to his letters or phone calls, what other choice did he have? But there was no reply at the little cottage, and he spent more than two hours hanging around the garden and pressing his nose up against the windows. He made friends with one of the cats, though, a gorgeous hairy beast that wound his way round his legs and meowed when picked up.

'Who are you, then? Freddie or Fitz?' he asked. The toffee-coloured creature just purred. 'Tell your mistress I'm sorry, will you?' he said, stroking the furry head that she herself must have stroked a thousand times.

After that, he drove in to Oxford but when he tried to get into St Bridget's College, he was told it wasn't open to visitors. He spent an hour walking around the city but its beauty left him cold. There was only one thing of beauty he wanted to see, so he drove back to Katherine's once more. There was a car in the driveway, and he knocked and called until he was hoarse and a next door neighbour came out and glared at him, a dangerous-looking broom in her hand.

The event was thoroughly depressing. He returned to West Sussex and his writing.

Chapter 41

'YOU'RE GIVING US YOUR NOTICE?' BILL CARTWRIGHT ASKED ROBYN.
'That's right,' Robyn said with undisguised glee. 'I'm leaving.'

'But you've been here for…' He paused as he looked through her file.

'Forever,' Robyn finished for him.

'Yes,' he said. 'Why leave now?'

'I'm moving,' she said.

'Leaving Skipton?'

'Yes. I'm going to Hampshire.'

'Hampshire?' Bill Cartwright said sounding the word out as if it were foreign. 'What's in Hampshire?'

'My new life,' Robyn said.

It had been easy to hand in her notice at work and easy to tell her landlord that she was leaving her cottage, but then things got harder. Robyn learnt to drive a long time before, but sold her car shortly afterwards as it was too much of a luxury on an administrator's salary, and she hadn't driven since. All of a sudden, she had to transport herself, all her worldly goods and her chickens down to Hampshire. It was going to take time so while working out her notice at the college, she took a refresher course in driving and bought herself a second-hand van in which she could fit her books, TV, and chickens. A trailer on the back would accommodate their coop.

'Madness,' Judith, her neighbour told her. 'Sheer madness! I didn't mind your finally making a break with that boyfriend of yours, but why you want to leave Yorkshire, I don't know. What can you get in Hampshire that you can't get here?'

Robyn smiled by way of an answer and Judith nodded. 'Oh, I see! Well, I'll keep a lookout for my wedding invitation.'

Finally, after packing up two dozen boxes with her precious books, films, and crockery and persuading her chickens that they really did want to spend the next few hours in a crate in the back of a van, Robyn was ready to leave. Was this how the Dashwood sisters felt on leaving Norland, she wondered as she hopped into the van and took a last look at the little terraced cottage that had served her so well. How strange it was to be leaving, but the last few weeks of thinking and planning had proved one thing to her: she was ready.

As she left North Yorkshire and hit the motorway south of Bradford, she thought again how amazing it would be to actually live in Jane Austen's county. Robyn would be able to visit Chawton whenever she wanted and walk in the same fields and woods as Jane and her sister Cassandra. She could sit in the little church at Steventon, and she could visit Winchester, where Jane spent the final weeks of her life.

But Robyn was a long way from Hampshire at the moment and some strange noises were coming from the back of the van. Robyn pulled over at the next service station. There were a few dogs being walked on a grassy slope, but one couldn't very well do that with chickens, could one?

'You okay, my darlings?' Robyn asked, looking at their thin faces and beady eyes and wondering what was going on in their feathered brains. Her rooster, Wickham, was looking particularly startled and Lady Catherine looked far from pleased but then again, she always looked like that. Robyn threw a bit of bright corn into the crate, but the best thing for all concerned, she decided, was to push on.

It was midafternoon by the time Robyn crossed the border into Hampshire. The late autumn sunshine was surprisingly warm, and she rolled the window down and breathed deeply. The trees had just started to turn colour but cottage gardens still blazed with flowers, joined by a few bright red berries. How Robyn was going to love seeing the changing seasons there! Maybe she could take Moby and Biscuit for long country walks and she and Dan could ride through the countryside together. She would become a marvellously confident horsewoman and bake scones and make jam like women in Hampshire probably did all the time. She'd introduce Dan to her beloved Jane Austen DVDs, and he wouldn't put his foot through the TV screen. It was going to be perfect.

As last she entered the village of Church Stinton and turned into the driveway that led to Purley Hall. How long ago it seemed since Jace had driven her up that very drive, yet it was only a few weeks before, and now here she was in her funny little van, hoping to make this place her home.

She parked the van and got out, stretching her arms towards the sky. Walking around to the back of the van, she opened the doors to let the chickens have a bit of fresh air and made sure they had fresh water.

'Nearly there, my dears,' she said, listening to their funny little chickeny murmurs.

She knew she should let Dame Pamela know she'd arrived safely but the pull of the stable block was too much and she walked towards it with eager feet, a whole meadow full of butterflies rising in her stomach at the thought of seeing Dan again.

It felt good to be out of the van and walking, breathing in the autumn air, and it felt great to be back at Purley again, especially with the knowledge that she was there to stay this time. She wouldn't have to pack and leave as soon as the weekend was over.

The clock on the stable block tower was still reading quarter past two and probably always would. Robyn entered and inhaled the sweet aroma of hay and horse, but nobody was around. The stables were empty. There were no familiar heads hanging over the doors in the hope of having their noses scratched and no mad dogs came charging towards her in waggy greeting.

'Hello?' Robyn called. 'Anyone here?'

Perhaps Dan was indoors. It was late in the day, and maybe he was taking a shower before dinner.

She crossed the yard until she reached the door under the clock tower and knocked on it.

'Dan?' she called, biting her lip. The butterflies had risen in her stomach again as she wondered if he'd truly be pleased to see her.

Of course he will! Don't be silly. He asked you to stay, remember? she told herself.

Yes but that was weeks ago, a little voice told her. *He might have changed his mind. You haven't been in touch, remember?*

But I told him I needed some time to myself. He said he understood, she thought, desperately trying to reassure herself.

Her anxieties were getting the better of her, and when she

called again and there was no reply, she tried the door handle. It opened.

'Dan?'

Silence greeted her, and there were no dogs belting towards her in greeting either. She climbed the stairs, thinking she could always make herself a cup of that chamomile tea and wait for him to return but when she reached the living room, she realised he wouldn't be coming back. The room was empty. The sofa had gone as had the dog baskets and the pictures on the walls and the cookbooks that had lined the little shelves above the sink.

She walked through to the back, opening a door that led into a tiny bedroom but that was empty too.

She was too late.

Chapter 42

ROBYN LOOKED AROUND THE EMPTY ROOMS ONCE MORE AS IF she might have overlooked something. Had he gone back to London? There were no clues, no letter propped up against a mantelpiece, and no forwarding address left anywhere. Why hadn't Dame Pamela said something? Perhaps she thought Robyn wouldn't come to Purley if she knew Dan had left and didn't want to risk losing her new PA.

With legs that felt like lead, Robyn returned to her van. She'd never felt so hopeless, as if all the life had drained out of her. What was she going to do? She'd moved to Hampshire! She left her job and her home, and here she was in the middle of a strange county with just her chickens for company. Sitting on the floor at the back of the van, legs dangling, she wondered if she should just get back in and drive home.

'But I've not got a home,' she told herself.

There was only one thing to do: she *had* to make this work. She still had her new job as a PA, and Dame Pamela had promised her a little cottage on the estate where there was ample room for her chickens. She had to make the best of things, and maybe—just maybe—she'd see Dan again when he visited his sister and they would work things out.

'Miss Love?' a voice broke into her thoughts. It was Higgins, and Robyn smiled when she saw him. He was wearing a russet waistcoat as if in recognition of autumn.

'Hello, Higgins,' she said, jumping out of the van and shaking his hand.

'Good evening, Miss Love. I hope you had a pleasant journey.'

'Very pleasant, thank you.'

'Good. Can I get you some tea? I'm afraid Dame Pamela's been called away from home and can't be here to welcome you, but she wanted me to make sure you had something to eat before you unpack.'

'Oh, that's very kind, but I think I'd better get myself sorted out. My chickens—'

Higgins looked into the back of the van. 'Of course,' he said. 'I'll get your key but you must come up to the house later and have some supper.'

He disappeared for a moment, returning with a bright silver key. 'Horseshoe Cottage,' he said. 'You turn left out of the driveway and follow the road through the village until you come to the church. There's a track to the left. Turn there and drive over the cattle grid. Horseshoe Cottage is the house on the right.'

'Thank you,' Robyn said.

'If there's anything you need, give us a call.'

Robyn nodded and smiled, but the smile faded as soon as she got back in her van. She suddenly felt very tired, and the excitement of coming to Purley had melted away. She took a deep breath and manoeuvred her van and trailer with the skill of someone who'd been doing it much longer than she actually had, careful not to knock into the stone balustrades or reverse onto the immaculate lawn.

Turning out of the driveway, Robyn drove slowly through the

village, passing a row of thatched cottages. She saw the ancient stone church, its spire shooting into the evening sky, and then she spotted the track and slowed down to turn into it. It really was a track rather than a road and was likely to get very muddy during the winter months. Robyn was glad she'd bought a good, practical van, and she made a mental note to buy a new pair of Wellingtons too.

As she rounded a corner, she saw a tiled roof peeping over a large beech hedge. Horseshoe Cottage. It was built in the same rosy red brick as Purley Hall but of course it wasn't on as grand a scale. There was a sweet little porch, and three big sash windows promised the cottage would be light inside.

The first thing Robyn did once she stepped out of the van was to open a little gate that led to the back garden. It was a beautiful space overlooking fields between the cottage and the village. She quickly got to work setting up her chicken coop in a suitable spot and once it was ready, she was finally able to release her darling birds. With great trepidation, the six of them left their crate, necks straining as they ventured outside. Lydia was the first to brave the new surroundings, but the others followed and were soon pecking around at the corn Robyn fed them.

Fishing the front door key out of her pocket, she returned to the cottage and had just entered the porch when she heard the sound of a car coming up the driveway. It was a Land Rover, and the distinct sound of barking came from its open windows.

Robyn watched as the vehicle pulled up and a tall figure emerged.

'Dan!' she cried, rushing towards him and flinging herself at him before she could think of a more respectable, heroine-like way to behave.

'Robyn!' he cried in response, taking her face in his hands and kissing her deeply. When they finally broke apart, Robyn looked up at him, surprise and adoration in her eyes. The sun had deepened his tanned face and arms, and his eyes shone even brighter than ever.

'I thought you'd gone back to London,' she said.

'London? Why did you think that?'

'You weren't in your flat below the clock tower. I didn't know what to think.'

'I was here, getting the cottage ready.'

'You're living here?' she asked, her eyes wide.

'I'm not being too presumptuous, am I?' He suddenly looked very shy. 'I mean, I can move back to the stables if you prefer. It's just… well… Pammy's not very good at keeping secrets. As soon as you rang her to take the job, she came to tell me, and I thought… well… I wanted to be with you. You don't mind, do you? I haven't overstepped the mark?'

Robyn placed her hands in his and smiled up at him. 'I thought I'd lost you,' she said. 'I thought I'd be living here on my own with just my chickens for company.'

'I could hardly bear it when you left Purley,' Dan said. 'It was the worst few weeks of my life not knowing if you were coming back.'

'Did you really think I wouldn't?' she asked.

He squeezed her hands and shook his head. 'I knew we were meant to be together. I knew it from the first time I saw you. You *had* to come back.' He bent down to kiss her once again. 'I love you, Robyn Love!' he said.

'And I love you,' she said.

'Do you want to see your new home, then?'

She nodded and watched as Dan walked back to the car and opened the tailgate. Moby and Biscuit leapt out, jumping around Robyn's legs and barking madly.

'I hope they won't mind the chickens,' Robyn said above the noise.

'They'll be fine,' Dan told her. 'Come on.' He took her hand and they giggled as they both produced front door keys.

'You first,' he said.

'No, you.'

He grinned and opened the door for her but then he stopped, blocking her way. 'There's just one thing I want to ask you,' Dan said.

'What's that?' Robyn asked, suddenly anxious.

'Would you be here right now if I hadn't read *Pride and Prejudice*?'

Robyn hesitated. It was a strange thing to ask her but judging by his expression, he wanted an answer. She swallowed. Would she be here right now if he hadn't read *Pride and Prejudice*?

She smiled. 'But you *did* read it,' she said.

Dan smiled back at her. 'You're right,' he said. 'I did! And do you know what? I think it would make a great film.'

'It *is* a film. It's several films *and* a brilliant TV adaptation.'

'Is it?' he asked.

Robyn nodded.

'I don't suppose you've got it on DVD?'

Robyn laughed. 'If you help me unpack, we might just be able to find one or two.'

Chapter 43

How quickly the months slipped by when one was writing a book! After an almost impossible time, Warwick finally got himself sorted out, shunning further publicity and focussing on the new book. Week after week vanished in a mad flurry of words, until one day, Warwick looked out of his study window and noticed that the lawn was white with frost.

It was the middle of December.

His new heroine was called Katherine and she had pale, luminous skin, dark eyes, and a mass of dark hair that she wore loose over her shoulders. She was strong and intelligent and never let the hero get away with anything. It really was a very thinly disguised character but he couldn't help himself.

'As least my hero gets his happy ending with her,' he said to himself as he looked out across the garden towards a holly hedge stuffed with scarlet berries.

He worked through his novel, the daylight hours shortening until it became necessary to have his desk lamp on throughout most of his working hours. One day when he was hunting for a booklet about a stately home he felt sure would make the perfect house for one of his characters, he came across Katherine's letters. He thought they were safely shut away from view and that they would no longer torment him but when he opened that filing cabinet, all the feelings he felt sure he'd banished came tumbling out again. He still loved her and he missed her more than ever.

His novel forgotten, he sat on the floor of his study with the letters spilled around him and he read them.

> *It was wonderful to get your latest letter. How I look forward to them! They are the highlights of my very dull weeks. Last week I was rereading one in class. I'd hidden it in a copy of* Jane Eyre *so that my students wouldn't see and when I read that bit about that squirrel running off with your sandwich, I burst out laughing! I told my students that they should be focussing on their work and not concerning themselves with what I was doing.*

Warwick smiled as he finished reading the letter and then picked up another one.

> *I know we've been writing to each other for only a short time but I really do feel as if I can tell you things—things that nobody else knows about me. I don't think I've ever trusted anyone as much as I trust you.*

Warwick swallowed hard. He could hardly bear to read those words again, so picked up another letter.

> *Winchester is such a special place. I love it for Christmas shopping and I always go there on the 16th of December because*

that's Jane Austen's birthday. Have you been to the cathedral? Her grave is in the north aisle. It's the most amazing place and draws so many people to it. I love my trips there.

December sixteenth.

Warwick scrambled up from the floor, grabbing his desk diary. That was tomorrow! Katherine was going to be in Winchester Cathedral tomorrow. She couldn't hide from him there like she could in St Bridget's College or her home. She would be in public and in plain view of him. She'd have to talk to him then. She'd *have* to listen to him.

There was only one question hovering in Warwick's mind as he held her letter in his hand. Could Katherine ever forgive him?

How on earth could it be December already? Katherine wondered as she looked out of the train window onto the misty fields of Hampshire. It didn't seem a minute since term had begun in September. Katherine always loved the bright promise of a new academic year and this one had been particularly splendid.

And now it was December. How had that happened?

She sighed. It was strange but although time had flown by in many ways, Purley seemed like a lifetime ago and Katherine had done her very best to banish it from her mind. She spent her time in quiet solitude in her little Oxfordshire village, surrounding herself with books while she researched her next Jane Austen nonfiction title. This one focussed on the letters between Jane and Cassandra, and the wonderfully witty pages she read almost banished Warwick from her mind. Almost but not quite.

There'd been that awful day when he called at her house. She hadn't expected it and hid in the hallway with all the doors shut until her neighbour had come to her rescue.

'I chased him off wiv me broom,' Mrs Rushton told her. 'He didn't look happy to see me, I can tell you!'

Katherine dared to smile at the memory.

Things had gone quiet after that. Warwick's letters stopped and there were no more hammering-on-the-door incidents. Of course she tortured herself rereading his letters and reading them with a new perspective and spying all the little white lies dotted throughout them. How easy it was to see, now, she thought.

But how she missed those letters from Lorna! As Katherine read them again, she couldn't help thinking that all the qualities she'd loved so much in Lorna were actually Warwick's qualities. Or had Warwick faked everything? It was hard to tell the truth from fiction, and Katherine finally gave up trying, but how she missed her old friend and all their wonderful confidences!

She looked out of the window and saw that Winchester was fast approaching. She dwelled on the fact that she not only lost her lover that autumn, but she also lost her very best friend. She had to move on, though, and what better way to banish miserable thoughts than with a bit of Christmas shopping?

'There are so many good shops here… one can step out of doors and get a thing in five minutes.' That's what Mrs Allen had said about Bath in *Northanger Abbey*, and Katherine felt the same way about Winchester. Once she ticked everybody off her Christmas list, she'd visit the cathedral. It was her annual treat and she wasn't going to let anything get her down that day because it was a Jane Day.

The sixteenth of December was Jane Austen's birthday. Katherine had always thought it rather wonderful that she'd been born so close to Christmas Day. Wasn't that the most perfect gift to the world? Katherine would walk the length and breadth of the great building, pay her respects to her favourite author and light a candle in her memory.

Hopping off the train, she made her way to the town centre, determined that despite the upsets earlier in the year, she was going to do her very best to enjoy the Christmas holidays.

Chapter 44

WARWICK ARRIVED AT THE CATHEDRAL AS SOON AS IT OPENED and had soon seen all there was to see—twice, paying his respects to every single grave, including one that belonged to a dear fellow called Francis Francis. Warwick's feet had echoed up and down the stone tiles and he needed to sit.

It would be easy to miss Katherine in such a huge building. She could be in and out in the time it took him to walk down the nave but he had an advantage. He knew exactly where she would be and there were seats to ease his waiting near the very spot.

Jane Austen's grave was in the north aisle and Warwick took a seat in the nave. It was partially obscured by a great pillar but he wouldn't be easily spotted because she wouldn't be looking for him, would she? He just had to make himself as comfortable as possible and hope that she arrived before he dropped off to sleep. He was positioned near a great fat radiator that was doing a good job of warming his little corner of the cathedral, and it would be terrible if he fell asleep and missed his big chance.

He spent a while reading, first the cathedral information leaflet and then the children's guide which he thought much more interesting. He then got his notepad out and started writing a short story, all the time looking up to make sure he didn't miss Katherine.

The low-backed wooden chair was comfortable enough for a few minutes, but it wasn't long before Warwick felt his bum going numb. He picked up the small green hymnal in front of him and flipped through it, reading the words of Percy Dearmer.

> *A brighter dawn is breaking,*
> *And earth with praise is waking*

'Let's hope so, Percy. Let's hope so.'

What if it all went wrong? What if Katherine screamed at him and made a big scene in front of the whole of Winchester? What if she threw chairs at him across the nave? Or worse—what if she didn't show up at all?

He looked at his watch. There was time yet. He mustn't panic.

It was cold enough for snow.

The sky was darkening when Katherine made her way to the cathedral. Strings of white lights threaded through the trees overhead. She'd managed to tick everything off her Christmas list and got a few gorgeous extras besides. The Christmas market, with its tiny wooden huts huddled around the cathedral, had been addictive, and Katherine bought a red berry wreath for her front door, the softest of shawls for her aunt and an indulgent bag of creamy fudge she couldn't resist plundering as she watched the skaters on the ice rink.

And then it was time.

As she entered the cathedral through the great red door, she breathed a sigh of relief. There were a few tourists around but it wasn't nearly as crowded as the shops had been. Katherine was always surprised that other people should want to visit Jane Austen's grave. Selfishly she wanted Jane to herself, but her grave was a popular spot with tourists whose toes strayed onto the sacred spot and cameras flashed at the words on the gravestone. Katherine would wait patiently for her turn, lighting a candle for Jane not because *she* was religious but because Jane had been. She waited for the crowds to clear and then walked towards the aisle, reading the familiar words etched into the stone.

Every year was the same. Katherine felt a sudden swell of emotion and had to blink rapidly to avoid tears falling, and then she'd sigh. How could she get emotional about a person who died two hundred years earlier—a person she didn't know at all?

'But I *do* know her,' Katherine said to herself.

And each year, the same things upset her. The grave above Jane's belonged to a Frances Dorothy Littlehales, who had died at the age of seventy-one. That was thirty years more than Jane had been given. How unfair that seemed to Katherine! She always wondered what Jane would have done with so many more years. What wonders would she have written?

Warwick's eyes and thoughts wandered. He gazed up at the cathedral's astonishing roof. Imagine the weight if it all came crashing down, he thought. How many houses could you build with the masonry?

He turned around to look at the view behind him. He liked the huge West Window. The colours were so sparse that the window was almost completely transparent but there wasn't much light to be let in that day, and what little there was, was fast fading. An enormous Christmas tree stood under the window, sparkling with white lights. Together with the groups of tiny bright candles, the lights did their best to brighten up the dark spaces, but it was a losing battle and, by four o'clock, the north aisle was almost in total darkness.

He was just thinking how easy it would be to slip under the spell of religion and superstition in such a place when he saw her. She was wearing a bright pink hat with matching gloves and scarf and her long dark hair was loose. An icy little wind had nipped her nose scarlet and her cheeks were flushed with colour too. She was laden with shopping bags when she stopped by the grave of Jane Austen.

At first he couldn't move but stared at her as if she were some kind of mirage. She had no idea he was there and he remained seated, half-hidden behind the great stone pillar, watching her as she looked down at the grave in the aisle. This was the moment he'd been waiting for but suddenly he felt unsure of what to do.

Then, swallowing hard, he got up and walked towards her.

Chapter 45

KATHERINE WASN'T SURE WHAT MADE HER LOOK UP AT THAT moment but when she did, she saw him standing there. Her name was formed on his lips but no sound came out.

'Warwick?' she said, watching as he walked towards her, stopping just short of the gravestone.

'Got anything in there for me?' he asked.

'What?'

'Christmas presents,' he said, nodding to her bags.

'No,' she said.

'Oh.'

There was an awkward silence for a moment. Warwick was the first to speak. 'There are a lot of bishops here,' he said. 'I've never seen such amazing monuments. Have you seen them all?'

'Yes, I've seen them all. Warwick, what are you doing here?' she said in a tone that suggested that Winchester Cathedral was in her jurisdiction and that he did not have visiting rights.

Warwick raked a hand through his hair. 'I came to talk to you.'

'I didn't ask you to.'

'But you gave me no choice. You wouldn't answer my letters. What was I meant to do?'

'But that was all weeks ago. You stopped writing me letters weeks ago.'

'I know. What was the point of writing more if you weren't reading them?'

'Then you should have taken the hint,' she said. 'I've got to go.' Katherine made a move towards the exit.

'Katherine!' Warwick suddenly leapt forward to block her way. 'Listen to me—*please!*'

For a moment she didn't look at him but then she raised her dark eyes to his, her face a mixture of sadness and annoyance. 'What do you want?' she asked him.

He looked at her and there was real longing in his eyes. 'I want us to be the way we were at Purley. I want my dear friend back. I want to hold my lover in my arms again. I want to say I'm sorry.'

Her gaze met his but she was unable to speak. She simply shook her head.

'Katherine—I'm more sorry than I can ever say. You believe me, don't you? Say you believe me!'

'Warwick... I...' she stopped. 'All those things you said to me—the way you used my letters, the endless lies you told me— you were making fun of me.'

'*No!* I wasn't. I wasn't *ever* making fun of you. It was wrong of me—*so* wrong. I just wanted you to like me for who I really was.'

'Have you any idea how it made me feel when I found out who you really were? I've never felt so used in my life. You really hurt me,' she said.

Warwick looked down at the floor. 'I know, and I hate myself for it. I never *ever* meant to hurt you. Things just got out of hand.'

'Yes, they did,' she said. 'You let them get out of hand. You arrived at Purley knowing exactly who I was but you didn't give me the opportunity to know who *you* were—who you *really* were. Not once did you say to me, "Katherine, there's something I should tell you" or "Katherine, I've been lying to you this whole time, but I want to tell you the truth now." Not once, Warwick. You could have said something at any time, but you didn't.'

'And I really want to make up for that. Please, give me a chance.'

They were silent for a moment, but then Katherine sighed. 'Look, I can't fight here. It's not right—not so close to Jane,' she said, making a move towards the great door.

'Then let's go outside.'

'I'm not sure I want to go anywhere with you.' Katherine stopped again.

Warwick gave a sigh and raked a hand through his hair. 'Darcy got a second chance,' he suddenly said.

'Pardon?'

'Darcy. Elizabeth gave him a second chance. If she hadn't, they might never have married and lived happily ever after.'

'Yes, but he redeemed himself.'

'And if you had any sisters I could rescue, perhaps I could redeem myself,' Warwick said.

'That's not funny.'

His shoulders slumped. 'I'm sorry.'

They were silent again for a moment.

'I wish you'd read my letters,' Warwick said at last. 'They were full of all the things I should have told you at Purley—*before* Purley. And all the things I've thought to say since. I haven't stopped thinking of the way I behaved and the way I *should* have behaved. I can't believe what a fool I was to jeopardise your trust. You were my best friend. More than that. You were my... my—' he paused and took a deep breath, seeming to inhale all the air in the cathedral before letting it out in a long sigh. 'I was in love with you. I *am* in love with you.'

He stood perfectly still and something in the way he spoke moved Katherine and she looked up at him. His face was pale and he looked agitated, as if he'd missed a week's worth of sleep.

'You believe that, don't you?' he said.

Katherine didn't know how to respond. This encounter was the very last thing she expected that day, and she had no idea what to say to him. 'How did you know I'd be here?' she asked.

'You told me,' he said. 'In one of your letters.'

She nodded as she remembered, and she couldn't help thinking that her letters betrayed her yet again.

'You shouldn't have written so many letters,' Katherine suddenly found herself saying. 'You should've been writing your next book.'

'I was. I am. And I've got my latest one too,' he said, digging in a carrier bag and pulling out a hardback and handing it to Katherine. 'It's out next week.'

As much as she wanted to ignore him, she found that she couldn't, and the Lorna Warwick fan she'd kept hidden away for many months got the better of her, and she reached out and took the book.

It had a beautiful young heroine on the cover, as all the books did, and there was a Gothic castle in the background and a black stallion rearing.

Christina and the Count, she read. Katherine smiled and wondered if she could run away to a quiet corner of the cathedral and read it.

'Open it,' Warwick told her.

She looked at him.

'Go on,' he said.

She opened the cover and flipped through the pages, wondering what he wanted her to see. On the fifth page, she found out. It was the dedication.

To Katherine—forgive me.

Despite all common sense, better judgement, and the strength of her willpower, Katherine felt her eyes fill with tears.

'Your favourite novel's *Persuasion*, isn't it?' Warwick said. 'So you know what it is to make a mistake. Just look at Anne Elliot. But you forgive her, don't you? You want her to have her second chance at love and a happy ending, don't you?'

'But Captain Wentworth still wants Anne.'

Warwick stared at her. 'You don't want me?'

Katherine's mouth narrowed into a line of indecision. 'It's not that I don't...' she paused. What was she trying to say? She looked down at the two simple words he'd written to her. *Forgive me.* She wanted to, she really did, but something was holding her back.

'You hurt me, Warwick, and I've been hurt so many times now. I don't want to go through that again.'

'But I couldn't possibly hurt you again!' Warwick's eyes were wide. 'There are no more nasty surprises. I *promise* you! You know all my dark secrets now. They're all out there. You've found them all out!'

She couldn't help smiling at that.

'I miss you,' he whispered, his words almost lost in the enormity of the cathedral. 'I really miss you.'

Katherine blinked away her tears and willed herself not to produce more. 'I miss Lorna,' she suddenly said.

'You don't have to. She's right here.' He gave her a little smile. 'And Warwick? I hope you miss Warwick just a little bit too. You do, don't you?'

She avoided his gaze and instead looked across the nave to where a woman was lighting a candle, a tiny perfect beam of light in a dark world.

'Has it been awkward for you, since people found out Lorna Warwick was really a man?' she asked, carefully moving away from answering the question he'd posed her.

'No,' Warwick said, shaking his head. 'It's actually been quite good fun. I expect you've seen some of the press. Sales have rocketed. I actually owe you a considerable cut in royalties.' He leant his head to one side. 'It's good to see you smiling.'

'I'm not smiling,' she said.

'No? You sure?'

There was another silence-filled moment.

'I've been back to Purley,' Warwick said.

'Oh?'

'Yes, last month. Robyn's living there now with Dan. She even moved her chickens down from Yorkshire. They're getting married in the summer.'

'Really?'

Warwick nodded.

Katherine smiled; there was no disputing it this time and she had to admit that it felt good.

'There's going to be a film adaptation of *The Notorious Lady Fenton,* and Dame Pamela's going to star in it.'

'Really? That's brilliant! That's my favourite book!'

'I know.'

She blushed, remembering that she wasn't really speaking to him.

'They're going to start filming in May. It's all happened really quickly,' he said.

They began walking slowly towards the door together, neither of them knowing what would happen next.

'Oh,' Katherine said as she realised she was still holding Warwick's book. 'Here.'

He shook his head. 'It's yours. I brought it for you.'

'Thank you,' she said quietly. 'And for the dedication.' She dared to look up at him again.

'I'm going to dedicate all my new books to you, Katherine, because I'm completely and irrevocably dedicated to you.' His expression was gentle yet intense, and there was no doubt in Katherine's mind that he meant what he said.

'You shouldn't do that,' she said. 'And you shouldn't say such things.'

'Why not?' he asked. 'I mean it.'

He held her gaze for a moment. 'I don't know what to say,' she whispered.

'Say you'll give me another chance. Say you know I'm an idiot but that you forgive me anyway. Say you'll let me hold your hand and that we can start again.'

Katherine bit her lip. She felt suspended for a moment, as if she were floating somewhere high above the nave looking down on herself. What was she going to do? What was she going to say?

She took a long deep breath. 'Okay,' she said.

Warwick's eyebrows rose. 'What?'

'Okay,' she said, adding a smile so the word would make a little more sense.

Warwick smiled back. 'Really?' he said.

Katherine nodded and a light filled Warwick's eyes that made them so beautiful that she actually laughed.

She turned around to take one last look at Jane Austen's resting place and then the two of them left the cathedral together and, when Warwick held out his hand, Katherine placed her own inside it.

Acknowledgments

To my wonderful writer friends who shared their knowledge and love of Jane Austen and the Regency period with me: Monica Fairview, Amanda Grange, Melanie Hilton, Nicola Cornick, Sheila Riley, Jo Beverley, Kate Allan, Jay Dixon, Eileen Hathaway, Juliet Archer, and Stephen Bowden.

Thanks also to Pia Tapper Fenton, Henriette Gyland, Naomi Tydeman, and Maureen Lee.

To the real Katherine Roberts for letting me use her name! And to Allan Forsyth for naming my hero.

To Linda Marsh and Rose Baring at Ardington House for answering my questions and making me so welcome.

To the staff at Chawton Cottage and Chawton House and to the History Wardrobe for allowing me to use their wonderful Undressing Mr Darcy presentation.

To my dear friends who kept me going with kind messages and support: Bridget Myhill, Deborah Wright, Linda Gillard, Kate Harrison, Sarah-Jane Pearson, Kerrie Smith, Debbie Downes, Kate Boden, Sue Reid, Alex Brown, Debs Carr, Brent Pemberton, Pat Maud, Helen Wilkinson, Janet Brigden, and Carol Drinkwater and my lovely pals on Facebook and Twitter who keep a writer company.

Also, thanks to my Let's Talk about Love gals: Janet Gover, Jean Fullerton, and Juliet Archer—I so enjoy our events. And to the fabulous RNA—happy fiftieth anniversary!

To my wonderful agents: Annette Green, David Smith, Laura Langlie, and Ronit Zafran and to Kate Bradley and the team at Avon and Deb Werksman at Sourcebooks. I love working with you all.

And, as ever, to my husband, Roy, for chauffeuring me around Hampshire and beyond in search of this story.

About the Author

Victoria Connelly was brought up in Norfolk and studied English literature at Worcester University before becoming a teacher in North Yorkshire. After getting married in a medieval castle in the Yorkshire Dales, she moved to London, where she lives with her artist husband and a mad springer spaniel.

She has three novels published in Germany and the first, *Flights of Angels*, was made into a film. Victoria and her husband flew out to Berlin to see it being filmed and got to be extras in it.

Her first novel in the UK, *Molly's Millions*, is a romantic comedy about a lottery winner who gives it all away. She's now writing a trilogy about Jane Austen addicts which is a wonderful excuse to read all the books and watch all the gorgeous film and TV adaptations again.